FIRE AND KNOWLEDGE

Fire and Knowledge

FICTION AND ESSAYS

Péter Nádas

TRANSLATED FROM THE HUNGARIAN
BY IMRE GOLDSTEIN

FARRAR, STRAUS AND GIROUX
NEW YORK

Farrar, Straus and Giroux
19 Union Square West, New York 10003

Copyright © 2007 by Péter Nádas
Translation copyright © 2007 by Farrar, Straus and Giroux, LLC
All rights reserved
Distributed in Canada by Douglas & McIntyre Ltd.
Printed in the United States of America
First edition, 2007

Library of Congress Cataloging-in-Publication Data
Nádas, Péter, 1942–
    [Selections. English. 2007]
    Fire and knowledge : fiction and essays / Péter Nádas ; translated
from the Hungarian by Imre Goldstein.— 1st ed.
        p.   cm.
    ISBN-13: 978-0-374-29964-4 (hardcover : alk. paper)
    ISBN-10: 0-374-29964-1 (hardcover : alk. paper)
    1. Nádas, Péter, 1942—Translations into English.   I. Goldshtain,
Imri, 1938–   II. Title.

PH3291.N297A2 2007
894'.511334—dc22

                                                        2006036749

Designed by Jonathan D. Lippincott

www.fsgbooks.com

1   3   5   7   9   10   8   6   4   2

Contents

FIRE AND KNOWLEDGE

The Great Christmas Killing

Twice, on two recent consecutive evenings, I watched how the former president of Romania and his wife were sentenced to death and how they were executed.* I saw two different documentaries, but since they both used the same original footage from 1989 to illustrate the ritual event, the effects of the two films differed very little.

The films made me ruminate over fundamental moral and aesthetic questions to which over the last ten years I have had no answers. Dispassionately I watched myself enjoying the tyrannicide. I kept observing that although I should have been ashamed for enjoying the sight, I was not ashamed at all. I found no mercy in my heart; I felt no pity for the couple.

I believe in just, legal procedures. Despite this belief, my conscience was conspicuously silent. I do not believe in capital punishment. Still, the brutality of the procedure I was witnessing did not offend me. Being vaguely aware that there had to be something I should object to in this outrageously unlawful, dilettante farce—though I had no objection—and that there should be another law-abiding and humane person within

---

*On December 25, 1989, Nicolae Ceauşescu and his wife, Elena, were shot by a firing squad after a secret military tribunal had found them guilty of crimes against the state; the charges against them included genocide and undermining the national economy. Their capture on December 22 had followed a week of increasing violence and an upsurge of mass protests against Ceauşescu's brutal regime, which had been in power for twenty-four years—Editor.

me to protest my moral indifference and oppose my aesthetic naiveté—though there was no such person to be found—created a strange vacuum.

Base enjoyment is dangerously close to the noble kind. Perhaps this is so because we have no separate sets of nerves for the two different kinds of enjoyment. Carnal pleasure and pain can also overlap—and not only in humans but also in animals. Any kind of pleasure tends to speed up or even disrupt breathing, causing the sensation that circulation is momentarily arrested. Hyperemia blots out consciousness with the feeling of sensual breathlessness. The physiology of mammals is a closed system. The graph of great political excitement or religious ecstasy does not differ greatly from the rising graph of lovemaking. When one is in this state, moral judgment is suspended and self-reflection takes a long break. Vision and other sensations are not blocked by inhibitions. A tension builds up, not only in the limbs but also in the groins and belly, in the intestines, and in the radial, annular sphincters controlling the anal orifice. This occurs whether I myself am doing the killing of a tyrant or if I watch others commit tyrannicide. Opposing, convulsive muscle contractions and muscular tensions become all-pervasive. This is the reason political or religious ecstasy on a mass scale is such an enthralling spectacle. And this is why mass hysteria is so frightening. Ultimately, it is only a matter of deciding what it is I want to make public and what it is I want to conceal. Dogs have erections when frightened; when happy, they urinate and whimper at the same time; anger makes the hair on their spines stand on end. Criminology is familiar with these phenomena. Burglars, thieves, and murderers evacuate compulsively in their pre-action sensual excitement and may actually ejaculate while carrying out their criminal acts.

In everyday circumstances one keeps in check the effects and emotions associated with base pleasures, and with good reason. If one does not guard well the delicate and sensitive border between hatred and love, between base and noble feelings, if one's closed physiologic system is not preserved for the more noble pleasures, then the chaos of suspicion, of being insulted, of the unquenchable thirst for revenge, of covetousness, envy, selfishness, vanity, and greed will quickly swallow one up. Sometimes one person with hysterical tendencies is all that is needed to drag the rest of a group along. This sort of chaos swallowed up Yugoslavia quite some time ago. The membrane that still protects Ukraine, Russia, Hungary, Romania, Slovakia, and Croatia has grown very thin.

A dreaming mind may give birth to nightmares, but hatred's fancy, uncontrolled by the mind, will engender vampires. From the danger I pose to myself nothing can protect me except the last remaining patches of my mind that I have managed to keep alert and rational.

The captors of the dreaded Ceauşescu couple, as if the two might somehow have broken out of the dreary room in which they had been tried and sentenced to death, forced them into a space between the wall and two steel-legged tables. Either it was cold in the room, or the uniformed members of the summary tribunal did not permit the tyrant and his wife to take off their coats. They were in a hurry. They wanted to get it over with as quickly as possible. They had no lawful authorization. And even if they had had it, they wanted to slaughter the two tyrants exactly the way they would one winter dawn slaughter their cherished, fattened hogs they used to scratch with such pleasure. Political consideration also entered into their haste, of course. While the tyrants were alive, any attempt to restore them to power might be considered legitimate, in which case they, the judges, would end up dead. Who would kill whom first? That was the question.

Elena Ceauşescu wore a fur-lined, light-colored cape. Gathering it tightly about her, she hoped to defend herself. She was shivering, more likely in fear than from the cold. Yet no one can say she did not remain self-possessed until the very end. She knew what was going to happen, and she said so too. Nicolae Ceauşescu was not quite so self-disciplined, though he eventually realized that his end was imminent. And I am sure it was not only his obtuseness that helped delude him. The man was seventy-one years old at the time; for forty-four of his years he had been a member of the Central Committee of Romania's Communist Party. That is much too long a time for even a single, tiny patch of one's brain to remain rational. No one had wanted to kill János Kádár when he was removed first as general secretary of the Hungarian party in 1988 and then entirely from political office in 1989; still, at the moment of truth he managed to save his mind by throwing himself into the dark abyss of dementia senilis. Ceauşescu just kept looking at his wife, rolling his small, shifty eyes and grinning nervously; you could tell he couldn't grasp what was really happening or figure out how he might gain the upper hand.

He was wearing a very heavy dark gray overcoat. The wearing of these wretched, ungainly overcoats had probably been ordered by a secret clause in the Warsaw Pact. János Kádár had the largest one of all; Mrs. Kádár had a pretty big one too. In Bulgaria, Todor Zhivkov's was too small. President Gustáv Husák of Czechoslovakia wore one with a dreadful cut. The mandatory headgear to go with these coats was a large, dark hat. On Christmas Day 1989 the Romanian head of state chose to wear an astrakhan cap. And to follow the example of his more disciplined wife, he stretched his arm across the table and held on to this astrakhan cap, kneading it, mangling it. He looked at his watch, wondering whether his rescuers were on their way. He looked at his watch as if to say, All right, I don't understand what's going on right now, but the real party conference is going to start anyway.

The cameraman aimed now at the two of them, now at members of the summary tribunal. In the whole room he found no angle from which he could frame all the participants. And he seemed unable to get close-ups either. He wobbled, jerked about, the camera shaking in his hands, and kept turning in different directions, undecided. And not only because he was no professional but also because he could not suppress his own fear and thirst for revenge. He could not reconcile his personal feelings with the task at hand.

Complete, total dilettantism lends perfection to this documentary film. You can cut it, edit it this way or that, nothing changes; its harmony remains perfect. None of its subjects, light effects, participants, sounds, or means of filming is anything but base, ugly, and amateurish. In this film the windows are blacked out, and no door is seen. There is no exit from this dictatorship. Even today we don't exactly know where we are in these shots. The cameraman can't step out of the picture either; to do that, he would have to have something in mind besides the murder. Freedom is not something one receives as a present. The cameraman identifies himself with the emotional outbursts of the horror-stricken summary tribunal, and we follow his unpredictable, fitful roving. This might conceivably lead to a cathartic realization—if only we could experience, together with members of the tribunal, the emergence of truth. But that is not what happens. Narrow-minded and driven by their petty thirst for revenge, they condemn the two tyrants to death.

It cannot happen any other way because the judges and tyrants are so much alike. They are equally witless, ugly, unlettered, coarse, and common. Perhaps most important in terms of justice, their behavior and their words are completely devoid of anything that might lend a person dignity. And no one has ever seen true justice that lacked dignity.

A decade has gone by since the execution of the Ceauşescus only three days after they fled Bucharest. As I followed the camera's undignified shifts, flitting to and fro among these people, who had lost all dignity and understood nothing, I failed to realize that my indignation, satisfaction, and enjoyment arose from my desire not for justice but for revenge. And it's even more embarrassing than that. Tyrants go to their death without dignity, but at least they can bridle their fright. The members of the tribunal that tried the couple, however, not only feared that they wouldn't have enough time to kill the two tyrants, in which case they themselves would be slaughtered by other avengers, but, even more, feared the very prospect of having to slay two such giants. They could not rid themselves of the image of their own dwarfishness. When looked at with the naked eye, in the entire course of world history we have never seen ourselves quite this way.

Just before the execution, when the tyrants' hands are tied behind their backs with some coarse clothesline, we hear the drama's single human sentence issue from the mouth of Elena Ceauşescu. Although ready to die, she and her husband still protest the treatment they're getting. Even now they fear not the loss of their human dignity but the loss of their fame and prestige. The terror gripping the soldiers, however, is so profound it seems doubtful whether they can properly carry out their odious mission. "What are you so afraid of?" rises the female voice from the depths of the scuffle. And to make this self-portrait of dictatorship even more complete, in the very last scene the character who should have remained silent makes himself heard too: it is the cameraman, talking to the doctor from behind the camera when they're already out in the courtyard where the execution by firing squad has taken place. The doctor's hands are shaking so violently he cannot guide his stethoscope to the jugular vein. If only he could look into the eyes, under the lids. All his fingers, his whole body, everything is trembling; he cannot do it.

"Raise his head. Let us see he is dead."

The doctor hesitates for a moment. He is not sure the cameraman's request can be granted. If he steps out of his role as physician and does as he is told, he'll be breaking the circuit of thousands of years that, with a last little puny string, still ties his person and his profession to Hippocrates.

If he obeys and does as he is told, he'll be carrying out the most terrible sentence of all dictatorships: nothing is sacred. And then he does obey. He raises and shows us Nicolae Ceaușescu's lifeless head. He pulls down the lower lids so we can look into the dictator's dead eyes.

With this devastating sensory experience we carry the logic of dictatorships into the next millennium.

First published as "Nagy karácsonyi gyilkosság" in *Talált cetli és más elegyes írások* (Pécs: Jelenkor Kiadó Kft, 1992, 2000).

Liar, Cheater

It was springtime, and I already knew how to write.

On my way to school I saw something strange. In a large black cart, a thick black mass was boiling. The cart was being fueled with wood, and then the mass was let into a wheelbarrow. It was stinky. I didn't know then that it was tar. But it was interesting to see how they were fixing the road with it. And how it was gradually cooling off. I was on my way to school.

In the first recess it occurred to me that it would be better to watch the roadworkers than to sit in the classroom for no good reason. After all, I already knew how to write. I tore a page out of my notebook and wrote on it the following:

DEAR TEACHER PLEASE RELEASE MY SON BECAUSE TODAY IS HIS BIRTHDAY AND WE WOULD LIKE TO CELEBRATE IT

And I signed my father's name. In nice block letters.

As the lesson got under way, I took the page to the teacher. She read it, nodded, and let me go home. I was very happy. And didn't go home. I stood for hours on the edge of the sidewalk, until the roadworkers stopped their labor and began to wash up. They did this stripped to the waist, using a tin washbowl in front of the toolshed whose door was open. They were pouring water out of large cans onto one another's arms. But that wasn't so interesting anymore. Not like the way the black mass turned into pavement. I think that even today I'd make a pretty good roadworker should my services be needed. I recorded everything. Every single move. Including the washing up.

That evening our doorbell rang. My parents sent me to open the door. A very elegant lady was standing in the dark stairwell. A hat on her head, gloves on her hands. She looked a lot like my teacher, but my teacher had never dressed so elegantly. She always wore simple things. And it was rather incredible that my teacher would be standing at the door. Yet she was the one who rang the bell.

With her gloved hand, she stroked my head, and then a bit more strongly she squeezed my neck. The way my teacher usually did. And she handed me a chocolate bar. But why? And she said that she wished me well on my birthday, and, she said, she had thought she'd visit me on my birthday and celebrate it together with us, and that is why she put on this pretty dress and her hat, and that is why she brought the chocolate, said the teacher, and she laughed so gaily as people do on festive occasions.

We were standing in the dark hallway.

The door was still open because I couldn't close it. Somehow, I couldn't move my hands, though I knew I should close the door. And I couldn't say anything. Though I knew I should say thank you and ask her to come in. But I couldn't say a word. The teacher pretended not to notice anything. Though I saw that she did. And with light steps she began to cross the hallway as if she had visited here many times before.

Light was coming out from under the living-room door. The teacher's high-heel shoes approached the door; then she stopped and, with her gloved hand, knocked on the door. She did not bend her fingers; she knocked with her clenched fist. She opened the door, and in the sudden light, she hesitated for a second to see if I'd follow her. But I could not move. I would have liked to move, if she hadn't been going to the living room or if something else might have happened. Then she closed the door behind her.

And in the dark hallway I was left alone only with the narrow strip of light coming from under the door. I felt something dreadful was about to happen in there. There, where the light was coming from. Something so dreadful I couldn't even imagine it. I did try to imagine it. But everything was quiet. As if my parents were not in the room and the teacher had not gone in at all. Perhaps there was no one in the living room. Only the light still coming out of there. And I did have the chocolate bar in my hand. Even though this was not my birthday. It was still to come. Sometime. I'd still have to wait for it.

I ran into the bathroom. The door slammed with a loud noise. I realized it made a loud noise because I slammed it behind me. But I could not calm down. In there it was even darker. The chocolate turned soft in my hand. I bumped into the bathtub. My palm felt the gap between the tub and the wall that, during my baths, I always peered into but could never see the bottom of. It was a very deep gap. And the gap helped me. I threw the chocolate into the gap, but unfortunately it made a thump behind the tub, I heard it clearly, though I didn't want to hear that thump, because I would have liked the gap to reach all the way to the main floor and the chocolate to fall all the way down there.

The chocolate behind the tub: this made everything worse.

I ran further, into my own room, and there too the door slammed with a bang because I slammed it hard, though I shouldn't be slamming doors; I should be very quiet and try to hide in the dark, among all the objects in my room, somewhere. I stood in my room, motionless. As motionless as if I did not exist at all.

But I did exist. Because from the adjacent room I could hear voices, and quiet laughter, but no matter how hard I tried I could not make out what they were saying. And why were they laughing?

And the dread would not pass. And the chocolate behind the tub. I was shaking. And I was afraid, but in vain, because nobody was coming to get me.

To this day I've no idea what I was afraid of. And I don't remember how I got from the middle of the room back to the door and, still shaking but more bravely, put my ear to it. I don't know what I could have been so afraid of; my parents had never beaten or punished me. Could it be that I wasn't afraid of them but of myself, as I pressed my ear to the door? To this day I don't know.

There was no sign of any excitement on the other side of the door. A kind of calm conversation. As if the teacher had not been there at all. And even if she had, the conversation sounded like other evening conversations. A kind of lulling, relaxed exchange of words. The kind that could put you to sleep because it sounds like a fairy tale being told. And quietly I pressed down the doorknob. Blinking, I stepped into the bright room.

The evening brightness of the chandelier. They were having tea. They were smiling. As if nothing had happened. As if they had not noticed what was happening inside me. As if they did not see how I stole over to the table, sat on the armrest of the big stuffed chair, and inclined my head under my mother's hand.

And my mother's hand stroked mine. And my head. Just like that, by the way, while she was talking. And then I withdrew a little. But they spoke to me, and I knew how to reply. Only no one uttered a word about my birthday.

The teacher left, and everything remained as if that evening had been like all other evenings. We had dinner. I washed up. I was put to bed, but my mother did not tell me a story, and I didn't dare ask for one. But she kissed me. And that too felt as if it had been preceded by her telling me a story.

Still, everything changed.

To this day I don't know what they talked about in the adjacent room. But it's not important.

And the chocolate behind the tub? Did it turn up during the next housecleaning? Or was the gap really so deep? For a long time I kept looking for signs, to see what would happen. Because I could not retrieve the chocolate from behind the tub. But nothing happened.

First published as "Hazug, csaló" in *Gyermekünk*, 1974.

The Bible

"No innate principles in the mind."
(John Locke, *An Essay Concerning Human Understanding*, Book II)

1

The rust-eaten roses with their loosened roots, the hanging plants, and the fancy acanthus leaves rattled long and noisily whenever the huge iron gate, so hard to move in either direction, was opened or closed. The jumbled sounds of unoiled metal forced their way through the quiet garden and then reverberated wearily from the stuccoed wall of the single-story villa.

The villa, proud of its ostentatious dimensions, spread out in a leisurely way above the garden, but its builders had exercised enough moderation not to show its haughtiness to the street. They masterfully hid the facade among tall pine trees, ornamental shrubbery, and rock gardens.

The jutting terrace and the winter garden, however, behind intricate bars, had an open view of the city's hazy outlines.

The six rooms, clearly designed for a lifestyle alien to us, seemed shabby when compared with our apartment in the city, and we were amazed at the marble-covered foyer and the enormous blue-tiled bathroom. Our furniture appeared lost in the six gigantic high-ceilinged rooms that could not be heated, and so the wonder and amazement gradually turned into a headache.

The garden was large.

All day long I roamed in it purposelessly. I would smoke stealthily or drag the deck chair out and read.

I was bored, looking for things to do, but I did put some order in my days. After coming home from school, I'd eat lunch, then walk in the garden, slapping my legs with a stick, strut among and glance over the flower beds, with the short-haired fox terrier stepping smartly behind me.

Having made several rounds of the entire garden, I'd change, put on an old sweatsuit, and run back out again. Meta would be waiting by the door, sitting on his haunches and happily wagging his tail. What usually followed was the "bullfight."

I'd brandish a red rag and start running. Meta would jump after me, catch and pull the rag, let it go; I'd spin it over his head, and he would follow it with his whole body in a frenzied spin. He would yelp, whimper, growl, and catch the rag again. I'd shake it, and then he'd keep yanking it with his teeth. I wouldn't give in, would tear it out of his mouth and run away, the dog after me; he'd knock me down, we'd roll around in the grass, he'd catch my wrist, jump on top of me, and then gallop away with the rag . . . and that's how it went day after day. We'd keep on doing it until the running and laughing made my sides ache.

Meta sometimes forgot the rules and took our struggle seriously; he'd bare his teeth, growl, keep snapping, and with his frightening pink gums and spotted palate snarl at me threateningly.

But fear also made me bristle, and even more than he. I wouldn't play the game, wouldn't relent. It was on such an occasion that he attacked me.

The fabric got stuck in his teeth; I held on to it and lifted him up into the air. He howled with pain, tensed his body, and tore himself free. A piece of the red cloth was dangling from his mouth.

He snapped at my foot. I felt all but unconscious for several seconds—from fear, because I felt no pain; the only trace left afterward was a scratch. There was a hoe lying nearby on the grass. I reached for it slowly, with a clear mind. Meta, with whimpering eyes, was cowering, flattening himself against the ground. I began to hit him. Blood was flowing from his body. During the first blows he'd still howl; then his eyes closed, and he quietly suffered his skin and flesh to be ripped up by the sharp hoe.

Nausea made me stop. If not for that sickening feeling, I don't know what I would have done, driven by my strength and my revenge. I left him where he lay.

We didn't find him for days. Father stumbled on him Saturday afternoon at the bottom of the haystack. He pulled him out and took him into the foyer.

The dog's eyes were shiny with fear, his body was burning with fever, hay was stuck in his wounds, and clotted blood was drying on his fur. It was hard for him to breathe, his tongue was hanging out, and he kept licking his chops.

My mother washed him, bandaged him, gave him water, and then my parents tried to figure out who could have done the brutal beating . . . maybe it was Meta's fault, if he stole a chicken . . . I said nothing.

The next morning, on the way to the bathroom, I tripped on Meta's nearly stiff body. He must have dragged himself toward the door, maybe wanting to die outdoors . . . With a tragic expression on my face, I walked into my parents' bedroom. They were still in bed. It was Sunday morning.

"He's dead," I said, and burst into tears. I slipped in next to my mother, but I yanked my head away from her caressing hand. I did not feel the need for any consolation.

2

For days I couldn't find a place for myself. I climbed up to the attic and found new treasures—trunks full of old letters, photographs, and newspapers—the only legacy of the former owner of the house, who had been a big landowner. I rifled through the dusty documents and enjoyed reading the ponderous, long-winded letters written in a scratchy hand. For hours I'd sit on a dusty beam, reading about soirees, servants, love affairs, fashion, gallants, and seashores.

I looked at photographs of smartly dressed gentlemen and ladies on the decks of grand ships, on the backs of camels by the Egyptian pyramids, under arcades in Rome, and in Venetian gondolas.

From the narrow attic windows came a steady stream of golden dust. Only rarely would a noise from the netherworld reach me—a shoutlike voice or the city's constant, monotone buzz, which anyway I couldn't hear because I was so used to it.

Some of the letters made me daydream. My imagination would put me too on horseback, not as an adult but as I was, a child, seated smartly with a riding crop in my hand. Or I would find myself in a huge marble hall, by the piano, like little Mozart; huge double doors were festooned with red velvet draperies, and from time to time letters of congratulations would be delivered on a silver tray by the maid dressed in black and white.

Sitting idly like that, in undisturbed indolence, I propped my head against a beam. Suddenly a female voice crashed into the golden haze. It came from the end of the garden, from the tennis court.

"Évaaaa! Come out of the waaater . . . !"

I climbed up to the window, but because of the thick foliage, I could not see into the neighboring garden, and Éva must have come out of the pool because it was quiet again.

Her name made me excited.

Quickly I threw my treasures back into the trunks and ran downstairs.

In the early-afternoon hours silence reigned everywhere. My grandparents were resting in the farthest room of the house.

They had the daily newspaper, *Népszava*, delivered; my grandfather had been subscribing to the same paper since his days as an apprentice. His profession had ruined his eyes, and by now he could not make out even the largest letters. For ten years, every day, my grandmother had been reading the paper for him. She'd sit by the window, push her wire-rimmed glasses high on her nose, and the words would pour quickly, flatly, from her mouth. Grandfather needed either infinite patience or infinite resignation to listen to Grandmother's prayerlike recitation. And while he always managed to distill the essence from this fog of words, as thick as sour cream, Grandmother could never remember anything except the weather forecast, and that only because she claimed her waist and legs could signal any change in the weather better than the Institute of Meteorology.

During these afternoons everything was mine. Time and space. I was free to poke around in drawers and read forbidden books.

When I ran down from the attic, prompted by Éva's name, I headed straight for Father's closet and pulled out a few of his neckties. I could not conceive of meeting the girl without wearing a necktie.

I started running toward the tennis court. The closer I got, the slower I ran. I was trying to imagine Éva: strolling around the pool, wearing a pink tulle dress and carrying a white parasol, holding her head high under a straw hat, just as I must have seen it in an illustrated novel for young girls. And the anticipation sent my heart into my throat.

I approached the fence cautiously and looked through the parted lilacs, but I saw no one. In the middle of the lawn, in an elevated rock garden and fully exposed to the sun, stood a greenhouse made of glass. The swimming pool, built from natural stones, was lower down, and next to it a smaller pool full of water lilies.

I sat in the shrubs for a long time. Nothing stirred. And this fascinated me even more. I imagined that Éva was sitting in a shuttered room, playing the piano. But there was no sound of a piano. This of course did not change the images in my mind. I had been sitting quite a while when a girl's powerful voice broke the silence.

"Goosy, goosy, goosy," I heard, and the girl appeared, carrying a handful of corn, followed by hungry waddling geese.

She kept coming closer to the fence. She was teasing the birds, throwing a few grains here and there; the geese swooped down on them, then resumed their waddle.

The girl—it didn't occur to me that she could be Éva—was wearing a skirt she must have outgrown for it barely covered her skinny legs, and she was barefoot. Finally, not far from my hiding place, she emptied her hand, and all the corn was on the ground. By then I had lost all fear and yelled to her. "Hey!"

She turned around, and I thought she'd be a little surprised, but her thin face was rather hostile. "What d'you want?" she asked.

"Nothing."

"Then what are you looking at?"

"Why? I'm not allowed to look?"

"Idiot," she said, and turned back to the geese. I was taken aback, but I didn't move. She pretended to be looking at the geese, but from the corner of her eye, she kept glancing in my direction, and then she burst out, "Are you still here?"

"Yes, I am," I answered timidly, because she started back toward the house, and she merely said over her shoulder, "Then I'm leaving!"

Involuntarily I shouted my words: "Don't go yet!"

She stopped, turned around. "All right," she said.

I plucked up my courage. "Come over here, closer."

"What for?"

"Let's talk."

She didn't reply but came a little closer. I was still squatting by the fence.

"Sit down."

She sat down. She held her skirt down with her feet and looked at me. That look confused me again. My glances kept jumping between her eyes and her knees pressed together. She had dark brown, calm eyes.

"Let's be friends," I moaned.

"Idiot," she answered again. "I'm a girl, I can't be your friend."

I was staggered by this response. I couldn't say anything. I thought she was right because I felt the urge to argue, but she kept looking at me. We were silent. Then she got up, dusted off her skirt, and in her deep, intimate voice said, "See ya."

I would have liked to ask her to stay, but she strode away with such confident steps that I didn't have the courage.

3

Like all the other rooms of our apartment, the foyer was special and very large. Ornamental marble columns divided it into two parts. To the left of the entrance door one could reach the walk-in hall closet and the three bedrooms; to the right, where the marble columns stood, the foyer widened into a round space, with huge windows from floor to ceiling on one side and the brown stained-wood door that led to the attic on the other. Also from this side opened the kitchen, the pantry, and the servants' quarters. Pushed against the attic stairs stood a table covered with oilcloth and five chairs. This is where we had our meals.

Both Mother and Father worked late hours. It was usually eight or nine in the evening before I heard the slamming of the car door, then the miserably squeaking gate, and then Mother's short steps on the sloping garden path. I'd run to open the door. She'd kiss me, wash up, and then, while Grandmother heated up supper, we'd sit in the living room. Mother would either mend socks or knit, and I could make my report of the day and of what happened at school. Mother would always come home before Father, but she'd always wait for him.

We'd spend a quiet half hour, sometimes a whole hour, before we heard the second set of slams, first of the car door, then of the gate. Again there would be steps on the concrete path, this time not so reserved, but hurried and forceful. Mother would open the door, and I, standing between the living room and the foyer, would watch them and try to make out their lips, offered to be kissed, in the semidarkness. (I was greatly interested in their physical encounters and their relationship in general.) Then Father would put his beige briefcase under the coatrack and go through the closet and into the bathroom. On his way he'd stroke my head with his palm. He looked down at me from a distance and every evening asked the same thing: "What's up, kiddo? How was school today?"

But he never waited for an answer. He couldn't, because he was already washing his hands, holding his face under the gurgling water and at the same time talking to Mother. I wasn't offended—it was all such a routine, and I didn't expect anything more from him. Ever since we had known each other (from the time I could talk), his interest never extended beyond his unanswered question of "What's up, kiddo?"

Of the father-son relationship I knew nothing more.

In the course of these evenings I hardly ever said anything. The two of them would talk about work, politics, and colleagues as if I weren't there at all. My job was simply to understand everything, without asking questions, to take apart and put together in my mind the people I was getting to know from their words. I actually liked this silent participation in their conversations. After all, they were talking about officials, secretaries, presidents, and ministers.

Sitting on the attic steps, I would watch them eat their supper. They would keep talking during the meal. Father sometimes would put his spoon down and, forgetting about the food, in a sharp tone argue with some unknown person. When that happened, Mother would look at him and smile, and Father would catch himself and continue eating.

Grandmother would also hover nearby. She was waiting for them to finish up so she could wash the dishes. She would also manage to tell them that peas were no longer available in the Közért, the state-owned food store, meat she hadn't been able to get for more than a week, and in the bread there was more potato than flour, it just fell apart . . . and in her urge to unload her entire litany quickly, she didn't seem to mind that my parents paid her no heed.

My grandmother, my mother's mother, was a short, corpulent woman; she was an old woman used to work and therefore never disgruntled, but she carried her heavy body with ever-increasing huffing and puffing.

She'd massage her waist while cleaning, sighing loudly whenever she bent down to pick up something. She was extremely proud of her daughter. Whenever she went somewhere in the car, she'd press her face to the window so everyone could see that her daughter wasn't just anybody but was somebody who took her mother in her car.

She had once been a housemaid. That's how she met my grandfather, who, as a clockmaker, had come to repair the undersecretary of state's musical clock. Grandfather made a very decent living; he wouldn't let her work.

She often talked to me about her young days. She railed at the undersecretary and his family, but she always added, "They were fine folk."

After we moved up to the house on the mountain, she felt worse. She had no one to talk to. That's why she took to spending long hours in the Közért, ignoring the varicose veins in her aching legs, standing in long lines for almost anything whether she needed it or not. She veiled her passion in long complaints; if she managed to get two eggs, she'd declare that one had to push and shove one's way through terrible lines for everything. She would talk to everyone about my mother, and because she didn't really know that much about her, she invented a lot of stories, sometimes so ingeniously that she actually believed them to be true.

Now she was bringing the next course: larded potatoes and fried kale (instead of meat).

Mother handed her the soup plates. "I'll see if I can find some meat in the city," she said.

"Get about three kilos," Grandmother said. "I'll deep-fry it so it'll keep." And she marched out with the soiled plates.

"Mama!" Mother called after her. "Come sit down for a minute. There's something I want to tell you."

Grandmother quickly returned and put new plates on the table.

"Géza and I decided to hire somebody. The house is getting to be too much for you."

"Oh, no. There's no need. I can manage." My grandmother pleaded, but her plea contained joy that somebody had thought about her, jealousy that someone new would be coming to live in the apartment, fear that there might be nothing to complain about, pride that she could still perform all the necessary tasks, and a practical sense that one should not throw money around unnecessarily so long as she was still around.

"Out of the question. The girl is coming tomorrow, and that's that," my father said sharply, as if to cut short any argument.

"All right," said Grandmother, already resigned, and immediately showed her willing cooperation. "Then I'll clean the small room tomorrow."

"The girl will clean it. You won't have to work anymore." Thus Father.

Grandmother was amazed. She weighed her position and then asked, "Is she reliable?"

"Dearest Mama, why wouldn't she be? A country girl. One of my colleagues recommended her. A woman."

"And is she young?"

"Seventeen."

"That's trouble," Grandmother said, seriously considering the proposition.

"Why should there be trouble?" Father burst out again. "We'll see to it that there won't be any trouble! She'll be coming tomorrow, early in the afternoon. If we aren't home by then, show her everything."

"All right, I wasn't saying that . . . it's just . . . I'll show her everything . . . but usually with the young ones there's always trouble . . . the—" But she didn't continue because Father gave her a look that demanded silence.

"There won't be any trouble," he said, in a tone with which one usually calms oneself as well. "We'll try to be home by then. Her name is Szidike Tóth. Right?" And he resumed eating, considering the case closed.

Grandmother sighed, signaling that she was convinced in her belief that there was always trouble with young ones, and this belief was unshakable, but seeing that she could not prolong the conversation, she rose and took the dishes into the kitchen.

They sent me off to sleep. I made my bed, picked up a book, but could not concentrate. I was trying to put together Szidike in my mind. A peasant girl. And peasant girls I knew only from books. I turned off the light, closed my eyes, but couldn't sleep. I was listening to the familiar nocturnal noises. Under Grandmother's heavy body her bed was creaking. Then I caught a few words: she was praising my mother to Grandfather, what a considerate daughter she was, how she wanted to spare her mother. But I couldn't make out Grandfather's reply; his voice was too soft.

Water was running in the bathroom. I could sense exactly how the tub was filling as the sound of the running water changed. I also heard when my mother stepped into the tub, I heard when she threw the nail-brush back into the soap holder, I even thought I could make out the gentle grating of the towel, but the walls were thicker than to let such a sound penetrate them.

Grandmother kept tossing for a while, then said something, and my mother closed their door. She and Father spoke in low voices for a while, and slowly the world quieted down around me. The distant barking of a dog was heard, and from somewhere in the city the horn of a factory.

4

The next day Grandmother was waiting for me at the door. She made me wipe my shoes and emphatically warned me not to make a mess in the apartment. She was wearing a black silk dress, which she had got from my mother and put on only on festive occasions; I looked at her some-what amazed.

The freshly polished doorknobs were dazzling, and everything seemed in painful order.

She hurried me through lunch, and she washed the dishes with care-ful, elegant splashes so as not to soil her dress. Then she came into my room, carrying a book that she had never had any intention of reading, and settled down by the window. She didn't even put on her eyeglasses. That's when I realized why the fancy dress and the spick-and-span apart-ment; from where she sat she could see the main gate.

I ran to the fence at the end of our garden. The girl was sitting on the edge of the smaller pool, kicking the water lilies. I crouched down in the shrubs. She spread her toes, and using them like tweezers, she caught the stem of a lily, gave it a fast yank, and the lily's head flew a good dis-tance behind her. She repeated the same actions until there were no lilies left within reach of her feet.

I was thinking how to begin and finally called to her: "Let me have one!"

She didn't even turn in my direction, as if she hadn't heard me at all, but she did pull her feet out of the water. Seeing that I had managed to surprise her, I pressed my advantage and yelled even louder, "Let me have one!"

She quickly turned and pretended she'd just noticed me. "Oh, it's you!" she said. "Hi."

She gathered the flowers, came over to the fence, sat down facing me, and pushed one water lily across. She began to pluck and tear at the rest.

"Why tear them to pieces?" I asked.

"Why not?"

"You could put them in a vase."

"We don't put flowers in vases."

I smiled indulgently. "You probably haven't got a vase!"

"Yes, we do!"

"And do you have a girl?"

It was her turn to be amazed by my question.

"What d'you think I am?" she replied.

"I mean," I insisted, "a girl who cooks and cleans instead of Grandmother."

She pulled her lips to the side, indicating that she understood, and said instructively, "You mean a maid. That we don't have, because my daddy doesn't let my mother go to work and she does everything in the house."

"My mother works. And a car comes to pick her up."

"My father gets picked up too! And . . . and . . ." She thought for a while. "And he takes Mother too, if you really want to know!"

"But my father works in the ministry."

"Mine too."

"Then they're the same," I declared, but she wouldn't let it go at that.

"My father is greater because our house is nicer."

This I had to admit, but just as the day before, it made me want to argue.

"Are you Éva?" I asked.

"Yes," she replied. "Let's get properly introduced, shall we?"

Standing on tiptoes, we shook hands above the fence. She had a strong grip, and now I noticed that she was a lot taller than I was. I held her hand for a long time. It felt good.

"Let go! The wire hurts," she said.

I sat down, but Éva remained standing.

"I'll be going then," she said. "Come over tomorrow. We'll play."

Happy at the invitation, I jumped up. "I'll bring a ball, all right?" I asked.

"I've got one, but bring it if you want to."

I heard the gate slam in the upper part of the garden.

"I'm going," I said, and already running, I yelled back happily, "See ya!"

"Wait for me here, by the fence," Éva shouted after me.

5

Grandmother was still sitting stiffly by the window, reading, holding the book in her outstretched arms.

"Szidike?" I asked as I burst into the room.

She looked at me with undisguised glee and made a face.

"Oh, it was only the neighbor."

I left, disappointed, and sat down by the fence near the gate. The early-afternoon sun was cutting a path among the foliage and poured tufts of light on the empty pavement. From my hiding place I could see all the way to the bend where the road turns down toward the station of the cog railway. By the sounds reaching me, I could tell when a down-ward train would leave or one from the city come up to the station. From time to time I'd climb on top of the gate to see even farther; if someone approached, I'd withdraw into the shrubs.

The girl came alone. She was wearing a wide skirt with lots of under-skirts, the kerchief on her head was tied under her chin, and she was car-rying a string bag. There must have been folded clothes in the bag, wrapped in newspaper. She stopped at the gate, peeped in, looking for the number, then unbuttoned her blouse and produced a much-wrinkled piece of paper. Her lips were moving while she read. She looked at the number on the house, but still she hesitated. She took a step back, put her bag on a stone, and fixed her kerchief. Still, she didn't dare reach for the handle. She looked for the bell. She barely touched it with the tip of her finger, and there was an immediate response from inside the house: nothing was stirring.

I couldn't understand why Grandmother wasn't coming to the gate or why she didn't shout "It's open!" from the window, as she usually did.

The girl stood still for another second, and then she tried the handle of the gate. With great noise, the creaky gate opened, alarming her; she closed it behind her very carefully. Slowly she made her way down the path.

When she passed me, I jumped up and went round the house, then climbed in through the veranda window. I stole over to the door of my room. Grandmother was still sitting calmly, pretending to be reading. Outside, the girl stopped in front of the window and greeted Grandmother. "Good day, madam. I'm looking for the Till family."

Grandmother glanced up and gave her a cold smile. "Well, my dear, you are Szidike Tóth, aren't you? Come, come on in. I'll get the door right away." And heavily she headed for the door.

I don't know why, but I happily threw myself on my bed, while listening hard to Grandmother's voice.

"Go ahead; put your things down, wash up, my dear. You must be tired. Did you find us easily? I'll show you your room. Let me know when you're done, I'll introduce you to my husband and my grandson. Well, come on then . . ."

The prospect of being introduced scared me; I quickly grabbed a book from the night table, opened it somewhere, and started reading. Of course I couldn't concentrate on the words. I was waiting for the door to open and Grandmother to appear with Szidike. But I had no patience for waiting. I ran out into the foyer. My grandfather was already there. Smiling, he held Szidike's hand in his own but said nothing except his name. And then I introduced myself too. Szidike was smiling happily; moreover, I felt she would have liked to stroke my head, and when she didn't, I looked at her angrily. All she said was, "Your name is Gyurka, right? My kid brother is also Gyuri!"

There we were, the four of us standing in the foyer, and my parents also showed up. They greeted Szidike, Father very curtly, as was his wont. I was asked once again, "What's up, kiddo?" and to indicate that Szidike's arrival would cause no change in his habits, Father put his briefcase under the coatrack and went into the bathroom to wash his hands.

"I'll show her everything," Grandmother said to Mother.

"No need, Mama!" Mother replied. "Just relax, you can go to your room. I'll show her everything."

Grandmother gave Szidike a painful smile and then looked at Mother with a hateful and offended air, smoothed her dress on her chest, and, with her shoulders pulled up to her ears, marched into her room.

6

They sent me into the garden to show her everything there too. I was so proud of my mission that I even changed my posture. I got hold of a thin flexible stick and, using it as a riding crop, swatted my legs with it. When Szidike addressed me in the familiar form, I felt offended. I retorted by telling her that never in my life had I heard such an impossible name such as hers. But the expected reaction would not come. Szidike informed me that in her family every girl was called Szidónia, and it was a very common name in her village.

This wasn't the way I had imagined our relationship. She even tried to hold my hand. But her attempt failed because I ran ahead on the red clay garden path, and she kept up, staying right behind me. Maybe she thought I wanted to play catch. But reading the frozen expression of my face, she soon learned that I did not consider her my playmate.

And so we strolled, strangely, somewhat stiffly, side by side. She was happy to see the flower beds; in very practical terms, she held forth on what should be planted and where, something she would be willing to do, provided that she had the time. As she overcame her initial shyness, I saw that she was a girl with self-confidence. And that too was contrary to my expectations. I should have liked her awkwardness to continue, for her to keep on moving the way she had outside the gate.

She was looking for the vegetable patch. Separated from the flower garden by meticulously pruned lilac bushes was a stretch of soil for vegetables, but we hardly made use of it. In the spring, with Mother in the lead, my parents would plant a few green peppers and tomatoes and, a little farther on, some potatoes, but in the summer they realized that even if they could find the time for hoeing, the whole thing didn't make much sense. It was getting to be late autumn, and we had only a few new potatoes. At the end of the patch stood a hothouse with one wall against the fence. It was heated with the kind of furnace that floral gardeners used. We didn't use the hothouse either, and during the two years since we'd moved to this house on the mountain its windows had been broken, its iron frame grown rusty, and the heating apparatus fallen apart

Szidike seemed to be in her element here. She smiled tolerantly at the neglected plants and was enthusiastic about the possibility of revitalizing this piece of garden. After that it was no use showing her the "tulip tree" with its red flowers or the weeping willow that so bravely aimed for the sky only to fall back, humbled, and bow to the ground. Nothing made any impression on her. In her thoughts and words she kept returning to the vegetable patch.

It was getting dark. We went back to the house. Mother was heating up our supper; Father was sitting behind her, talking about something. As soon as we came in, he fell silent. He left off in the middle of a sentence and turned to Szidike. "Well, how did you like the garden?" he asked.

Szidike gushed effusively—how she had never seen such a large garden with so many different kinds of trees and roses, only— She stopped, but at my father's prodding she blurted out that the vegetable patch was in terrible shape, but she could put a spade to it, in the spring plant everything, and we wouldn't need to worry about vegetables anymore. Mother, setting the table, protested that there was no need for the vegetable patch, and Szidike would have enough to do with the cooking, cleaning, and washing; we should be glad if she managed to do all that properly.

This forceful statement saddened Szidike, but she kept saying she'd probably have enough free time to take care of the vegetables—after all, it would be fun for her.

There were six settings on the table and five chairs around it. The sixth plate Mother put in front of the attic stairs, and we all sat at our places, except for Szidike, who was still busy between the kitchen and the "dining room." She was bringing salt, and from somewhere she produced yellowed toothpicks, setting everything before us.

Grandmother was working her spoon, staring stiffly into her soup. Grandfather sat at the head of the table. His silence didn't surprise me; ever since his asthma had overtaken his heart and lungs, he spoke less and less, though his eyes, sunk deep in his gaunt face, still shone brightly.

"Come, sit down already," Mother said to Szidike.

"No, no!" the girl protested. "In the kitchen, after you finish eating," she said, and I was happy to see how quickly she was losing her self-confidence.

"Please sit down here!" Mother said, half commanding, half joking. "What do you think, you'd be eating leftovers in the kitchen?"

Apparently even more confused, Szidike sat down, but she took her plate on her lap. This was something Father wouldn't stand for.

"Come on, relax and eat the way you're supposed to. In this house you are not a servant . . . as of today you are a member of the family."

The girl put the plate back on the table. She had to lean forward sharply to reach it. She held her spoon in a fist and made soft slurping noises.

The silence deepened. My parents weren't talking, the spoons clanged against the plates, and I could hear the gentle splashing of soup drops falling back into the plates and Szidike slurping. These were unusual sounds. And I soon discovered why they bothered me: because of them, I might not be able to hear my parents' arguments, and the thin thread that tied me to them would snap. Szidike kept slurping her soup right next to my ear. I could hear nothing else. I kept moving my spoon automatically between my mouth and the plate, and while staring at my mother, I kicked Szidike's leg under the table.

In fright, she dropped her spoon onto the plate. Soup spattered in my face.

"Excuse me . . ." I turned to her, smiling.

7

In my pajamas, barefoot, and on tiptoe I was approaching her and then stopped right behind her. She was at the doorstep, bent over, picking something out of a crack in the floor.

"What are you doing?" I yelled. She shuddered and dropped the washrag.

"Can't you see?" she answered back angrily, and then laughed. "You scared me."

"Got a good fright, didn't you?"

"I don't frighten easily."

"Not even in the dark?"

"No. At home we have no electricity. I get scared only in the cemetery."

"Not me. I don't get scared anywhere."

"You're a boy. You're not supposed to," she said, and rinsed the rag in the bucket, poured out the water, and shoved the bucket under the sink. "There, it's done." She straightened up. "Why aren't you asleep yet?"

"I couldn't fall asleep because—don't be angry—because I kicked you . . . I really didn't mean to . . ." Innocently I lowered my eyelids, and inside I was glad I could say this so calmly. I looked up again.

"Never mind, it doesn't hurt. Only the fright made me squeal."

"Should I run the water in the tub for you?" I asked.

"I'll just wash up a little."

"We always take baths. I'll run the water." I walked into the bathroom.

I put on my slippers. Szidike was coming after me.

"Look, this is how you turn on the heat," I said, showing her the gas boiler. "You let the water run, turn on the gas, and when you have enough, you turn off the gas and shut off the water."

"I'd like to get undressed," she said, embarrassed. "Would you mind leaving?"

"I could stay, though."

"No, you can't."

"My mother always lets me."

"But I—I don't . . . so, please get out . . . please . . ." she said, imploring.

"All right," I said magnanimously, and left for my room.

I sat down on the edge of my bed and waited for the familiar splash. In the meantime, I took off the slippers and put on my sneakers. In the adjacent room my parents were talking softly. I stepped up to the door contemplating whether I should walk in, but they never let me stay up and bother them in the evening. And I hadn't said a word to them all day. I pressed my ear to the door. They must have been in bed because their voices sounded muffled by their cover. ". . . She's got a cross around her neck . . ." I heard my father's voice. ". . . So what, as long as she does her work all right," Mother replied. ". . . We could pay some special attention to her once in a while . . ." "When do we ever have time for that, but if you can see your way . . ."

I heard the splash. Quietly, watching my every step, I walked to the veranda window. It was open. I jumped out into the dark. For a long time I stood among the petunias, my feet sinking into the soft ground. The night air was mild, with motionless clouds in the sky. I was listening to the little nocturnal noises, staring wide-eyed at the two white figures I knew to be flower baskets carved of marble, yet I waited for them to approach. But only the wind was rustling the foliage.

As I stepped out of the flower bed, I stubbed my toes on a rock. The light went out in my parents' room. I stopped short, and then, with my feet feeling the way to the path and the steps, I started to go around the house.

The bathroom threw light on the lawn, with the shadowed patterns of the fancy iron grating. I ran toward this spot. I stopped under the window and listened again for sounds from the bathroom, but the distant barking of dogs and the humming of the city all around me overwhelmed the noises of Szidike's tiny movements. Like a large eye, the glass of the window stared at me, cold and stiff. I should have liked to see something, maybe a blurry shadow, move behind the grating, but the windowpanes remained empty.

The two lower panes of the bathroom window were fitted with translucent decorative glass, while the two ventilating panes above them were transparent. I would have to stand on the grating's second crossbar to see inside. With one leap, I caught the rusty, cold iron and pulled myself up. I had a good foothold on the tin windowsill. That's when the shadow inside made a move. I froze. I thought I had been seen. But after my initial fright, I realized that Szidike had simply stood up in the tub. Now I'll see her better—this thought flashed through my mind, and I stepped up on the first crossbar. I moved on, but fear made me stop. Then curiosity egged me on. Up onto the second crossbar. All I had to do was straighten up to see the whole bathroom, but my hands and legs kept shaking, and I clung to the bars peeling with rust. Suddenly, I don't know why, I remembered the gleaming, sharp hoe, its smooth, shiny handle in my hand, and Meta's yelping, frozen stare. I could already hear Szidike inside. My ears registered the familiar sounds of a body's being washed (maybe I just imagined I heard them), but my thoughts got away from Szidike's body. Again I was seeing Meta, the clumps of clotted blood mixed with straw on his fur, and somehow I was also hearing

Mother's voice and, coming from somewhere further inside me, my own voice as well.

"Aren't you disgusted?" I asked. Mother, while continuing carefully to wash the dog's body and dipping a sponge in the water, looked at me and said, "If you only knew the things I've already done! My goodness! Like dragging on a sled the bodies we scraped out from under the rubble."

Again, I heard my own doubting voice. "When?"

And I heard my mother's instructive, cheerfully proud voice as she replied, "When we were liberated."

Noisy splashing, and behind the decorative glass the blurry shadow straightened up again. I heard her step out of the tub and bend over again, and the water gurgling down the drain. This sound, with the force of fear (that I might miss something) propelled me forward to the crossbar. My back straightened, and my head was inside the frame of the transparent ventilating panes. I was sweating.

Szidike was standing on the wooden mat in front of the tub. She reached back for the towel; strangely, she bunched it up and began to dry her neck. She was smiling. She gathered her braids into a wreath on top of her head, and she showed me her body with all its freshness, muted light, and gentle colors. She opened the towel and rubbed her back with it. She threw back her head, and then her gaze directly caught mine.

For seconds, while the wall of fright was shattered by the realization, we both stared motionless. First, she let out some inarticulate sounds, brought her hand before her mouth, and continued looking with the fear of defenselessness in her eyes.

I kept gripping the crossbar, my body pressed between the uprights of the grating. Then Szidike crouched, making herself as tiny as possible and tried to cover herself with her own body; in a hollow voice, as if from within herself, she yelled in my direction. She motioned with her hand that I should go because she couldn't stand it anymore and she might scream, and she was moving her hands to cover her breasts.

Dizzily I jumped, or maybe fell, from the window and found myself flat on the ground. I felt I'd broken every bone in my body, and the fear that she might tell my parents had me in its grip from neck to loins, in a vise I had never experienced before.

I dashed into the darkness. Fear was overcome by a yet greater fear; dread of the night was dissolved in an inner fright.

Much later, in bed, I recovered my senses. I heard Szidike's door slam. I tried to conjure up her body but could recall only her whimpering, defenseless gaze. And my anxiety made both her body and her eyes seem inimical to me.

8

We cut out the bottom of a string net shopping bag, spread its two handles between two tree branches, and used it to play "basketball." Éva was ahead. She'd leap up with ease and with her arms extending forward gracefully sink the ball. Every time she found the basket, she'd yell happily and announce the score. Then it was my turn to jump up and catch the ball falling from the net bag.

My muscles were signaling failure. Anxiously I'd run back, away from the basket, take off from the starting position, and make a show of pretending to count the all-important steps toward the basket. While running, I felt more relaxed because I pictured myself flying through the air, but at the decisive moment, as if something were holding me back, I stopped short and just stared at the basket.

Bumptiously Éva was encouraging me. "Come on, come on . . . do it . . . Now!"

I felt like throwing the ball into her narrow, mocking face, but this feeling remained only an inner urge. Instead I also smiled, bumptiously. "I didn't pace the steps right," I said, and made a face.

I ran back again and counted the steps aloud, then took another running start, left the ground with one foot, and flew toward the basket. As if new dimensions had opened up inside me when I did that, I saw myself from the outside—with Éva's mocking, squinting eyes, my awkwardly jumping, clumsy, thickset body—and at the same time I saw Éva with her knitted brow, and I also saw the basket at whose center I was supposed to aim the ball. I missed.

Éva was already running to retrieve the ball when she squealed, "Look at this, I'll show you!"

And she sank the ball.

She had more than forty points and I hadn't reached ten when I proposed to end the game. We lay down by the fence. The fallen leaves were like a thick blanket under us. We were panting, our faces toward the sky streaked with yellow light. Éva was perspiring heavily. I was very sensitive to smells, but hers did not bother me. Huffing hard, I sniffed her, hoping she would notice, but she did not turn in my direction. I looked at her from the side. She closed her eyes, tiny pearls sat on her yellowish, oily skin, and her nostrils widened in rhythm with her breathing. Her small, protruding upper lip sometimes left the lower one, like some valve, to let out the air, and then the lips closed again. I followed the path of the pearls running down her smooth forehead as they approached and rolled into her seashell-like temple and disappeared in the thick brownish red strands of her hair.

I felt light and pure and suddenly thought of bending over her and stopping one of those rolling pearls with my tongue. But just then she spoke.

"I beat you, after all. Of course you're at a disadvantage because you're shorter than I am and I'm more flexible. My gym teacher said I was very flexible." She didn't open her eyes while she spoke; her eyelashes rested calmly on her flawless skin. Her voice was relaxed, deep, and so convincing that I could not protest.

Thinking how strong and calm she was, how confidently she dominated me, I pulled closer to her. I closed my eyes too and enjoyed the moist heat of her skin.

She moved. The dusty leaves rustled under her, and I was afraid she'd pull away from me, but she snuggled closer. I did not dare move.

"It's nice like this," I said so softly that only her inner senses could have heard, but I saw that she understood, because her lips parted and formed a lovely smile. I turned over, put one arm carefully around her, and pulled her toward me. Her body turned obediently. She opened her eyes.

"Nice, isn't it?" I whispered into her face. Her lovely smile continued, and she nodded that it was nice.

"I love you very much," I said.

"Me too," she answered, but the moment she said this, there was another flash of Éva's hard face that had disappeared somewhere in a great distance.

I yanked her to me. I put my mouth on her lips but felt nothing. I withdrew my mouth and found her lips again. In the meantime, I moved my head the way I saw my parents do it in the semidark foyer. Again I felt nothing. Éva opened her mouth, and I pressed myself on her more forcefully. She jumped up, looked at me, frightened, and I thought she'd be upset, but I saw that her face hadn't changed. Pouting contemptuously, she kept looking down at me.

"You don't even know how to kiss! In Németland everybody knows," she said, picked up the ball, ran to the path with it, and kept bouncing it.

I had no idea why I didn't know how to kiss. I thought I should learn and the only person who could teach me would be Éva, but seeing her impassive face while she kept bouncing the ball on the pebbled path, I lost interest. I kept lying on the ground, hurt and alone, just the way she had left me when she jumped out of my arms.

"Return game!" she yelled, loud as if nothing had happened, and raised the ball above her head. "Aren't you coming? What are you lying there for?" She kept urging me.

I knew I could change expressions easily, but I found it hard to get up and look at her the way I had during our earlier game. Slowly I got up on my knees and, driven by a sudden idea, began to do push-ups.

In a flash she was right next to me.

"Well, who can do more?" she asked, and while she raised and lowered herself, she kept counting aloud.

It was hard to complete the sixth push-up, my arms began to shake, the seventh I managed out of sheer willpower, and I pushed myself up for the eighth time too but felt that my bones had twisted out of their joints, and I collapsed.

"Ten . . . eleven . . . twelve . . ." She counted loudly, and then she stopped too.

"I won again!" she said, and clasping her hands above her head, she began to roll down the sloping lawn, shouting in disconnected phrases, "Bring the"—she stopped because her face was to the ground—"ball . . ." and kept rolling, faster and faster. "We'll . . . con . . . tin . . . ue . . . the . . . game." She jumped up, panting hard.

"Come on," she commanded while dusting off her short skirt.

"Now? I'm tired," I said decisively, hoping she'd relent, but she laughed mockingly again.

"You're a worm! A worm! Are you tired, little worm?"

The blood rushed to my face. "Your mother is a worm!" I yelled wildly.

She stiffened, took a step forward, and, nailing me to the spot with a hard stare, slowly approached me; her movements indicated that she was confident she'd catch me; defenselessly I waited for her. "Whaaat did you say?" she hissed.

I could see only her threatening eyes, and frustrated anger just burst out of me. Her spotted ball was lying next me on the ground. I picked it up and repeated, "Your mother is a worm!"

"What did you call my mother?"

I backed away. I raised the ball and with all my might threw it in her face. In the last second she drew her hands in front of her eyes, but it was too late. She staggered a little at the impact and then rushed at me furiously.

"You miserable beast! You sonofabitch bastard!" she screamed.

I turned and ran toward the fence. I fought my way through the shrub and slipped through the hole in the fence. My shirt got caught in the wires; no matter how hard I yanked it or grabbed it from every direction, I could not free it. She was catching up with me, I could hear her angry panting, and I gave one last yank with my whole body. A small part of the shirt stayed dangling on the fence. Inertia propelled me forward, all the way to the middle of the tennis court. There I turned around. She leaned over the fence and yelled at me, her voice fighting her urge to cry. "I'll have you taken away! By my father! I'll have you taken away!"

9

The car door slammed unusually early. Mother's hasty steps were pounding on the concrete. I lay on my bed, my fear slowly dissolving, and listened to her approaching steps. I did not run to open the door. She was alongside my window, her shadow passing one pane after the other.

My hands were about to move, to make me go, stand before her, and cry or just quietly to press my head against her breast and own up the matter with Szidike and tell her about my fear, the kissing with Éva, but my mind told me to be still. She'd come into my room anyway, sit next to me, make me face her, and ask, "What's up, my little Doydi?"

The lock clicked, the door slammed, and I heard Mother's voice as she said quickly to Szidike, "We're going to a reception. Don't wait for us with dinner."

Then I heard Szidike mention my name and felt as if someone were tightening my stomach with a string.

Silence. I did not move. The car's engine kept humming in front of the garden gate, and running water hit the tub with alternating strength.

For a while Mother was rummaging in their room; then she came into mine.

With soft steps, she walked to my bed and asked me in a whisper, "Are you asleep?"

"No," I answered in an artificially colorless voice.

"Why are you lying down then?" she asked, in a loud tone.

"Because."

"Do you have a headache?"

"No."

"All right, you'll tell me if you want to. Uncle Sanyi is waiting at the gate. Your father and I are going to a reception."

I felt I couldn't tell her anything now. I looked up at her. She was wearing a dark blue suit and a white blouse.

"Sit down for a little bit." I begged her. Nervously she sat on the edge of the bed and stroked my head.

"What's with you?" she asked again.

"You're so beautiful, and I love you so!" I blurted out, and I snuggled close to her. She held my head, looked at her watch, and jumped up.

"I've got to run! Father is waiting for me, and I'm late. Szidike tells me you didn't eat your lentils!"

"She's lying."

"What are you saying?"

"I'm telling you."

"I've got no time to listen to your cheekiness!"

"Just come here again, for a little while." I implored her.

"Can't you understand I'm late?"

"You're late, you're late, you're always running." She had nothing to say to that. She took her leave, calling back from the door, "Do as Szidike says, and eat your lentils!"

She closed the door. Her steps passed by my window again and then along the garden path. Uncle Sanyi revved up the engine, and the car took off.

10

I went to sit in the kitchen, to be with Szidike. She was washing dishes, her body bent over the sink; the cross on the thin gold chain around her neck swung back and forth with her every move. She paid no attention to me as she scrubbed the bottom of a pot. Whenever her powerful movements made her braids slip forward, she would give her head an irritated little shake and the braids would fly behind her back.

"Do you believe in God?" I asked.

She made a few more scrubbing strokes at the bottom of the pot before lowering her arms. She leaned against the sink and looked at me, alarmed. "No . . ." she said softly.

"Then why are you wearing a cross around your neck?" I asked triumphantly.

"My mother gave it to me for my first communion," she replied.

"But why are you wearing it if you don't believe?" I repeated. She didn't answer and resumed rubbing the bottom of the pot.

"Take me, now. If I weren't a Communist, I wouldn't wear the Lenin badge."

"You're a Communist too?" she asked, raising her eyes to look at me.

"Of course!" I answered proudly. "That's the difference between us. You believe in God, and we are Communists. You do believe in God, don't you? You can tell me . . . I also studied religion."

She looked at me again, and I could see in her eyes that she would have liked to ask me how come Communists also study religion.

"I studied it because it was compulsory," I added.

Silence followed. It irritated me that I couldn't rile her, and I said, more as a statement than a question, "So you believe in God."

"Yes," she replied, and proudly threw her head back. I was glad to have this answer.

I attacked immediately. "Then why do you squeal?"

"I squeal?"

"And lie."

"No, I don't lie."

"Yes, you do, because you told Mother I didn't eat the lentils, and I did."

"I said it because you were only playing with the food and in the end left a lot on the plate."

"That doesn't mean you have to squeal on me. Doesn't your God forbid it? The good little Heavenly Father?"

She swallowed and left my question unanswered. Grandmother shuffled into the kitchen. She stopped in front of Szidike and crossed her arms under her heavy breasts.

"If you're finished here, it's time to do the ironing, sweetie!" she said.

"The lady said I could have the afternoon off because guests are coming on Sunday . . ."

Grandmother looked at her angrily and wouldn't relent. "First of all, as I have told you before, it's not 'the lady' or 'madam,' but simply 'comrade.' Second of all, you may take some time off tomorrow, but today you have to do the ironing."

"All right. I only said it because the madam comrade told me." Szidike sounded apologetic.

"Have you been studying?" Grandmother turned to me, somewhat appeased.

"No. What guests are coming this Sunday?"

"How should I know? You think your mother tells me things like that?" Grandmother answered with a question, insulted. "Go ahead, you just do your homework, my little Doydi."

"Must be the Pozsgais . . . they think this is a holiday resort . . ." I mumbled, pretending not to have heard Grandmother's exhortation to study.

"Am I talking to the wall?" she snapped.

"I'll study later. Now leave me alone!"

"I should leave you alone? Very well, I'll leave you alone . . . he's getting impertinent too . . . I should leave him alone," she grumbled, and marched out of the kitchen.

Szidike finished washing the dishes in silence.

She wiped off the table, put on the blanket for ironing, and, while the iron heated up, sat on the kitchen stool, her hands in her lap.

"Aren't you going to sprinkle it?"

"Sprinkle what?"

I got up and showed her. She sighed and with listless arm movements spattered water on the clothes. I found something else objectionable about her work and then left for my room to do homework. But nothing came of studying. I wanted to be around people, to tell somebody everything. The silence was drumming in my ears. I looked into my grandparents' room. With his elbow on the radiator, Grandfather was listening to Grandmother's monotone reading. I stood in the doorway for a while, but the uniform drone of the words made me even more restless. Quietly I closed the door.

I went out into the garden. I found nothing to do there; I wandered around aimlessly. I walked along the shrubs by the tennis court. I won't say I got there unintentionally. My heart was beating aloud. It was getting dark, and I saw through the sparse foliage that the lights went on in Éva's villa. Maybe her father is coming home now and I'll be taken away, I thought, and ran back to our place. I climbed up on the gate with its fancy decorative flowers and stared out at the street, but nothing was moving. If her father had come home, his car would be leaving just about now, and I should be able to see it! I was trying to calm myself, but Éva's yell, on the verge of crying, seemed stuck in my ears. I climbed down and ran into the house.

Along one wall of the living room was a long bookcase. I started rummaging among torn old books thrown in behind the others. This is where my parents kept their notes from political lectures, various brochures, a few yellowing trashy novels, and books for young girls as well as the books that had become historically obsolete and, having lost their timeliness, useless.

I stood up on the edge of the bookcase, and from behind the books on the top shelf I fished out a black leather-bound book. In its upper-right corner gilded letters said THE HOLY BIBLE. I held it in my hands, looking at it with awe and curiosity. As I always did. I read it a lot; I loved it because it moved my imagination, and for other reasons too . . .

I kept on walking in front of the church for a long time. I looked up at it, its towers inviting me to distant heights. I knew I had been baptized there, but I didn't dare enter.

I sat down on the sidewalk across the street, put my ball on the ground, and kept looking at the dark, cool arches of the entrance.

A woman with heavily dyed blond hair came along, swaying on her high heels, and headed for the entrance. I knew her. She lived below us on the second floor. I said hello. She nodded and disappeared in the semi-darkness of the church.

I picked up the ball, put it under my arm, and followed the woman.

With reverential patience, I pushed open the swing door and stopped. She stood before the font with holy water and then walked on between the rows of chairs disappearing in the dimness. I leaned against a marble column and watched her from there.

As confident as if moving in her own apartment, she went up to a saint whose head faced upward. She crossed herself and knelt. With her head bowed, she murmured her words. Not for a long time. Then she stood up to leave.

I looked for a place to hide, but she already noticed me and made straight for me.

"How dare you come in here when you're so filthy?" she whispered, and passed in front of me. I looked at myself, waited for her to be gone, and slunk out of the church.

My mother bought the Bible in 1944. My father, along with three of his friends and a printing press, were hiding behind a hastily erected wall in the cellar of a house near the Danube. A solitary window at the back of the house was their only contact with the world. Through that broken window my mother would throw down food every evening and pick up the flyers every morning. The window gave onto a deserted little alley, which my father showed me once. My mother would stop, and if no one was around, she'd drop something through the cellar window. That meant that she was ready to get the flyers. They'd put the package out on the sidewalk as close to her basket as they could, and she would hide it under the vegetables or other packages in her basket, put the Bible on top, and walk on as if nothing had happened. They could not exchange words, because everything had to be done within a few seconds, taking the dangerous chance of being seen by someone from any of the bathrooms in the house opposite.

Mother would take the tram, staying on the platform, holding her basket tight, like a regular housewife taking hard-to-obtain food to her family; the Bible on top suggested that good woman as she was, she might even stop in at a church on her way home. Around her neck, on a thin gold chain, she wore Grandmother's cross. That's how she rode home, her stomach in knots.

Once a priest in a black cassock got on. Only the two of them were on the platform. In the old days Father and Mother played the game of having to hold one's button if they saw a chimney sweep or a priest. Out of habit Mother reached for a button. The young priest followed her move-ment, and then his eyes strayed to the Bible and stopped. Slowly, as if trying to hypnotize her, he looked deep into her eyes. My mother caught herself and in her nervousness almost laughed out loud. The priest went up to her and, looking at her face still fighting the laughter, asked her re-provingly, "How can anyone be so superstitious?" They were coming to a stop. Mother felt that if she didn't get off, she'd burst out laughing. She spun around, and in the last possible moment, almost knocking over the priest, she jumped off, holding on to her basket in which, hidden under the Bible, she had the underground flyers.

Curled up in the stuffed chair, I was flipping the thin, delicate pages. I was looking for the Ten Commandments. I found a few interesting de-tails, then nervously and quickly kept turning the pages, but the law that prohibits lying and talebearing I couldn't find anywhere. I vaguely re-called something about Judas, only I didn't quite know what he had to do with lying, and of the Ten Commandments I could remember only one: thou shalt not kill. These words kept drumming inside my head, and I turned the pages ever faster, slowing down at parts about who begat whom. Then I jumped up and with the Bible in my hand walked into the kitchen.

Szidike was ironing, and the whole kitchen was wrapped in a warm mist.

"What is this?" I asked, putting the book on the table.

She looked at it. As if afraid of a new attack whose purpose she could not fathom, she did not answer for a long time. "The Bible . . ." she said finally.

"You see? And it's written in it that one should not lie! Your beloved Bible says so!"

"Gyurika, please let me do my ironing . . ." She pleaded gently.

"You go around lying, but I should let you do the ironing, is that it?" I snapped. She looked at me imploringly, and I looked back at her an-grily, unsmiling, stern.

"Gyurika, I didn't even tell the madam that you peeked in on me last night . . . it's not squealing."

"Oh no!" I forced myself to laugh. "You're imagining that I peeked in. Where did I peek, when? You see, that's all you can do, lie and lie, right along with your rotten, goddamn Bible!"

I was bursting with anger and fear. I picked up the book, and while tearing its pages, I kept screaming, "There, take this . . . shit . . . you see . . . there you have it . . . you liar!"

She put down the iron and grabbed the half-destroyed Bible out of my hands.

"Why are you doing this?" she asked with stifled dread, and pressed the book against her body. I fell on her, yanked the book from her hands, and threw it against the wall. It landed flat in the corner, its pages spread open. "Why are you doing this to me?" she asked, crying. She walked over to the Bible, picked it up, shook it, and took it into her room. She didn't close the door behind her. I heard her crying.

Next to me, one of Grandmother's nightgowns began to smoke. I didn't reach for it. Some inexplicable vengeance was prodding me to let it burn. I didn't know toward whom or what I should direct my revenge, but in the tension of my jaw I felt accumulating rage. The rose-colored flannel gradually turned brown along the edge of the iron. That calmed me down; taking care to pronounce each word clearly, I yelled into the room, "The house is on fire!"

Szidike sat on her bed, the Bible on her lap. She wouldn't even look in my direction. She thought some more humiliation was coming, and she submitted to it without a word, without any defense.

"Don't you get it? The nightgown is burning!" I shouted.

She sprang up, hid the Bible under her pillow, and raced toward the kitchen. By then the iron had made a solid brown iron-shaped spot in the fabric.

"There, you see?" I said sarcastically.

She stood motionless before the kitchen table. From the rim of the iron, brown smoke rose with a menacing hiss. Her smooth, round face slowly turned red. She was beautiful. I grabbed the iron and put it back on the iron well. She didn't even notice. Her dull gaze seemed glued to the brown spot.

This silent bewilderment infected me too. Cautiously I stroked her hand. "Szidike . . ."

The hand fluttered, reached out for the spot; it felt the spot's contour. Now I was stroking her arms; under my palms, the blond fuzz was purring imperceptibly. In a sudden burst of emotion, she clasped my head. As I looked up, I saw two tears about to leave the corners of her widening eyes. I pressed my head to her breast.

"My sweet mother told me"—her voice broke, but she forced herself to continue—"to make no trouble . . ."

"Szidike . . ." I ran my hand over her face, her soft neck, and her breasts. Her eyes, full of tears, quivered with fear. She shoved me away from her. For a few seconds I looked at her angrily.

"Idiot," I mumbled, and left the kitchen.

11

Grandfather shook his head, motioned to Grandmother to stop her reading, and asked me, "What do you do with yourself all day?"

I was lying on their bed, facing the ceiling, and did not respond. I don't do anything, I thought, only wait for something to happen, always. I imagined that Szidike would come through the door with the burned nightgown on her arm and would start stuttering, Grandmother would yell at her, maybe fish her bunch of keys out of her pocket, and in her anger throw it at the girl. And I would continue to lie on the bed and calmly watch her retreat, slink out of the room, whimpering.

My grandfather turned to me fully and, narrowing his eyes behind his thick glasses, looked straight at me. "Really, my child, what do you do with yourself all day?"

". . . told him to do his homework, but you think he listens to me? . . . Just like his mother," grumbled Grandmother, and kept crackling the newspaper with her fingers. Her glasses slid to the tip of her nose as she blinked at me too.

"I read a lot, Grandfather, and I also study," I answered calmly, continuing to look at the ceiling.

"When I was your age, I was already working as an apprentice. I'd already learned a trade. It's not good what you do," he said.

" 'When I was, when I was,' " I said mockingly. "What's not good?"

"Lying around all day. You'll be a softy!" Grandfather burst out, but Grandmother gave him an angry look, shoved her glasses up to the ridge of her nose, and turned on Grandfather.

"The doctor ordered that he rest. He's so anemic it's hard to look at him."

"The doctor said that two years ago. Since then there's been nothing wrong with him."

"Nothing wrong?" Grandmother exclaimed, sucking on her teeth, and she seemed ready to loosen the reins on her words, but Grandfather turned red, tugged at the clump of silvery hair at the top of his head, and motioned to her that she should continue reading. She huffed a little longer and then, changing her tone, resumed her task. I was listening, and watching the door, but Szidike did not appear. I closed my eyes. Soon the reading ended, Grandmother put down the paper and noisily got to her feet. I felt her leaning over me, and she covered me with a blanket. The unpleasant odor of old age hit my nostrils, but I had no strength to protest. I fell asleep.

The lights were on when Grandmother started to wake me up. "Get up, Doydika . . . you've got to go to bed . . . that rotten maid! . . . come on, get up, dear," she kept repeating. "She burned it . . . well, we'll make the bed and go to sleep . . . you too, go to bed."

I opened my eyes. The burned nightgown was spread out on top of the ironed laundry. But it didn't interest me anymore. I let Grandmother make the bed and help me untie my shoes, and for a minute I thought of the homework I hadn't done, then slipped under the eiderdown.

Water was running in the bathroom. Szidike is taking her bath, I said to myself. The thought brought me to full wakefulness. Without any fear, I could now recall her matte skin, the towel she had gathered into a knot . . . I forced my eyelids shut, to hold on to the image. Gradually I fell asleep again.

The dream brought calm with it.

Szidike, all curled up, is crouching on the wooden mat in front of the tub, but her eyes are smiling at me. She straightens up and comes bouncing toward me. I don't dare look at her. With the tips of her fingers, she raises my head. She laughs. Like my mother . . .

12

Gloomy gray clouds were hugging one another. It was raining hard. Thick streams of water were bubbling from the torn eaves. From time to time the wind raced through the shriveled-up leaves and hurled against my window water that seemed like columns of ice. Plants, trees, and the rusting leaves of bushes lost their color; the lively green of the lawn, the screaming yellow of the tulip tree all surrendered and blended into the grayness.

My room was cool. I had been lying awake for a long time, peering out into the confined world. I didn't feel like crawling out of the warm bed. I'd doze off, some noise would pull me awake, and whether I'd slip back into the soft layers of dreamless sleep or listen to the harsh noises of the wind, from somewhere at the bottom of my consciousness fear kept creeping up. I was afraid of the rain, of Szidike, of not having done my homework, and that I might be taken away, because I didn't know how to kiss or because I left one of my father's books in the garden. These small fears were not attacking me separately; somewhere inside me they swirled in an undefined way, and all of them were gray, like the mist above the grass.

And that's when I felt that I could probably find a solution for everything. If I got out of bed, I'd still have time to do my homework; if I told Szidike everything, she might understand me—but the thought of getting out of bed made me shudder.

Near my head the alarm clock went off. Six-thirty. I felt like crying, but I made myself get up. I quickly pulled on my clothes and on the run I threw some water on my face and hands.

Someone had turned on the oven, and the space where the dinner table stood began to be filled with a welcome heat that smelled a little of gas. My mother, all dressed, was humming as she briskly set the table, lobbing the utensils in a good mood I hadn't ever seen before. Szidike was in the kitchen, standing in front of the stove and concentrating hard on the milk, making sure it wouldn't boil over. The pot was filled to the brim and the skin of the milk, tautened in a large bubble, was inflating, about to spill over. But Szidike shut off the gas and the skin bubble slowly deflated.

"Top o' the morning, you grumpy teddy bear," chirped my mother, bending down and planting a loud kiss on my face, but all I could do was grumble a "morning, everybody."

Szidike tried to carry on Mother's light tone. "He's like a man already, always grumbling," she said.

Mother had a good laugh at this. "Of course he's a man! A sweet little man. Coffee . . . tea . . . cocoa?" she asked, bending down. Then she closed her eyes, deepened her voice, and asked, "Or some soup?" And she laughed.

This didn't put me in a better mood, and I expected that, as happened on other occasions, she'd fly into a rage, but she kept laughing.

"None of these!" she shouted. "Do you have any idea what you will have for breakfast?"

I looked at her inquisitively as I sat down at the table.

"An orange!" she blurted out.

"Stop fooling around," I replied irritably. But Mother couldn't even hear this because she was producing a huge orange from the cupboard and holding it up triumphantly. Curiously, Szidike stepped up close to her.

"An orange," she said incredulously.

"You know who sent this?" Mother asked, her face glowing, and answered immediately, "Comrade Rákosi!"*

I was filled with joy and honor.

"How did this happen?" I asked. "And you talked to him too? And he sent it to me?"

Mother did not bat an eye, but I felt that her smile was phony. "He came up to me and asked if I had a little boy. I said I did, and then he said to take an orange for him."

Then I knew this wasn't true, but I wanted to accept her sweet lie. Only now, many years later, do I try to imagine Mother again as she stands in line at that reception to shake hands with Rákosi; having done so, she moves on and notices oranges on a tray, thinks of me, and quickly, looking around stealthily, slips two of them into her bag. And she might even smile because she is thinking of those flyers.

"And I also told Rákosi that my son is no ordinary boy; he is a good student and a Pioneer. And if he makes the effort to improve his marks in mathematics, he'll be a straight-A student."

By then I felt sure she was lying; how could she have said anything bad about me? If she had said anything, it had to be something good. She put the orange in front of me, stroked my head, and kept cooing and babbling. I was offended.

"And this one is yours, Szidike!" my mother said, shoving the other orange into the girl's hand. While I was peeling mine, Szidike was staring wide-eyed at hers, resting in her palm. She said nothing, but then her

---

*Mátyás Rákosi was general secretary of the Hungarian Communist Party and leader of Hungary from 1945 to 1956—Editor.

glance bounced between Mother and the orange as if asking whether it was really hers. I had never eaten an orange before either but would have been ashamed to let Szidike know it.

"Go ahead, eat it!" I called to Szidike.

"I'll take it home," she replied quietly, "to my mother and Gyurka."

"Go ahead, take it, it's all right, Szidike. They haven't seen one before anyway," Mother said cheerfully.

I left off peeling and put the orange on top of the fragmented peels. "They haven't seen one before anyway." I kept turning Mother's words in my head.

I looked at her, as if expecting a correction, but immediately realized she was right. Szidike's mother and Gyurka couldn't have seen such a fruit. I had only seen colored drawings of oranges in my botany book. Mother's sweet lie turned bitter in my mouth, and I could not accept it. Her patronizing tone when she said, "They haven't seen one before," made her incomprehensible, distant, and repugnant. Suddenly—all this was in a matter of seconds—I couldn't understand how I could treat Szidike with such superiority. I thought of Father telling her, "In this house you are not a servant . . . as of today you are a member of the family!" My father appeared to be a giant to me then. Maybe because he was always out of reach.

Szidike took the fruit into her room, walking cautiously. Grandmother appeared in the doorway. Holding her head high, she threw a pained look at my mother and responded to her only from the corner of her mouth. "I'm taking Papa's coffee to him," she said.

"Leave it, Mama," chirped Mother. "I'll do it. Light or dark? I'll get yours too!"

"Leave it," replied Grandmother. "Don't trouble yourself."

Mother was startled by Grandmother's sharp tone. With stiff movements, Grandmother poured the coffee into the cups, and Mother pottered about at the stove, cutting some bread, spreading butter on the slices. Then Grandmother took the tray and started out. Over her shoulder, she hurled her words back toward Mother. "I shall want to talk to you!"

Mother made a face, and Grandmother turned around fast enough to notice it. "That's all right too," she said, even more offended than before, and stormed out of the kitchen.

Mother winked at me impishly and asked, "Is she always this angry?"

I shrugged my shoulders and buried my head in the dotted coffee mug.

Szidike came out of her room and with a still emotional expression stepped up to Mother. "Please forgive me, I haven't even said thank you . . . it's just that I've never seen a real one before."

"Oh, it's nothing," Mother replied, and ran her hand over the girl's hair.

Grandmother stormed back into the kitchen. On her arm she carried the burned nightgown. "There you are, look at it!" she said, and threw the nightgown on a chair. Mother looked at her, not comprehending, but Grandmother was too furious to engage in long explanations. Grandfather's gaunt figure appeared behind her in the doorway.

"No, Mama, don't—" he said quietly, but the old woman silenced him with a sweeping theatrical gesture.

"Here is your handiwork!" she screamed. "Making faces, yes, *that* you know how to do really well, behind my back, eh? To make fun of the old woman . . . I told you—didn't I?—but then too I was just a dumb old hag no one had to listen to!" Her voice turned to a screech. "Didn't I tell you we'd have trouble if we took a young one? All my clothes get burned. . . . I've got no money to buy new ones every day . . . and that one gobbles up an orange . . . what am I supposed to do with this thing? what . . . ? what?" Her voice became shriller; she grabbed the nightgown and thrust her fist into the brown spot, where the damaged fabric gave way and tore into a hole. "There you are! The work of your maid!" she said, and threw the nightgown to the floor.

"Mama, shut up!" my mother shouted.

Szidike flattened herself against the doorpost, frightened, clasping the white ornamented grooves of the painted woodwork, and with her eyes— that's what I felt—looking for me. I closed my eyes. I knew I should speak up.

Grandmother gasped and under my mother's gaze rapidly retreated to the door. The veins stood out on Grandfather's forehead. He started to cough, and bitterly repeated again, "No, don't . . . no need to . . . leave it alone, all of you . . ."

"All right, all right!" Grandmother said breathlessly, grabbing the old man as she left, and slamming the door.

For a while Mother stood motionless, and then she picked up the nightgown and with stiff, awkward movements began to fold it. She went back to the utensils on the table. She turned to Szidike. The girl was still standing against the door, frightened, apprehensive. "You ought to be more careful! I don't like this sort of thing."

That's when Szidike looked at me.

I took a section of the orange and popped it into my mouth.

13

By Sunday morning the rain had stopped. The dim yellow disk of the sun appeared vaguely behind the clouds; then a dark tattered cluster swam before it, and it disappeared, as though it were playing a game. Nothing moved. It seemed odd that in the sky the clouds were moving and down here everything was so calm. Calmer than usual. Morose ivy leaves were crawling high, gripping the sumac tree in a fatal embrace. Drops of water were gliding from one shiny, oily leaf to the other, reaching the ground as if descending from floor to floor. In the grass, puddles of water were plashing. The concrete paths were like taut bright strips on the incline, all headed toward the gate.

I was standing by my window.

Beyond the gate, on the street, nothing moved. The dull clamor of the cogwheel train, reviving and dying off, was also a reflection of time. On Sunday morning it ran only every half hour.

From the kitchen I could hear the familiar clattering of dishes. The foyer door opened and Father, in his bathrobe, with his shoes on but without socks, his hair disheveled, ran along the concrete path, took the newspapers out of the mailbox, and on the run, careful not to slip, headed back to the house. He noticed me; with the rolled-up newspaper he waved to me and disappeared behind the door.

I stood by the window for a long time. I was stalling. I felt that if I moved, if I washed and put on my clothes, I would have to enter the day, and whatever had until now been smooth, easy, and light would be all scrambled up, would turn hard and merciless.

I put my forehead against the window. My arms were folded. My breath spread a light mist over the glass. I drew figures in it. Then I blew new misty spots and crossed them with new lines.

The door was pushed open. It was Grandmother with two empty water mugs in her hands, which she took to their room every evening.

"Hi, Doydika," she said, and smiled while she crossed the room.

"Hi."

"Get dressed quickly. They'll be here soon."

I didn't even look at her. I was concentrating on the figures on the windowpane as they were slowly disappearing. It's all over, I thought.

I washed up. Carefully I got dressed, put away the bedding, and lay down on the sofa. I was engrossed in my reading.

The first car stopped at our gate around noon. I got up, and from the window I saw the driver jump out of the car, run around to the other side, and open the passenger doors.

A thickset man and a wiry woman got out. They waited. The woman said something to someone inside the car. She seemed very familiar. Maybe because of the way she held her head. Then the front door popped open too, and with a graceful movement Éva stepped out. She was wearing a blue woolen dress, with a small white collar, and white stockings. They were arguing about something. Éva looked into the garden and petulantly shook her head. The wiry woman moved very close to Éva, and now they resembled each other even more. In every one of their gestures.

In the meantime, the driver returned to his seat and let the engine run. The three of them stood there, outside the car. Then, nudging Éva before them, they started up the path.

I jumped away from the window, threw myself on the bed, turned toward the wall, and closed my eyes. Are they going to take me away now? Or are they coming for a visit, as guests? But then why did they come in a car? They live right here, one street below ours! Why is the car waiting? For whom?

For me . . . I curled up. From somewhere far away I heard my mother's loud greeting. The foyer door slammed, and they all walked into the living room. Maybe the car was gone! Because I couldn't see it from the bed, I looked out the window. Indeed the car was gone . . .

I let out a huge sigh. My legs were shaking. I plopped back down on the bed and grasped my knees; they were still shaking.

And now more cars were coming in quick succession. Engines stopped, doors were slammed, followed by the garden gate slamming, engines roaring loudly again, the sound of footsteps, shadows passing by my window, loud greetings everywhere, the scraping of chairs in the living room.

In different circumstances, these noises would have seemed very simple, but now they seemed to have coagulated, piled up. Everything was familiar, as if it all had already happened once before. Because I had been waiting for it.

Where could I hide? How could I disappear from their eyes? The garden is wet. I can't go up to the attic. They'd notice me.

I stayed lying on the bed.

Grumbling, Mother walked into the room. "Maybe you'd be kind enough to make an appearance, would you?"

I pretended to be asleep.

She shook me. "What are you doing? Everybody's here already. Is Count Till making everyone wait for him? What's going on with you?"

I changed my expression. "All right . . . I'm coming . . . don't shout."

Reconciled, Mother looked at me and said, "The children are in the winter garden. You should go there . . ."

Before opening the door, I changed my expression again. I tried to smile.

In a cane chair turned toward the window, Éva sat with her back to me staring rigidly at the garden. The two Pozsgai boys were standing over my scattered toys; the older one was kicking the pieces of my Erector set.

"Why are you kicking it?"

"Because," he answered, and panted while puckering his lips.

"Is it yours?"

"Mine has a lot more pieces."

I was watching Éva. I knew I had to talk to her. I couldn't avoid it. Either I'd walk up to her or I'd leave the room . . . but that I couldn't do. I felt my mother's piercing look in my back. Slowly I went up to Éva. I said hello.

She nodded.

The Pozsgai boy was still kicking the Erector set.

Angrily I spun around; only then did I notice the Ungvári girls under the giant ficus. They were thin, prim, and haughty. With graceful gestures, they were showing off in their spectacular dresses and barely deigned to look at me.

"Hi, you two." I greeted them. Their lips moved, but I heard no sound. Should I go over to them? I turned my head and looked at Éva. No. I won't go. They were whispering to each other. I shrugged my shoulders and turned my back on them.

"Hello," I said to Éva.

She looked at me but did not reply.

"How did you get here?"

"By car," she answered mockingly.

"To visit us?"

"Yes, if you don't mind."

"Don't be angry with me."

"You insulted me."

"I'm sorry."

"You bore me, like the rest of them. I'm going to skip out of here."

"Me too," I told her, and thought she'd be glad if we did it together.

"You stay right here. You are a coward."

"I am not . . ."

"Don't think I forgot everything. But sometimes one has to keep things under cover. By the way," she added casually, "I had my father report you."

"We'll set up the swing," said one of the Pozsgai boys.

"Go ahead," I said, and walked out.

14

I felt like laughing. I knew she was lying. She wanted to scare me. She was wrong! I am not a coward. I don't like to fight. That's not cowardice. Cowardice would be to run away. I am strong; I can look at my parents calmly in the eye.

That made me think. Fear, like a cloud, passed over me. Maybe I couldn't face them calmly. Maybe she wasn't lying, and had told on me . . . I'd go into the living room; her father would stand in front of me and say, "I'll have you taken away now. The car is waiting outside." The car had left. "I'll have you locked up." "You can't do that!" Mother would shout. But he could, because he's more important. Their house is more beautiful.

My dislocated senses refused to labor further. They were rebelling. All

I wanted to do was to cry. But I didn't dare lie down because anyone might walk in. At any moment.

I was stumbling further in the night that was suddenly descending on me.

Szidike . . . I'll tell everything to Szidike . . . But Mother called from the hall, where she was kneeling before the hastily opened closet doors. Tablecloths, sheets, napkins, and towels were strewn all around her. She kept throwing more and more things on the floor.

Her proximity had a calming effect on me.

"What are you looking for?"

"That damned white tablecloth! Have you seen it?" She looked at me.

"Where would I have seen it?"

"Just asked," she said, and with her whole upper body leaned into the closet. "It's not here . . . not here . . . I can't find it!" she railed. "Get Grandmother."

"All right," I said, and started out.

"Wait, I'd better do it myself," she called after me quickly. "Call Szidike."

"All right."

Szidike was in the kitchen, standing over a large pot of steaming, bubbling water, watching the dumplings.

"Szidike, Mother wants you, come on," I said. My unusually soft voice seemed to confuse her. She wasn't sure she should come immediately or finish her job first.

"Gyurika, the dumplings will overcook. Tell madam comrade I'll be right there."

Mother and Grandmother were standing around the laundry hamper, its contents all over the floor. They both had their hands on their hips. With puzzled looks, they were shaking their heads.

"Well?" Mother turned to me.

"She's coming, but the dumplings might overcook."

"This is for sure," my grandmother said.

"I don't think so."

"You always trust people, until you have to pay the price."

"Come on, Mama! What would she do with a damask tablecloth for twelve?"

"Her corporal gets mustered out and they'll get married."

"Mama!"

Mother was thinking but didn't say anything. And suddenly I felt guilty too. As if I had stolen the tablecloth. I felt myself blushing. Szidike couldn't have stolen it! Why not? I certainly hadn't. Nervously I said, "It must be someplace else."

"Gyuri, you're blushing. You know where it is!" Mother turned on me.

"I don't."

Szidike came in. Mother was facing away from her; she put on a smile before turning around. "Have you seen the white tablecloth, dear?"

Szidike was at a loss.

"The white cover, the white tablecloth."

"I haven't seen it."

"Because we've looked for it everywhere, and it's nowhere to be found," Grandmother put in.

"And Gyurika doesn't know either."

"Wasn't it in the laundry to be ironed?"

"No, it wasn't. I would have remembered."

"We've looked everywhere," repeated Mother, and poked at a pile of clothes. "You're sure it wasn't among the ironed clothes?"

"No, I'm telling you, it wasn't." That is when Szidike must have understood Grandmother's thinking. She grew pale.

"If you burned it, you'd better tell us!"

"I've got nothing to put on the table . . ."

"It wasn't burned . . . because it wasn't there," the girl moaned.

"It wasn't with the clothes to be ironed!" I shouted, beside myself.

Mother walked up to me and slapped me in the face. Her thick ring cut my lip. "There," she muttered, "you'll learn when to shout!"

I stared at her. Szidike jumped over to me. Grandmother grabbed Szidike's arm and yanked her close. "You stole it. Need it for your new home, don't you?"

I brought my hand to my mouth. It got bloody. I didn't know what I was doing. I couldn't pay attention to myself. I smeared it all over my face. It was like licking steel.

"No," Mother muttered again, "don't," and she freed Szidike's arm from Grandmother's.

I went to the bathroom. There was no fear in me. Now people were pure before me. I understood them. I was afraid of them only when they spoke.

Szidike was standing stiff.

"Let's have it," said Grandmother, leaning into the girl's face.

"Mama, don't," Mother said listlessly.

The girl shuddered; then with steady steps she started out, biting her lips.

"Wait," Mother called after her weakly. "Come on, stop, wait! We didn't mean to—"

They went after her. Szidike sensed this and changed directions. She walked into her room, leaving the door open behind her. The two women stopped. The girl's face was rigid, more severe than frightful. Like the face of a dead person. And just as pale. With slow, deliberate movements she opened the closet. There was hardly anything in it. Two silk blouses, one turquoise and one white. She threw them out of the closet to the floor. She swept her underwear off the shelf and threw out two skirts. She did all this in silence.

She walked to the sofa and folded it up. From the bedding bin, she dumped the quilt, the pillow, and the sheet. There was nothing under them. She moved to the night table.

Mother signaled with her eyes to Grandmother. The old woman walked away, her face frightened.

Mother stepped up to the girl and held down her arms. "No, Szidike, don't," she said gently.

The girl tore herself away and flung open the door of the night table. Mother looked anxiously at the girl's face, which seemed insane. Mother clasped the girl's shoulders and pressed her down on the bed. She sat next to her.

"Don't, Szidike," she said.

Szidike lowered her head, as if exhausted and destroyed. She was crying silently. Her tears flowed down her round face, along her nose. She let them. Mother was stroking her head. I stood, numb, in the doorway.

"Go, tell Grandmother to put on the pink tablecloth," Mother whispered to me.

"All right," I said.

15

Monday morning Szidike took the train home. She was to come back Tuesday. But she didn't. We thought she had missed the train. We called the train station; there were no more trains until early Wednesday morning.

She didn't show up on Wednesday either.

It was around nine o'clock in the evening when I heard the car door slam. I was sitting at my desk doing homework. Then the gate creaked miserably, and Mother's steps could be heard on the garden path. I didn't go to open the door. She didn't even take off her coat.

"Doing homework?" she asked, looking at me.

"Yes."

"Szidike?"

"Didn't come."

"That's what I thought."

"Something must have happened."

"Yes. She's afraid to come back."

"Because you attacked her, all of you."

"What do you mean, we attacked her?"

"You kept accusing her."

She waved her hand and started out. "Are you coming to the living room?"

"No."

She stopped, came up to me, and stroked my head. "What's going on with you lately?"

"Nothing."

"Doydika, I can see it. Why don't you tell me everything? Sometimes I'm very nervous, I admit. Have I hurt you?"

"No."

"Don't sulk! My sweet little Doydi." She leaned over and kissed my head. I felt I had to hug her. I put my arms around her neck and got frightened. I realized I was unable to love her. It was my fault. She kissed me again and seemed to have calmed down.

"Are you coming?"

"Yes."

She left. I stared at my notebook. I finished the problem I had been

working on, then listened to the water rushing in the pipes and to the little noises of the bathroom. I also heard when she went to the closet. I got
up and joined her. She was putting her sewing box on the table. "Got
anything that needs mending?"

"No."

She took her knitting out of the box, looped the yarn around her finger, leaned back, and, while her hands worked rapidly, looked at me and
smiled. "What happened in school today?"

"Nothing."

"Did you have to report in any subject?"

"In Hungarian. Got an A."

She nodded. "And you didn't even study for it."

"Hungarian I don't have to study. I just listen during classes. That's
enough for me."

"Well, it wouldn't hurt to study too."

Grandmother stuck her head in. "Hello, darling."

"Hi, Mama. I hear Szidike didn't come back."

Grandmother pushed herself inside. "I didn't think she'd dare come
back. And I also know why."

"That's what I thought too."

"Didn't I tell you?"

"What?"

"That there would be trouble."

"Don't start again, Mama. I beg of you."

Grandmother made a solemn face. "I can't find my blue terry-cloth
towels. Three of them."

"Mama, please look for them—"

"I *have* looked for them. And I know why she isn't coming back."

"Mama, I don't believe—"

"Did she take her clothes with her?"

"I don't know."

"I do. She did. She didn't leave here anything. I looked into her
closet."

"No, Mama, I don't think so."

"The towels disappeared! I looked for them everywhere."

Mother stood up. They left the room. I did not move. I could see how
they once again emptied and turned over the contents of the linen closet

and the hamper and went through all the clothes waiting to be ironed. And I could also see how Mother's skeptical expression turned into one of anger.

They came back. Grandmother was smiling, as if to say, See, I told you so! Mother clenched her lips, sat down, picked up her knitting, and then threw it down.

"One of the sheets is gone too," she said, mostly to herself.

"I don't think Szidike would have taken it," I said.

"What do you mean, you don't think? Then who else?"

"Mom, didn't you see her face on Sunday?"

She looked at me incredulously. "There are facts," she answered.

The gate creaked. Vigorous steps on the garden path. With tired movements, Mother got up.

"I'll go warm up your dinner," said Grandmother with the old enthusiasm.

Mother opened the door. Father entered and let his eyes get used to the dimness. Then he bent down to Mother's mouth. "Hi, sweetheart," he said.

He walked by me.

"What's up, kiddo? How was school today?"

"All right, kiddo," I answered.

He knitted his eyebrows and looked back at me. His bag stopped in midair. He didn't put it down.

"Three of Mother's terry-cloth towels and one of our sheets have disappeared," said Mother.

"Did she come back?"

"No, she didn't."

"Well, that's absurd," Father exclaimed, and threw his bag under the coatrack. He was shaking his head.

"Did she write?"

"No."

"You have her work permit."

"As if she really needed it."

"That's true."

"Tomorrow I'll go visit her ladyship."

"How will you go?" I asked.

"By car. You want to come?"

"There's school."

Father looked down, smiling at me. "Even you can be absent once. We'll write you a note that you were sick."

"All right," I said, and I was all smiles. That's how I looked up at Father.

16

Everything was milky white and infinite. Along the road, broken by heavy horse carts and cut up by countless grooves, the bare poplars stood like the intricate towers of Gothic churches.

We had left the concrete road a good half hour earlier. The car was bounding in the potholes, throwing itself in all directions. We had to hold on hard.

The driver was grumbling. Small whitewashed farmhouses stood kilometers apart. All shabby, as if thrown out into nothingness. On both sides of the road, grooves of plowed land ran toward the houses. There was hardly any shrubbery. Here and there we passed some marshy stretches. At the bottom of large depressions, full of reed and bulrush, there was no water, only frozen sand.

"We should ask somebody," said the driver, keeping his eyes on the road.

"Let's go in somewhere," Mother replied.

We turned in toward a farmhouse. The driveway was wide, covered with grass. We drove up to the yard and stopped.

Nothing moved.

"Does anybody live here?" Mother asked, probably of herself, and we got out of the car.

We took a few steps toward the house. The doors were closed, and the windows, dusty and grimy, stared back at us. Then a pug-nosed, square-faced old man came shuffling from behind the house. An oily fur jacket hung off his shoulders; a fur cap was on his head. His jacket was unbuttoned; he had on no shirt under it, only a dirty sweatshirt. Black stubble covered his face. He gaped at the car.

Fear gripped me suddenly. Maybe this is where she lives. Why did I have to come? Szidike couldn't have stolen anything . . . she is not like that . . . or maybe she is?

"Good day," Mother said cheerfully, and extended her hand.

The old man rubbed the black, cracked skin of his hands and then fee-
bly shook Mother's hand. He was still looking at the car.

"Uncle, we're looking for the Tóth family. Could you tell us where
they live?"

The old man was swaying his head. He didn't answer. From among the
hoary daisies, a skin-and-bones dog rose to its feet. It was obvious that
walking took great effort; slowly it limped toward the old man, its rust-
colored short fur standing up on its back. When it reached the old man, it
rubbed against him. The man looked down at it and kicked it aside.

"You wouldn't know where they live?" Mother repeated her request.

"There are lots of Tóths around here," the man answered, his words
drawn out.

"They have a daughter named Szidike," said Mother, raising her voice
as if talking to someone hard of hearing.

"Here everybody has one. But not in this neighborhood."

Mother seemed confused. She looked at me, puzzled.

"But where then, uncle?"

The old man started to sway his head again. The door behind him
opened a crack. A young woman stuck out her sleepy head. She must
have just gotten dressed because all her clothes were in complete disarray.

"Father, get out of there!" she screamed wildly at the old man.

The old man heaved up his pants, turned around, and, shuffling away,
rounded the house.

"Who are you looking for?"

"The Tóth family!"

"There are lots of Tóths."

"With a daughter, Szidike."

The woman was thinking, and mumbling, "Szidike . . . Szidike." Suddenly she said, "The shop assistant, or the other one, in the school?"

Mother shrugged her shoulders. "I don't know. The one working in
Budapest."

"Oh, the one that's gone to be in service?"

"That's the one."

"She came back."

"That's the one we're looking for."

The young woman, still in the doorway, arranged her clothes, blinked
at the car, and stepped outside.

"You take the big road to the school," she said, and pointed, "then turn left. It's there by the woods. You'll see it."

We thanked her and got into the car. The woman stayed put, looking at us. The old man stuck out his head from behind the house.

We turned around and headed to the paved road. I looked back and saw the old man come out from behind the house. The dog took off and, barking wildly, tried to keep up with our car.

The two of them kept standing there, motionless.

We covered a long way but saw no woods. Then a sparse acacia grove appeared. Beyond it was a long house. No driveway led to it, only a trail-like path. We got out of the car and continued on foot. Frozen sand stuck to our shoes. Chilled, Mother gathered her coat about her.

"Terrible," she said.

"What's terrible?"

"The way they live."

I didn't answer.

"They don't even have electricity here," she said, looking up into the air.

As we left the stunted acacia grove, the forlorn farmhouse seemed to turn to face us.

Mother stopped. She gave me a look before moving on. A stable without a door was gaping darkly at us. We stepped on a veranda-like gallery running along the front of the house. Mother stopped again, hesitated, then knocked.

There was no response. She opened the door. We stepped into a small entrance space. Opposite the door, under the table, a wooden pallet stood covered with a coarse, threadbare blanket. A crucifix hung on the blue wall. From here another door opened. Mother knocked again.

Someone called out. It was Szidike.

We walked in.

Szidike was sitting in front of a high clay oven, peeling potatoes. A small boy, naked from the waist down, was squatting next to her and eating the raw potato peels.

The knife stopped in the girl's hand. Her head stiffened. On an iron bed behind her lay an old woman, an eiderdown pulled up to her neck. Seeing us, she raised herself to her elbow.

"Good day," Mother said quietly, and closed the door.

Szidike blushed and stammered. She jumped up from the kitchen stool and grasped Mother's hand. She kissed it.

Mother turned red, and yanked her hand away. "What are you doing?"

The girl ran to the old woman lying in the bed. She started arranging the pillows and at the same time was whispering, "Dearest, this is Madam Till and—"

The old woman was looking at me.

"That's Gyurika."

The little boy stopped munching on the peels and blinked at me with amazement. Then he continued munching. Szidike jumped over to him and took the peels from his hands.

"You shouldn't, Gyurika. Please sit down, over here," she said, and wiped off the kitchen bench. "Sit here, please."

We sat down. Mother unbuttoned her coat.

"How did you—how did you find your way here?"

"We came by car."

Silence. The old woman propped herself up a bit more and turned to us. "It's because of me that Szidi didn't go back. I'm alone, and Gyuri—" Her voice cracked, then turned into a whistling cough.

"No matter, it's just that we were expecting you and didn't know what happened to you," said Mother.

"I wanted to go, but I couldn't leave them here alone . . . or the animals."

"We were waiting for you—"

"Yes, but I couldn't."

Mother lowered her head. The wrinkles on her forehead were running into one another. Then she lifted her face and took a look around the room.

A blackened chiffonier between the two fogged-over windows. Above it a faded mirror. The chiffonier covered with a white cloth, on it a devotional picture in a tinfoil frame. Next to it a Bible, bound in black leather. And the orange, still in its wrapper.

I instantly recognized the Bible. My heart began to beat very hard. Mother did not notice it. Szidike was following our glances. She rushed to the chiffonier. Hesitantly, her hand reached for the Bible. Her face twitched; she looked frightened.

"I didn't . . . really . . . please believe me, I didn't—" she said, and suddenly brought her hand before her mouth.

As if sensing something, Mother stood up. She picked up the Bible. She opened it. Szidike bit her finger and whimpered something I couldn't understand. Mother's brow darkened. Her powerful cheekbones were jutting out of her face. "This is ours," she said gravely.

Szidike silently, with trembling legs, lowered herself to the stool, then sprang up and held on to the edge of the chiffonier.

"I don't steal . . . we're not Gypsies . . ."

Mother appeared not to have heard. "How did this get to you?"

"Well—" she stammered, and turned her frightened eyes on me.

"I gave it to her," I whispered, though I thought I was shouting. "Mommy! I gave it to her! She doesn't steal, believe me! I gave it to her."

Szidike plopped back down on the stool, let her hands fall in her lap, and cried. The little boy stumbled over to her and babbled something incomprehensible. She shook her head.

"I gave it to her," I kept repeating.

Mother let the Bible drop on the chiffonier, then picked it up again. She opened it, kept turning it in her hands. From its covers she carefully wiped off invisible dust. The little boy took a peeled potato from the pot and rolled it against Mother's feet. Mother looked at him and slammed the book shut. The little boy glanced up and, like a beast of prey, pounced on the potato.

"Mine," he said, and began to nibble.

Mother looked at me and Szidike. "I believe you," she said hoarsely. Then, raising her voice, she turned on me. "Do you have any idea what a memento . . . what this means to me?"

"I do, but I thought we wouldn't want it anyway . . ."

She made no reply. Szidike raised her apron and wiped her eyes. She didn't look at us. The old woman lay in the bed, her face rigid; save for the inner sounds of her body, nothing reached her anymore.

Silence, except for the tiny noise of a raw potato being chewed by the little boy's tiny teeth.

"Szidi didn't go back because of me . . . I'm alone," the woman whispered, her eyes fixed on the ceiling.

"Will you come back to us, Szidike?" Mother asked after a long while. The girl shook her head hesitantly, indicating that she couldn't, and gazed at her mother.

"Then I'll leave your work permit here, all right? And let's have no hard feelings toward each other."

Szidike shook her head again.

"But I will take the Bible . . . it's an important keepsake," said Mother, almost apologizing.

The girl did not respond. I was the only one looking at Mother. She put the black, leather-bound Bible on the edge of the table. She took the work permit, a little booklet, from her bag. She wrote something in it, put money between the pages, and handed it to Szidike.

We stood up. Mother extended her hand to the girl. She held Szidike's hand for a long time, mostly out of absentmindedness. She forced a smile on her face. It was as if her thoughts were already elsewhere. She started out.

I saw that Szidike would like to bend down and kiss me. I offered my face. When we were very close, some unpredictable force pulled both of us back. We only stared at each other. My eyes clouded over. I reached out with my hand. It took a while before she accepted it.

As we were walking out the door, I looked back. There on the table, hiding its torn pages under the heavy binding, lay the Bible. Mother had already reached the path. I didn't call after her. With wavering, swaying steps she was making her way over the clumps of frozen sand. From time to time she looked back, as if asking for a respite, but my eyes did not respond.

With a stubborn resolve to avoid any response, I followed her.

First published as "A Biblia" in *A Biblia* (Budapest: Szépirodalmi Könyvkiadó, 1967).

Homecoming

for Miklós Mészöly

In the fall of 1973 I traveled from Berlin to Rostock and from there to Warnemünde. I had not a thing in the world to do in either town, where I knew no one and no one knew me. I wanted to see the sea and wound up looking at it from the tenth floor of a cheerless, boxlike new hotel.

The water was almost perfectly calm, the sky heavy, overcast, and the air humid. The food in the restaurant was bland and boring. At night the temperature dropped below freezing.

This must have been during the last days of October, which is always a special month for me, as if every year I were reliving the tribulations of my birth. I feel it as a joyful season of pleasant objectivity. Spring's germination, budding, flowering, and fresh starts make me irritated, unpleasantly restless; summer, with its hastiness, its limp heat waves and furious thundering, I find much too hysterical, as if nature wished to finish off something in huge contrasting strokes; and in the winter we never get enough snow, and I weary of the grayness of bleak prospects. Autumn is my season. With its dazzling sky, morning mists, its smells of burning, protracted rains, colorful berries, its leisureliness, swarming flies, early frosts. My mental attitude, with preferences for parting and enjoyment of transitoriness, may have to do with the fact that because of my somewhat sour historical experiences, I regard the future with ominous premonition rather than with hopeful images radiating energy and strength; the long and short of it is that I'm not a spring person. On the other hand, action is not one of my strong suits, which might account for my resentment of summer, while death is something I fear too much and know too well to enjoy its eternal winter, though I admire its isolation, strictness, and the geometric precision of the blooms of its icy flowers.

I was born to be an onlooker, or to be more precise, the month of my birth has restricted my life to the boundary between life and life's passing. Neither here nor there, I live in a state of in between.

As though on a regular schedule, I fall ill almost every autumn. Still, runny nose and fever, teas, and handkerchiefs notwithstanding, that is when I feel spiritually whole in the world. This is the artful wholeness of transitoriness, perspiration, feverish nightmares, and not yet fatal unpleasantness. In the clear autumn air, with the summer hysteria of the will to live gone, one hears better the distant tolling of the bell.

Some think of me as reserved, others as cruel, yet others as objective. In truth I am as sentimental as a piece of bread spread with butter and honey, much too sentimental to release what is ephemeral and condemned to death within me, and it always crumbles before my very eyes.

That is just how it is with emotions.

I keep forgetting all this, and every autumn illness catches me unawares.

In Warnemünde, for example, on my first night there I went down to the hotel's sauna and then, without waiting for my heat-soaked body to cool off, immediately made my way to the beach to stroll among the abandoned wicker sunbathing chairs. A wool scarf around my neck and a light coat did not protect me well enough, but my feet so enjoyed the fine soft sand I could not stop walking in the sharp evening fog. The result was not long coming; that very same night I came down with a high fever.

I have no regrets because that evening and during the night the possibility dawned on me of a work whose realization, with all its joy and pain, filled up and fulfilled every single day and night of my life for the next ten years and more.

Two days later I continued to Heiligendamm, where my fantasies, fueled by feverish hallucination, received a material, topographical frame.

In those years I was struggling with serious professional problems. This meant having to cope with the most basic questions of my life, with fateful questions that kept giving birth only to more questions, to which I had no hope of finding answers. This was a great dark forest in which I found not the true path but, rather, all the false, slippery, alluring, and misleading tracks and trails. I was not looking for the so-called truth; no, I simply sought security, the antidote for my anxieties, which were becoming unbearable. Or death. Nothing occupied me more in those years than the thought of extinguishing my own life.

I was taken ill with a love come true.

I was nineteen when this illness first spread throughout my body. So by that time it had been eating away at me for eleven years. My rashes had festered and were oozing; they itched, and I scratched them; they hurt deliciously; I did not want to live any longer.

I did not want to live another minute, though I was very much alive.

If the circumstances of my birth and childhood had been other than what they were, or if I had been born into this life with different sensibilities—which is to say, if I had been given the chance to reach my youth in times of peace, without the sight of death and piles of corpses—most likely I would not have been so sensitive to the love of the body.

In the natural course of life one remains for a very long time totally deaf to death; one comprehends it, but it does not turn into a close experience; one may surround it with rituals, make light of it, and approach it very cautiously. Only when past the age of pleasure extracted from one's own body, past the age of having found beauty in another's body, and way past the romantic experiences of trying to blend one's self-induced pleasure with another's beauty, when arriving in the desert of adulthood, does one truly begin to deal with death, to grow up in time for death, if one is capable of growing up at all.

I was not sheltered from death, from deterioration and decay; as a result, I began to live my life in a precisely reverse order.

Union with another's body affected me the way others are affected by the unexpected loss of a dearest being. It awakened me not to life but to devastation. I should have learned to speak in a new language, but my mother tongue was death. It is well-known that only a mother tongue can be spoken with perfect naturalness; my studying the language of love was in vain so long as death was speaking in my dreams.

I well remember that nineteen-year-old fragile youth who only a few weeks earlier had become acquainted with the body of a woman. He cannot have enough of her, yet he dreads his own insatiability. But he considers himself lucky to wake each dawn from his horrible dreams to the sight and touch of this body. Still, he considers the deliciously delayed explosion of fulfillment exaggerated and illicit; it is at once him and her, reality and illusion, as is the road leading to her, so rich in nuances it knows no repetitions though it's nothing but repetition. Sometimes he also finds himself engulfed by disgust, which he does not understand.

I recall going swimming one morning. The cool water washed my love out of my pores. I was slicing through the water with big, energetic, youthful strokes, as one who can confidently entrust all his thoughts and every part of his body to the water. Except for my loins. My body had become a separate being, utterly aroused even when in a relaxed state. That is when I thought that this body, which with the strength of my limbs I was dragging from one end of the pool to the other, should die at the very first opportunity. It should have perished in the substance of the other body, for it could endure nothing else. It had become vulnerable. With the knowledge of the other body, it would not be able to endure life. It wanted to die. Thus I kept swimming to the opposite end of the pool.

As I have said, I am an autumn person. Far be it from me to voice any complaint, self-pity, or accusations. I have no desire to blame anyone for my inside-out life; I accuse neither my fate nor history. Precisely because my life is turned so strangely inside out, I simply try to observe its realities.

The realities are hollow. It is the observation of them that provides real or imagined, useful or useless contents.

In those years my narrative style gave me the most trouble. Not that I couldn't write plain sentences that others believed to be authentic; I was the one who did not sense a complete, perfect inner credibility, the kind that could be measured against my being. I felt in my own sentences as if I were walking around in strange clothes, now in this kind, now in another, always in some costume. Of course fate had blessed me with a certain penchant for mimicry, but it seemed that this gift, which is indispensable to understanding and living the lives of strangers, would deny me the means to express the relationships and attractions that interested me most. In vain did I hit on some style or tone that at least appeared close to my temperament and mentality; in vain did the narrative engine start up in the adopted mode, if after a few cleverly spun sentences it stalled on the clods of my own boredom and resistance. In my sentences I was imitating writing. The spacious, full-blooded structure swarming with myriad details yet lucid and transparent, a hallmark of every narrative work, could not come into existence from the monkey tricks of my sentences. At the same time, I was successful, and that made my situation all the more dangerous. Critics, comparing my descriptive talents with those of great writers, publicly showered me with praise. But fortunately I listened more to my pains; in other words, nothing could have guided me better in this literary entanglement than my own torments.

These torments increased to the point where after the execution of a few polished short stories, not only did I become dissatisfied with my sentences, but I also felt the punctuation of my sentences was invalid and false. Commas and periods, dashes and question marks: they were all false. I found paragraphs even more repulsive because I could not decide when or why I should begin a new one, and when I did, did I really have to believe it appropriate?

I felt I was putting punctuation marks here or there because that's how others were doing it, without comprehending their relation to me; so my marks had only a global meaning but no personal value. And the more faithfully I served this consensually accepted global sense, the more I distanced myself from my personal requirements.

Like love, my work did not awaken me to life either; rather, it devastated me into life. I saw no other possibility to solve my problems except to kill myself.

I made several attempts. What held me back was neither fear nor a guilty conscience but the thought that going through with it would mean shifting the compounded torments of my life onto the person I loved most. I knew that this happened in ordinary life, that among themselves people barter with the feelings they receive, but I was excited about accomplishing the all but superhuman task of not doing that, of leaving no pain behind for her, but of bearing my fate without moving a single muscle of my face. Until the moment of my death. For I was still hoping to die. Since I could neither die nor kill myself, I had to work. Work meant writing slick, safe, calm sentences—in my dazed and half-dead state—sentences whose sense or sober punctuation would convey nothing of my real emotions, thus making me face once again the urgent notion of having to kill myself.

I kept struggling with these thoughts for long years, until about the age of thirty.

During these long years, with a gradualness I was hardly aware of myself, I developed my particular system of punctuation. First, I left out the conventional notations of speech; as I did not think the frequent insertion of question and exclamation marks was proper, and not wanting too many commas, for every kind of monotony repelled me, I restricted myself to simple sentences. Today I would say I had returned to the most ancient form of simple declarations. Of course one must consider well what one wants to declare. Anxiety causes cramps in the stomach, lumps in the throat. I needed to express the simplest things. For example, I needed courage to call a table a table, which others also hold to be a table, though I know that the word "table" is merely a conceptual aid, alluding to the morphological identity of all tablelike objects in the world, and incapable of expressing the peculiarities of my table. And adjectives cannot solve the problem, either, because the situation is the same with them. These seemingly foolish questions become questions of vital importance in periods when the universality of a culture is assured only by the universality of its uncertainty and turmoil. Had I put this in the form of a question or exclamation, I would be letting others make the decision. I spewed knots and lumps into the declarative mode. However, my parallel declarations lent my text a body that assumed its shape and inner thematic structure not through punctuation, such as an excellent student would apply automatically, but through the manner and rhythm of parataxis. I learned that in this way sentences acquire their own rhythm, and the text as a whole a peculiar kind of breathing. From the reader's point of view, this means that he reads not only with his eyes but also with the rhythm of his breathing and, consequently, with his blood pressure as well. Punctuation has a direct relationship to physiology.

The music of the text, resulting from the inner rhythm of the sentence and the relation between the sentences, proved to be a very malleable means that could be used in a multitude of ways. On the one hand, it had a most profound and intimate connection to me, as a living, breathing person in possession of a definite life rhythm, and on the other hand, it had an equally powerful connection to the situation of the text in which I made use of it. In tune with the inner needs of a scene, the rhythm could be sped up or slowed down; it could dissolve, roll up in knots, turn into a saccharine melody or a hammering beat; it could pant or become winded, and yet it all remained me, without the text's losing any of its objectivity or becoming boring and repetitious in my own critical eyes. I discovered for myself one of the most obvious traits of the language. The found music carried me away and led me to thrillingly wild and not at all inauthentic associations of images. I became aware of the two-way mutual relationship that links the phonetic form and the meaning of the word. I ascribed an atomic existence to the word, in which phonetic form and meaning had the same function as that of the electron and proton in an atom. I arrived at a situation in which not only was I thinking of words, but also the words began to think for me and along with me. This phenomenon may also be observed among so-called loquacious people. Because their thought-controlling apparatus, their inhibitions, work very sluggishly, they pour out not what they want to say—if there is anything they want to say at all—but the linguistic schemes of their physiological system and psychological state, and in the pleasures of intonations, in the acoustic downpour, they create surprising links among seemingly very distant phenomena of their lives. Now I had to be careful not only that any declaration or statement of mine have a credible meaning, but that the declaration, inspired by the text music, also think of itself as appropriate.

My texts became more objective, aesthetically well ordered, but no matter how attentive I was, their orderliness stemmed from the musical organization of the text. My friends' warning that I was making music rather than speaking did not come as a surprise. Having taken a different road, perhaps a higher one, I was back where I had started. There was a problem with my narrative style.

As if while searching for the method I had forgotten what I really wanted to write about. But this was not quite true, either, because finding the music of the text brought me closer to the object that attracted me. Still, it seemed I was only giving my voice a bit of a workout—true, on a particular scale. Without a doubt I found some sort of principle of form, but I was still far from the experience and the insight that in a complete form there must be proportionate room for the formless, the raw, the deformed, the irreparably ugly, the awkward, and the magically contingent. I felt the objects of my interests and attractions to be formless, not given to beautification, ugly, and contingent. Yet these were the reasons I busied myself with stylistics. It was like pulling the devil's leg. Although my stylistics managed to develop certain muscles, they weren't adequate to execute the movements I wanted to perform. In this period of my life anxieties about my narrative style turned into thematic questions.

I had to find for myself a rather delicate thematic point from which I could take off—with the help of my discovered stylistics, which I thought inadequate and too loyal to theories of form—and head toward the narrative of my own formlessness.

Nothing excited me anymore except my own total formlessness or, more precisely, my unshapable formlessness that lived in a form, my in-betweenness, my raw will to live feeding off my death wish, my easily aroused sensuality that plunged me into the most vulgar adventures, my brutality that kept mating with refined attentiveness, tenderness, and sentimentality, only to give no satisfaction and to remain ungratified.

I may have been considered, until then, a moderately oppositionist political writer who, while keeping to the silently and consensually ac-cepted rules of literature of his time and with an average innocence, walked into the china shop of political manipulations and caused no small amount of enjoyment for his tiny audience busy with everyday problems. My interest turned first toward stylistics, then, on the path of stylistics, toward eroticism. I reached an area in which the politician loses all influence. Unless he is a tyrant. This change of direction, which may have been a turning point, had been prepared in me to such a degree that I also understood its political ramifications.

A politician, if obeying the compulsion of his calling, becomes a per-son who assumes a conjunctive, instrumental, stylistic, and nonthematic relationship even with his death, since he must look even at his death as a unique factor that will influence politics. As opposed to this, I, who ever since I can remember have been in a subordinate relation to death, have thought about everything from death's point of view; I think of eroticism also from the final standpoint of death. That is why death for me cannot be a means, not for a moment, not even if I were to wish for my lover's death. If therefore I occupy myself only with my death, as practically I deal with nothing else, then I manage to wrest life's most sensual territory from incompetent and highly irresponsible hands.

I did not have the chance, nor did I intend to separate myself from history or politics; on the contrary, I wanted to cling to them, in some obscene way, by descending to the most common and mortal regions of my self. And like all converts, I wanted to be extremely radical—

immediately. I did not long for rolling heads, human sacrifice, gurgling blood, or washed-out brains; I wanted only parched lips, the fine fragrance of genitalia, sperm, slick and slippery vaginas, intercourse with people of all races and social strata, the smelly sweat and protracted moans of love. What every living being discovers in him or herself as the primal chaos and the attraction of mortality. At least in the culture we live in.

There was therefore a longing for a form that would gain its strength from formlessness; a stylistics, with muscles not developed appropriately, that imagined itself capable of following the breathing of various human conditions; a relatively good penchant for mimicry, readiness for empathy, some psychological objectivity—for me new at the time—and some ability for abstraction, though not enough to break away from its own practicality and become a philosophy.

This is how things stood when, still hot from the sauna, I went for a stroll on the Warnemünde beach, and by nightfall I had a fever.

Ever since my early childhood my reveries have had two definite forms. Either I would brood over death, about its expectant approach, its form and possible sensation, a little bit as though I were watching everything from a time beyond my own funeral, or to allay the tension evoked by these thoughts, whether comic or tragic in nature, I would make up stories, complete series of actions, fables, tales, and yarns whose resolution was, once again, a death. A story would calm me, of course, because it would be not about my death, therefore not about personal death, or, because it is impossible to live through it, about abstract death, but always about one case of death.

On that stroll I was imagining that the retired Thomas Mann was walking on the beach. My brain turned Warnemünde into Travemünde, which I knew from his novels, letters, and memoirs. So then, Thomas receives a union-paid holiday in the summer resort at Warnemünde and, by chance, is accommodated in the very building where he had once loved a boy with true love, a boy who in the end was murdered by another youth out of jealousy. That is what he is remembering now. "Thomas Mann at Breakfast in Warnemünde" is the culinary title I would have given to my imaginary short story. I kept on fantasizing, but imagination is never allowed to cross the borders set by reality. I learned how true this was only when, years later, I began to read the unendurably long-winded diary of the master whom I so greatly respected—and therefore regarded with no small amount of derision. In one of his notes, Peter de Mendelssohn, the diary's editor, informs the reader that Thomas Mann, in his Munich years, indeed had a romantic relationship with the painter Paul Ehrenberg, and of this tragically broken-off love affair the master wrote half a novel, which, after his marriage to Katja Pringsheim, he destroyed.

In those days I was longing for something that others, for any number of reasons, could not set down on paper, or would not want to, something that, in their stead, I would have to write.

I thought then that the literature of the century was full of lacunae of this sort. Even in the works of the greatest writers you can spot the points of truncation. In my view, these were no accidental, instinctual, or irresponsible gestures but, rather, results of our culture's prohibitions. Anyone who can read in this culture will therefore not only comprehend the truncation but also see which limb has had to be sawn off.

My profound understanding and grandiose plans had a thematic hitch. By submitting to the same cultural prohibitions that caused Mann and many other great authors to truncate their works or at least to refrain from speaking freely, my "I" would be left out of this nicely devised stylistics game. But what would happen, I fantasized further, if alongside this game, already developed to the point of plagiary, idiotism, and parody of parodies, I were to place nicely and innocently the sources of my own ribald game? What would happen if in the most uncouth and most formless manner I piled high the simpleminded documentation of my life right next to the stylistically very demanding ones? It would be very nice, I enthused feverishly, because in this way I might be able to serve up what is bloody serious as something like a game. The shapely and the shapeless, the direct and the indirect would face off very nicely, and I would gain a structure that had a striking resemblance to that of the classical novel. But it would also differ from the classical structure because the chapters of varying stylistic values not only would have their independent meanings but also, like a bridge, would link what was so contradictory and different within me. There would emerge a reassuringly transparent structure in which I could create the interplay of various elements and motifs with contradictory contents, without the appearance of contradicting myself. Whatever I could not relate this way, I would relate that way; now I would satisfy my stylistic tendencies, now my thematic ones, almost arbitrarily or, more precisely, by conforming to those rules that make one loquacious or taciturn, brazen or humble. Therefore I would not be tied to a single tone or manner, would not have to narrate the whole novel within a single scale; I could be like this or like that, I could wiggle out of this or wiggle out of that. Freely and with head held high, I could strut about in borrowed feathers because this heightened formlessness could become the form not only of details but of the entire work.

When I got home, sobered up, cured of my illness, I began to work.

I tried to hit the stylized note. I ran up against it once, twice, three times. I could not do it.

My search for a handle on the stylistics of the two great truncators was in vain because I was not thinking correctly about them. I took their indirectness for truncation. Comparing the facts of their lives and of their aesthetics, I suspected lies—that is to say, I was evaluating form from an ethical standpoint. Both Proust and Mann wrote in a style much too parodic to make them the object of my parodies. Later I came on the cheap fin de siècle romantic novels that had fed their parodies, and I too took a sizable gulp from this murkily bubbling spring. Back then, however, the truly obvious solution—that the most subtle effect derives from the most trivial one—was still out of reach because I was far from the insight that direct speech conceals at least as much of the object as does indirect speech. In my youthful daring I wished to entrust myself to direct speech, had nothing but contempt for indirect speech. It bothered me no end that I was still busy with questions of stylistics. I did not want to read or look for sources; I wanted to write. In a word, I had a seemingly unavoidable desire to write everything I had failed to write about the few moments of an evening in the life of my hero Thomas—not about him but, without any distancing or transference, about myself. Not the way I am writing these lines. In those days I would have liked to write the way things were.

But how exactly were those things?

I began this new effort at the dawn of my father's suicide. I wrote that a teenage lad, who I was then, is startled out of sleep at dawn; it's getting light outside, he looks at his watch, it's only four-thirty, but he can't go back to sleep.

It is four-thirty. He calms his anxiety the only way possible: with pleasure squeezed out of his own body. There is nothing exceptional in this; that is how he had done it before, and that is how he will do it later, though his father, who caught him at it once, emphatically warned him that it was forbidden. His pajama gets slightly wet in the front, there will be a stain, which makes the paternal prohibition not quite without danger, but at least he manages to fall asleep again. It is Sunday, April 15; he does not have to go to school. Later, around nine-thirty, he is awakened by the bell. He opens the door. His aunt and uncle, deadly pale, are standing before him, and they give him the news of his father's death, which occurred at four-thirty.

In this approximately twenty-page typed manuscript, I left not the slightest crack for my imagination. With my bent for mimicry, I was imitating not a person or even a possible person, but rather my former self. I gave no free rein to my love of telling a tale; I limited myself exclusively to the most objective description of the situation as I was able to see it.

By no criteria could I have found the result uninteresting. During the writing I already felt how swiftly I was being carried toward the limits of madness. Like a drug addict deprived of his drug, I withdrew myself from my only drug, the story. A simple rereading of it was enough to reinforce the feeling.

At the time I was living in complete isolation; I worked for four or five hours and had no contact with anyone during the rest of the day. In the lonely week and a half that it took me to write those twenty pages, an imaginary bell jar, absorbing all outside noise, descended on me. I could have thought this wonderful, but trusting the need for some final sense of equilibrium and for an innermost protest, which in fact contradicted the rules of my profession, I felt that if I continued this way, a very ominous error might make inroads within me. I stopped in mid-sentence. The text had reached the bottom of the page, but I did not bother to start another page. I lay around helplessly for a week.

I probably should have looked for some other activity, but the bell jar would not let me. And no matter how many times I read and reread the text, it did not seem uninteresting. At most it may have been tasteless, but at the time I could not have said why. Neither could I decide why I had wound up, so tragically, in a confrontation with my intentions, while I felt I had arrived at the place I wanted to be. I only knew that I could not live under the same roof with this text. I burned it.

Today, without being able to recall this text word by word, I see that the reason for its disturbing, or at least not uninteresting, tastelessness was that its maniacal insistence on authenticity and truth created a direct connection between a man's voluntary death and a boy's autoeroticism. Like the already mentioned loquacious persons, I said something but did not know what I had said.

The temporal concurrence of the two series of events is not in question; they might be called historical facts. When the father sends a bullet through his own heart, the boy starts up from his sleep. When the father falls back, the boy puts his hand on a sensitive part of his body. These are mythic facts and need no moral comment of any sort. However, my text was dictated by a belated guilty conscience, which in that moment thwarted my insight into the mythic value of the moment, and I also did something that according to my father (by then already dead), I should not do at all. Going against his mythic prohibition, I unconsciously disgraced the dead. The tragic tastelessness of my text derived not from the objective description of my self-gratification but from my using moral standards when trying to interpret the mythic connection between two distant, unrelated facts.

Still, I would not call the experiment useless. Because I discovered once and for all how important it was for me that the moments when certain events occur can be judged morally too; in a word, how immeasurably sentimental I was. It also became clear that the mythic connections of existence cannot be measured by moral standards. If we approach them with moral standards, any real emotion degenerates into false and useless sentimentality, and we are dealing no longer with existence but only with its contingent moral projection. It further became clear that the reality of a text brought to life on paper should not be confused with the reality of a life we may call up from memory, because just as remembrance lives in its own shades and nuances, so must the text too have its shades and nuances. A text may receive its distinctiveness only from the imagination; imagination is life's only means that can ensure passage over the abyss between the uniqueness of personal experience and the generality of the experience that is common in each individual. In our culture, imagination guards the balance found at the boundary between the mythic and the ethical; thus it has also become clear that anyone who, in the name or interest of any kind of truth, is willing to abandon imagination is likely to give himself over to madness or immorality. I had a single choice left: with a selfishness bordering on paroxysm, to go beyond the personal.

As we know from others, a manuscript does not burn up. And it was not really the manuscript I burned but, with the barbaric act of a fire sacrifice, my infantile longing for the truth, which had produced a falsehood producing more falsehoods. At the same time, this was the first gesture of my adult life made against annihilation. I did what I did against my own death wish, against my own final negativism. For the first time I said straight to my demon that I had no intention of going insane or of killing myself; oddly, by doing this, I found myself closer to rather than farther from death.

I realized that to reach or understand any kind of truth, we need some intermediary. The demons carefully conceal my open self and remove their hands a little bit only if in my fear of death I entrust myself to my imagination. Please listen and understand well: entrust myself neither to my will—the will ties you up in knots and drives you to madness!—nor to my sober calculations based on experience, because calculations make you relax and lead you to depravity! If I choose neither of these two ways, if I manage to avoid the Scylla and Charybdis of our culture, then the demons mediate willingly, as does my imagination, and let me see what I cannot possibly see.

Until that time, because of some instinctive choice, I wrote almost all my texts in the first-person singular. From then on I began to hate this first-person singular, and this hatred helped me try consciously to speak of myself so that the speaker would be not only me but, in equal parts, my self and what is common to others within this self.

Of course all this was not nearly so theoretical as it sounds now.

What happened, simply, was that a single word took shape, or rather crystallized within me: memoirs. I shall write memoirs. The parallel, temporally slightly out-of-phase memoirs of several people, somewhat like Plutarch's lives. And these several people could all be me, without being me. That is how I arrived at a common, generally accepted form I thought I could fit into.

My imagination took off. Characters, faces, bodies, gestures, clothing flooded toward me with all their words and smells. I thought I would fly away in my happiness or drown in this abundance. I would need a miraculous, mute secretary who would hear my thoughts and see my sights and put it all down on paper. I became infinitely wealthy, I was living off the fat of the land. I lay about, lolled in bed, and did not even try to sit down in front of the white sheet of paper anymore. I felt that my game had some nice mysterious rules. I should let my imagination go wild, spend its fury; if we are so deep in the goodies, I can easily afford to let the chaff fall by the wayside. I didn't even take notes. A word written down ties you down, and I did not want to be tied down. After a while my imagination indeed began to be selective; it organized, regrouped, and the continually rearranged order created new details and pages.

Two years had passed since the stroll in Warnemünde. I mostly lay abed. An outside observer would assume I was in deep depression. For the first time in my life, and I hope for the last time, I lived on pills. I took sleeping pills to sleep, tranquilizers to stay calm, uppers to stay awake. I was really ill. I had never stared at walls so doggedly.

My imagination did nothing but—with colorful bursts of enthusiasm, and giving free rein to hitherto restrained or stray energies—go about processing the fundamental experiences of my thirty-three years. Had I thought of myself with such enthusiasm, I probably would have become very dizzy, but my imagination was thinking for me. In the meantime, my body, the real one that could not be substituted, did nothing but slumber, doze off, drag itself around. It had no appetite, ceased to have any desires.

Soon, after about three weeks or a month, I gave up the pills. They had weakened me and invaded my mental state. Imagination probably needed a certain amount of pain to be able to function.

In those days we lived on the eighth floor of a building in a housing project. Opposite us a concrete monstrosity similar to ours was going up. Day and night the work continued, complete with the noise of cranes, mixers, and dump trucks. I assumed it was the Inferno's noise, though I did not believe the author of *The Divine Comedy* could have imagined it like this. Whenever I couldn't get away, despite my cunning and trickery, from the editorial office where I worked in those years and go to Kisoroszi, in the country, which meant that regarding my planned novel I was condemned to inactivity, my imagination and I had to hole up here, in this concrete but otherwise not badly furnished box on the eighth floor of this concrete hell.

I am exceptionally sensitive to noise; my entire adult life has been filled with the battle against, the fleeing from, and the mental suffering caused by noises.

Oddly enough, it was in the midst of this hellish construction noise that I decided I could not wait any longer for my circumstances to improve; therefore I could not defer the matter. My imagination had grown tired; inertia had forced it to keep plowing its way through its own products again and again. I was afraid this process would begin to bore me. One afternoon, with earplugs in my ear, a soft velvet-covered pillow pulled down on my head, I tried to ignite the usual séance of my imagination; it was no go. I got up, sat down at the table, and began to work.

Of course this "began to work" is not an exact phrase. It would be more correct to say that somebody, for the first time in his life, began to speak in his natural tones. I was that somebody, but at long last I succeeded in writing sentences that were stretched out between the rawest demands of self-knowledge and the subtlest form of imagination, without slipping over to tasteless confession or mere fantasizing. I am extremely proud of this. The demand of confession burdens the sentence with an exaggerated objectivity; it imbues the sentence with meanings that, although comprehensible, may not always be decipherable. In reality, such sentences contain more than what they say. Just the opposite is the case with sentences born of sheer imagination; their lack of objectivity makes them ungraspable; they say more than what they contain. And while the former sorts of sentence are too close to reality, the latter are too far from it.

My imagination is also a phenomenon of life; therefore it cannot possibly produce facts that might not be true. However, in literature only those facts of the imagination can be accepted as authentic whose place and value I can feel because I have traced them back to the phenomena of my everyday life. If my imagination and my dreams produce something whose place and value I don't recognize in my life—judged to be rational—then for the time being I should not yet write these scenes, sentences, images, or feelings, no matter how attractive and aesthetically pleasing they may seem to me. I should include them in the blacklist of "suspect" and "to-be-solved-later" problems, because such a phenomenon means nothing more and nothing less than that in this case I am not in control but defenseless and at my own mercy. And my sentence would be equally defenseless. But it would be also a mistake to let the phenomena of my own life bypass my imagination and enter my sentences directly. This would mean that I wasn't aware of their place and value among life's other phenomena, or at least that for the time being I hadn't had a chance to find their place and value. It would make for a puffed-up sentence dominated by moral judgment; therefore it could not possibly speak of life or existence. Better to leave such a sentence for better days.

The ideal literary sentence may be born of imagination or experience, but it must gauge its imagination within its experience and its experience within its imagination. For my imagination it is my experience, and for my experience it is my imagination that will become the only possible worldly means that will help me get to the outside of what I am on the inside of. In a world without intermediaries, it is impossible not only to live but also to write regular sentences.

When I began to write my novel and for ten long years afterward, always, I prayed to God as fervently as I could and begged him never to let me stab a single sentence from above. I could not help thinking of Saint George raising his lance and gracefully running the dragon through. Not like that. Please.

The honest sentence might make one mighty, but one may not act mighty with the sentence.

In an honest sentence two forces are at work simultaneously. Imagination is galloping ahead, while experience is plodding behind, checking, sometimes restraining the galloping, and it is good that this is so. Imagination makes you swell, spread out, sprout tendrils in all directions, grasp everything around you, while experience cuts it all back, gives you direction, prunes what is superfluous, and it is good that this is so. This statement refers to the sentence born of imagination. The one born of experience is slower from the outset, drier, occasionally downright gray or awkward. Imagination gives it a nudge and little licks, once in a while even attempts to dress it up, stick a few sparklers on it, give it a bit of fragrance, yet the sentence born of experience keeps standing on its terrible clay feet, and it is good that this is so. Experience keeps the sentence rooted to the ground; it is sensible, immovable; imagination carries it away, infuriates it, and drives it mad—and it is good that this is so.

In an honest sentence no son of man can define the proportions of intuition and consciousness; the tension between these opposites is precisely what creates the inner proportions of the honest sentence. It is honest because it is tense—because of these opposing forces—but it does not want to be tenser or slacker than it can be according to the value of its location; therefore it is proportionate.

The honest sentence follows neither existential nor moral theories; its existential theory may be deduced from the degree of its tension, the quality of its language, and its mode of intonation, and this is also its only possible moral theory.

And then ten years went by.

First published as "Hazatérés" in *Játéktér* (Budapest: Szépirodalmi Könyvkiadó, 1988).

Little Alex

Alex Kovács had been given a Spartan upbringing. When the invitation arrived, therefore, his parents, though not too pleased, did not let him see how they felt. They decided he would make the trip alone, and on foot, on the road between the two mountains. After a lengthy explanation about how to go, they thrust a good-smelling box wrapped in tissue paper into his hands, drew him a map on a page from his notebook, and on Sunday the little boy set out in the early afternoon.

Wearing his black felt pants reserved for festive occasions, white shirt, and red sweater, he stepped out of the gate of their villa. He felt pretty gloomy. Partly because of the thick felt pants, which had been altered from his father's uniform and dyed dark blue—the blue turned out black—and partly because he did not feel like going to the party to which his parents, not he, had been invited. For reasons unknown to him, they excused themselves but made Alex—perhaps for the same reasons—make this visit.

The bullnecked little boy thrust forward his head, which was always sheared bald for health reasons, and, kicking at fallen leaves, made his progress through the still-familiar streets. He passed the Clock Villa, where, as he had been told, the traitor General Görgey had held his war council, though at the time he had not yet betrayed Hungary.* Alex

---

*Artúr Görgey was the general who ended the war for Hungary's independence when in August 1849 he surrendered to the Russian army that had intervened on the side of Austria; his capitulation was regarded by Louis Kossuth and his supporters as tantamount to treason—Editor.

glared with great contempt at the building contaminated by the traitor, and turning back several times, he kept looking at the shabby, squat row of columns. He could not understand how people could live in this house. Yet people did live in it, in this villa marked by history; on lines strung between stately columns, bedclothes were drying, pink bedclothes.

From the villa the road declined sharply. Alex was no longer on familiar ground because this area fell outside the territory of the children's ramblings and skirmishes; only in the winter, during their wild sled chases, would they venture this far. With a ducklike gait, he was descending slowly; by the time he reached the water-worn bottom of the road, he looked disheveled, his shoes were dusty, his shirt soaked through with perspiration, but he felt good this way. Only the thick pants with their sharp creases bothered him a little. He kept jumping in and out of the roadside ditch, saying hello to strange pedestrians, and laughing at the humorless grown-ups with wonderment and concern on their faces.

He correctly identified the street and matched the house number to the one listed on his map. When he stopped in front of the yellow villa— its exteriors made impressive by the French windows and wrought iron balconies—and looked at the neatly divided areas of the lawn in the garden, Alex, instinctively aware of a contrast, looked at himself before pressing down the handle on the gate. With the creases long gone, his pants looked like stovepipes and were dotted with some prickly weed; on his dusty shoes, which showed no sign of their earlier, careful shining, there were two or three droplets, indicating that he had had to stop on the way. No definite notion had formed itself in Alex's mind, but he sensed the dissonance between his attire and the environment he'd come from and the one he would now have to enter. The difference wasn't great—an adult would probably dismiss it with a wave of the hand—but Alex's world, like the world of children in general, was too narrow for his imagination to overlook even a small shade of difference. The villa he lived in was massive, overadorned, and run-down, while this villa was friendly, simple, and well cared for; while his family's garden, witness to romantic adventures, was overgrown with shrubbery, in this garden everything was finely planned out and cunningly pruned to look natural.

In the world of adults this difference did not mean much because we might say it was chance that determined who used this garden and who used that one; in fact adults thought that the whole thing, in a certain sense, was fairly transitory, not tied to any particular person and therefore interchangeable at will and at any time. But in this seeming uncertainty Alex discovered certainty; in his eyes the current situation was the final one, the only situation in which his consciousness might get its bearing and find its way. He reasoned therefore that if this house was more beautiful (and however reluctantly, he had to admit this, standing at the gate), its residents had to be of higher standing. And in this naive, childish hunch—deserving of a smile—a simple truth took shape.

He pressed down the handle, crossed the path leading to the entrance of the house, and, looking at the small droplets on his dusty shoes, walked up the few steps. He let the bell ring for an impolitely long time; no one came to open the door. He walked back down the steps and, being familiar with the life and layout of these villas, without giving it a second thought walked around to the back.

In front of the building's facade, on chairs set up on a deep green lawn, a large company was sitting under the clear sky. They were deep in conversation.

Nobody noticed the approaching little boy.

A tall man had the floor. None of the men wore jackets, and the only difference between them and the man talking was that his shirt sleeves were rolled up to his elbows. He was gesticulating vehemently with his hairy arms, and perhaps because of that, he seemed wilder, more desperate, and more undressed than the rest of them.

From among the familiar faces, Alex sought out the one he thought belonged to the mistress of the house; this was a buxom, freckle-faced woman with thick legs.

His head thrust forward on his ruddy bull-like neck, the pebbles crunching loud under his feet, Alex headed straight toward the woman as if to gore her.

The hairy man's arms stopped in midair, then lowered themselves to the armrests of his garden chair. The whole company turned toward the little boy, and on every face appeared the smile obligatory when looking at small children. Alex did not see this; with a quick glance at the woman's freckled face, he stopped in front of her. Before muttering his low greeting, he shifted the small packet from one hand to the other, quickly looked around at the adults, interrupted in their conversation, and felt some headstrong rage that immediately distanced him from those sitting on the chairs.

"Good day," he said quietly.

As a response, here and there among the company, well-intentioned but somewhat rusty laughter was heard.

The word "fools," spoken in his father's voice, ran through Alex's mind.

The woman got up from her chair, ran her thick hand over Alex's head, clasped his neck, and led him toward the house. Halfway there they stopped.

"Go on, Alex," she said, flashing her huge buckteeth. "Your little friends are waiting for you . . ."

Alex looked at the door he would have to go through, and shrugged his shoulders imperceptibly.

"Yes," he said.

The woman returned to the company, and Alex walked to the nursery.

This was a large, light corner room; the sun came through a wide window facing west, but it did not illuminate the entire space, so that Alex, in the first moment, saw only one little girl in the wide strip of light. She was wearing a little ballet costume of pink tulle and tiny pink ballet slippers. The little girl was toddling, spinning on the shiny parquet floor inside the strip of sunlight; she was puny but not ungainly. When she noticed him, she stared straight at him with the large gray eyes in her mousy little face. But Alex did not deign to look at her long; he looked around quickly and noticed five or six little boys and girls in dark blue or colorful dresses, sitting on the floor or on chairs in the darker part of the room, looking at the performance with obvious boredom on their faces. Alex had no idea what he was supposed to do and therefore felt an immediate dislike for those sitting in this room too; he also did not know to whom he was supposed to hand the tissue-wrapped box, which had become dirty and tattered in his sweating hands. Everyone was looking at him, and he stood motionless in the doorway. He ran the tip of his tongue along his lips, thrust the box forward, and hesitantly said, "Who wants this?"

The little girl in the pink ballet costume pirouetted closer to him.

"I do."

"Is this your birthday?"

"Yes."

"Then here you are," Alex said, and handed over the box.

While the two were talking, the others jumped up, relieved; a fat boy began running around in circles, and the girls took a doll off the shelf and argued whether to dress or undress it. Then the fat boy leaped over to the girls, grabbed the doll, and galloped away, and the squealing girls took off after him in hot pursuit.

For a while, motionless, Alex watched the chase. The sound of stamping feet, screaming, and yelling filled the room. The little girl in the tulle costume jumped up on the sofa—one could see her underpants, which had slipped to the side—and in a whiny but commanding tone was shouting so hard the veins on her skinny neck protruded.

"Give it back to them! Give it back!"

When the fat boy ran past him, his face flushed and happy, Alex, without moving any other part of his body, stuck out his foot. The fat boy tumbled full length to the floor.

In the sudden silence that followed, the tulle-costumed little girl burst out laughing, ran to the boy on the floor, retrieved the doll, jumped back up on the sofa, and rolled her eyes wildly. "I'll give half my kingdom!" she yelled.

This sentence seemed so pointless to the others that they turned away from the fat boy, scrambling to his feet, who was sniffling loudly, and stared at the little girl. But there was neither continuation nor explanation. With a softened countenance, the little girl jumped off the sofa, letting the doll drop from her hands, danced across the room, and disappeared.

Alex withdrew to the corner between the pink lacquered closet and the cold glazed-tile stove. He was sweaty and covered with dust. He propped his back against the wall, as one who is on the defensive while also preparing to attack. No one paid attention to him; the movement getting under way in the nursery was the natural movement that must begin in every human community whenever people who do not know one another find themselves in the same space. Those who belong together band together, and those who feel they have nothing to do with one another turn their backs to one another; the lonely ones remain alone.

In a few seconds the little girl reappeared, jumped up on a chair, from there to another, and from that chair stepped on the sofa to gain the windowsill, where she sat down and observed the throng beneath her. From time to time her gaze also ran across Alex, standing in the corner. At first as if she would not notice him, then with a sarcastic smile on her lips as if to emphasize her separateness from and power over the others. When this gray glance flashed at him a third time, peremptorily ordering him to move away from the corner, Alex surrendered to the little girl on her windowsill throne and lowered his head. This compelled gesture sufficed to shake him out of his state as a calm observer and make him feel humiliated and vulnerable. He pressed himself harder against the wall—the traces of his open palms would be seen there for a long time to come—but this movement, which could be construed as defensive, was in direct contrast with his fury. Not consciously, only with an animal instinct, he sensed that there were only the two of them in this room—he and the little girl—who in their souls carried the loneliness of rulers and of chosen ones, and they must clash.

Meanwhile, the nursery showed the tranquil picture of children at play, the kind that never fails to move adults peeking through the crack left by an open door. Toys lay strewn everywhere, pieces of furniture had been moved from their places, the fat little boy was now making a phone call from under the rug to his friend who was riding the bookcase, straddling it with widespread legs, and must have been in a great hurry for he kept digging his spurs into the horse's groins. Each time he did this, the bookcase became a magic steed, a transformation that did not interfere with its rider's ability to receive instructions via the telephone and to scan the horizon with his binoculars at the same time.

"The Germans surrounded the company," came dimly from under the rug.

The little riding boy responded by making a combative face, saluted, and was about to say something when the little girl rolled off the windowsill, her tulle skirt quivering around her waist; she jumped over a few chairs and knocked the rider from his seat.

"You will not sit on my shelf!" she said, her words flying like sparks.

The little boy, before he realized what had happened, found himself on the floor, but he couldn't quickly return to reality; he aimed his arm at the little girl's head, closed one eye, and began to rattle like a machine gun. The little girl pushed the bookcase back in place and then gave a sharp tap on the barrel of the machine gun. The little boy jumped up, and they probably would have been at each other's throats if not for the drawn-out sound of a female voice behind them coming from the direction of the door.

"Children! Cocoa is ready . . . come on!"

The birthday girl's mother spread her arms as if to embrace all the children hurrying toward her. Alex was still standing in the corner. When the little girl passed in front of him, he raised his head. They looked into each other's eyes. Alex leaned very close to her, which made him perceive her gray eyes glittering behind the lids, narrowed to be especially sarcastic.

"Your mother's cunt!" he whispered to the little girl, and yanked his head back.

In the little girl's face everything changed. Her eyes opened wide, and lines of the most profound astonishment collected on her forehead, but this lasted for only a second, and then the face readjusted itself. A new being, different from its former self, was standing before Alex; the brazen features vanished; the countenance of someone who had wanted to rule everything lost its edge and took on a gentle mien, as if the obscenity had given birth to the person the little girl would one day become. But they had no time to continue the searching and gauging game of their eyes, and thereby to understand the alteration that had occurred—the little girl was now ready to bow to Alex's will—because the woman at the door spoke again.

"Klárika, put on something decent this instant. Whoever let you wear *that*?"

Klárika looked at her mother, but most likely without grasping the meaning of the words; she understood only that an order had been given and, like a sleepwalker, started out after the other children standing in line in front of the bathroom.

"Are you deaf? I'm talking to you!" The woman's voice snapped and then, as adults know so well how to do, suddenly turned sugary. "Alex, dear, come on over here, we'll wash your hands."

Klárika trudged back into the room to take off her little ballet outfit, and her mother guided Alex to stand with the other children. At the sink a very tall, very gaunt woman was doing the job; she would put each child's head under her upper arm and say, "Well then, let me have your hands!"

When he heard the same sentence for the fifth time, Alex looked at the woman's face. Actually, it was a young face, though it seemed old to the little boy because of the many wrinkles running under her eyes and around her mouth, and while she washed the dirty hands, her jaws moved as if she were talking to herself or her gums were grinding food. Alex did not wait for the sentence; he raised his head, smiled at the woman, and said, "I'll wash them by myself."

But no matter how scared or disgusted he was, his head also wound up under the woman's armpit, and the sentence was heard: "Well then, let me have your hands!"

When the hand washing was over, the children were herded into an even larger room, where even more windows gave onto the garden and where a huge long table, covered with a pink tablecloth, was set with a variety of cakes and pastries. Out of a gold-rimmed bone-colored pitcher the hostess was pouring steaming, thick, slowly trickling cocoa into sparkling porcelain cups. The children's procession went around the long table. Klárika burst into the room behind them, gave Alex a shove, and said, "Sit over there."

Alex sat down; the hostess again snapped at her daughter, "Stop running around! You'll be all sweaty!"

The little girl shoved aside somebody who was about to take the chair she had had her eyes on and settled down opposite Alex. The gaunt woman put a trayful of stiff whipped cream in the middle of the table and looked silently at her mistress, who responded with a smile, flashing her large buckteeth. As silently as she had come, the gaunt woman left the room. The hostess dished out the whipped cream and also lit the six little candles on the cakes. Klárika blew out the six little candles, and they all had to clap; then the cake was cut and everybody got a slice, and the room was filled with the pervasive smell of the tallow candles, and the cake was also smelly on the plates; and the hostess smiled continuously, throwing a word now this way, now that. Alex squirmed in his chair, picking at the stiff bristles on top of his head, and at the same time trying to avoid Klárika, who had been regarding him with transfigured admiration, unable to take her eyes off him.

When the woman finally left the room, Alex tasted the hot cocoa, and then with the tip of his finger he scraped a little icing off a cake and licked it while sending a cautious glance in Klárika's direction. With her nose deep in the cup, Klárika was slurping her cocoa, but her eyes were searching Alex's brown face. After taking another gulp, Alex looked up.

"What are you staring at?" he asked aloud.

Klárika laughed, nicely, freely, and for a long time.

"What are you laughing at?"

Klárika continued in bursts of laughter, infecting the other children, laughter spreading around the table; the fat little boy laughed so hard that pastry and whipped cream, mixed in a mush, came churning out of his mouth. Alex laughed too and looked around. Everybody's laughing, he said to himself, and he let his voice boom: "Well, what are you all laughing at?"

His shout turned out to be so loud everyone fell silent. Alex looked around again and now felt he was the center of the company's attention. He took his cake from the plate, put it in his palm, jumped up on his chair, and said, "Look at this!"

Everybody looked. Alex sought out Klárika's eyes and slowly began to bend his fingers. There was complete silence, except for the increasingly louder squeals of Klárika, which began to sound like a siren. Alex suddenly clenched his hand, and whipped cream gushed out between his fingers. He licked it up. But no one laughed at this either. He plopped down on his chair and, as if imitating a dog, began to lap up the flattened cake on his open palm. All around the table the children stopped eating and waited quietly for what might happen next. Klárika kicked out the chair from under her, dashed around the table, and stopped behind the overfed little boy.

"Lick it for him!" She pointed to Alex's hand.

"I won't," the boy said, insulted.

Alex looked at the little girl, and he stood up slowly too.

"Lick it, I said," insisted the little girl.

"I will not!" the boy screamed.

With his arm stretched out, Alex stood between the two and thrust his palm under the boy's nose. The little girl stood facing him, the fat boy between them. Alex's and Klárika's eyes met for a second, they understood everything, there was complete agreement between them, and Klárika pushed the boy's head so that his nose sank into the remains of the cake. Resounding laughter. Somebody's elbow knocked a cup off the table, the cup smashed noisily. In the same instant the two boys were at each other, but it was immediately obvious that Alex was the stronger one. With a few hits and shoves, he proved his superiority and then smeared the cake all over the boy's face. Klárika was rolling with laughter. The party was thrown into total disarray; the children, as if gone mad, ran wildly around the table, and the fat boy, sobbing aloud, retreated into a corner, wiping his face in his sleeves. Alex was standing in the middle of the circle; he looked around again to assess his situation, and his eyes again met those of Klárika. "Shut up!" he screamed.

Silence followed.

"Now we play dog!" Klárika said, and got down on her knees.

"We won't play . . . anything!" screamed the fat little boy from the corner, still wiping from his eyes the cream that had mingled with his tears.

"Shut up!" said Alex, now a little more softly. "We are going to play dog!"

The children knelt submissively and then lowered themselves on all fours.

Klárika sprang up. "Everybody, stay like that! Whoever asks nicely might get something to eat," she said and picked a cake from the table. "Come on, beg . . ."

The girl kneeling before her begged. And then, from the depths of the house, from the great silence, they heard the sound of approaching steps. All movement ceased. Alex looked around quickly and darted toward the door, in the opposite direction from where the footsteps had been heard. Before going through the door, with a single movement of his sticky hand he grabbed one corner of the pink tablecloth and gave it a good yank. Cakes and the porcelain service went flying all over, shards landing on the floor and on the heads of the kneeling children; whipped cream was splashing; cocoa was dripping everywhere. He took in all this and then flew out the door. Tearing open many other doors in the labyrinth of the unfamiliar house, he stumbled through rooms and alcoves, across rugs and stairs, until he was again out in the open on the street. But he would not stop there either; trembling, and with unexpected lightness, his legs carried him along, as if he were flying—only he did not know where.

First published as "Sanyika" in *Kulcskereső játék* (Budapest: Szépirodalmi Könyvkiadó, 1969).

On Thomas Mann's Diaries

The unprecedented interest in the works and the person of Thomas Mann among Hungarian readers since the early 1920s is probably due not exclusively, or primarily, to the literary significance of this man of considerable stature but also, and at least in the same measure, to the representative role that has emerged from the innermost peculiarities of his essential character as a human being and a writer. Behold—come and see, one and all—this is the image of the well-educated, well-to-do burgher who in every respect has completely realized himself. He is modestly proud of his mature personality, has been properly tempted by his demons, is always tolerant and understanding, and is well acquainted with the ways of good and evil. Every single day he performs his tasks in a meticulous and exemplary manner; at the completion of his diurnal labor he effortlessly and with great delight mixes in illustrious company. And let us admit that such a personality would be enviable even if he only played this role—throughout a long and arduous life Mann was able, relatively consistently, relatively tastefully, relatively flawlessly, therefore relatively authentically, to play a role that he cut from nothing but the fabric of his own self—but in fact he was the living image of the role he tailored for himself.

And perhaps I'm not mistaken when I claim that it was the surface of this role, in no way enviable but in every way finely honed and detailed, that provided the opportunity for the relatively unproblematic acceptance of his writings by the Hungarian public. In other, less privileged cases, the literary output has to be tasted first, has to be chewed and digested several times; and only after these actions are carried out will it become clear what roles the same author's other works might play whose lack we had not felt before. And we would still not be talking about the personality who stands protected in the safety of the works.

Thomas Mann's works did not have to go along this difficult road; his person did not have to struggle for acceptance among Hungarian readers as did his contemporaries such as Gide, Hesse, Kafka, Joyce, or Musil, who in more than one respect are more significant than he and to this day are less known and in the same measure less accepted. If the Hungarian publication of Proust's works had not bogged down after the first volumes, or at least if the translation of these first volumes had not turned out to be so mannered and overrefined, perhaps Proust too would have an important, eminent place in our literary consciousness. But this process has remained in the conditional mode probably because the literary activities of this other great stylist lacked—as did those of all the other writers I have mentioned—the ability to play a role. The literary awareness of a public whose background is not personal freedom but the ideal of national independence, even exploiting the former to make a case for the latter, is necessarily more sensitive to literary achievements in which the personal role is in harmony with the sociological or historical one.

In his entire private life, Thomas Mann kept up the appearance, was a representative, of what he presented in all his literary activity—as opposed to writers who, much more faithful to the bourgeois traditions of the novel, tried to present exclusively and rigorously a kind of self who has no inclination or legal claim to be in any way representative. Proust, for example, chose a completely reverse method when he presented the traditions of a hierarchically arranged, aristocratic, and representative life culture as coming from a persona that represented nothing beyond his own person. He accepted as palpable reality only the conditions and relations of a single person, and that is how he became the last great writer in the intellectual orbit of the Enlightenment.

We are dealing with a world in which one thing has more than one explanation, where through an infinite chain of explanations every part of an arbitrarily chosen thing is in need of new explanations. In a writer's world, where details cannot even explain one another—at best they allude to one another, to the extent they can be peeled out of their mutual concealment—hierarchy cannot have a privileged meaning, and one thing cannot be the representative of another any more than parts can represent the whole from which they were allegedly torn. Proust styles himself an aristocrat so that he can establish the analytical ideas of his own personality free of bourgeois restrictions. Thomas Mann, however, hoping for a hierarchically well-arranged world, styles the technique of his own way of thinking and living as representative of such a world. He revives the historical nostalgia, tied to utilitarian ideas, that Proust finds painless to part with.

Let us not consider it a coincidence that Hungarian publishing, lacking all prudence and balance, had the ambition to acquaint us with the complete works of Thomas Mann, in all its details, while it failed to make available the comprehensive works of Gide, Hesse, Kafka, Joyce, Musil, or Proust. Of course I do not mean to say we have too much of Thomas Mann. I could not say such a thing, especially now that a barbarically truncated edition of his diaries, courtesy of Europa Publishers, is lying before me on the table.

These diaries, whose first volumes Peter de Mendelssohn began to publish ten years ago at S. Fischer, legal successor of Mann's original publisher, show fairly clearly and transparently what that fuller personality was like, the one from whom the life role was wrenched and then presented with great literary integrity.* "My fears now concern primarily and almost exclusively this plot against the secrets of my life. They are weighty and serious," he writes in April 1933, when he has good reason to fear that the diaries he has just rescued from his house in Munich, seized by the Nazis, have unhappily disappeared at a railway station in Switzerland. "Terrible, even murderous events might follow."

In the end the notebooks in which he had kept his diaries up to 1933 are returned untouched to their owner. But probably prompted by the experience of these fear- and anxiety-filled days, on May 24, 1945, carrying out a long-ripening decision, he burns almost all these diary notebooks in the garden of his house in California. And this was not his first burned

---

*Mann's diaries, edited by Peter de Mendelssohn and published by S. Fischer (Frankfurt), appeared as follows: *Tagebücher, 1933–34* (1977); *1935–36* (1978); *1919–21* (1979); and *1937–39* (1980). Selections from these appeared in English: *Diaries, 1918–1939*, selected by Hermann Kesten and translated by Richard and Klara Winston (New York: Harry N. Abrams, 1982)—Editor.

sacrifice. At the age of twenty-one he had burned the diaries he'd written until then, and after that other diaries found their end in garden trash fires. He spared the diaries written between 1918 and 1921 because he made use of his notes there in his work on *Doktor Faustus*. Which in itself is a telling comment on the nature of the diaries. Thus, after the mandatory waiting period specified in his will, only the earlier diaries spared by the fire and ones from after 1933 (and kept almost until his death in 1955) could be published.

A person familiar with the diaries in the original may accompany with frequent nods the dread aroused by the deep secrets of the author's life; Mann did well to burn what he burned, and he did even better when he had mercy on what he had relegated to a different fate. The earlier notebooks give an ample taste of the secrets he had planned to destroy; the more carefully written, later notebooks refer to the proportions of the personality image from which, determined by the scale of his character, he forged the role to be played, thereby alluding to the possible whole that he did not feel necessary to preserve after all. With this burning, Thomas Mann probably performed the greatest deed of his life: he destroyed the documents of that intimate, personal, and indispensable mental process without which he could not have continued his work. What remained were the diaries that agreed completely with the role he played in life, but these left only allusions to the tracks that had led Mann to this life role. Still, the attentive reader's dread cannot be an ethical one. Unless I am Perseus, at the sight of the Gorgon's head I freeze with fright but am unable to judge.

The most surprising experience in reading these diaries in the original German is that the texts disregard or evade the sentence-building techniques so characteristic of this author's works. These techniques, elaborate and finely tuned, at once cautiously and mercilessly detailed, are rich in hypotaxis and parataxis, embellished with structures of multiple adjectives; their rhythm may be unhurried or deliberately complex, thereby revealing no small amount of self-enjoyment in the techniques themselves. But in his diaries Mann records things briefly and comments a bit more copiously; he creates no connection between the recorded and commenting parts because these connections are obvious, and therefore he has no need to arrange his themes in any stylistic relationship. He writes hurriedly, often using only abbreviations, speaks in incomplete sentences, uses a surprising number of colloquial terms, and allows himself set phrases that otherwise he would never use. This is not to say the jottings are rough or constructed without the same rigors of style and structure he observes in his books. But this style, so unlike the styles of his novels, may best be characterized by its lacks and deliberate incompleteness.

It is possible that we are talking only about the results of an obvious technical problem. When he must set down everything he considers important or even vital besides his work and social life, he is exhausted by the latter. Done with what the public considers his workday, the man who makes his diary entries in poorly dressed sentences is the same man who otherwise writes only in well-dressed, occasionally overdressed sentences or speaks thus as the self-created persona he presents to the public. Yet in these texts, although more loosely woven, his ability to distinguish matters referring strictly to his person must function more keenly because he has to relinquish the mental and stylistic manipulations with which humor and irony would distance the raw facts of life from himself. Indeed the diaries wholly lack the humor characteristic of his public voice or public appearances, also his famous irony. Because of a decided lack of composition and of stylistic relationships, there seems to be no qualitative difference between the individual phenomena of life or between the most varied facts and events. It is as if in this extreme seriousness every phenomenon and event have the same weight, or as if the only reason all the entries are not considered uniformly insignificant is that their writer considers himself exceptionally significant. He treats the phenomena of his own body and his own soul as if he were sticking so many insects, pierced with safety pins, onto a piece of paper.

Whatever happens, and however anything might happen, I must keep my distance. This is the sole psychological gesture, repeated ad nauseam, that marks the background of Mann's diary style. Of course the distance is now smaller, now greater, now more successful, now less so, but as a result, the dynamics of the text are very small, monotonous, and, one might say, nobly boring. Regarding his topics too, he is given to repetition, and because of the different stylistic levels and disparate stylistic gestures, repetition throws no new light on his topics. If we are informed of everything but the diverse elements are kept on a level of no stylistic expectation, the field of vision necessarily narrows. It is as though we see how flat and boring such a great life is; through the net of his repeated topics we see not his personality but how, by this narrowing, he has kept his personality in his net. Catching his topics by the ear, at the repetitions and along the monotonies of his personality, he can then easily separate them or put them into groups.

He gives account *of the state of his health*, his indispositions, imagined or real illnesses, sleep, appetite, digestion and the quality of his bowel movements, use of medications, sedatives, and stimulants. He tells us *of his physical and mental stamina*, his zeal for work, his moods, the length of his walks, including their places and duration, his eating, drinking, smoking, and the nature of his sexual manipulations. He treats as a totally separate theme *his erotic fantasies* about boys and men, the daydreams evoked by the sight of known and strange ephebes. In a similar manner he reports the events *of the household and housekeeping*, acquisitions, prices, shopping—with his wife or with the children—and matters of the family's financial situation and those concerning the servants. Other recurrent themes include *weather reports, daily political events*, and *social events*, for example, fair weather and revolution, rain and war, also lunches, teas, appointments, visits, concerts, theater attendance, official meetings, and conversations with friends—and with similar regularity he informs us *of his travels, readings*, or *correspondence*. If we categorized these topics attentively enough, we might see the structure of his interests. The schematic repetition of his topics and the stylistic monotony of their presentation reveal the psychic compulsion of a person who exercises this compulsion not in accordance with the principles of his personality but by confining it to the constraints of the conventionally accepted conditions of bourgeois lifestyle and conduct. Not even as a conjecture would it occur to him that there might be other conditions of life, other techniques of living, not even when completely unable to identify his own way of life with a good or significant one. For these rare cases, he reserves the quiet resignation with which he can completely give himself over to the compulsion of predetermined life conditions. "A life of luxury amidst pains."

This style of Thomas Mann the diarist is no less telling than that of Thomas Mann the novelist. Progressing along this fixed, in every way pretuned system of conditions, he accomplishes tasks, does his work, fulfills his obligations. He is possibly the most upright child of his times, and for this distinguished title he pays with a tragic lack of individuality. To pay the price, he barely allows his immeasurable tragedy to reach the threshold of his consciousness. On his lonely walks he is often wracked by sobs, and even more frequently he suffers from insomnia, from a brooding, tense, and gloomy dejection. The deeper level of his life, as revealed by his

diaries, is a dark tangle of flight and suffering. Yet he must act the role
that he wants the world to perceive—cut from the whole of his personality by these fulfilled obligations and accomplished tasks—with an elo-
quence that keeps him from even thinking about a possible rebellion
against it. This must never occur, not even once. And what else could possibly stop him from doing this if not his very compulsion? Even while
reading his diaries, people might believe that Mann's was the best of all
possible lives. He suffers and therefore takes refuge in presenting himself
in the role of the successful man. Success lends a palpable meaning to suffering, but the suffering does not diminish; on the contrary, it increases.
Because the constant, pendulous movement between suffering and success
also exacts a heavy price, he can surrender to neither passion nor emotions,
and into his vocabulary he admits only the most distant, refined synonyms
of words that might express anger in relation to things he lacks or misses.
With this technique of sublimation, he is indeed unique among his contemporaries. He is the hero of the technique of liberal thinking and living, and he could not become this hero if he did not refine and sublimate
all the martyrdom he must endure in the very interest of this heroism.

To dispel the illusion resulting from this role-playing, we need not
necessarily turn to literary works that drifted out of the opposite current
of the same cultural tradition, like Gide's diaries or Kafka's letters. The
bankruptcy of liberal individuality, its catastrophe and tragedy of mythic
proportions, as we discover following the style of Thomas Mann's
diaries—and maybe exactly because of the nature of omissions, the placing of abbreviations, the manner of juxtapositions, and the contingency
of the whole—provide abundant data for this.

His diary is a means of doing the job of refinement and sublimation.
The diary is not made for us; it is necessary for the writing of his novels,
with its written reminders of psychological work already or yet to be done,
a barely stirring inland sea among the promontories of his works and his
life. In the diaries he reminds himself of what he has created out of what
and what he might or should create in the future out of what source. His
thinking and the technique of his life's conduct create a vault between the
columns that are meaning of work and significance of personality.

It is impossible to imagine a function, phenomenon, or manifestation
of life that Mann would not observe from the standpoint of these concepts,
these supporting pillars. This is where everything originates and what
everything returns to; only through the significance of the author's work

or personality can anything qualify as worthy or worthless. In a world like this every phenomenon and manifestation of life should be accepted, yet anything that might upset the carefully achieved balance of values is omitted. Such a world must not include any passion that has value only for the self; even love and sympathy are unusable feelings. Indeed there is no trace of these feelings in Mann's diaries. Perhaps he must read so much Tolstoy so as not to miss so much what is otherwise utterly absent; Mann's feelings are present not in their mere existence but in their stylized form, according to their usefulness or uselessness. He has no feelings he would not calmly acknowledge, and therefore there can be no doubt about his integrity as a writer, yet he also has no feelings that he would not stylize from the standpoint of his own significance. Thus whether or not he puts on a tuxedo for dinner has no more or less significance than the fact that he can barely suppress his permanent disgust at the sight of his youngest child. The local value of such feelings is determined by how and where they take their place in the hierarchy leading to significance.

In a world where, in the interest of significance, everything and anything must equally be accepted, thinking must also reject everything that is extreme. It is probably for this reason that in the years of writing his diaries his political ideas shifted tangibly to the left, disgusted as he was with fascism, yet his sensitivity to social matters remained equal to zero. He has erotic urges, powerful attractions, but no feelings of friendship for anyone. We understand precisely the incommutable place and function of Katja Pringsheim in his life, yet only with the greatest difficulty could we establish any connection with the feeling that might be called love. Love in general does not issue from his pen; the word itself appears only rarely, or rather, he explains to himself the single and long-gone feeling resembling love in a roundabout way, in exclusively synonymic terms that exclude all passion. We may categorize his paternal feelings for his children as a false rarity; this sentiment is most spurious not when he does not notice one or maybe any of his children, but when regarding one of them he believes he is obliged to feel something he might feel genuinely, but being otherwise engaged, he cannot.

This psychologically educated liberal mind cannot yield completely to hatred, the negative passion of love, either, it can only make good use of the refined, sublimated vocabulary of this emotion. Of course there is a plethora of rejection, contempt, disdain, disparagement, not to mention disgust and nausea. These carefully cataloged and pleasurably sampled psychological manifestations form a negative hierarchy at the summit of which stands the antiseptic, idealized image of the significant personality, his ambition justified by his own successes.

With Mann, the metaphysical notions of a world that would allow for thinking and speaking free of stylization are completely absent, and the intellectual world of humanism is called upon to fill the gap. Unhappy, raving Nietzsche is the one who like a tortoise carries Mann's humanistic intellectual world on his back; it is a world populated with gods, demigods, and mythological heroes according to Wagner's insane stylistic method, and enthroned in the seat of the supreme deity is none other than wise Goethe. I do not intend to make fun of Mann. He might deserve it but would need it only if he had not sensed much more strongly than I the tragic contingencies of this basically idolatrous notion, which lacks all reality.

He is aware of the enormously dangerous nature of a worldview exposed to human intelligence; this is the other side of the same coin that testifies to the integrity of the writer. Perhaps the most shocking piece in his diary—because it is an entry that demolishes his entire way of thinking—is dated October 19, 1937. While reading Max Horkheimer's review of a book by Karl Jaspers, he comes upon a sentence by his beloved Nietzsche defining the Germans as "a people that submits itself to the intelligence of a Luther!" And after a pause no longer than the time it takes to insert a dash, he cries, "No! Hitler is not an accident, not an illegitimate deviation. It is from him that the 'light' reflects back to Luther, and this must be recognized in him without hesitation. He is a true German phenomenon." Still, he has no realization painful or awkward enough to block his permanent, psychic compulsion to style himself, somehow, alongside Goethe. Moreover, this means that he must style Goethe as at least the regent of the human spirit on earth. And that of course says more about Wagner's bad taste, to put it mildly, than about Goethe's organic way of thinking, whether Goethe is singing or going and coming from other worlds. Mann knows this; he knows everything; but given the hierarchically arranged system of thinking that he creates and compulsively represents, he must erase the critical and protesting spirit that should permanently animate this thinking. The toppled idols, the expelled saints, taking on the countenance of living and dead people, return to the carefully whitewashed walls.

It can be seen how Mann, observed in his own diaries, fills the lack of metaphysical notions in his works with stylistic notions, or how, with the help of humor and irony, he turns negative psychic contents into positive, meaningful ones. He tames his doubts but leaves faint traces of his perturbation. His diaries record this mental work. In them, he relates to every secret of life only from the standpoint of his work, and therefore he has no personal secret that might not leave some detectable trace in his books, but neither does he have any secrets that might appear in their complete, original length in his diaries.

In his works Mann appears in the role of the benevolent, well-groomed, sympathetic, fragrant, gentle, matured-in-enlightenment, and mollifying father. Those who flaunted similar virtues could celebrate themselves in him, and so could those who, with their minds tortured by the loss of personal freedom, yearned for just such a father figure who might guide their existence. Although the mouth was that of the poet Attila József, it was I, and you, all of us in Hungary who asked Mann to sit down on the edge of our nursery beds and tell us a story. However, the one who did sit on our beds—and in light of his diaries this circumstance is as clear as daylight—was not Hermes but Cronus. The same Cronus who gained world domination by castrating his own father, Uranus (i.e., heaven!), and who will devour his own children too.

Just as we cannot reproach Cronus, we must also restrain our moral judgment regarding the storytelling Thomas Mann. He did not deceive us, not at all. He had no soothing tale that did not include visible warning signals. Look out! Now I am bluffing! Now I am cheating, now I am enticing! In our immaturity, we were the gullible ones, and what we did not notice was what we did not want to notice. His own children, with a word for domestic use, called him the magician, which satisfied the universal ambitions in the family and, to boot, was true. Some people know a great deal, and however difficult it may be for us to admit, some other people know everything knowable. These diaries, recording much or perhaps all knowledge, show us Thomas Mann's works, which we thought we know thoroughly, as well as the author's public persona, in a new light. What becomes visible in this new light—if not another person or another person's lifework—is the suffering man who stands in the shelter of the most jealously guarded secrets of liberal thought. This proved to be very timely and modern in the eyes of the generations that rejected his stylistics and, by following rigorously his way of thinking, based on hu-

man intelligence, ejected the very concept of suffering from the dictionary of literature.

I must emphasize that this Hungarian edition of the diaries first edited by Peter de Mendelssohn is abridged, though in the preface the editor claims he did not shorten the material from the surviving notebooks.
He immediately adds that given the sensitivity of very private matters,
he considered it his duty "in a very few places" to remove "a few sentences, or a word here and there," and he marked these places by brack-
eted ellipsis points. In the notebooks for 1920, we find two passages that
in part—and we cannot tell how great or small a part—fell victim to
Mendelssohn's editorial dread, though otherwise he deserves all our admiration and appreciation.

In 1920 Thomas Mann was forty-five years old. At the end of the
July 5 entry, we find this brief and surprising announcement: "During
these days I have fallen in love with Klaus. Promptings for a father-son
short story.—Intellectually lively." Klaus Mann, nicknamed Eissi in the
family, was not yet fourteen. The truncated sentence renders incomplete
an entry made nine days later about Mann's most intimate relationship
with his then thirty-seven-year-old wife. We can read, however, his reflec-
tions on the missing details. He writes that he is unclear about his situation: impotence can hardly be a factor; more likely it is the usual
confusion and unreliability of his "sex life." In this sentence he puts the
phrase in quotation marks, as one who does not seriously think that anything like that could exist as a function separate from his entire personality, yet the quotation marks serve exactly the purpose of separation.
Undoubtedly, he writes in his next sentence, his excitable weaknesses are
carrying him toward wishes that "originate on the other side." What
would happen, he asks—again putting into quotation marks the very
suggestive words that may be twisted in two directions at once—if a boy
"were lying in front of him" or "were at his disposal"? He doesn't need to
write down the answer to the rhetorical question: he would be successful;
he would not prove to be impotent. It would be senseless, he goes on, to
let his failure, whose causes are not new, depress him. To be lighthearted,
whimsical, indifferent, and self-assured would be the proper behavior as
well as the best salve for something like this. In the following days, when
his will to work is "very poor," he responds to the call he directed at himself. And subsequent entries leave no doubt who that certain boy could

have been and what sort of reversal of his attention may have caused his impotence. He is "ecstatic" about Klaus, who is "alarmingly handsome in the bath."

To solve this situation in his life, he must have superhuman abilities, or lacking them, he should resignedly collapse in the tragedy. He has no other choice. If obeying cultural demands, he separates his sex life completely from the whole of his personality and regards his potency as a measure of success, then he must expect failure, the crumbling of the image he had created of himself. If, however, he considers his attraction to his own son an inalienable part of his personality, then he must negate his entire culture. And he cannot make this latter choice, for then the restrained spirit of negation would burst out of him.

"I find it very natural that I fall in love with my son." From a stylistic standpoint, this sentence is a logical solution of his attraction. If it is natural, it cannot be extreme, and if it is not extreme, there is no need to be afraid of it; this will be the artistic success, smartly evading cultural demands, that could lead him to the short story to be written. A few lines on, already in possession of this accepted feeling and free of embarrassment, he is on the train to Munich, engaged in a brief conversation with a young man in white trousers sitting next to him. "Glad about this. It seems I am completely done with the feminine?" In his question, meant to be a statement, Goethe's eternal feminine ideal greets us in a lighthearted and whimsical style that the author asks himself to adopt in the interest of solving the situation. But he cannot develop this style further because he has arrived home. "I greeted everyone after the journey for which I paid 20 M. With naked, suntanned torso, reading a book, Eissi was lolling on the bed, which made me flustered.—Yesterday, K's birthday. Morning, giving of presents; he received the new bicycle. At noon, I took Eissi for a brief stroll and talked to him about the article. To K's parents for chocolate. In the evening, garden party at Dr. Mannheimer," where "I spoke with a lot of people, they were all men, among them the being who finally 'got to know me.' Walked home, very late and very tired, to bed." The words in quotation marks (in the German original as well) are not easily interpreted; their textual environment and the manner of the writing lead us to conclude that they refer to a potential or a consummated erotic adventure.

In any case, the writer of the diary calms down somewhat, for he had sidetracked his attraction and thereby lived up to the suggestion he made to himself. He furnishes evidence of his success, and thus he might end without moral injury the adventure of the original attraction that he managed to draw into the sphere of naturalness. Still, this is what we read two days later: "Last night I read Eissi's short story, full of agonizing weltschmerz, and at his bedside, amid tenderness and affection, I gave him my critique, which I believe he was glad to receive." Aware of the preceding events and relationships, no great imagination is necessary to realize what critical limits the diarist's passion must have reached amid tenderness and affection. Perhaps it was the paternal criticism resting on the writer's integrity that protected him from what he had protected the boy from. The semblance must have been paper-thin.

In an entry dated three months later, we learn how he dealt with the passion he had stifled within himself. "I heard noises from the boys' room, and I surprised Eissi while he was fooling around, completely naked, in front of Golo's bed. Deep impression at the sight of his splendid body on the verge of manhood, a shock." Now he is gazing down from the heights of his paternal authority, though this does not cool his attraction. We are at the mercy of conjecture here, because the German editor once again interrupts the text. We still manage to learn from the closing section of this entry that when he returned to the bedroom, he could trust his tendency to overcome his own passions, and he might rely on his wife's understanding behavior, but in his relationship to her, the desired readjustment would not be possible.

In these hastily analyzed entries, mentioned only as mere examples— and heavily censored in the Hungarian edition—Thomas Mann proves to be one who knows cultural relationships about which European literature and psychology until now have kept utterly silent and will continue to be just as silent in coming times. In a culture based on the authority and achievements of male divinities, the fact and daily practice of the sons' love for their fathers must be held necessary and desirable, but of the other face of the same love, fathers' love for their sons, we must be utterly silent in order to protect the fathers' authority. This is the point where this culture is undermined. The sons' father-love assures this authority and stimulates the very achievement that the fathers' secret love for their sons crushes to smithereens and extinguishes. Mendelssohn's blue pencil goes to work where in the most positive way we might have been informed of the details of this cultural relationship that defines all our lives.

The first volume of the Hungarian edition of the diaries goes much further in the process of truncation. It obeys not cultural prohibitions but a much simpler necessity: not only are sentences missing from the daily entries, but whole days and weeks are gone. In my rough estimate, about two-thirds of the diaries are omitted, and a proportionate amount is gone from the accompanying notes, making our orientation especially difficult. It is thus questionable whether the Hungarian edition has a right to use the same title given on the title page of the original edition. The unsuspecting Hungarian reader takes in hand not the first volume of Thomas Mann's diaries but, rather, a selection—prepared according to dubious viewpoints—from them.

I am certainly not the person to tell scholars what an edition of such a significant work, carefully prepared and uncompromising in its fidelity to the original text, ought to be like. But I have thought a great deal about the guiding principles that may have produced this incredible, unjustifiably large truncation. Antal Mádl, the publisher of this Hungarian edition, reveals only that the selection, "within the framework limited by size, attempts to provide a cross section of the original material that would introduce the reader to every essential trend, in condensed form." I readily admit that the selection introduces the essential trends of the diaries very proportionately—to readers who are familiar with the original. These proportions are achieved exclusively by complying with one constraint: to cling to the known, well-cared-for, and innocuous image of Thomas Mann and plod along with the representative principles of form; that is how this edition creates its own version out of the system of original relationships among entries. It bases its infidelity to the text on fidelity to the person it presents. Thus this version of Mann's diaries saves Hungarian readers from the very novelty whose knowledge might help them reevaluate their false image not only of the writer but of the art of living and the styles of an era. With some sternness, I must declare that whoever reads the Hungarian edition of Thomas Mann's diaries may claim that he knows these diaries less than anyone who has read not a word of it or of the original German.

First published as "Thomas Mann naplóiról" in *Holmi*, 1989.

The Lamb

For Ladislav Fuks

János Maczelka positively hated Rezső Róth.

"These people always manage to grab the best of everything," he would often say to his wife.

"And always what's most comfortable," Mrs. Maczelka would reply.

"And they always make you feel sorry for them," Mr. Maczelka would continue.

"On top of everything else," Mrs. Maczelka would add.

From the very beginning Rezső Róth was a thorn in Mr. Maczelka's side. Perhaps because he was an attractive man, tall and lean, with his naturally wavy silver gray hair following the shape of his oblong head, and because no matter how humbly he was dressed, on his wide shoulders and slender hips his clothes seemed tasteful and elegant, whereas Mr. Maczelka's pants would sag limply on his protruding belly and short spindly legs, and in the summer, when he wore no headgear, his bald skull shone like a watermelon.

Rezső Róth had large, clear cat's eyes with long lashes. János Maczelka's eyes were deep-seated little beads with short lashes. Rezső Róth walked softly with straight, long strides; Maczelka waddled, and no matter how careful he was, his shoes always clacked noisily on the pavement.

"That's how they are, all of them," Mrs. Maczelka would often say.

"All of them are like that," Mr. Maczelka would reply.

"He's already got money even for his coffin, but nothing is enough for him," Mrs. Maczelka would say.

"He's pinching pennies as if he were a twenty-year-old," Mr. Maczelka would reply.

They talked a lot about Rezső Róth. True, they also talked a lot about the Kelemens and about Mrs. Herbst, about Imre and Jancsi Zsudi, and about all kinds of people they had met in their lives; they talked a lot because Mr. Maczelka had nothing else to do. Mrs. Maczelka had been busy in the kitchen for forty years, and for thirty-nine of those years she had seen Mr. Maczelka only in the evenings, so for thirty-nine years they had had very little time to exchange unhurried words.

And Rezső Róth was indeed a man worthy of hatred.

He was smooth as a sheet of marble, taciturn, and brutally simple. No one ever saw him smile; he only laughed. But even in his laughter there was something that provoked hatred, because laughter would burst suddenly from the calm superior air of his countenance and then vanish just as suddenly from his mouth and eyes as if it had never been. And he always laughed unexpectedly, with a quick panting, the one thing that connected him to his fellow humans because it indicated that he needed, just like other people, to breathe in order to get air. When he was not laughing, he did not pant, hawk, cough, smack his lips, or click his tongue, as others did; through his large nostrils he silently supplied his lungs with oxygen. Did he have lungs at all? Or did Rezső Róth carry his separateness to such an extreme as to make do without lungs or a heart, which other mortals possessed?

They knew nothing about him. Yet he was one of the original residents of the housing settlement. There were the original inhabitants, the latecomers, and the intruders. The three groups lived in a strictly maintained segregation. Rezső Róth was accused of associating himself with the intruders, but this was a baseless accusation, since he did not fraternize even with them except insofar as persecuted people instinctively flee toward safety and he may have been a shade less adamant in rejecting their approach than he was toward other residents.

Rejecting? What elicited hatred for Rezső Róth's person was precisely the fact that he was not a rejecter, nor could he be accused of indifference, discourtesy, or lack of compassion. On the contrary, he was more considerate, more compassionate than the average person, but these positive traits were filtered through a peculiar character (hard to define because peculiar) that changed the established norms and categories of goodness,

consideration, and compassion to the point where it did not occur to anyone to call Rezső Róth a good man. It would be easy to say that he did
not care what people thought of him; in fact it may have interested him
greatly, but if anyone approached him with words either to flatter or to
abuse him, if the conversation tried in any way to pry into events in his
life, Rezső Róth clammed up and became smooth and flat as marble.

It seemed that he held the basic form of human contact, words, to be
worthless, that he did not believe in them, nay, that he would run from
them as though fearing they might lure him into a labyrinth from which
he could not emerge. Unlike those who defend themselves against life
with words, he drew boundaries around himself with his appearance and
mien, with his gestures and unexpected laughter, creating an image of
himself that in his little world made him a figure both hated and, though
unapproachable, respected.

The closer the boundaries around a person and the harder to see behind them, the greater the irritation of the outside world, especially of
people who with endless chattering and babbling destroy the wall of individuality around themselves, apparently easing human contact thereby;
but while they strive to expand their borders as much as they can, they in
fact do away with them altogether, failing to notice that with their feverish talk they are eliminating their own character.

But what does character mean to those who know nothing of the values inherent in its peculiarities? What does character mean to those who
consider character a scourge of God because ignorant of their own, they
see in others' only a hindrance to their own existence? What does character mean to a person whose own character develops through a series of un-
principled, characterless bits of behavior?

In a word, in his world, Rezső Róth was like a lesion, an ulcer that
could affect the whole body, a malignancy that everyone tried in various
ways to remove: the surgeon with his scalpel, the quack with herbs, the
superstitious with incantations.

But a man, whatever he may be, cannot really be compared to an ulcer. Therefore his removal, in times of peace, may encounter irksome
obstacles.

We children feared Mr. Róth, and if he hadn't been a Jew, and if our
parents hadn't brought this up so often as the ultimate argument against
him, we might have discovered at the bottom of our fear some attraction

to him. We were children; in our eyes the object of our fears was worthy
of respect because instinctively (while we rejected him) we would have
liked to emulate it. We did not yet know that there were differences
among the objects of our fears, because we did not yet know that to be
frightening was at least as terrible as it was to be frightened. So instead of
being attracted to Mr. Róth, we were attracted to our drunkard fathers
and to the strange tramps, whores, tavern brawlers, and loudmouth bul-
lies from the edge of the city who loitered around our settlement; with
our instinct to emulate authority and threatening behavior, we looked
down on Mr. Róth the way we scorned our mothers, always disheveled,
always smelling of dishwater, whose powerful slaps we nonetheless
dreaded.

Although I did not know Mr. Róth well and he has grown into a figure of symbolic proportion in my eyes only since I've come to understand
him, there was a difference between the way I feared him or my mother
or my grandmother, the latter forever exiled to the kitchen, and the way
I feared my father, who constantly exuded the bitter smell of coal dust.
And I feel a little guilty too. Not because of what came to pass, for these
events had absolutely nothing to do with my own intentions; I feel
guilty—maybe more than a little—because in my thoughts at the time I
was trying to become like my loud-talking father. With the other boys
we drank brandy on the sly, we smoked and swore openly, and as if re-
hearsing our future, we tried to overcome our fear of our mothers with
secret, stealthy kicks, words, and gestures.

It was as if we were trying on for size the kind of power we would
have in the future because we were male, and with our mothers these attempts were successful because they screeched, sulked, took offense, and
made up with us exactly as they usually did with our fathers. The difference was that we were not yet men, only children, and often the response
to our power-testing efforts was an even greater terror: merciless blows
from our fathers. How well I remember the sound of bawling or restrained hissing issuing from our houses and apartments!

"What did you dare say to your mother, you little shit?"

Only the adjectives varied. And the peculiarities of human traits further increased our guilt about our belatedly recognized complicity, because in the wake of these words and paternal punishments we were the
more convinced that we must strive for male power and authority. And if

I own up to this striving of ours, I can't claim with complete certainty
that I had no hand in the events that followed.

In every moment of one's life one strives for harmony. I believe this is
the reason people talk so much, as if with various forms of argument, al-
tercation, and confession, by talking they could create a harmony between their inner and outer worlds. But this harmony cannot be created
by simple communication. People have no confidence in themselves,
however, and want to explain everything; at every point they want to
force their own views on their surroundings; and instead of bringing
them closer to a solution, or, if not to a solution, to a momentary tran-
quillity (which is related to safety) that takes them ever further from harmony. Every uttered word gives rise to more conflicts and contradictions
that need resolution, and thus they link up in a chain that leads people
astray and into dead ends.

Of a ruined relationship no one can say how and when it was ruined. A
ruined relationship is always full of the little thorns of insignificant words.
Although these little thorns to some extent express a person, they are far
from being able to express a person fully, for words cannot do that. Yet
people trust words blindly. They trust blindly their own words and wait
for the words of others, ready to pounce on them and tear them to pieces,
to injure themselves and to inflict injuries in the name of their presumed
righteousness. If nature had not seen to our attributes as wisely as it has, I
believe we all would wind up in insane asylums. As it is, only those with
whom nature has dealt less wisely wind up there. If one lived one's entire
life with the same energy one had between the ages of twenty and forty, by
the time one was seventy, one would be living in a net of offenses and injuries from which the only escape would lead to insanity. That is why I
think that loss of energy is a blessing. After some time and the accumulation of a certain amount of received offenses, one realizes it is impossible to
resolve the chain of contradictions one carries from infancy (one has long
forgotten what should be resolved), and therefore the intensity of activity
is reduced; the number of phenomena one accepts without demur continually increases, and then comes the period when one grumbles only about
trifles, and after a while one stops that too and saves up enough to cover
the expected funeral expenses and gives oneself over to death.

It was trifles that annoyed the Maczelkas. They had forgotten most of
the verbal battles they had waged so persistently and enthusiastically

during the forty years of their marriage, but neither had they so lost energy or come so close to death that some events could not fire them up and magically evoke the fervor of their youth. Five years before the time of our story, Mrs. Maczelka had ceased to be a woman, or, more correctly, she believed that after thirty-five years, twice a week, having more than fulfilled her conjugal duties, she was no longer willing to be a woman; this was the last reason for their quarrels, sometimes wildly vehement, sometimes insidiously smoldering, because in the wake of Mrs. Maczelka's decision manly desires still raged in Mr. Maczelka for a while, but then, suddenly, as though his entire life had been spent in rigorous self-restraint, sexual urges died away in his body. The Maczelkas sank into the emptiness of quiet vegetation, and this state, which after the stormy periods could be called blissful, was disturbed only by Mr. Maczelka's retirement. But not much: in the fortieth year of their marriage he did not use quarreling with his wife to mitigate the helplessness and anxiety of emptiness caused by not having to work. No, forty years had evidently been long enough for them to get used to each other. Still, this form of being accustomed to each other causes boredom, and no one likes to be bored; therefore, beyond the simple pleasures they derived from their apartment and from eating, the Maczelkas entertained themselves with what was going on in the outside world. They were still far from the big moment, the moment of death, when they would finally reconcile themselves to the futility of struggling with existence. But they had already lost the kind of awareness that would have made them turn to their own inner world and become able to generate new experience, moment to moment. Deprived of this human trait, which at times may seem horrible and at other times loftily beautiful, they therefore mulled over and became entangled in phenomena occurring around them.

As I have said, it took a few years—not that many, really—for the figure of Mr. Róth to become crystallized, become a symbol in my eyes. I grew up. And much as I would have liked, I could not follow in my father's footsteps. Maybe that is why today I am so drawn to Mr. Róth's memory. As the years go by, I am becoming a taciturn man myself, and I too feel what Mr. Róth may have felt, that strange and contradictory circle of hatred and respect of those around me. If I were to seek the reasons for wanting to be taciturn, I would have to say a few words about myself, but I want to write about Mr. Róth. And that won't be easy because I didn't really know him. Of the reasons for his taciturnity, therefore, I know only as much as I know about my own, though no doubt on the level of the phenomenon's manifestation there are great differences between us. Still, I wish to write about him (though I know I am writing about myself), because I feel he was the only person in my life, no matter how I failed to notice it at the time, who precisely because of his inconspicuousness made a profound impression on me. His existence and the lesson of his fate infected me. He infected me . . . perhaps with the knowledge (I find it hard to put this in the right words) that no matter how man may want to prove the opposite about himself and mostly about other people, and no matter how he is bothered by this realization, he is a mysterious being. He is mystery itself. Thinking back on my childhood now, I see that my grandmother, mother, and father were also mysterious beings, because it is impossible to decipher their lives or the motives for their actions, but at the same time, they fought this mysteriousness in every way possible and especially with their loquaciousness. They waged their little battles before my eyes just as openly as they lived their love lives. I think it was because of this difference (beyond the fact that Mr. Róth was Jewish) that I, like the others, also looked down on and hated Mr. Róth. My world opposed and negated Mr. Róth. People in my world, except Mr. Róth, lived open lives. It took many coincidences and the passing of many years for me to understand that our inability to accept the laws of nature, and most particularly the enigmatic nature of man, can lead to tragic consequences. And we can expect the same if we try to make an individual blend into a community of individuals who are not true individuals. In my view, only true individuals, like Mr. Róth, can make a community. I may be contradicting myself here, but neither Mr. Róth's nor my own solitude contradicts the fact that we, he and I, would be the most appropriate candidates for membership in a community; there is no contradiction because, I believe, the cause of our solitude lies not in us but in the world. It is therefore to be sought in the particular situation that compelled Mr. Róth to resort to silent, proud resistance, as it does me too—more and more.

Now that I have alluded to myself so agreeably, let me list my doubts as well. It is possible that I, the person putting these words on paper, am simply a weak man, weak and afraid of life, and my feelings have nothing to do with Mr. Róth; I am merely using him to justify myself. Perhaps.

Perhaps it is only a strange coincidence, and when looking for the reasons of my ever-deepening taciturnity by groping around in Mr. Róth's character, I may be on the wrong track. Perhaps I have grown unaccustomed to communicating with my fellow humans through words only because coincidence steered my life to the more abstract world of numbers, of formulas made up of numbers and letters, and perhaps abstraction, in the form of madness, has taken possession of me. I say madness because at the same time that I speak of the absence of words I am trying—with words—to decipher the painful anxiety of my life, my alienation from words. Could I be mad?

Perhaps.

The housing settlement was built on a garbage dump. Its oldest house was not more than fifteen years old. It was surrounded by fume-spewing factories, iron-cutting workshops, and junkyards. When the lots were distributed, ten families and Rezső Róth began to build their houses out of scraps and remains, which weren't easy to come by. After the houses had already gone up, it turned out that the official in charge of selling the lots had pocketed the money. He was jailed, and the residents were ordered to tear down the houses for safety reasons, having to do with the instability of the land. At the turn of the century the whole area had been used as a garbage dump and waste disposal site, and even now it was covered with only a thin layer of windblown sand. A single rainfall could make the landfill shift and bury all the houses along with the people in them. But by the time the official order to raze the houses came, another fifteen families (the latecomers) were in the middle of constructing homes on the ridiculously inexpensive lots, and despite the authorities' repeated notices, no one was willing either to halt construction or to tear down the completed houses. The authorities could not guarantee housing for twenty-five families, so they applied an emergency measure. They made everyone sign declarations whereby the signatories conceded that for any possible tragedy they would hold no one but themselves responsible.

The declaration was signed by everyone except Rezső Róth and duly placed in the archives. The next year another fifteen new constructions got under way (the intruders), and for selling lots illegally again someone was thrown in jail.

From then on the population of the settlement increased only by sub-tenants. Numerically, the settlement had forty-one houses. Some had lit-tle towers or gable roofs, but most were uniformly simple little houses. The forty-one buildings, arranged in a semicircle, skirted a large empty area, which indeed remained empty for a long time; even weeds did not grow more than a few inches. But if it was no delight to the eye, its use-fulness for soccer-playing children was indisputable. In the whole settle-ment, which in time managed to fashion odd-shaped little streets, narrow here, wide there, no trees grew. The residents planted shrubs at the base of their fences, a few fruit trees in their gardens, but more delicate plants could not take root in the soil.

In a few years the authorities realized there was no chance of disman-tling the settlement, and as a result, in another few years they also forgot their fear of the unstable ground. They decided, in line with the demands of the "On with the Race for Garden Cities" campaign, that they would create a park in the large empty area that had been used only as a soccer field. With the new park the settlement would become, officially, a fully authorized part of the city.

Still, our settlement remained completely outside the law.

Everyone felt this but mainly those, like my family, whose houses stood farthest from the large empty lot: the intruders. The settlement's earlier residents, as if to justify their own presence, claimed we had pur-chased our lots illegally. By the time our parents found out that these people had bought their lots the same way, it was too late to use this in-formation as a fresh argument; the old residents considered both our exis-tence and our presence illegal, the separation of the groups had become permanent, and the fact that the oldest residents had also acquired their lots through real estate speculation became public knowledge only be-cause of the consequent infighting. But perhaps it wasn't this twice-repeated and double illegality that placed our settlement outside the law, but rather its location. The forty-one houses rose in the midst of a very dusty flatland. The nearest building to the south was a long-abandoned brickyard, beyond which lay a pulp-processing plant, but not far enough away to spare us its awful stench, and even farther was the paper mill, with only its smokestacks visible to us. To the east and the west there was nothing. To the north there were the ironworks, a few junkyards, and far-ther still a market gardener's cabbage and cauliflower fields. But the latter were so far away that we did not even bother to steal from them; this was already where the city began, the city which meant law, oppression, and authority. We freely associated and identified the city with the building and the spirit of our school, because to attend school we had to go to the city.

To an outsider, especially to a city dweller, our settlement was a dreary sight, but I—and I'm sure that's how the others felt too—cannot recall greater happiness than a spring or early-autumn day when away from our teachers' prying eyes and in the company of the other boys, I would hurry home toward the little houses in our settlement. In small groups or alone, brandishing our schoolbags, we'd amble past the cabbage patches where every day around noon the wary gardener turned loose his shaggy dog with its gruff bark; then we'd make our way across the flat rubble-strewn central area. From a distance, the settlement houses seemed to huddle together, isolating themselves from everything, and this enormous isolation under the wide sky was broken only by two wires strung between the brickyard and our houses, which connected us to the world. But I remember that I was so charmed by the sight before me that I filtered out even this umbilical cord so that I might believe that having left the slavery of school behind, we were approaching a world—the world that was also our home—that was even freer.

All of us, young and old, bore our status as outcasts proudly (at least among ourselves). Maybe that was the reason for our general and unanimous consternation when one nice spring day four or five giant dump trucks showed up. They struggled over the potholes and, accompanied by the frenzied barking of dogs, dumped their loads in the middle of the area surrounded by the houses.

We all ran out of our houses and watched as the trucks disappeared and then returned with fresh loads of black dirt, unloading them at different points on our soccer field.

Nobody dared ask what was going on.

The piles of black dirt stood out sharply against the sandy yellowish white soil, and they stayed there for weeks without anyone knowing what would be done with them. Our parents kept walking around them, examining them, and then, after many days had gone by without anyone checking up, they had us haul bucketfuls of soil from them into our gardens. By the time another truck arrived with a few men and various pieces of equipment and tools, there was nothing left of the dirt piles. The men

swore and threatened, but finally they went off. The next day a few more
dump trucks showed up, along with the truck carrying the men, and in
the settlement everyone lay low, fearing that the fine-smelling, light,
springy black soil—already carefully tamped down in our gardens—
would have to be returned, but nothing like that happened. The laborers
went to work with their shovels and rakes, and by evening the basis of the
park had been laid out. The barely visible spring weeds had been up-
rooted, the thick topsoil brought in the dump trucks had been evenly
spread out; the men worked efficiently and quickly and asked Mr.
Maczelka, who after a while ventured out of his house, for some drinking
water. As they worked, they sometimes quarreled or swore loudly; they
were just like our fathers; still, the residents of the settlement stayed away
from them. Although it was obvious what was going on, it was as if people, sensing the interference of a higher authority, felt this might be a
precedent for further unasked-for intrusions in their lives, and the plan of
the park became repugnant to everyone. Even the arrival of saplings and
the gardeners' broadcasting grass seeds from their burlap bags failed to
soften people's hearts. The settlement withdrew into itself.

Only Mr. Maczelka fraternized with the gardeners. Since they had
asked him for water, he may have felt he had gotten closer to the higher
authority that worked invisibly but arranged and guided everything. On
the second day, with quiet little laughs and confidential words he fawned
on and hung around the gardening men; on the third day they were offering cigarettes to one another. I would say those three days changed Mr.
Maczelka; if in the evening a woman showed up at the Maczelkas to
sound him out about the day's events, he would respond only with long
silences, leisurely smoking his cigarette, an all-knowing smile on his face.

The grass sprouted, pansies bloomed in the flower beds, though the
saplings, set deeper into the ground, struck no roots. Judges of the "On
with the Race for Garden Cities!" campaign, accompanied by city leaders,
came to inspect the newly established park.

As the judges walked up and down the narrow gravel footpaths taking
notes in their little notebooks and city leaders enthusiastically gave them
pointers regarding various improvements to gain a better place in the
competition, an elderly man approached them. His face was shining with
a smile. He bowed and said, "I am János Maczelka, the oldest resident of
this settlement."

"Oh," said a city official and turned to the judges. "The oldest resident of the settlement . . . but of course we already know each other . . ."

For a moment the smile disappeared from Mr. Maczelka's face, but seeing the official's encouraging look, he assumed it would be improper to ask where they might have known each other from, or to reveal that any doubt about their acquaintanceship had arisen in him. "But of course we do." He smiled again.

The official let a slender hand drop on the old man's shoulder, and blinking and seeking the judges' eyes, he asked, "And as the oldest resident of the settlement, are you satisfied with this nice new park?"

"How could I not be? We are very happy that the city has chosen to remember us with such a nice new park."

The official's palm rose, and twice it patted Mr. Maczelka's shoulder, but the official was no longer looking at him; in hopes of a well-deserved reward for his resourcefulness, he was searching for an appreciative look from his immediate superior. Having received the reward in the form of a dignified nod, he placed a narrow hand on his hip and, holding it there, joined his colleagues and moved on. János Maczelka, with ungratified wishes in his heart, remained alone in the middle of the grassy field and then sadly followed behind.

When the group finished its job and, led by the chief judge, its members headed for their cars, Mr. Maczelka managed to get in front of them. He knew that what he was about to do was wrong, but he couldn't contain himself; he would never have another chance like this. He hesitantly touched the young official's arm.

"Is anybody going to water this nice new park?"

The city leaders indicated reprovingly that this question should not have been asked at this time, the judges let their eyebrows crawl up on their foreheads, and the official's slender hand slapped János Maczelka's shoulder.

"Aren't you people watering it every day?" he asked loudly.

"Of course," said Mr. Maczelka quietly, and smiled.

"There you go!" said the official in his loud voice.

The officials got into their cars and were driven away.

After that, nobody cared about the park. Quietly, when in the evening Mr. Maczelka joined his wife at the window, placing his elbow next to hers on the windowsill, and gazed at the slowly drying lawn and the weed-ridden gravel footpaths, he would remark, "I told them, didn't I?"

I would have to relate a great many things to make comprehensible not only the simple event that took place many years ago in our settlement, but also the effect it had on me and perhaps on others as well. Since I have made this my goal, I must once again consider both the value and the lack of value in words.

Jew. I thought about this word for a long time, scribbled it on paper many times before putting it down here in its final form. And the reason is that this word means many things, and it means each of those many things in many different ways. I get into conflicts with words. The value of this word is so varied in the world; it has meant so many things in the course of millennia that I fear, when I write it down, it will produce a different idea or image in each reader.

If I resorted not to writing but, say, to speaking my thoughts into a radio microphone, my situation regarding this little word would be incomparably easier, if not completely easy. Because with my organs of speech I could express the myriad shades, differences, value judgments, hatred, contempt, respect, isolation, gloating mockery, and sorrow my ears have absorbed and my brain has stored up during thirty years of hearing this little word being pronounced. And then there are these other words: "Mother," "dogs," "park keeper," "settlement." I have to explain them all, submit myself to the compulsion of explaining so as to make clear how I understand and interpret a word, what it means to me. But if I don't wish to be accused of contradictions, I should be glad I have no opportunity to convey my thoughts over the radio, because ultimately I have made clear—and I haven't changed my mind—that I attribute far greater significance to a gesture than to a sentence, more meaning to a glance than to a syllabic emphasis. Therefore, pronouncing with various emphases the words "Jew," "mother," "dogs," and "settlement" would only carry me further from my objective.

My mother never pronounced the word "Jew." Had I scrutinized more closely the words I heard when they were spoken out loud back then, I'd probably have noticed the absence of this word from her vocabulary, because it was otherwise ever present, in my world, gaining different meaning with each different emphasis, and from my earliest childhood it was judgment itself, not the condemnation of anyone but an implication that the person to whom it applied—for some don't-ask-me-what kind of crime—already had his neck only inches from the ax and, that being so, must have well deserved what was coming to him. Perhaps it was the peculiar edge of the emphasis put on it, in whichever context it was heard, that drew my attention to this word very early on and to the contents concealed in it; maybe that's why it became fixed in my mind more clearly than anything else.

"I'll beat that rotten Jewish blood of yours right out of you!"

My father uttered this sentence, and if it hadn't been uttered, I would not now remember the hideous distortion, the vein swelling in his neck, his face reddened by fury and drink, that came over him whenever he got ready to beat me. This was the sentence that fixed his face in my mind, and because I could not have been more than ten years old at the time and because those around me gave me no clue as to how to deal with my uncertainties, I carried this sentence within me for months, even years, and even more than the others, if that was possible, I looked down on, despised, and tried to expel Mr. Róth from my soul.

As if softening my rigid attitude would suddenly shed light on what my father had been screaming within our four walls, and perhaps thanks to my compounded fear, a few years later my interest was drawn to the more abstract world of numbers and formulas, for by then I feared not only what all we children feared, but also the fate I might be carrying in my blood.

My mother, who never uttered the word "Jew," was also the only one among the settlement residents who once, and only once, crossed the threshold of Mr. Róth's house.

What this house was like on the inside—this place where Mr. Róth spent the last days of his life (what a banal expression this is; no one knows which days are his last)—I shall never know because my mother gave totally contradictory reports on the arrangements of the rooms and furniture. When she came home on Easter morning, my father, in a drunken stupor, was still snoring in the large family bed, under a painting of Christ among his disciples. Mother sat down in the kitchen and said only, "My God, the poor man."

And we moved away from her as from a leper. My grandmother eyed her hostilely, and because the air was filled with the promise of scandal after my mother's rebellious act, we kept quiet and asked no questions about what she had seen in Mr. Róth's house. Our curiosity came later, after things had quieted down, but by then my mother was incapable of giving any objective response; terrified by the only bold act in her life and by its consequences, she babbled aimlessly and described the interior of Mr. Róth's house however the given moment required.

And now another word rises from the sea of letters: "events." This forms a huge and coherent complex within me, and I should like to convey all of it to you in great detail, but I know from experience that this is as impossible as it is for two people to understand each other completely, profoundly, and mutually; I consider my own effort in this direction to be quite futile, and it essentially goes against my principles because I'd be trying to dispel the inherent secretiveness of human action.

It began, or rather continued, with something nobody dared do until the middle of the summer: to go near the old empty lot now turned into a park. And that included us children, though we liked pitting ourselves against the law—and immensely enjoyed breaking it. We avoided the park and looked for a new playground in the pits at the brickyard, not because we were afraid of actual retaliation—that sort of fear only made our law-challenging experiments the more exciting—but because we rightly saw the park as the embodiment of a strange higher authority that it was neither possible nor permissible to contest. We felt this way only for a few months, however, until we realized that nobody was taking care of the park. Weeds covered the narrow paths, grass and flowers dried up; authoritative power had evaporated, abandoning this piece of artificial nature, and with the help of the wind blowing the sand, it slowly retransformed itself and returned to something like its former self; it became ours again.

And with increasing enthusiasm we reoccupied it, trampling underfoot whatever had been left of the park, letting the footpaths and flower beds run together; in a splendid little game we snapped the saplings in two, and the whole space again became a soccer field, including the dry, tamped-down, round spot in the middle where the dribbling mostly took place.

But by the time spring came around, the authorities seized the reins again; the landscaping brigade returned and, without calling anybody to account for the vandalism, rebuilt the park. But this second intervention, which included the puzzling phenomenon of the authority's not even deeming us worthy of reprimand and planting new flowers and trees as if nothing had happened, jolted us out of our apathy (and not just us but all the settlement residents). And this was the more emphatic because for reasons completely unknown to us, Mr. Róth was made the park guard and caretaker, he of all people. This began a multidirectional shift of nearly immeasurable complexity in the general mood of the settlement. I might say that while the old life was continuing, a new life began.

The dog is a peculiar animal. It resembles man. It is an animal born to obey no other laws than those of its own instincts. Still, a dog's being is controlled and kept in hand by human regulation, regulation that, for the dog, materializes in the form of human interests. The dog, understanding what is in its own best interest, conforms to the human laws and makes them its own. It even adapts itself to some regulations that are in conflict with the laws that govern animal life. And dogs become like their masters in that they form different castes and classes.

The dogs in the settlement were mongrels that, like the residents, formed three castes. There were original dogs, latecomer dogs, and intruder dogs.

Still, an animal is an animal. During the mating season the caste differences disappeared, though it was doubtful that a mongrel from the settlement could have entered into a marital relationship with, say, a purebred Russian wolfhound. Because of the enormous differences among the classes, this kind of fanciful thinking is absurd, and anyway, in the majority of cases, dogs mate where the first opportunity presents itself.

The caste differences were nonetheless inherited because dogs, in the earliest stages of ontogeny, became aware of their own interests and adopted the human regulations that this awareness had made seem reasonable to them.

The three-layered stratification of our settlement's residents had a strictly nonmaterial character based on the human desire to know that there are others below them in the hierarchy, and those on the very bottom, thirsting for revenge, wait for the chance to rebel against both the nonmaterial and material stratifications. We the children were at the bottom, but below us were the dogs, and below them the cats, mangy, scrawny cats so far down they aren't worth mentioning. But the dogs still lived within striking distance, partly our allies, partly our enemies, and partly living creatures over whom we could wield power. Hence, dogs had a very special place in our lives. Mr. Róth had no dog. But the Maczelkas did: a huge, filthy, komondor-like beast. We hated it. And partly to annoy its master, partly to annoy the beast itself, we invented a silly little game. Dogfights we called it. Holding them by twine we tied around their necks, we'd drag five or six of the "intruder" dogs to the Maczelkas' house; the miserable animals would be irritated by the ropes cutting into their flesh, aggravated by the frustration-driven snapping and scratching among themselves, and by the time we were at the Maczelkas' fence, they had reached the level of ferocity needed for a fight. But we didn't turn them loose yet. The huge komondor mongrel, shaggy and lazy but not without a measure of dignity, would sense the approaching attackers, sidle up to the fence, gently wag its thick-furred tail, and, unlike our dogs, calmly wait for developments. The five or six mongrels, tied on the same line, would bark wildly, snap their jaws, bare their gums, and try to jump at the fence. Then we'd yank the line back (the pain would increase the dogs' fury), the barking would be heard everywhere in the settlement, and at this point Mr. Maczelka would usually appear in the doorway, add his dreadful howls to the cacophony, and chase us away. Throughout the years he never realized that he could spoil our game simply by not coming to the door. But he always did. And we'd let go of the line, take a few steps backward, feigning retreat, and the dogs, finally freed from their painful bondage, would charge the fence. Mr. Maczelka would flail and yell, bang on the fence, but he could not stop what was happening because we, in relatively low voices amidst the deafening cacophony, would egg on our curs with cries of "Sic 'em! Sic 'em!" though they hardly needed encouragement; biting one another and tearing at the fence, they'd run up and down it while the frenzied komondor did the same on the other side. A real clash would occur only if the komondor mongrel managed to widen the gaps in the fence that Mr. Maczelka had tried so carefully to patch up; elongating its body, it would slip out under the fence, the others would pounce on it, turning themselves into a single growling, whimpering, and scrambling hairy ball. For days after the din of battle ceased the dogs would lick the wounds they'd given one another, and we'd cut into one another's words as we heatedly evaluated the outcome and maybe here and there rub our faces where slaps had landed when meted out by our parents in front of Mr. Maczelka. After his departure, though, we'd all have a good laugh.

When Mr. Róth was made the guard and caretaker of the park, we thought that finally we'd have a chance to crack his calm, proud character. We moved the location of the dogfights to the newly sprouting lawn. It would have been truly mean for any of us to initiate such a thing on purpose; we acted purely out of instinct, though having said this, I should add that this does not absolve one of responsibility. In my view, instinct is nothing but a system of habits and rules stored in the deepest layers of consciousness, inextricably intertwined with the wishes, desires, and aggressiveness inherent in human nature. If there is anything that needs to be exposed, it is human instincts. And let no one think of making excuses because making excuses is nothing but passing on responsibility. But to whom are we passing it on when we blame our instincts and plead to be excused? We pass responsibility to communities, to systems made of people, and to everything beyond these systems: to the stars, to the solar eclipse, to the slump in the market. This kind of attitude is but a cover for simple lies and fears. We'd like to absolve ourselves by means of the sins of others, not believing that man, even a single individual, is a totality. The self's totality is to be found not in one's instinctual life, in the genes, or in the subconscious but in our dependence on others and on ourselves; in the fact that one's epidermis conceals a very exceptional being, unlike any other, that is identical with the universe. Its bone structure is constructed on the same principles as the bridges it builds, and its material nature is as infinite as that of everything else in the world.

With our instincts, therefore, we did represent something of the world, but because we had been raised to be instinctual beings, nothing interested us except having some fun—at any cost.

Mr. Róth stood at the edge of the lawn, on the narrow footpath, his body erect, his beautiful eyes resting on us, and because it was mating time for the dogs, we were rolling about in the middle of the lawn, convulsed with laughter, around the dogs that were glued to each other by their rumps, staring dumbly ahead, and we weren't laughing because this was very funny or because it was the first time we'd seen such a thing; we were laughing *for him,* hoping he would sense the hidden, titillating rebellion in our laughter and also the fear of rebellion, fear of his stick with a large nail at the tip and his straight gaze, and also sense the contempt that lurked behind our intentions and for which we had two reasons: he was a Jew, and he was an adult. While two of my buddies, howling with laughter, tried to yank apart the copulating dogs, I kept thundering in his direction: "Mr. Róth! What are these dogs doing?"

He neither answered nor made a move. He did not yell at us to get off the lawn, either, and this made the situation all the more infuriating.

"Mr. Róth! These poor dogs are stuck together!" I said.

Mr. Róth finally made a move, and I was ready to react to anything he would do while the rest of the gang fell silent with anticipation, but the old man did not answer us. He laid his stick down carefully at the edge of the lawn and with slow steps walked over to the spigot, fastened the end of the rubber hose on it, unwound the hose, and, careful not to step on the grass, began to pull the hose after him along the winding narrow paths.

This was a very special moment, like those moments when we made sly attempts to express our contempt—similar because our intentions, with no word of response from him, were never realized. Later these unrealized intentions were to gel into a single harmonious entity, convincing me that one can only humiliate someone who himself humiliates others, and the world is made up of humiliated people in whom, after each insult, the insatiable desire arises to humiliate others. But this enormous ambition of global proportions came to naught with Mr. Róth and turned into the odd feeling that made one realize that with one's humiliating ambitions one humiliates first of all oneself.

Mr. Róth was pulling the hose, careful of the new grass; in our helplessness we continued to fool around for a while, and the dogs, glued together, were still in the middle of the lawn. Mr. Róth went back to the spigot, the hose jerked a few times like a dying snake, and I was gripped by the urge—I remember this very clearly—to help him by getting hold of the end of the hose and keep the water from spraying in every direction so the old man wouldn't have to run back to it himself. But I did not hurry, nor did the others. Mr. Róth began watering the lawn while we slowly, nonchalantly moved away. Quietly we watched him work. In the meantime, the dogs uncoupled. They circled and sniffed each other for a while and then trotted off. But I couldn't leave it at that.

"Mr. Róth, don't you think these stinking beasts will get sick from all this . . . from being stuck together."

The boys around me sniggered.

"What happened to them, Mr. Róth?" I asked, trying to get a rise out of him.

And then Mr. Róth told us exactly what the dogs had been doing. He used the same word we had been using as a conjunction—our parents not far behind us in this practice. But coming from Mr. Róth's mouth, the word had a very special effect on us.

It sounded distorted, disgusting, and also seemed as if we were hearing it for the first time.

"But this, I believe, you boys already know," he added quietly after a short pause.

We were silent. Then one of us piped up: "Mr. Róth, will you let me do a little watering?"

Mr. Róth handed over the hose.

I got angry. Rotten traitor, I thought. That's what the rest thought too, but unusually, nobody said anything. According to the gang's code of honor, a traitor should be abandoned. And so we slunk away. But in fact we were also jealous of the boy because he got to use the hose. And we never spoke of this incident afterward. We herded the dogs together on the lawn a few more times, but then we gave that up too.

The week before Easter the settlement's atmosphere was already poisoned, germs of the illness had found an ideal breeding ground, and the events that followed attested to the inevitability of the sickness. There was no antidote. Could there have been? No, there could not have been. If one day the human brain turns into something like a microscope-cum-telescope, it will be able simultaneously to discover and evaluate the most general phenomena as well as the tiniest events of the world, and maybe then it will be possible to avert epidemics of self-destruction. For the moment the human brain can be compared only with a sponge, a sponge that indiscriminately absorbs any liquid, and then the same liquid, in a slightly altered state, can be squeezed out of it. At the moment the human brain is capable only of experiencing events first and evaluating them later.

My wisdom is of the same kind: it came after the event. Let it be said in my defense that I was only a child then. Since then science, whose servant I have become, has accustomed me to analyzing phenomena. But how far we are from the stage in which we might rigorously follow ev-

ery movement of our lives with the strict attention of our minds! So far
this ability has been developed to exceptionally high levels only in the
freakish skills of dissemblance. But is dissemblance the same as self-
knowledge? Although dissemblance may develop one's sustained concentration—since it requires great self-discipline, as one gauges the exigent
demands of every situation and compares them with one's own, the goal
of a dissembler being not the impartial evaluation of facts and phenomena but, rather, conformity and assimilation, and life producing many
different and contradictory situations—the continually conforming dissembler, so adept at altering his image, will awaken one day and realize
that he has lost, in fact with his own hands destroyed, his own individuality. If only he would awaken to *that*! But with his self-knowledge he
never gets that far; he never realizes that with no nervous, agitated defense of his own individuality and interests he has annihilated himself
with his own hands. He cannot recognize this because he is not the only
one who lies; everybody around him does, and in the voices and lies he
sees himself just as if he were looking into a mirror. He sees himself, and
he calms down. He has accomplished his goal; he has become like the
others.

Not only did we not know Mr. Róth, but we had not the vaguest notion how he had spent his days before the city entrusted him with the duties of a park keeper. What we knew about him was that he was getting a
fairly small pension, and the mailman who supplied this information, and
who was always slightly drunk, could not be trusted. He was talking
about letters mailed from Israel. I remember he mentioned something
like that just before Easter because my grandmother, on my return from
school, announced: "Rezső Róth got a big money order. From Israel."

This money order—I have no idea whether it was real or only con-
cocted in the Maczelkas' kitchen by the mailman's alcohol-clouded
brain—gained special significance and became the starting point of a
campaign whose leaders and spiritual guides were the Maczelkas.

When we gathered again behind the brickyard that evening, the sum
mentioned had risen to ten thousand dollars. We speculated on what we
would do if we had ten thousand dollars. The cool semidark air and the
filthy ruins of the factory became populated with the figments of our
imaginations; our personal desires intermingled as we kept interrupting
one another in trying to dream up a bright, glittering world around us.

But after a while, after we had revealed our dreams, modest or grandiose as they might be, we fell silent, and without anyone's saying a word, our thoughts turned toward the man in our settlement who was master of the power behind such a vast sum of money. And when on our way home we ambled past Mr. Róth's little house, one of us gave appropriate expression to our feelings when he first hawked loud and long and then spit across the fence.

Although we were children, mere tools in the hands of a higher authority—the society of adults—and even if in our rebellion we did nothing but try to acquire or at least approach this authority that oppressed us, we did have a sense of being mere tools and that our hatred of Mr. Róth was only a pale imitation of what we saw around us. And if not all of us sensed this, I myself was forced to be certain of it.

I don't remember exactly when it happened, the same day or a few days later, but in any case, one evening when I got home from our get-together at the brickyard, I was surprised to find Mr. Maczelka sitting in our kitchen, opposite my father, a bottle of wine before them, and my mother filling their glasses. It was a little smoky in the kitchen; pleasant warmth was emanating from the stove, and with a familial hominess Mr. Maczelka's round body and dimly glowing bald head blended smoothly into the general atmosphere. Mr. Maczelka and my father were looking at each other like old friends, and my mother was humbly wiping the glasses as if we had been granted a great and unexpected honor and privilege. I muttered some sort of greeting under my breath, but Mr. Maczelka, who usually insisted on a clear, loud salutation, did not grumble this time but hailed me warmly, even tried to pat me on the shoulder.

"Go into the room," my father said.

I went into the room.

"Close the door," my father said. Because I made no move, my mother closed the door for me.

The door was old and cracked—it must have come from a demolished peasant cottage—and the light filtering through the cracks drew stripes in the dark room. I did not turn on the light, just leaned against the table while the adults continued talking in low voices. I felt the urge to eavesdrop, but the feeling that in the kitchen very important things were being discussed, that if I planted my ears to the door I might become party to them, not only increased my curiosity but also aroused my fear; although I went up to the door, I was seized by an involuntary shaking and did not dare put my ear to it. Maybe a whole hour went by without my being able to make out a single word; then Mr. Maczelka finally left. Mother came into the room, switched on the light, and gave me a strange and, I thought, slightly abashed look. "Come, have supper."

"Don't want any."

"You haven't eaten anything."

"Can't you hear I'm not hungry?" I muttered angrily.

My mother stood there, hesitating, her hand still on the light switch. I went past her into the kitchen. Grandmother was dozing on the edge of her bed in the corner, while my father was making round movements with his fist stretched out before him. I stopped in front of him like an animal waiting to be thrown a few leftover morsels from a sumptuous meal. Father did not even notice me; his head was red from the wine and the heat; he poured for himself and downed the drink in one gulp, then slammed the table hard.

"'Cause what? God damn it, I'll show . . . Holy goddamn mother!" Again he poured for himself.

"Don't . . . Józsi! Don't," Mother whispered, and it wasn't clear whether she was begging him to stop drinking or stop talking as he was.

But my father wasn't listening. He downed the wine, shuddered, stood up, and without as much as a glance in our direction stumbled into the other room with heavy, unsteady steps, shedding and scattering his clothes as he went, and lay down on the made-up bed.

If I still had any doubts that my own mood was but a pale reflection of the adults' mood, they were dispelled when, a few days later, after having gone around the whole settlement, Mr. Maczelka put a sheet of paper on our kitchen table and without a word pushed it at my father. My father was a poor, slow reader. His bony face showed his embarrassment at the sight of the sheet ruled with squares, but Mr. Maczelka was tactful enough to take it back and read out loud what was written on it. Maybe because I was busy watching these hesitating and slightly shameful gestures of the men and Mother's furrowed brow along with Grandmother's eyes, which expressed almost physical pleasure, I didn't catch as well as I should have the words of the text, meant to express the unanimous opinion of the settlement. It said something to the effect that we, residents of the settlement, considered it unfair that the city leaders had entrusted care of the park to a man who, considering his financial situation and foreign correspondence, very understandably did not feel this work to be his calling and who, as witnesses could corroborate, on several occasions had made disparaging remarks regarding the park and its builders.

The text was followed by signatures; my father also signed, and then, after some hesitation, so did my mother. After Mr. Maczelka left, Father did not start banging on the table again; he asked for his supper, and while Grandmother was setting the table, he grumbled: "Why does that old fart stick his nose into everything?"

Mother, as if she had been thrown a life belt, clutched at the sentence. "Shouldn't have signed it, Józsi!"

"Shouldn't have . . ." Father repeated the words mockingly and slapped his thigh. That gesture put an end to the discussion, and I believe it also put his conscience at ease.

The feeling that we children were only tools was reinforced when we saw to our great surprise that our parents had their doubts and hesitations and even gave expression to them, if not very bravely, but we children neither hesitated nor had doubts.

And this was so not only after the petition was submitted, but before that, after the first round of Mr. Maczelka's visits, when there had been no cracks in the unanimity of our parents' opinions. And because we had no doubts, we could express our opinions more openly. While the adults simply turned the other way whenever Mr. Róth's lean figure happened to appear or made obviously hostile and jeering remarks behind his back, my friend Jancsi Zsudi, when sent with the garbage pail behind the brickyard, emptied its contents in front of Mr. Róth's house. We staged another dogfight on the lawn and in the flower beds, and an unknown perpetrator, using chalk, scribbled the word JEW on Mr. Róth's house. It was evident from the wavering letters that it was not an adult who had done this; besides, no adult would have risked climbing over the fence to get to the wall of the house.

The park changed Rezső Róth's life too. In a certain sense it made it public. A part of his life was now taking place in the area ringed by our houses. In the morning, when he first appeared, he would pause for a moment, and before taking off to gather the rubbish with his spiky stick, he would look about with the pride of a proprietor. Once the paper bits had been collected, he raked together the dried-out grass and then swept the narrow little footpaths. Sometimes, by noon, he'd produced several small piles. In the afternoon he would burn the piles and clear away the ashes. And at sunset, if it was not raining, he would uncoil the hose and, without getting his clothes wet or dirty, water the lawn. On rainy days he did not leave his house. The work was quiet and monotonous, but he did it with obvious pleasure.

I often heard adults express dismay about the cruelty of children. But I don't feel we were crueler than our parents; it was that their views and opinions about Mr. Róth, developed and ripened over the years, became embodied in our actions. We were even less aware of the meaning of our acts than were the more mature members of the community. And without a doubt, the openness that distinguishes the cruelty of children from the more concealed, more treacherous cruelty of adults did quicken the pace of events, and this because the adults saw in our acts a vindication of their own thoughts. But instead of recoiling from what we exposed, they were emboldened by it. This had to be the case, because when that word appeared on the wall of Mr. Róth's house, no one became indignant, on the contrary, people took it in their stride as naturally as if they themselves had scrawled it on the wall. And since the perpetrator remained unknown and no one tried to find out who it was, this word written in chalk was considered to have some sort of approval by a higher power. The day the word appeared, the mood of the settlement changed. News of it traveled by word of mouth; from behind windows or from close up, we all stared at the defamatory word. Everyone felt that any moment now the sentence that the word implied would be carried out.

I consider it impossible that Mr. Róth could not have noticed that it went on like this for days. Counting on his noticing it, we curiously waited to see the countermeasures he would take. But no matter how Mr. Maczelka kept strutting around his garden all morning pretending to be busy with his plants, no matter how many side glances he cast at his neighbor, Mr. Róth did not wipe the word off the wall of his house; not a muscle moved on his face as he walked around the pile of rubbish dumped in front of his garden gate; he showed not the slightest sign of dismay, shock, or anger. He did not touch it. He strolled across the park and spent the mornings tending to his work as he had before.

At noon, however, he left the settlement. We were on our way home from school, and the moment we saw his erect, attractive figure approaching from a distance, we fell silent. The closer he came, the more strongly I was seized by anxiety, but this didn't stop me from exchanging mocking and conspiratorial looks with the other boys. He smiled kindly and wisely, as if he were aware of all our emotions, and seeing this kindness, we became as submissive as herded animals. Jancsi Zsudi was walking behind me—he was the smallest and the wildest of us—and when the rest of us said, almost in chorus, "Good day, Mr. Róth," he said, "Good day, Mr. Jew!"

For an instant fear and malicious disdain got mixed up within me. But Mr. Róth did not seem to have heard the dissonant sound in the general chorus. Or he did not want to. Tilting his torso slightly in our direction, he doffed his hat.

Then he stopped. And so did we. Mr. Róth stepped before Jancsi Zsudi and raised a hand to his breast. Silence. In our fear, several of us turned our heads away. Some hint of irony crept into Mr. Róth's gentle smile, and he looked straight into Jancsi's eyes. "No need for you to remind me. I haven't forgotten it."

Jancsi bit the edge of his lip and then, as if faced with a terrible thought, looked up at Mr. Róth, but no sound escaped his throat.

"Well?" Mr. Róth smiled gently again.

Strange, fitful sounds burst from Jancsi's mouth. "I wasn't the one who wrote that on the wall! Please believe it . . . it wasn't me."

Now Mr. Róth's enormous gentleness should have led to a forgiving gesture, but instead a flushing redness traveled across his skin, and his lips curled into a disdainful pout. He gazed into the distance and back at us again, and then without a word he walked on.

We just stood there, devastated. Everything had changed around us and within us because now we understood that we were cowards. Or rather, we felt that one of our mates, the smallest one, whom we coddled as lovingly as if he had been our own child, coddled as we had never been, and as only children can coddle one another—the object of our love, Jancsi Zsudi, was a vile coward. We continued silently on the empty road to the settlement. This defeat might have been the final one if we had stayed as we were, together in one group all of us who sensed our own vileness, but we parted; our roads led us separately to our uniformly shabby homes, where our mothers or grandmothers would thrust into our hands slices of bread smeared with lard or warm up the previous evening's leftovers for lunch and once again infect us with their poison. Here, in these kitchens, the world once again ran according to the old system. We'd quarrel with them, and they'd threaten us or maybe stroke our disheveled, school-smelling hair. With their words and gestures they'd guide us back into the fold.

That afternoon Jancsi Zsudi did not show up behind the brickyard; only his older brother Imre came.

"Jancsi?" someone asked.

"How should I know?" said Imre sullenly, shrugging his shoulders.

That afternoon we didn't play soccer, but we didn't mention Mr. Róth either; we spent the time, with great gusto, reviling our teachers. It was getting dark when Jancsi Zsudi finally arrived.

We pretended this was perfectly normal, and so did he. He sat down on a pile of bricks and looked at me. I was smoking a cigarette.

"Give me a drag," he said, making his voice sound infantile.

We liked this kind of voice, which made us more conscious of the relationship in which we had accepted him as our child, we, who had grown taller and were in fact a few years older than he.

Without a word I passed the cigarette to him; everyone watched my movement. He took two puffs and gave it back to me.

"You guys know where the Jew went today?" We all looked up. Jancsi narrowed his eyes and made a face. "To the police. To squeal on us."

The grin did not leave his face. This grin was addressed to us who had abandoned him there, on the road, to us who had backed down under Mr. Róth's gaze. The grin was meant for us who were cowards. And because of this grin, I believe, everything got all mixed up in me for a long time. When had I become craven and vile, I wanted to know: back then, on the road, when I felt myself vile and cowardly, or now, here, in a brick-yard pit when again I felt craven and vile? There I had betrayed Jancsi and my earlier conviction; here I betrayed the old man and my new conviction. In the pit of the brickyard I believed that Jancsi was the strongest of us all; the smallest was the strongest. The following morning three new piles of rubbish turned up on the park lawn.

Vacation! The sun was shining, our feet kicked up the dust in the road; it was as if a giant blue dome had appeared above us. Only the angels were missing. Here, even in our desolate landscape, nature meant much when it joined forces with freedom, and our minds, once terrified by countless school obligations, could calmly absorb everything our barren wasteland had to offer. We didn't dawdle, as we generally did, but ran toward the settlement yelling and jostling; here and there we'd stop suddenly and, laughing our heads off, spin and spin with our schoolbags, letting the laws of centrifugal force take their course and our schoolbags fly off in the air.

A whole week's vacation! It seemed so long a time we imagined it would never end. More precisely, we were optimistic enough not to think of the moment when once again we'd have to cross the school threshold. And in this optimism, which came not from the world but only from our ignorance, we forgot—we shed like soiled clothes—the tiny fears and anxieties that usually filled our days. We also forgot Mr. Róth. At home we flung down our bags somewhere, received our slices of larded bread, and ran to the back of the brickyard. What a wonderful feeling it was to play without guilt lurking at the depth of each moment! It was late in the evening by the time I got home, and the next day it started all over again. We scouted our favorite places, pried open the door in the abandoned factory building, climbed up on the steel ladder along the smokestack, shoved one another at the edge of the abysslike pits, and whenever we found a secluded spot we'd discuss things quietly, interrupting one another all the time. Everything that happened that day reached us only as if from afar. We attributed no special significance to the fact that a man came looking for Mr. Róth and Mr. Róth allegedly threw the man out of his house and even threw the park keeper's stick and armband after him. Nor did we care about the dogfights we had once staged to annoy Mr. Maczelka or the rubbish heaps Jancsi Zsudi had dumped on the park lawn—we were free. In the evening we built a fire. I stole some bacon from home. But there was more smoke than fire because rotted old planks and shelves don't burn as well as dry twigs do. Since we were unfamiliar with the taste of bacon roasted over an open fire in the woods, we were satisfied with what we had. Harmony was never greater in the gang than in those first days of our vacation; we were so immersed in having a good time that we failed to notice how late into the night we'd stayed out.

We went home as if we didn't care, though for reasons incomprehensible to us, staying out late usually brought retaliation. An ominous silence reigned in the kitchen. Grandmother was lying in her low iron bed; Mother was putting things in order in the other room. The smell of pastry and roast meat wafted in the air, but there was no sign of cooking or baking; the holiday meal was most likely already put in the pantry for tomorrow.

"Where have you been?" Mother called out, but feeling this sentence to be a superfluous introduction to a well-known routine, I did not bother to reply.

I felt the sentence was superfluous because it was part of a transparent, petty power play, a game in which my mother, who was never the least interested where I had been knocking about, chose to play the role of the loving, caring mother. Had I been a stay-at-home—and there had been a period when I was—my parents would have found other reasons to discipline me. My mother disciplined me not because she was worried about me but because she herself was constantly under watch.

"Can't you hear me?" she said, stopping at the door.

This question could not be answered. My grandmother sat up. Her dentures were no longer in her mouth, and she made peculiar lisping sounds when she spoke. "Always loafing around . . ."

But the scene could not continue as usual because somebody delivered such a powerful kick to our kitchen door that two of its little glass panes fell out and shattered on the floor. Mother grabbed the doorpost. Another kick followed, and my father let out a loud roar outside the door. "Are you sitting on your ears?"

I opened the door. He was standing there, drunk, with inarticulate words dribbling out of his mouth. His eyelids were half closed, as if he were about to fall asleep. And under one arm he was holding a small lamb; in his other hand he had a bottle of wine. The lamb was making pitiful bleating sounds and with its powerful legs kicking Father's hips. As if not feeling those kicks at all, Father managed to stagger to the middle of the kitchen.

"So this is how my little woman is waiting for me, eh?" he asked quietly.

Dread appeared in my mother's face, and I knew I mustn't stick around. I started for the other room, but Father let out another horrific roar. "Is this the way I am welcomed here? The door, even that god-damn door . . ." He slammed the wine bottle down on the table; the lamb convulsed under his arm and fell to the floor, but he did not even notice it.

My mother screamed, "Oh, God! Don't hurt me!"

Hard as Mr. Maczelka strained his ears while pretending to be busy with the flowers in his garden, Mr. Róth's shouting was not loud enough for him to make out the meaning of the words; still, he smiled because he felt that his case was proceeding well. In a few moments a lucky coincidence would also assist him. Suddenly the door flew open, and the young city official who had disappeared inside a half hour earlier now appeared in, or rather jumped through, the doorway. He ran along the narrow footpath, but before dashing through the open garden gate he turned, brandished his briefcase at the house, shook his fist, and, with his face like chalk, gasped: "I resent this!" His lips were trembling, though he seemed to be talking only to an empty doorway. "I most emphatically resent this!"

He may have wanted to say something else, but then the attractive figure of Rezső Róth also appeared, his face pale but determined, in one hand clutching the park guard's stick and in the other waving the armband, his office badge; he hurried after the young man. He appeared to have a definite plan for the stick. The official leaped out of the garden and slammed the gate shut behind him; his next steps were more like running. But Rezső Róth, as if awakening from a daze, stopped. They looked at each other.

"You have forgotten your stick, my dear sir," he said. "And this whatchamacallit too," he added, waving the armband.

The young man did not move, though his lips were trembling. Rezső Róth had by now completely calmed down. With unhurried steps he reached the garden gate, opened it, threw both the stick and the armband on top of the rubbish heap by the fence, turned on his heels, and returned to his house.

The official now noticed János Maczelka, and a painful, forced smile appeared on his face. "Oh, hello, it's you again," he said sociably.

János Maczelka was grinning, but this offended the official, who felt that the recent scene, which the older man must have witnessed, had considerably damaged his reputation.

"We do know each other, do we not?"

"Of course we do; when you were here the last time . . ." said János Maczelka, and stepped up to the fence.

At this moment the official noticed the word scrawled in chalk on Rezső Róth's house: JEW. For a brief moment he once again lost his almost regained composure. "What on earth is that?" he asked.

János Maczelka, as if he could not see well, came out of his garden and at some distance from the official, pretending to be surprised, looked at the wall. "It must have been one of those swine . . . You see what hooligans they are . . . to scribble something like that." He pointed to the house and then to his forehead, indicating that the resident of the house was not all there. "He wouldn't wipe it off. And I did tell him to. I said, 'Mr. Róth, why don't you wipe it off?' "

The official, eagerly acknowledging Maczelka's small gesture, with some dignity shook his head. "This Mr. Róth is really not all there," he said.

"Of course I've got no problems with him, and otherwise he keeps to himself," Mr. Maczelka responded, almost sadly.

"I see."

"He didn't insult the comrade, did he?"

The official considered it beneath him to reply to this question. He merely looked at Mr. Maczelka.

The old man was becoming confused under the official's gaze. "Because if he did, the comrade should not take it to heart . . . He is usually quick to anger . . ."

"I see."

"Otherwise we have a good neighborly relationship with him," said Mr. Maczelka, and stepped closer. "But he's a little crotchety. They say that over there, in the concentration camp, his nerves were shot."

The official pretended that his interlocutor's words did not interest him. He looked at the stick and the armband lying on the rubbish heap. "May I ask you to do me a favor?"

János Maczelka said nothing, but his eyes sparkled.

"Keep these things until further arrangements are made."

"The stick?"

"And the armband."

"With pleasure. By all means."

"Would you mind picking them up?"

János Maczelka moved to the rubbish heap and picked up the named objects.

My mother did not sleep that night. I myself tossed and turned. The bliss of vacation was over. Again I had to face the question, Which of the two adults was right? It was all the harder to decide because I loved them both, and they both disgusted me. It's a hard thing, but I have to say it. I was disgusted by the artery swelling in my father's neck, but I was also disgusted by the helpless cowardice with which my mother accepted his blows. I was disgusted by my father's fist and by my mother's shrieks. I was disgusted because my father, whose fist symbolized family authority, demanded absolute respect, and if I unconditionally submitted to his authority, I would have to banish my mother from my heart. But if I unconditionally took my mother's side, I would have to deny my father's authority, and because his behavior embodied the prevailing order of my world, I would have to deny that order too. When I was disgusted by the one who was humiliated, it meant I was on the side of the authority, and when I was disgusted by the authority it meant I was siding with the humiliated one. Rejection demands confrontation and action, and because I was incapable of acting, I was incapable of making choices. More precisely, I had a mistaken notion of action. Not that I was a foolish or unfeeling child, but because my world—the very one that rejected Mr. Róth—recognized nothing but the right of might and authority, I had to believe that if I sided with either parent, I would have to use my fist against the other. My fists were still small. I thought to myself that when I grew up, I would gain authority over my parents. And that might well have happened, but it didn't. By the time I grew up I understood that they were as much a part of, and tools of, the system as we children were, and there was no authority that could rise above this system except the system itself—another system. And unless I am mistaken in this, then it is also true that because we are tools, parts, and partakers of this system, it was not one another we had to conquer in the battle of fists but the system itself—whenever it tried to get the better of us.

And now I have arrived at the point where it may become clear why the figure of Mr. Róth grew so excitingly great for me and why, after so many years, I learned to love my mother for a single thing she once did that at the time seemed incomprehensible.

My mother, as I have said, didn't sleep that night. In the morning, when I got out of bed, a couch pushed against the foot of the family bed, and went into the kitchen, she was sitting at the table. In front of her on the floor, in a large cardboard box lined with rags, lay the Paschal Lamb. With glazed eyes it stared into space and held stiffly away from its body a leg, the one that had broken in its fall and that Mother had put in a splint during the night. Its little muzzle was incomprehension itself. I stood over it and watched how from time to time the almost transparent fur twitched along its belly.

"Must be hungry," my mother said, whispering.

From the other room we could hear my father's snoring.

"You could get him some grass," Mother continued, looking at me pensively. "D'you know what it eats when it's still so little?"

"No."

"Maybe milk. But we don't have any."

"No milk?"

"No. But you could get some grass from the park. It's nice and green there."

"Yes."

"And when it gets better, we could take it out to graze."

"Yes."

"Well, go . . . That's why its belly is twitching . . ."

"Yes."

Quietly I closed the door behind me. The settlement was quiet, the sky a little overcast, but the air was clear and fresh, since because of the holiday, the factories were not spewing out their heavy smoke. I stopped at the edge of the park but did not bend down to pull out any grass; I simply stared ahead of me. I was not interested in my mother's quiet anxiety about the lamb because I did not yet understand that it wasn't directed at the lamb. And I didn't care about the lamb either, though in fact my father had brought it for me. I stood there for a long time and then, as if pursued, slunk in between the dilapidated buildings of the brickyard. I sat down; I was sleepy, miserable, sad. I even thought of never bothering to go home again, of just taking off right there and then, trying my luck in the world; one fine day I'd return and stand before them as a powerful and famous man. I was hallucinating. And the hallucination—because so far from reality—numbed and lulled me, so much so that I forgot why I was sad. I don't know how long I stayed in the brickyard; by the time I started back, the houses were full of the rhythm of everyday life—the sounds of radios, conversations, and the clanging of dishes—though the crooked little streets were still empty. I would have stopped in the park and picked some grass, but my mother appeared just then on the other side of the street, dressed in her holiday best, carrying the lamb in her arms. As we approached each other, I kept my head down, pretending indifference, but in the meantime I was trying to think of some acceptable lie. But my mother didn't call me to account.

"Lambs don't even eat grass," I said.

"They don't?"

Her voice gave me a start. I looked at her. Her narrow face, which at other times hardened in fear or anger, was soft and calmly cheerful.

"I'll take it then."

"To where?"

"To Rezső Róth."

I gaped at her, speechless.

"It'll be good for it there," she said, and in this sentence there was no hint of apology.

We looked at each other for another moment; and then she moved on with the lamb to Mr. Róth's house. I turned after her, still not understanding. Nor did I understand why I started to run in the opposite direction, homeward.

After the Easter holiday the settlement became quiet. The Maczelkas stayed in their kitchen. Mr. Maczelka tried on the park keeper's armband, picked up the stick to see how it felt in his hand, and turned his small shaving mirror so he could see himself in it. Mrs. Maczelka was serving the lunch she had prepared from the holiday leftovers, and she stole stealthy looks at her husband, totally absorbed in contemplating his image in the mirror.

"Say," Mrs. Maczelka said suddenly.

"What?" Mr. Maczelka asked, but did not look at the woman.

"Did you see Róth yesterday?"

Maczelka looked pensively at the woman, who had hurried to the window, opened it, and was looking out at the neighboring house.

"I haven't seen him since Easter Sunday," she said.

"No wonder . . . After what happened!" he said.

They looked at each other and then turned away. Later they sat down to lunch.

"He probably shut himself in," said Maczelka, and made loud noises while chewing the food he'd stuffed into his mouth.

"He got insulted," said Mrs. Maczelka.

Maczelka shrugged. There were all sorts of leftovers on the table: half a roast chicken, stuffed cabbage, a plateful of aspic, pastries with walnuts and with poppyseeds, a few dried-out cabbage strudels, boiled eggs, pickled peppers. Dutifully, slowly, the two of them were finishing off everything. Maczelka looked up from time to time as if to say something; he even opened his mouth but then went on chewing.

When he was full, he spoke. "If they don't come by tomorrow, I'll take them myself . . . They should tell me what to do with them."

"They'll come. The man said so."

"He said so. But he forgot about it."

"True. Going in is a good idea, because maybe they're thinking about you for the—"

Mr. Maczelka did not respond but was glad his wife had said out loud what he was thinking. He stood up from the table, placed his hands on his belly, and between two hiccups said: "I'm stuffed like a goose."

"Lie down and rest a little while."

We finished our lunch; my mother and grandmother were arguing about something; the water was being heated for washing the dishes; the vapors escaping from under the lid were gliding like sparkling pearls on the kitchen furniture. I was sitting on my grandmother's pallet, my mind wandering in the world beyond the door, in the gray sky from which a light rain had been drizzling tediously all morning. It was such a sleepily calm time that mother and daughter did not become belligerent or show readiness to fight. But the next day was working on me like a guilty conscience, because our vacation—whose end we did not believe would come—had evaporated, leaving behind only the taste of its first hours. Restless and anxious, I was frittering away the last minutes of freedom. I was restless because the time in which I had placed so much hope, expecting relief and respite, solved nothing; on the contrary, the events of Easter Sunday had thrust our family, however invisibly, into a deeper abyss. If my parents pretended to be standing merely at the edge of the precipice, in reality they had stepped over the last rock and begun their plunge into the void. In my dreams I envisioned the pit at the brickyard, except I could not see its bottom because that was an impalpable darkness, and the four of us, tied together with a rope, were hurtling downward like clip-winged birds.

That weekend my parents had consumed the last morsels of their mutual respect or love. The rope that held us fast in the dream may have been symbolic. After my mother's last and greatest act of rebellion our paths should have diverged, because it had become clear that the four of us were held together by nothing but the simple, cruel law of the stomach.

If my mother's deed had been driven not only by instinct but by sense and reason, or if my father had recognized in it that the one who rebelled against him was striving not to challenge his authority but to rise to a loftier, more dignified existence, then perhaps our lives might have gone in a different direction and the rope that in my dream so meaningfully bound us together would have been the symbol not of coercion but of rational love. But in our world, the conditional mode that goes beyond the limits of necessity is superfluous; its sole purpose, it seems, is to express the illusions of a few puritanical souls. The events themselves left no ambiguous gaps and spoke for themselves.

Is the way we live the only way to live? Couldn't my parents have lived differently?

My mother was dependent on my father, and after her irrational yet rightful and beautiful rebellion she bowed her head even lower, if that was possible, before him. She didn't even notice that for her this meant total self-annihilation. And because my father felt his authority threatened, he expected this of her, yet still not fully satisfied and fearing further rebellion, he changed his tactics: open brutality was replaced by a slier cruelty in whose recesses lurked the possibility of new outbreaks of the old violence. And at this point the tragedy ended, because my mother was grateful for not being beaten and pretended not to notice that for her any possibility of a new life was over forever. *The defeated rebel gratefully kissed the hand of her adversary, and the authority took great pleasure in being able to do as it pleased, to play with her as a cat plays with a dead mouse.* And although in the depth of their souls they knew they were adversaries, my parents were allies, the perfect servants of each other's interests. They were forever deprived of the bearing and dignity that make human beings human. The walls of their individual personalities lay ruined in the dust of the struggle for power.

The warm, mysterious light of my mother's personality flashed one more time on that tediously drizzly afternoon of the last day of the Easter vacation when our neighbor pushed the kitchen door open, her voice trembling with excitement and from the exertion of running, and managed to announce, her tone not completely free of malice: "Something happened to old Róth . . ."

Mother's movements following this announcement were few, but the unexpected news fixed them precisely in my mind. With both hands she grasped the dishwashing pan on the stool and heaved it to the table, spilling most of the water; her lips parted, and with her wrist, glistening with grease, she smoothed her forehead as if to readjust an unruly lock; then, lowering for an instant her thin and almost transparent eyelids, she took a step toward our neighbor. By the time she looked up and was able to formulate her question, my grandmother was there too.

"Not really?" she said, leaning toward the neighbor, expecting confirmation and some elaboration on the news.

"I don't dare go over there," whispered the neighbor, waving her open hands in all directions.

My grandmother's curiosity reached the limit beyond which she could not help asking, "But what happened?"

"Nobody knows yet."

During this exchange my mother's face was undergoing a transformation. She wrinkled her forehead and looked at the two other women as if she were really wondering about something, and then this expression disappeared from her face, leaving only a quiet sadness. Absently she slid her hand down the doorpost and stepped back to the table. Again she grasped the handles of the dishwashing bowl, and this time I saw only her back, which was slowly arching forward. I thought she was crying.

The neighbor ran off, and my grandmother, throwing an old coat over her shoulders, ran after her; the two of us were left there in the vaporous dimness, Mother still motionless. As if trying to test her feelings, I said, "I'll run over there too."

Now she looked at me. Her face and her gaze were cold and indifferent. She was not crying. On the contrary, it seemed now that it had not been shock that prevented her from speaking moments earlier but the realization that she should not interfere with events unfolding.

"You're not going anywhere!" she said.

I walked to the open door and with my back to her leaned against the wall.

"I said, you stay here!" she screamed.

"I can't even stand in the door?" I screamed back, turning only my head in her direction.

Finally she lifted the dishpan and without a word walked past me to empty it outside. When she disappeared behind the house, I broke into a run toward Mr. Róth's house. Rebellion carried my feet: rebellion against her, the coward, the one who had surrendered. This was a dialogue we repeated daily, and my rebellion against the prohibiting words continued daily too, but because this particular prohibition had a most profound meaning, or content, my rebellion became deeper too; it was not curiosity that was carrying me toward Mr. Róth's house but the contempt I felt for my mother.

I did not yet know that this running was down a road to a different kind of life toward which in fact my mother had pointed the way, which was something she too had desired. And because I did not yet know exactly what I was doing or know that fear would accompany me all along the route, after a little distance I slowed down. Between two fears I found myself on the small, muddy settlement street. A feeling akin to guilt was rising in me because in the house toward which I was hurrying a tragedy awaited me, and I already sensed that I had something to do with it. I thought of turning back. By the time Mother would return to the kitchen I could be back, standing by the door again, leaning against the wall as if nothing had happened. In my mind I was running forward and then back, but in fact for long minutes I had been standing in place while all around me people were running, driven by curiosity, with their coats pulled over their heads against the rain. Like the criminal whose feet take him to the scene of the crime, I followed them.

There they were: men, women, and children standing under the gray skies, lashed by the rain. From a distance it looked like a small crowd, a faceless crowd that nevertheless consisted of familiar individuals to each of whom I had some sort of connection. And all the individuals of this crowd, led here by God knows how many different emotions, were now filled, overwhelmed by, if one may put it in these terms, compassion trembling with excitement.

"But what happened?"

"Is he dead?"

"They say he disappeared."

It was as if profound anxiety and solicitude quivered in the curious, excited voices, and that anxiety and solicitude set me apart from the group assembled here. Although I did not move from my place, and from a distance it may have appeared that I was part of this faceless crowd, I was separated from them by my thought that there was nothing constant in these people or in people in general. The reverse side of the hatred they felt for Mr. Róth was marked by compassion and anxiety—all their feeling had a reverse side—and now they were rotating the leaves of their feelings on the stems of their habits. And I could feel this all the more because I was no different from them; I *was* part of this crowd. Mr. Maczelka was the only one who did not succumb to the general mood; he was at the head of the throng, shouting.

"You'll find out everything in good time!" he thundered, waving his hands. "Nobody can go near the house before the police get here!"

"They reported it to the police?" somebody asked, and someone else replied immediately, though nobody knew exactly what had to be reported, "You bet, or maybe you thought we should have waited for your advice!"

The boys were there too, the Zsudi brothers and the rest of my friends, standing at some distance from one another. It didn't even occur to me to talk to them because their faces reflected the same panic I was feeling. And then a police car, spraying us with mud, backed into the space in front of Mr. Róth's house with its siren blaring, and the crowd fell silent. A dread, cold numbness gripped me; I closed my eyes, daring to look up again only when the officer in charge and his two subordinates were inside Mr. Róth's garden. They walked around and inspected the house, exchanging meaningful looks. Mr. Maczelka trotted behind them; when he started to say something, the officer silenced him with his hand; they tried to open the door and the windows, but everything was shut tight. Their movements, which seemed ritualistic to us, were hindered by the drizzling rain; they would have liked to have been done with the whole thing as quickly as possible; pulling their heads into their shoulders, they huddled together and then parted again; one of them took some photographs, and as the whole procedure kept going on, a new wave of low whispering began in the crowd. I did not understand the words because I felt no need to pay attention to words; I just stood there trembling with the cold and with fear. Then there was silence again because the photographing policeman noticed the word on the wall, which was well protected from the rain by the eaves; he took a good look but showed no surprise, took a step backward, and clicked the shutter.

"They're going to break down the door!" somebody said.

"What are you talking about?" came a reply from someone else.

They did not break down the door; they simply opened it and went inside. We waited. For the certainty. But not for long: within minutes the officer in charge, holding a kerchief to his nose, staggered out of the house, followed by his two men.

"Good Lord!"

Mr. Maczelka was standing before us. The policemen exchanged a few words and then disappeared in the house, this time for a longer period. When they reappeared, the lamb was reposing in the arms of one of them. The policeman didn't know what to do with the animal. He looked around hesitantly and then put it down on the ground. Trembling, the little animal buckled. But the policemen no longer paid attention to it. They closed the door and ran toward their car, trying to get out of the rain. Mrs. Maczelka blocked their way.

"He's been dead for at least three days," said the officer, loudly enough for everyone to hear.

But this was not what Mrs. Maczelka wanted to hear. "Don't leave that poor little animal there," she said, pointing to the lamb.

"Take it out then," said the officer curtly.

"That's our lamb!" I heard my grandmother's voice from somewhere, but nobody paid attention to her.

"Good Lord!"

"Dead for three days?"

Several people broke into tears. Their weeping could be heard over the noise of the revved-up police car.

Pressing the lamb against her body, Mrs. Maczelka ran out of Mr. Róth's garden. Everything grew blurry before my eyes. Behind me, people were talking about wreaths and about what a kind person the old man had been after all. I did not believe that the whole thing was so simple.

János Maczelka and his wife were leaning their elbows on the windowsill as they sat next to each other. Outside, the enfeebled lamb lay below their window.

"It's going to kick the bucket," said János Maczelka.

"That would be a pity," said Mrs. Maczelka.

"And we can't really afford to feed it either."

"You could take it out to graze on the grass."

"How could I?" said Mr. Maczelka indignantly. "I've got to set an example."

"That's true."

"If I did, the next day these people would take cows out there to graze."

"True, that's the way they are."

"They don't know the meaning of order."

"I'd be sorry if it died."

Their gaze took in the whole park. They were quiet for a long time. Mrs. Maczelka spoke first. "Do you remember what a great mutton stew I made for our first wedding anniversary?"

"And you haven't made one since!"

"Of course I have!"

"But not with paprika."

"That's true, only with garlic. The way you like it."

"But that mutton stew with paprika was delicious. I still remember it."

"You've got to put in a little tomato and a bit of cherry pepper. The trick is to let the onions brown well."

János Maczelka's Adam's apple moved up and down. "I don't know about that, but one thing's for sure: you're a great cook."

First published as "A bárány" in *Kulcskereső játék* (Budapest: Szépirodalmi Könyvkiadó, 1969).

Hamlet Is Free

A dirty gray light pervades the dim stage. As if by mere accident some boring and meaningless lighting has been left on solely to avoid total darkness. Work light. Not theatrical light, which accentuates or conceals, emphasizes, unveils, or characterizes; but neither is this light imitating real light, because no real light, neither the sun's nor the moon's, reaches in here, here nothing is natural; this is a stage. And the huge open space is empty. It is empty not because all objects have been removed from it but because the lack of objects is demonstrated by the structure (and mechanism) of the stage. The stage has been opened to its full depth; the rear wall is a raw, white surface divided by crosslike stripes reminiscent of wooden planks stained medium brown. The left and right flies have been moved in front of the proscenium arch, and a forestage has been created that covers the orchestra pit. But the stage is divided not only in its depth but also in its height. The forestage is a good step lower than the main stage, and the vertical beams creating the different levels are not hidden. The play therefore will take place on the false stage; this is only theater, nothing is real. And there is another gaping depth, the third grade of depths. A grave. A rectangular hole cut into the wooden floor. A pit with black heaps of real dirt at its sides, prepared and ready for the imminent burial. Only the black dirt is real.

This space is empty because both its height and its depth are rigidly articulated. It consists only of planes and edges. It reminds us of nothing. Neither of life nor of theater. Though it could accommodate life, theater, and death. But the planes and edges have neither history nor age. This space does not turn on historical consciousness, and therefore nothing blunts the rigidity or lessens the bleakness. Neither does the lifelessly gray light. If anything, it makes the space all the more unfathomable.

In front of the stage right fly lies a rough-hewn log. Just the right size to fit into the grave. It could be a coffin or bench, but it could also be a bed. In the half-filled grave, a wide-hilted sword is stuck in the black dirt. And nothing else. Someone is sitting near the backdrop of the upper stage. His legs are spread, a guitar in his hand, his head lowered, motionless. He is Hamlet, prince of Denmark.

It is very important that this impassively bleak, hierarchically rigid scene, which the gray light blurs and smudges but warms not, persist for a long while in the eyes of the audience. An open stage makes sense only if it means something. Very important that in this preparatory phase a certain feeling take effect that one cannot delineate but that is made of insecurity, tension, anxiety, and also, because of mass curiosity, mild hysteria and what might be called a sense of something lacking. It is important for us to notice that in this world, emerging from stable illusions, everything is seen in the system of hierarchically arranged emptiness, planes, and edges. Once something appears within this framework, it has different gradations and levels, it emits and reflects light, creates an atmosphere; the atmosphere evokes emotions, and although all this is rather uncertain—since the framework itself is also mere illusion—there is one certainty: the end, the ground, the hole, the grave. And it is very important that we should be able to accept the hierarchy established in this emptiness, that we wait and continue to wait for something to happen in the emptiness and that whatever it is going to be, it should alleviate the feeling of lack.

Hamlet rises, comes forward, plays his guitar, sings at the top of his lungs; then others enter too: Bernardo and Francisco, Marcellus and Horatio. They are talking, but we are still swimming in the same uncertain light that keeps us from seeing what is visible, hearing what is audible, which in turn keeps us from feeling what might be felt, because the unstoppable march of events begins only when somewhere on high, between the gridiron and the obscured top of the proscenium, something creaks. It is a perfectly simple set of pulleys that traverses the ceiling grid arching over the entire stage, and, with the awkward lightness of a giant, hurls down a coarse, heavy curtain of knotted twine that fills the entire empty space. This is now the wall of authority. The tempting king. The broom of existence. And it knocks down and sweeps away everybody. In the moment of having executed its action with a triumphant simplicity, when having knocked the tiny human figures off their feet, it stops parallel to the footlights and fills the stage from floor to ceiling, from wing to wing, with its ugly and wild, dark and coarse beauty, as if a vessel had been filled with twice as much liquid as it can hold; the sense of lack is filled to overflowing and the aesthetic space of the play is completed.

In the theater of Yuri Lyubimov* this curtain is the most spectacular element. A lifeless object, yet in the space defined by planes and edges it seems to be alive. Because it is able to move with prancing lightness, it can run, make full turns, heave and roll, come and go, undulate, tremble, and grow rigid; it has feelings, it can remain modestly in the background, then push bumptiously to the front; it offers an escape route, hides, then cuts off the same route and exposes; with the unreliability of a living being it chooses its roles; it shows itself as gentle and lovely but is hard and ugly; it is soft and pliable but also implacable and aggressive, appears to be impenetrably dense but readily lets sound and voices through; it turns pale, then black; it becomes tediously or coldly gray, or warm brown, and it allows us to see its playfully varying protuberances, yet it is smooth like the wall, inscrutable. At the same time, it does not wish to seem more alive than it really is; it always remains an object, a stage element; all its movements are accompanied by the booming and creaking of the pulleys, though it has its own sounds as well: popping, sliding, scuttling, reverberating, and thumping. Its independence, however, is very limited; this curtain is but one of the elements in the hierarchy being constructed from stable illusions; it is not one of the main characters. It seems to be alive only because its environment is dead. It moves because it carries out the commands of programmed machinery standing in the background. And it can have emotions only because the

*The Russian actor and director Yuri Lyubimov was long associated with the celebrated Taganka Theater in Moscow, which he founded in 1964. (In 1980, after this essay was written, important Taganka productions were banned, and in 1984 Lyubimov was stripped of his Soviet citizenship, after which he worked in the west. His return to Moscow and the restoration of his citizenship in 1989 were considered triumphs) — Editor.

humans living in its environment—according to the woefully limited laws of thinking—presume to realize their own emotions in *it*. This curtain is a fetish.

Yuri Lyubimov is not a great theatrical innovator, but he is among those who have a great vision of the world. He sees the world as orderly, and therefore he knows the place of everything, even if he suffers from this final and extreme orderliness. His theater is not in the least theoretical in nature, which means not that it is without a solid theoretical basis but that every significant vision has a sensory character. Lyubimov's perception is arranged hierarchically. On its lowermost rung he sees an immaterially empty space untouched by human history; on the next rung appears the rustic curtain, which, although immaterial, appears to be alive and which does contain some references to human history even if only in generalities. The curtain, the macramé, can be seen on an Assyrian relief from about 850 B.C., but the technique was favored in the court of William of Orange, and it is fashionable even today. On the third rung of the hierarchy appear the actor and the text. The text places history in a concrete temporal framework, and the actors expand it not only with the director-created mis-en-scène but also with their costumes; they play in large-meshed pullovers and knitted clothes that refer back to the curtain and can be worn today, too. On this rung of the hierarchy, the live human being and the lifeless matter in the empty space are found in history's system of relationships. And finally, on the topmost rung of the hierarchy: light.

If the empty space is the basis on which the show is built, if the curtain is the most spectacular element of the show, if the actors and the text form the center in which the living and the lifeless are organized into a history, then we may say that in Lyubimov's theater, light is consummation and fulfillment, the means of going beyond the limits of history; it is infinity itself, possibly even God. But though light by its nature contains mystical elements, there is no mysticism here in the conventional sense of the word. With Lyubimov, light too has a sensory character. With lighting he fills up and empties the space. With lighting he gives concrete function to the space; with lighting he brings to life the mechanically moving curtain; with lights he lends character to human faces and bodies. In a certain sense, lights carry the feelings because he can multiply them, lend them rhythm, music, and multiply them into a mass that affects the entire play; *from the mass of the lights, every individual feeling is transformed into a mass feeling.* Lyubimov has neither inhibitions nor scruples about lighting techniques. He uses the blinding whites and dirty-sad grays of Brecht the same way he does the bombastic light orgies of Americanized music halls or the low angles familiar from Eisenstein's films, which throw demonically long shadows on the backdrop and distort the most innocent face into a devilish image. For Lyubimov, light is what color is for the painter, sound for the musician. Light makes Lyubimov free.

But he is not a slave of light either: the light sources are visible, and light is only a basic element, like the emptiness, the objects, the ground, the human being, a means with which he can top off the hierarchy. However, nicely constructed hierarchies are good only for proving their own impossibilities. Lyubimov reconstructs a hierarchically built world, makes use of it and plays with it, its being a natural enough form of identification, but paradoxically this does not pervade his way of thinking. He is free, meaning that he can also perceive from the outside what he has built, thereby preserving the sober purity of his instinctive perception that goes beyond every conventional framework. That is how the complex dramatic structure of his theater takes shape: a structure in which the hierarchy, made of *stable illusions*, pregnant with material, historical, social, and philosophical features, confronts the *unstable real* chaos of instincts and feelings, of individual, mental, and sensuous human relationships. And by any standard, the latter has primacy.

In this theater, sensuality does not of course take the spectacular forms we have grown used to in West European theater, which has exploited the liberating effects of pornography. Here nobody strips or exposes genitalia; no one masturbates or has intercourse. The sensuality of Lyubimov's theater is not narcissistic and exhibitionistic but covered and masked. And however strange this pronouncement may sound, it has a national character.

The national, specifically Russian, character of the sensuality manifest in Lyubimov's theater may be made plastic via a seemingly far-flung example taken from the world of ballet, if we compare Maurice Béjart's choreography for Stravinsky's *Le sacre du printemps* with the production choreographed by Natalya Kasatkina and Vladimir Vasilyev, which is showing in the Little Theater in Leningrad. This triple comparison is especially justified because ballet is the art form that gives social character to sensuality by conjuring it on the hairsbreadth-thin border area between absolute abstraction and absolute concreteness.

Béjart in many respects denies the guiding role of classical ballet's conventional movements. Yet despite all his so-called modern strivings, his ballet is classical because he breaks down manifestations of feeling and sensuality to dances of isolated individuals and isolated couples, and thus the superior-inferior relationship between soloists and corps is the same as it is in classical ballet. But this is merely an emotive approach and as such irrelevant in a certain sense. What is relevant is this: an enormously dynamic but senselessly murderous battle has been raging between the sexes; at the height of the struggle, when the game of attraction and repulsion cannot be continued, the couples break up; and on this summit of erotic loneliness, Béjart creates a peculiar picture in movement. Feet spread wide and planted rigidly, thrust-out loins rise and fall in strict rhythm, while head, trunk, and arms remain completely rigid and indifferent. This movement, with the exactness of a revelation, captures the schizophrenia of the senses. Béjart's approach is tragically shameless and anxiously self-referential.

Natalya Kasatkina and Vladimir Vasilyev's choreography shows a fundamentally different system of relationships. They use the conventional movements of classical ballet if only as analytically defined, meaning that the classical movements gain expression not in large arcs or generalizations but, rather, in synchrony with the music's tiniest dynamic details, and the movements become thereby a tensely rich unity of details, not an empty generality. But the Russian choreographers also change the traditional proportions by keeping a huge crowd onstage from the first scene to the last. The solos or pas de deux barely rise out of the massively unified sensual and emotional billowing waves of the corps de ballet. The stage concept is carried not by the solo and paired dances, not by the individual or individuals, but by the *dramatic relationship between the masses and the individual.* The classical division between foreground and background disappears, the crowd does not illustrate the emotions of individuals; the masses have feelings that must be expressed by the individuals too. Thus sensuality, though it has an individual face, is crowd size, and the crowd in turn is all but bursting the stage open. Therefore we must look for the power moving the crowd not onstage but outside the limits of the stage: in the rhythm, in the myth. There is something intensely grandiose and indulgently judicious in the sensuality of Kasatkina and Vasilyev's approach.

This is characteristic of the sensuality in Lyubimov's theater. It is not individuals he puts into motion; a single face gains its outlines from the sensuousness of the crowd. Everything begins in the crowd, and everything heads back into it; the drama takes place not between individuals but between the social laws of the masses, delineated in hierarchies, and the individual's longing for freedom, with which he hopes to break free of laws and hierarchies.

In the first scene of Act III of Lyubimov's *Hamlet*, the curtain, rigid and motionless, fills the stage from floor to ceiling and from right wing to left wing, parallel to the footlights, reducing the empty perspective of the stage. And there is the same nondescript gray work light we already know from the first scene of Act I. Behind the curtain the royal couple is eavesdropping. Hamlet is clinging to this same curtain at stage right, as if seeking protection. His black pants tucked into his short boots and his tight-fitting black collarless shirt, with his muscular neck protruding aggressively from the low-cut neckline, lend a neutrally sexless, purely sensuous effect to his strong body. He has already given the famous monologue that, on Lyubimov's stage, is not a philosophical piece about the problems of existence and its arbitrary ending but an everyday series of objective questions that, at certain crossroads of life, necessarily arise in everyone.

> *For who would bear the whips and scorns of time,*
> *The oppressor's wrong, the proud man's contumely,*
> *The pangs of despised love, the law's delay,*
> *The insolence of office and the spurns*
> *That patient merit of the unworthy takes,*
> *When he himself might his quietus make*
> *With a bare bodkin?*

The actor Vladimir Vissotzky poses these typical, let's call them typically Hamletian, questions, but it is obvious he is not philosophizing or struggling with the issue of suicide. On the one hand, by nature this Hamlet has no penchant for melancholy or philosophy, and circumstances do not allow him to be either melancholy or philosophical; on the other hand, his personal life ceased the moment the ghost appeared, after which his every step and word are an approach to death. Death for him is as natural as the black dirt of the open grave in the foreground; it is a fait accompli, no need to hurry with the "bare bodkin." And then Polonius, hiding at stage left, shoves his daughter, Ophelia, in front of the curtain. Natalya Sayko also clings to the curtain. They stare at each other. And the looks they throw each other, grazing the curtain, not only bridge the entire desolate stage space but also create a taut structure out of all the personal, material, and spiritual elements of the production. Actually, they are surprised, but the surprise pertains not to the situation but to themselves. Hamlet's desire peeks out from behind his suspicion, Ophelia's from behind her fear. And Hamlet, who in his monologue has believed himself to be sitting on the throne of finalized things—hence the monologue's ironic tone—now suddenly finds himself squatting on the stool of muddled instincts. He, who only a moment before thought he could find not a single vulnerable spot in himself, now, by the mere sight of Ophelia, becomes completely defenseless. Ophelia's existence ties him with a thousand strands to the world that, under the influence of his father's ghost, he has denied, but that cannot be denied. What they would truly like to do is to go at each other's throats. But all they can do is advance toward each other, slowly, clinging to the curtain, their hands groping, feet inching hesitantly. The huge curtain sags from the weight of their bodies, the hollows create a series of waves in the material, and the waves hinder their progress. Yet they are talking the while. It is as if they were making their way through a terrible gray morass, in which the stronger the desire to advance, the less achievable the goal. The symbolism is unequivocal: we are at the depths of the soul, in the malleable mass of desire, in that impenetrable sensual space that is common to them both, and this symbolism is not banal since in their words they maintain those social habits that cool the heat of glances and make impossible the gratification of desires. "Good my lord, / How does your honour for this many a day?" Ophelia asks, with the alluring, childlike charm of a young lady raised to be an informer, and Hamlet, with the haughtiness of a man who sees through everything, answers, but politely, "I humbly thank you; well, well, well." And stuck in the waving mass of the curtain, they grope toward each other.

Of all of Shakespeare's pretenders to the throne, Hamlet is the only

one who does not want the throne. He is interested not in power but in
the nature of power. "Let me not burst in ignorance," he cries when he
lays eyes on the ghost of his father. He longs not to conquer the world
but to understand it. In Lyubimov's conception, Hamlet is not a prince
but an intellectual with a Gnostic orientation who if he does not act, it is
because he is constantly thinking; he talks a great deal, but the attitude
he forms with his thinking and words has the value of action; it catalyzes.
"Your worm is your only emperor for diet: we fat all creatures else to fat
us, and we fat ourselves for maggots: your fat king and your lean beggar
is but variable service, two dishes, but to one table: that's the end." Hamlet thinks of life from the standpoint of death; therefore his ideas are as irrefutable and antisocial as are murders committed by kings. But thinking
is not the only thing Hamlet does. He is also a multiple murderer, and
Lyubimov does not cover up this fact. This Hamlet stabs Polonius with
raw force; with cold calculation he participates in Ophelia's death; in his
stead, he cunningly sends Rosenkrantz and Guildenstern to their deaths;
and he stabs the king with lusty pleasure. In the most common meaning
of the term, this is not a lack of action. Although he does not aspire to
power—murder is not his end or his means—in the interest of tracking
down the world's basically immoral nature, he must relinquish all social
agreement and custom, refuse all cooperation, must expose, tear out, and
stifle his own feelings, and perhaps these are the reasons that compel him
to carry out his actions in the antisocial mode about whose sense and legitimacy he himself has grave doubts. Nevertheless, Hamlet is free because he never identifies with his deeds. Although in his actions he
involuntarily reproduces the rules of the hierarchy, with his attitude he
resists; with his mind he distances from himself his own marginal attitudes the same way he does his possible reproductive actions. He opens a
crack in the hierarchy. He creates exceptions. With his being, he fills the
chasm that separates action from thinking. He is the demonstrator of
the chasm.

Lyubimov's Hamlet belongs in the category of clearsighted Hamlets
with a plebeian view. In a certain sense, this Hamlet from Moscow is the
twin of Richard III in Berlin. It seems that Lyubimov applied theoretical
statements to Hamlet that the German scholar Robert Weimann made
regarding Richard's plebeian views. He also seems to have achieved what
the Pole Jan Kott noticed when analyzing the dialogue between Prince

Clarence and the two hired killers: "This dialogue fragment is already the promise of Hamlet. For who are these hired assassins if not the grave-diggers of history? The two gravediggers in the cemetery of Elsinore also speak with a prince. And they look at general history and human tragedies from the same perspective; from the standpoint of those who dig the graves and build the gallows. From this perspective, there is no difference between a prince and the lowliest wretch . . . The king and the hired killer represent the world in its purest and barest form." The Richard of the slums with plebeian views, as played by the German ac-tor Hilmar Thate at the Deutsches Theater in Berlin, has no illusions about himself and illuminates with surpassing humor the "piping time of peace" in which he is forced to live. Similarly, the Hamlet in Moscow's Taganka Theater, played by Vladimir Vissotzky, shows no illusions about either himself or his prospects when, in the play's first scene, he steps into the empty space with the healthy enthusiasm of a populist intellectual. He has come to sing, in a crackly voice and to the accompaniment of gui-tar glissandi, Boris Pasternak's poem, the prologue of the production: "Fishing for distant echoes perhaps I'll understand / Whither the age in which I live."

They both live in death's perspective. Richard and Hamlet may be distinguishable only by their moral attitudes. Yet it seems to matter lit-tle that the quality of Hamlet's moral stance raises him above Richard. The hierarchical rules are identical. Hamlet cannot have any doubts about Ophelia just as Richard cannot have any regarding Lady Anne. They both know the nature of their world. They know everything about human be-ings. Everyone is capable of everything—and of its opposite.

For Hamlet, the scene of meeting his father's ghost is as vitally impor-tant as is Richard's conversation with Lady Anne. If this could happen, everything can happen. If a woman gives herself to a man over her mur-dered husband's body, then everything is permissible, then there is nei-ther morality nor love. And so it is in Hamlet's case, exactly! From the moment his father's ghost tells the story of how he was murdered, the feeling that dominates Hamlet is that of absolute mistrust and universal uncertainty. He is given a subject to cope with.

> *Yea, from the table of my memory*
> *I'll wipe away all trivial fond records,*

All saws of books, all forms, all pressures past,
That youth and observation copied there,
And thy commandment all alone shall live
Within the book and volume of my brain,
Unmixed with baser matter. yes, by heaven!
O most pernicious woman!

Although the last cry refers to his mother, it is projected onto the girl too; for Hamlet, the last and most essential trap is Ophelia. He must get out of it. For Ophelia is not only Ophelia but a living deception itself, preying on the senses. He did love Ophelia. And he knows there is no point telling her that. He is only groping in her direction, and in the meantime, as if talking to himself, he repeats those generalities that might distance his conscience from his own emotions.

I am myself indifferent honest; but yet I could accuse me of such things that it were better my mother had not borne me: I am very proud, revengeful, ambitious, with more offences at my beck than I have thoughts to put them in, imagination to give them shape, or time to act them in. What should such fellows as I do crawling between earth and heaven? We are arrant knaves all; believe none of us. Go thy ways to a nunnery. Where's your father?

The dirty gray curtain is sagging with the weight of their bodies. It laps them up. It is undulating, and they can only reach out their hands from under the waves.

This scene is the deepest point of the production. In this scene, with a last effort, Hamlet and Ophelia are trying to harmonize what cannot be harmonized: to match their feelings to their consciences. They believe that the tragic social schizophrenia separating them has not reached their feelings. After all, the desire propelling them to each other—to touch, to grasp, to hold tight—seems to function more strongly than the conscience. They want each other, even if Hamlet's conscience does not want Ophelia and Ophelia knows she cannot want Hamlet. In the prison of Denmark this is the only healthy spot left: sensual desire. And perhaps this will help. But they are the prisoners of the same sociopsychological trap. There is no way out. Their desire is also sick. Ophelia cannot free herself from the shackle, which is her father, just as Hamlet cannot break out of the fetter, which is his mother. Polonius and the royal couple are watching and eavesdropping behind the curtain. And just as Hamlet, in Lyubimov's conception, is not a melancholic philosopher, neither is Ophelia a blushing virgin. She too is deeply involved in the intrigues of the court. In this court everybody is an informer and a denouncer. Ophelia is no exception. Only a few minutes earlier Polonius showed the royal couple Hamlet's love letter while bragging thus:

> *This, in obedience, hath my daughter shown me,*
> *And more above, hath his solicitings,*
> *As they fell out by time, by means and place,*
> *All given to mine ear.*

And Ophelia works very precisely. She not only shows Polonius the letter but, with the dilettante enthusiasm of an excellent pupil, reenacts Hamlet's every gesture—the way he took hold of her hand above the wrist, the way he stepped back and began to scrutinize her face to see behind the face—and plays every tiny detail very precisely. Lyubimov richly motivates Ophelia's immoralities. His starting point is probably no different from that of earlier, romantic, weeping Ophelias, best expressed in Laertes's sentence about her, according to which "Thought and affliction, passion, hell itself, / She turns to favour and to prettiness," but Lyubimov shows the roots of this favor and prettiness, not their surface.

Natalya Sayko's Ophelia has three faces. Filled out and womanly, calm, cheerful, and enlightened, she speaks her mind when parting from her brother about to leave:

> *But, good my brother,*
> *Do not, as some ungracious pastors do,*
> *Show me the steep and thorny way to heaven;*
> *Whiles, like a puff'd and reckless libertine,*
> *Himself the primrose path of dalliance treads,*
> *And recks not his own rede.*

Most likely, this is the real Ophelia. But she is like a frightened little girl when talking to her father, and in Hamlet's presence, she writhes in the confusion caused by the struggle of these two attitudes. Ophelia loves Hamlet, but she is made of a material directly opposed to that of the object of her love. Ophelia is also an intellectual, but a realistic one. She knows exactly what is possible and what is not; therefore she knows well that in normal circumstances she cannot be Hamlet's, and she takes this into account. After all, her father told her, "I would not, in plain terms, from this time forth, / Have you so slander any moment leisure, / As to give words or talk with the Lord Hamlet." But she is a clever girl, finds a crack between the sentences, perceiving that her father is talking business with her, "Tender yourself more dearly; / Or—not to crack the wind of the poor phrase, / Running it thus—you'll tender me a fool." And a bit later: "Set your entreatments at a higher rate." She is justifiably hopeful, therefore, that if she obeys the cunningly contradictory command and, as a means to her own end, puts herself into her father's hands, the whole matter might somehow work out and she could become Hamlet's. To gain Hamlet, she betrays Hamlet. And herself. But in this new situation she cannot look into Hamlet's eye as a sweetheart, for she feels Hamlet sensing the political deception in her eyes. Sensuality and conscience, intuition and thought, word and movement: these wriggle to different rhythms in her too. And when she is thrown out in front of the curtain, like bait wriggling at the end of the line, the last words of her father are still ringing in her ears: "Be you and I behind an arras then; / Mark the encounter." As if seeking escape and safety, she too gives herself over to raw feeling. But the sensuousness that at the time of her brother's departure still seemed fresh and healthy in the meantime has rotted away under the weight of realities that she has taken on without distancing them.

The billowing curtain not only sucks them in but pushes them forward, roughly and wildly shoving them toward each other. And when, at stage center, the two bodies finally fall into the trough between two waves, and the hollow, under the weight of the bodies, sinks so far down as to hide them almost completely, and while Hamlet keeps talking— "God has given you one face, and you make yourselves another: you jig, you amble, and you lisp and nick-name God's creatures, and make your wantonness your ignorance. Go to, I'll no more on't; it hath made me mad. I say, we will have no more marriages; those that are married already, all but one, shall live; the rest shall keep as they are"—they get so close that body can touch body, and the wings of the curtain grow stiff. In their ignorant frenzy, the two fall upon each other. Yet in the same instant, repelled by the mere possibility of contact, Hamlet swings around and spins to the center of the stage. As if yanked by an outside force, he is on the very spot where just a while ago his mother and uncle have been consulting with the bespectacled Polonius above the open grave, and his last words snap like a verdict, "To a nunnery, go."

Ophelia remains in the deep lap of the curtain. Hamlet is free for good. They both have lost the last handhold.

In Lyubimov's direction, the system of relationships established among the dead king, Hamlet, the new king, the queen, Polonius, Ophelia, and Laertes is not free of the flavors and patterns of coarse Freudian psychology. The murderous relationship that ties his aging mother to his youthful uncle has confused Hamlet's sensibilities. Ophelia's sexual confusion, caused by her exaggerated devotion to her father and based on her fear of the father, means that emotionally she relates more naturally to her brother than to the man she really desires and loves. The schematized system of relationships alone would suffice to wrest the drama from the hands of bored philosophers and mawkish prigs, but instead of a superficial interpretation, this would in fact only offer a different superficiality. But Lyubimov is intimately familiar with the Elizabethan theater's understanding of the narrative concept. Therefore he does not follow the dramaturgical theories of the much later bourgeois theater; he does not create the picture of social hierarchy out of the system of mental functions of individuals. He goes in the opposite direction: he takes the hierarchy as axiomatic—the light is above, man is in the middle, and the grave is below—and within this seemingly orderly space he unveils those principles of pressure and coercion that the given social structure applies to the individual. Until the first scene of Act III, everybody's behavior is schematic because the pressure of hierarchy cannot squeeze more out of anyone than an archaic psychological pattern—but then, everything changes.

In the Danish court, affairs of emotions and of the state are secondary activities because every ounce of energy is engaged in making the traces of the latest murder disappear. For the royal couple eavesdropping behind the curtain, the question of whether or not Hamlet loves Ophelia is completely immaterial. If he does love her, they will make that fact a means to their end; if he does not, they will do the same with *that* fact. For both contingencies, they seem to have good ideas. If he loves her, maybe a wedding; if he does not, maybe a long sea voyage. Polonius too has prepared a safe position for himself, whatever Hamlet's feelings. If Hamlet does love Ophelia, Polonius will acquire a son-in-law with royal blood in his veins; if Hamlet does not love her, Polonius, for his efforts as informer, will enjoy the royal couple's special favor. But Hamlet's behavior does not enable them to answer the question, which in any case they could not have thought very important. Hamlet answers not their questions but his own, which, naturally enough, include their deeds. It is at this point that the archaic psychological scheme widens out into the actual social structure. Those who with their deeds conjure up Hamlet's spirit do not understand him because they also do not understand the meaning of their own deeds. As a result, Hamlet ceases to be a tool in their hands. He has slipped out of their grasp.

Now only the procedure of providing proof follows.

For this procedure, Hamlet has only one means, the theater, with the game of confrontation to prove that his mother is a whore and the king a fratricide. And in Lyubimov's theater the entrance of actors is one of the most wonderful and spectacular scenes ever done on stage. The curtain hangs parallel to the footlights in the middle of the upper stage, rigidly closing it off; the light turns blinding white; the hem of the curtain gently parts from the ground and, wrinkling into soft arches, rises into the air. From the bottom of the suddenly visible backdrop, a string of projectors throws light into our eyes. Footlights. The power of the light hitting our eyes makes the rear wall disappear, as if our gaze, beyond the lights, had entered the mellow darkness of an auditorium, into the darkness in which we are sitting. As if we ourselves had wound up on the stage as actors. The curtain has already risen, we are standing in the light, we are onstage, and the show has begun. The change is raw and revealing, oppressive and wonderful. And when the actors enter in a single file, turning halfway to the real auditorium and halfway to the even more real auditorium, we too are onstage, confronting ourselves and looking at ourselves, as we sit on that distant stage.

The strong effect of an audience hiding in a dark auditorium unexpectedly confronting another audience hiding in the dark of another auditorium and involuntarily identifying itself with what has become wedged in the light between the two auditoriums, with everything that is theater—actors, playing, stage fright—is matched by the roughness and strength of the next effect. These actors filing onto the stage, dressed in yellows, plum-blues, reds, and stripes, some with long scarves, top hats, obvious hand-me-downs with fringes and tassels, are somehow not what we would like to believe ourselves to be in their place. They have never confronted themselves; they will never be able to play in a real theater; they are an amusing, shifty, ragtag bunch, looking to make a living. They have been kicked out of somewhere, and they will be kicked out of here too whenever their services are no longer required; they are attractive and gross; they are barnstormers, the very bottom of society, artistic pariahs. And Prince Hamlet—with Polonius at his side and their backs to the audience—deals with them as an enlightened and wise director would. He engages them in his princely purpose, and he instructs them. As one profoundly familiar with the theater who is also a lover of theater, he gives them advice. They nod at his every word, though it is clear they think that what he says is superfluous nonsense; what they want is to make some money, have a roof over their heads for a little while, and maybe play a little bit. In their eyes there's no difference between the sensitive, astute observations of Hamlet and the insensitive, nonsensical croaking of Polonius. The prince with populist tendencies is still a lord and, along with Polonius, belongs among the powerful ones.

Beginning with this scene, the drama's entire system of dimensions changes. We might say that it is in this scene that Hamlet's world acquires its real dimensions. Everything he knows, feels, and wants becomes relative. Lyubimov, who has been observing Hamlet from close up and with his close attention has been supporting him, now withdraws, leaving Hamlet on his own. There is no more need to be with Hamlet; he is unstoppable. "If it be now, 'tis not to come; if it be not to come, it will be now; if it be not now, yet it will come: the readiness is all." And from then on we are at once inside and outside, already at death but still in life. We still cannot deny our identification with Hamlet, but we see the world no longer with his eyes but with the eyes of those who were left out of the battle of the powerful ones. The stage is empty. With their feet in the pit, the two gravediggers are sitting on the freshly erected mound. They are eating onions with bread. They are chatting. They are amiable and in a good mood. In the hierarchy everyone has his or her place. The king murders; the courtier informs. Hamlet creates an exception; the actors play; the gravediggers dig the grave. We are inside and outside at the same time, and greater human freedom than that probably cannot even be imagined. We are at once actors, gravediggers, kings, and princes. We feel the hierarchy on our own skin, yet we can also see through it. And we no longer have any doubts: no one can set aright the time out of joint. Fortinbras does not come with the army. He does not say:

> *Let four captains*
> *Bear Hamlet, like a soldier, to the stage;*
> *For he was likely, had he been put on,*
> *To have prov'd most royally.*

Hamlet did not want to be king; neither did he become a great one. There is no release. Fortinbras has been cut.

Creaking, the curtain turns to reveal the dead of the last act.

First published as "Hamlet szabad" in *Néző'tér* (Budapest: Szépirodalmi Könyvkiadó, 1983).

Lady Klára's House

"Where did you actually come from?"

"Actually, from Mágocs. Are you familiar with the place?"

"No."

Lady Klára was standing in front of the mirror. She was so short that her chin did not reflect in the glass, only the parts from the chin up: the wrinkled upper lip thrust forward by the false teeth, the nose that had long since lost its shape, and the dotlike brown eyes with the frozen stare, forming odd little circles in the spotty face. All sorts of other things were hanging in the picture against the background of the light blue tiles of the bathroom: small bottles, boxes, toothbrushes, and the lids of various little jars. From behind her came the steady grating noise made on the bathtub enamel by a rag dipped in scouring powder.

"Have you prepared breakfast, Jutka?"

Jucika straightened up. First her shoulder, then her head slid into the image in the mirror; she was so tall that her forehead was not reflected in the glass.

"Now listen to me," she said, and sighed deeply. "I must tell the comrade the whole thing from the beginning, but first I have to tell you right now that it wasn't my fault because he said he was going to marry me. He said it for sure, as sure as we are standing here in the bathroom."

Lady Klára lifted her short eyelashes to see the meek brown face in the glass, but her glance was casual, and she did not interrupt her massaging motions.

"And my sweet little Lacika . . ."

Making use of the momentary pause, Lady Klára said, "Your fiancé?"

Jucika disappeared from the mirror, and the grating on the tub enamel was heard again. "No, my little boy . . ."

"Oh, you have that too?"

"That's how my little Lacika was born . . . I will have to tell you in detail how it was—"

There was silence, and from this silence Lady Klára inferred that Jucika was occupied by one bitter thought or another and had left off scrubbing the tub. But her head did not reappear in the mirror; she must have remained bent over the tub in the position she'd been in when the thoughts had surprised her. Lady Klára finished applying her facial pack. The thick cream had a temporary soothing effect; it filled the wrinkles and glittered like enamel, and as she was gazing at the familiar face the world tipped (for only a second) under her feet. That's what I'll look like when I die? Then everything was steady again, the silence continued except that her heart beat a little more irregularly. She stepped away from the mirror and with a light movement, reminiscent of the human being that had turned into this wizened body, she gathered her long linen robe and sat on the folded-down lid of the toilet. Jucika straightened, though not fully, and stepped closer to Lady Klára, who could now see that her eyes were filled with tears.

"Because I want to . . ." Jucika said in a voice full of emotion yet flat, "because I always tell everything . . . because I want madam to know everything about me . . ."

Lady Klára lightly touched the girl's hair. "Don't cry, Jutka."

Pulling herself up to her full height, Jucika threw her head back and let out a short laugh. "Me, crying?"

"But you look so miserable . . . I can see," said Lady Klára.

"Me, miserable? I have never been miserable . . . All I want is that madam should know everything about me . . ." Jucika threw the rag into the tub. "I was a member of the Union of Working Youth, you know, the UWY."

"Really?"

"In Mágocs I was the UWY secretary."

"Really?"

"Really."

"Have you made breakfast?" Lady Klára asked again, and touched her face with her delicate fingers to check how the pack was drying.

"For two weeks I was UWY secretary in Mágocs."

"Really?"

"That's right. That's how it was. I'll have to tell you about that too. They didn't relieve me because . . . It's not that they relieved me . . . it's just that my Tibor got into the picture . . ."

"Your fiancé?"

"He was no fiancé of mine!"

Lady Klára shifted on the closed toilet lid. "You said so before." She raised her voice indignantly.

"Me? I didn't say—"

"You said that—"

"Well, yes. We were on good terms with my Tibor, 'cause that's all he wanted to be called, Tibor. Once, when we were already on very good terms, I called him my little Tibike. And you know what he did?"

Lady Klára raised her eyebrows questioningly, and the movement created tiny cracks in the smooth fields of the pack.

"Slapped me in the face. That's the only slap I got from him." Jucika laughed.

"But why?" Lady Klára wondered aloud.

Jucika shrugged. "I don't know. It was forbidden to call him anything but Tibor," she said, and, leaning back toward the tub, resumed her scrubbing.

Lady Klára touched her face again with her fingers and sized up the bending, stooping girl before her, the bony shoulders, wide hips, and shapely legs ending in red slippers. Out of a pocket in her robe she produced a cigarette, from the other a holder, fitted them together, and with a match that had been resting on the windowsill she lit up. She blew the smoke all around her, the pleasant fragrance mingling with the odor emanating from Jucika's clothes and body, sharp and acidy, the kind Lady Klára found irritating. However, having become a considerate and wise person, she would not have dared admit even to herself that she abhorred this sort of human exhalation. She had abhorred it even as a girl. Ever since she had left her rich parental home she had vehemently rejected her abhorrence; she struggled against it because she felt that her disgust would bond her with the people—capitalist, bourgeois, aristocratic—

from whose ranks she had come from, who had raised her, and whom, she believed, she had categorically rejected. As she was quietly musing, surrounding herself with the smoke of her cigarette while watching the thick-boned girl scrub the tub as if possessed, Lady Klára sank back into the loneliness in which she had been living for years. She could sit like that for hours on end, whether here in the bathroom or in her study, comfortable in her favorite armchair by the window where she could see the river, which seemed motionless beyond the row of weeping willows.

"That should do it; leave it," Lady Klára said after a while.

But Jucika kept scrubbing the tub as if she had not even heard the words. She had no system and did the work, in spots, here and there.

"And at the house of the artist"—she began a new story, her voice echoing inside the tub—"because I did that too for a couple of months. I will have to tell you how I got to know the artist's wife . . . They really insisted on a clean tub. Him, before I'd seat him in the tub, he'd conduct a whole examination . . . picking at it with his finger, leaning real close, and if he found something like a hair or a little stain, I had to let the water out, wash the tub again, and fill it up again. And he would bathe only if the water was thirty-eight degrees Celsius."

Lady Klára was paying no attention. Her thoughts were wandering. She sighed quietly and shook her head crowned with silver gray hair.

"So that's how you left Mágocs, my poor thing," she said.

"But it's true"—Jucika went on—"that a tub should always be clean. They made me wash it out in the middle of the day too."

"What?"

"The tub."

Lady Klára wasn't following. And she also felt that the pack on her face had dried and hardened. As she rose from the folded-down toilet lid, a boy, no more than seventeen, leaned in through the window; from his forehead, nose, and chin and from between his tender whiskers yet untouched by razor, huge red pimples were staring out at the world.

"Mornin'! Mother wants to know if you'd like some eggs because the hens laid a lot yesterday, and we got so many we might as well throw them against the wall," said the boy in one breath, and laughed. He looked not at Lady Klára but right into the armhole of Jucika's blouse, which had slipped forward, and he fancied he could see all sorts of other things below the protruding brushlike bunch of hair. Jucika noticed the look, straightened up, her gaze engaging directly with the boy's light blue eyes, now glazed over with craving.

Lady Klára did not reply right away, but to break up the game of the eyes, she said, "Ah, Jóska, there you are."

The boy blushed, and as his face reddened even the pale areas between the pimples became one with the hue of his lumpy ornamentation.

"Jutka will drop over to your place after breakfast," said Lady Klára, and turned away so the boy would not see her caked-on facial mask.

But there was no need to do that; after a brief and stealthy glance at Jucika he disappeared from the window. Jucika looked out after him and saw how with giant leaps he hurled himself over the flower beds and vanished behind the shrubs. She returned to the tub, paying special attention to a hand-size rusty spot, which she went over and over with loving care.

Lady Klára washed off her facial pack in the sink, dried her face, and applied a variety of creams to it; from behind she heard the steady grating noise and Jucika's heavy breathing. "Leave that, why don't you?" she said.

"I'm just about done," replied Jucika from the tub.

Lady Klára shrugged and left the bathroom.

"I'd really like it if the comrade and me could be friends," said Jucika, and downed a cup of tea in one gulp.

Lady Klára laughed but felt a little embarrassed. "Really?"

"And I knew the comrade's husband really well."

Lady Klára lost her hold on the slice of buttered bread in her hand, and the honey on top of the butter dripped on the tabletop. "My husband? You knew my husband?"

"In the UWY room in Mágocs there was a big picture of him on the wall. Whenever I was alone in the room, I would stop under Zoltánka's picture and I almost cried."

Lady Klára's lips quivered. "But where would you have known him from? You couldn't possibly. Zoltán died in '44."

"But I did, believe me. And as I stood before his picture, I even talked to him. I said, 'I'd like to be a hero just like you, Zoltánka.' Because we called each other by our first names, informally. And he'd reply, 'Just live a clean and honest life, my girl, and you'll be a hero.'"

"Zoltán would never have said such a thing," replied Lady Klára, irritated. She put the buttered bread on the small plate and licked the honey from her hand.

Jucika looked amazed. Her eyes were bouncing off the walls and the objects around her as if looking for but not finding the meaning of Lady Klára's words. Then she cut a piece of cheese and stuffed it into her mouth. Lady Klára was ashamed of her irritation and, smiling at Jucika, added, "Zoltán was a more rational being. We talked a lot about heroism, and he always said, 'What we need is not dead heroes but live ones!' "

"And tell me,"—Jucika went on, lowering her head shyly—"was it nice to live with him? In general . . ."

Lady Klára blushed. Her blushing was girlishly simple, yet her face turned red as an old woman's would, in dispersing spots. She picked up the remnant of the cheese from the plate and cut off the rind.

"You don't like the rind?"

"No."

"Let me have it. I like it a lot. In the artist's house they always collected the rinds for me. But I didn't like being there."

This time Jucika did not explain why she hadn't liked it at the artist's house because she was busy with her breakfast. Lady Klára kept looking at the girl and felt that she herself was undergoing a peculiar transformation. More correctly, she did not so much feel it as she felt that the transformation had been completed. The introverted, elderly wisdom that had for so long defined her life had been replaced by a childlike, wide-eyed astonishment. While she lived alone in this house and received her monthly not high but special national pension and kept working on her memoirs or, rather, the biography of her husband, who had fallen in combat, the world became simple, completed, final. When she glanced out the window while sitting in her armchair, she could see nothing but the rhythmic change of the seasons, the whimsical games of the weather. Beyond the age of sixty, weather and the changing seasons no longer seemed like inexplicable events. Nature's regularity, after the age of sixty, becomes one with a person. She did not rebel senselessly when it rained: she did not want to go out. She quietly acknowledged when the sun was burning too brightly: she was forbidden to stay in the sun anyway. And now she was merely watching Jucika's bony face and her thin, colorless hair twisted into rings, without putting her into a category, without assigning her to a preconceived class, stratum, or human type; she only looked at her, and the question kept running through her head: Was it nice to live with him? In general . . . She was completely preoccupied with this question and did not notice that Jucika had stood up and was now listening intently. In the wall above the stove something was making a knocking noise, like a dripping faucet only stronger.

"What's that?" Jucika looked at her, alarmed.

"I don't know." Lady Klára shrugged.

"Something inside the wall," said Jucika, and leaned across the stove to put her ear to the wall.

The knocking grew louder and faster.

"It's nine-thirty," Lady Klára said.

The knocking suddenly stopped.

"It always knocks at exactly nine-thirty," said Lady Klára.

"But what is it?"

"I don't know. Something."

Jucika sat back down and picked up a slice of toast, intending to spread butter on it. She halted the movement halfway, as if waiting for the knocking to resume, but nothing was knocking.

Lady Klára smiled. "Well, maybe it's time for you to go get the eggs, Jutka," she said.

Jucika stood up again, but her eyes were still on the wall, directly above the stove, where traces were clearly visible of last year's and earlier years' boiling of fruit for jam. She was staring with a frightened fascination as if she had stumbled into a haunted castle.

Lady Klára burst out laughing. "Go on, Jutka, go, get the eggs. Tomorrow you can listen to it again."

Jucika gave the old woman a quick look.

"At nine-thirty, exactly," Lady Klára added by way of explanation.

"Please don't call me Jutka," said the girl, annoyed.

"That's your name, isn't it?"

"Please call me Jucika."

Lady Klára, offended, drew up her shoulders.

"No problem at all," she replied.

While the girl combed her hair and also sprinkled her freckled face with Lady Klára's powder and even sprayed a bit of perfume on herself— all in preparation for going to get the eggs—Lady Klára cleared the

kitchen table. She puttered about slowly, awkwardly, with the move
ments of one who need not accommodate herself to anyone or anything,
one who is not driven by time. She was musing: Jucika . . . No problem
at all. Was it nice to live with him?

She hardly noticed that in the meantime she had washed the dishes.

Her daily schedule, as we shall see, had not yet been upset at this junc-
ture. At nine-thirty, when the knocking was heard from the wall, she
usually stepped into her room to spread out the pages of her manuscript,
together with the clippings from old newspapers and photographs that
helped her memory.

Now it was a quarter to ten, but she had been as late as this before, if
Mrs. Kalher, the fee collector of the chimney sweeps' collective, happened
to come over and they had a long conversation or if something in the mail
made her linger.

Although basically a lazy person, Lady Klára made serious efforts to
keep her life in some kind of order even past the age of sixty, and if once
in a great while she had visitors—old comrades and friends—she tried to
steer the conversation in a direction that would allow her to elaborate for
her guests on her ideas regarding punctuality and discipline.

CONVERSATION WITH MRS. VICZMÁNDY (RÓZSI)

"Lately I can't sleep at night. I sleep right through the morning, and
that's the end of my day."

"Only discipline can help, my dear," says Lady Klára, and tilts her
head to the side. "I get up at six in the morning, spread out the bedding
so it can air, brew my coffee—I have it here in the study—and then put
the apartment in order, eat breakfast, and exactly at nine-thirty I sit down
to work."

"And how do you get the time to do the shopping and cooking?"

"Oh, my dear, everything has its time. I work until twelve-thirty;
then I concoct something for myself, take a little nap, and after a snack I
do my shopping."

"In the afternoon?"

"Why would I stick to conventions if my way is more convenient for me?" Lady Klára looks into her guest's eyes, and at such a moment feels herself superior to everyone else. "Besides," she adds, "one shouldn't make a big deal of housekeeping. That is also a question of intelligence. Do you know Mariska Romsauer? . . . Well, my dear, this excellent woman, and this is what my poor Zoltán always said, almost drowns in her dishwater."

"She raised three children."

"Three children? And what about me?"

"But you have always been in a better financial situation."

Lady Klára shook her head. "No, my dear, no. The whole thing is a question of discipline and punctuality."

CONVERSATION WITH MRS. ROMSAUER (MARISKA)

"I don't even dare be seen by people. My son, my husband's son, who can thank us for everything . . . and not even a package, he sends us nothing. Not even for Christmas. You know, Klára, I'm fed up with the whole thing, everything, just everything. We have gotten old."

"The only thing that helps me, as much as that is possible, my dear, is discipline and punctuality." Lady Klára sighs and tilts her head to the side. "At six in the morning I spread out the bedding to air, brew my coffee—I have it here in my study—then I put the apartment in order, eat my breakfast, and at nine-thirty sit down to work."

"I often think about it: shopping and cooking. For forty years the same thing every day. What for? For whom? We've been left alone."

"Oh, my dear, you say this so lightly. You two have been left alone. I have been left alone all by myself. There is a big difference. For me, there is nothing left but memories. I sit with my papers until twelve-thirty, but to be sure I will remember something the next day, I concoct something nourishing for myself and then take a short nap, and after my snack I shuffle off to do my shopping."

"In the afternoon?"

Lady Klára waves a tired hand. "I know, only garbage is left by the afternoon, but it's good enough for me. It's all the same. One shouldn't make such a big deal out of housekeeping. The way poor Zoltán always said, the tragedy of women is that they drown in dishwater."

"I certainly have drowned in it. How true."

"You have raised three children," says Lady Klára.

"Three children? I've found no joy in it."

"That's our fate," says Lady Klára, and shakes her head. "Still, I tell you, my dear Mariska, only discipline and punctuality help."

These are Lady Klára's little victories.

Lady Klára's house stood on a small hill not far from the Danube. The garden surrounding it had gone rather wild with various perennial flowers, rosebushes, raspberries, currants, and uncared-for fruit trees. It was a quiet place, far from the highway; it was also windless because this was where the mountains descended to the river. And if a slight breeze stirred the air, it brought with it various scents depending on the direction. From the north, along with the murmur of the oaks, it carried the fragrance of the woods; from the east (the dominant wind direction) the breeze swept clear the stench of the Kalhers' pigsty.

So much for the garden and the smells.

Looked at from the front, the house, because it had its back to the foot of the mountains, was a split-level. Its ground floor (more precisely, its level on the ground) was taken up by a small closet-size room that, until Jucika's arrival, had served as a toolshed. The room's plank door opened directly to the garden; anyone who tried to look out of either of its two hand-size windows would wind up with his or her head stuck in the frame. A few months ago Lady Klára had cleared the room. With Jóska Kalher's help she put in a rickety sofa, an old closet, and on the wall that had a few wet spots she hung a Cranach reproduction.

When they were done setting up the room and Jóska Kalher brought the rag rug down from the foyer and they put it on the floor, Lady Klára looked at the boy and said, "Pretty nice."

Jóska did not reply, only looked somewhere above Lady Klára's head and stroked the pimples on his forehead. How dumb this kid is, thought Lady Klára; she gave him two forints for ice cream, which the boy did not want to accept, and then sent him away. Alone again, she looked around and now, half aloud, repeated in a voice that was meant to convince her too, "Pretty nice."

She straightened out the fringes of the rug, locked the door and put the key into the pocket of her robe, tapped the pocket to be sure the key was there, because she was forgetting everything. The key was there, in the left robe pocket. That's done, she thought, and left to go up to the house.

Let us follow her and become acquainted with the scene of our story.

Ten steps led to the entrance of the house; the living quarters were reached through a double door that at night Lady Klára made inaccessible to the outside world with the help of a lock, a chain, and a sliding bolt because like all lonely old women, she was afraid of villa robbers. Three doors opened from the entranceway in which, outside the two cane-bottomed chairs and a three-legged table, there was nothing worth mentioning unless we count the few Szőnyi prints and the two plates alleged to have come from Picasso's workshop. One door led to the kitchen, another to the bathroom, and the third, a double door with a striped silk curtain in front of it, into the so-called study. From the study another door led to the bedroom.

Lady Klára's study was a Biedermeier room. Biedermeier sofa, Biedermeier desk, Biedermeier chairs, little Biedermeier paintings, and under, over, on, in between, and above these Biedermeier objects that formed the basis of the Biedermeier furnishing were Biedermeier odds and ends strewn in all directions. Only a small oval table and two armchairs in the corner were not Biedermeier, but (Lady Klára to Mrs. Viczmándy: "The most eagle-eyed art expert has difficulty differentiating between a Maria Theresa and a Biedermeier") this did not bother anyone.

Silence reigned. The kind of absolute silence that is possible in the world. Lady Klára pulled the armchair to the window, pushed next to it a small table, on which she put the bundle of manuscript pages, covered with her angular black letters. Giving a final adjustment to the armchair's position, she settled down. First of all, she looked out at the river, and then she glanced at the manuscript. On the top page, written in her angular letters, it said IN THE FIRE OF LIFE. While she was reading, for about the hundredth time, the title of her book in progress, she reached into the pocket of her robe for a cigarette; out of her other pocket she would have taken the cigarette holder and matches, but they weren't there. This annoyed her.

She found the holder on the glass shelf in the bathroom, matches in the kitchen. She made herself comfortable again and lit up. When the match burst into flame, she had the feeling that the manuscript should be put to the fire. The match burned down to her fingernail because there was no ashtray within reach. She got up again, brought over an ashtray, and sat down again.

Quickly she turned the manuscript bundle over. This way, the last, half-filled page was on top. To be able to continue, she would have to read the last few pages. For two days, while busying herself with the preparation of the basement room for Jucika's arrival, she hadn't worked on the book, and she'd forgotten where she had left off. She picked up the last page, but the angular letters set her nerves on edge; it seemed as if somebody else had written them.

Maybe I should burn it after all, she thought.

Outside, the birds were chirping, and who knows where dogs were barking; inside the room the clock was quietly ticking. She glanced backward and realized that a half hour had gone by since Jucika went over to the Kalhers for the eggs. Where can she be for so long?

She took a deep puff from her cigarette and blew the smoke out the window. The telephone rang in the bedroom. She put down the page and quickly crossed into the bedroom. She sat down on the edge of the wide couch and picked up the receiver.

"Yes, I'll wait, thank you."

It took a few minutes for the connection to be made. Again she found herself without an ashtray, but she did not dare move, and so she flicked the ashes on top of the night table. When she heard the voice at the other end of the line, her features realigned themselves; she smiled. "Oh, hello . . . Yes, I can hear you all right . . . I'm working . . . The girl? Oh, very nice . . . I don't know. Out of the question, you know I'm working. But if tomorrow . . . they're waiting for the manuscript . . . Day after tomorrow? All right. But only in the afternoon, I work every day until half past twelve . . ."

The cigarette slowly burned down, and its embers were about to set the paper cigarette holder on fire too; it was smoldering badly in her hand.

"All right, then. All right. I am right in the middle of a sentence . . . No, it doesn't matter . . . All right."

As she replaced the receiver, the smile left her face. Angrily she threw the cigarette holder out the open window into the garden and walked back into the study. Before sitting down, she glanced at the clock. She picked up the half-filled manuscript page.

"If we were to play the movie of our lives for the youth of today, they would probably say such lives were not worth living. But they were. The movement demanded that we be ascetics. And we accepted that demand with complete enthusiasm because we understood that one must subordinate one's desires and interests . . ." Here the sentence broke off.

To what? she thought. And what is taking her so long? She looked at the clock again and pulled the little table closer. Then a cunning little smile crossed her face. I'll complete this sentence, and that will be the end of this chapter, she thought, grabbed her pen, and very properly completed the sentence. She sighed and reread the sentence. What idiocy, she thought, though it's true. Or maybe it isn't? What's an ascetic?

And then she remembered all sorts of things about Zoltán: the way they met, how she had left her family, and their first nights in Zoltán's flat. She had been awkward, she couldn't cook or do anything, and their friends would smile at her and look at her neck because it was covered with small red bruises slowly turning blue, and she realized the others knew where they had come from, and she began to wear dresses with high-necked collars. That's it, that's it. She smiled to herself, sitting in her armchair by the window. In that high white piqué collar, I looked like a nun.

Color rose to her cheeks; with a vacant stare she looked out at the river and the willows on the shore, and then suddenly she remembered an old picture of Zoltán . . . probably the one they hung on the wall of the UWY room in Mágocs; didn't Jucika say Zoltánka? It had to be a picture from his youth, the one where he looked his best. A brave look on his face, dark, his forehead high; it had to have been that picture; later he became completely bald . . .

Lady Klára burst into tears. With her hands she looked for a handkerchief but found nothing in the large pockets of her robe or in the crack between the seat and backrest of the armchair, where she would stuff small objects while cleaning the room. Tears trickled from her old dull eyes, and she did not hear the quick steps making the pebbles crunch on the path outside the window, or the opening of the hallway door and then the large glass-paned door; she kept weeping, withdrawn into the depth of the armchair upholstered with Biedermeier silk, still groping for the handkerchief. She was thinking that until now she had not really mourned Zoltán, because even when comrade Balázs told her about it on

Miklós Horthy Boulevard, she'd stopped only for a moment and then they continued talking, she couldn't remember of what, because they couldn't have been together for more than a few minutes, and they had to keep smiling. And ever since, she had been clenching her teeth, even though the earth was full of her dead: her father, whom she hated for his thousands of acres of land; her mother, who used to sit in this very armchair; and the whole world and this life—

"You're not crying, are you, madam?" Jucika asked.

"No, no . . . nothing . . . Would you give me my eyedrops; they're on top of the commode . . ." replied Lady Klára, and threw back her head.

Jucika hurried into the bedroom, and Lady Klára heard her walking back and forth, not finding the drops.

"On top of the commode," she repeated, and wiped her tears with her fist.

"On top of the commode?"

"Yes."

Jucika handed over the drops and watched as Lady Klára used the little tube to siphon the white liquid, drew back her eyelid with one hand, and let the white drops fall into her eye.

"How many eggs did you bring?"

Jucika did not answer the question. "I can see you were crying."

Lady Klára's eyes began to tear, but this was not real crying, only the medicine doing its job.

"And you are still crying."

Lady Klára felt great affection for the girl now. With her head still thrown back, she looked up, smiled, and stroked her hair. "Of course I'm not crying. You know, my dear, old eyes like mine are always teary. Whenever I work a lot, my eyes conk out on me."

"Whoa, conk out!" Jucika laughed.

"They do." Lady Klára laughed along with her and handed back the small bottle.

"Oh, with your permission I have to go downstairs and take a bath."

For a second Lady Klára did not understand what Jucika meant. "You had a bath this morning," she said.

"But I got stinky again, because of the chickens. Smell me," Jucika explained, and held out an arm close to Lady Klára's nose.

"From the chickens?" Lady Klára said, still not understanding.

"Oh, that Mrs. Kalher is so nice. She invited me over for this evening, because we had such a nice chat, and I should come over and help Jóska clean out the chicken coop."

"Is that what she said?"

"That's right. Because Jóska doesn't like to do it by himself. I've cleaned enough chicken coops; the gold ring wouldn't fall off my finger, especially since I don't have one. And Jóska said we got so stinky we should go down to the Danube."

"To the Danube . . ." Lady Klára picked up the half-filled manuscript page and looked at it with vacant eyes.

"And I've never bathed in the Danube. If you let me."

Lady Klára did not look up; instead she reached for her pen. "Don't bother me now. I always work in the morning," she said, making an effort not to sound hostile.

The girl left the room. And then a clattering began somewhere inside Lady Klára. At first it occurred to her that the girl was not quite right in the head; she glanced after her. From the bathroom and then from the hallway she seemed to be hearing muttering reminiscent of a song, and then fury began to rear its head in Lady Klára's brain. What can this Mrs. Kalher be thinking? What is she thinking? She became so angry that her thoughts became entangled. To clean her chicken shit, chicken shit . . . at my expense?

By the time Jucika returned from bathing, Lady Klára had composed herself a bit and knew what she had to do. When she heard the pebbles creak under her window, she settled back in her armchair and picked up the pen. When Jucika opened the hallway door, she looked up and called out, "Jutka!" And when the glass-paned door opened, Lady Klára leaned over the manuscript again.

"I've got to talk to you," she said, serious but calm, looking up at the girl. She wished she hadn't. This girl is not right in the head, not normal, she thought.

But she had no chance to say anything before the girl stopped in the middle of the (Persian) rug, wearing Lady Klára's blue and white striped linen robe, arranging her wet hair, and, with a slightly offended look on her face, said, "I asked you—didn't I—not to call me Jutka."

For a moment, Lady Klára thought she would faint, fly away, vanish, come to her end. But Jucika continued. "I've got very bad memories of that name."

The tiny body grew tense in the armchair. "Take off my robe, immediately!" Lady Klára screamed.

Jucika paled. "But nothing will happen to it!"

"Except it's getting soaking wet. Soaking wet!" Lady Klára ran out of breath. Her hand was shaking, and she dropped the paper and pen. Jucika hurried over, picked up both, and in a seductively polite manner placed them carefully on the small bentwood table. "If I only knew . . . Please don't make me miserable."

"You're making *me* miserable. Take it off this minute," Lady Klára said, then made a movement with her hand indicating there was nothing really wrong. "I should like to talk to you," she added.

The girl left the study. When she returned, the offended look was clearly set on her face again. And she was the one to speak first. "I would like to ask the comrade not to yell at me again."

Lady Klára did not respond. She felt she was now well prepared for Jucika's surprises. "Pull that armchair closer."

Jucika pulled the other armchair (upholstered with Biedermeier silk) to the window.

"Sit down," Lady Klára said.

Jucika sat down and let her eyes quickly sweep over the furniture in the room. She made herself comfortable.

"I'd like to talk to you."

"Yes, you've said that at least twice," Jucika replied, abstracted.

For the first time they looked into each other's eyes. Lady Klára held her gaze steady, as if to hypnotize the girl, but it took a long time and much patience to calm Jucika's wandering, meek glances. Quietly Lady Klára broke the silence. "Listen to me, my dear."

Jucika shrugged a little, which Lady Klára did not fail to notice. She toned down her voice as best she could to make her words sound even more intimate. "You came here yesterday, did you not?"

"Yes."

Lady Klára suddenly could think of nothing else to say. And what she did think of, she could not utter.

Jucika watched the old woman's quivering lips patiently, then spoke up. "I know what is wrong with me," she said.

"There, you see."

"But you misjudge me."

"I don't judge or misjudge you because I don't know you at all. All I know is that things cannot go on like this."

"Please believe me that it's very hard for me too."

"You've told me so. And I believe you."

"Sometimes I just can't resist."

"Resist what?"

Jucika clasped her hands and pressed them to her breast. "If I am asked to clean the chicken coop, I clean the chicken coop. That's how I am. Unfortunately."

"We're not just talking about the chicken coop."

They both wrinkled their foreheads.

"My robe, you shouldn't have—" Lady Klára went on, but got stuck because she wished to remain tolerant.

Jucika shook her wet hair, and her eyes widened. "That I don't understand at all. Because the artist's wife's robe or Mrs. Viczmándy's robe I wouldn't put on, I hated them so much."

Lady Klára felt she was headed for failure. She quickly lit up. "Listen to me, my dear."

"Yes."

"You came here yesterday, did you not?"

"Yes."

"You are a member of the Household Employees' Union, are you not?"

Jucika reached toward the cigarettes. "May I take one?"

"Go ahead, please."

"I understand what you're getting at, but I always need a few days to get to know a new place."

They were looking at each other. Lady Klára thought maybe this was the time to put an end to the matter before it was too late. She should get up, take the work permit out of the desk drawer, return it to the girl, and say she had changed her mind or something like that. Then help her get a decent place somewhere else. "I see, I can see you are a nice girl. Only you have a nihilist nature," she said listlessly.

Jucika's eyes sparkled, and for the first time she looked at Lady Klára with a sincere interest. This electrified Lady Klára too. The tables always turn when one thinks everything is lost, she thought, and felt that the opportunity had arrived. "And we must consider the realistic nature of life. You have a child. Who is taking care of him? And if you can't control yourself, who will take care of you? It takes no more than a few seconds and you can slide so fast down the steep slope of life that no power on earth can stop you."

Jucika's gaze turned velvety warm. Lady Klára felt this gaze was begging her, demanding of her, to share her life's accumulated wisdom, to help.

"What will become of your little boy? And what will become of you?"

"I know," answered Jucika quietly.

"You see then. And you know that the uncertainty of existence is hanging over your head."

"I know."

"And you must also know, Jutka, that people are bad." Jucika stirred in the armchair, but Lady Klára did not let her speak. "Look. Here, in my place, if you behave yourself, if you won't be a nihilist, you can cast your anchor. We could even come to terms about bringing your little Lacika here."

"Where would I bring him, to that hole?"

"What hole? That's a regular room. Many people would be glad . . ." Lady Klára retorted, offended.

"And how would I heat it in the winter? There isn't even a chimney hole."

Lady Klára thought about that. It was true. There was no chimney hole. And this nonexistent chimney hole turned into an existential question, a matter of life or death.

"Look, if you stayed with me, you might even have time to study, in night school."

The midday bell rang in the village.

"You look to me like an intelligent girl."

Jucika's eyes sparkled again, and she shyly lowered her head. Lady Klára felt she had won, felt a boundless love and responsibility for everything around her. This is life, she thought, and she had to sigh, long and deep.

Jucika was puffing awkwardly on her cigarette. Lady Klára took it out of her hand and stubbed it out. "It's hard to watch," she said, laughing.

Jucika raised her head. They heard the bell ringing.

Jucika said, "Maybe it's time to cook something . . . Now I can see . . . that . . ."

"What can you cook?"

"Everything."

"Well, that would be too much for lunch."

"What should I cook, then?"

"Let's see, what should you cook? We've got potatoes, onions, and some sausages in the icebox. There are also some cucumbers, for salad."

"Then I'll cook some potatoes with paprika and make a cucumber salad."

"That would be very good," said Lady Klára, and they both smiled. "How many eggs have you brought?"

"Oh, I forgot them."

She stopped in front of the stove. She looked around the kitchen, and since it was quiet in the apartment, she put her ear to the wall. She heard nothing. She opened the icebox and took the sausages out of the plastic container and one by one laid them down on the slate tabletop. She forgot to close the icebox door; cold was streaming out on her legs. She took a plate from the shelf of the kitchen cabinet, put the sausages on it, leaned against the table, and looked out the window.

From the kitchen one could see the Kalhers' garden, the imposing yellow house beyond the pigsty and the chicken coop. Mrs. Kalher was outside, in front of the house, with her thick arms patting and beating the eiderdown and pillows she meant to air. She was either singing or talking to someone; her voice could not be heard, but her mouth was moving continuously and rapidly.

Jucika pulled out the kitchen table drawer and looked into it. One can tell a lot by looking at the contents of a kitchen table drawer. Some people keep in it their cutting board for onions and meat, the tenderizer, wooden spoons, and rolling pin. Others make it the storage space for regular utensils. Sometimes everything is laid out in geometrical precision in neat spaces and compartments; other times everything is thrown in any old way and fished out again when needed. This drawer, the drawer in Lady Klára's pink kitchen table, proved to be below all expectations. Jucika shoved it closed because she remembered she had to peel the potatoes. She looked around the kitchen again and found potatoes in a large pot under the stove. She pulled out the drawer again, looking for a knife, but as she was rifling through the contents, she yanked and knocked out all sorts of things—pieces of string, lengths of wires stuck on fork tines; she could barely shove and stuff it all back in place. When she had the knife and the potatoes, she began peeling. She worked standing up, giving her a chance to see what was going on in the Kalhers' garden. Mrs. Kalher with her thick arms was no longer there; she might have gone into the house, but she could just as easily have moved to the vegetable patch in front of the house to put the hoe to good use there, doing her regular weeding, because she had said she couldn't stand weeds and all the other useless plants that just kept growing like crazy in the world, without knowing why or for whom they were growing.

And there is something to this, because it is the same with plants as with humans: the useless ones are either exterminated or thrown out.

The potato peels were coiling in nice even stripes from under her blade; her glances alternated between the potatoes and the garden, where now only the chickens were pecking and scratching about and the pigs, penned in the square of their wooden sty, were rooting in the muddy soil.

"Whoever eats and drinks undeservedly . . ." Jucika let her thoughts run on, but she could not recall the text. When she did, she said very quickly, like a well-memorized lesson, ". . . should examine himself, and let him eat from that bread, and drink from that cup accordingly, for whosoever eats and drinks undeservedly, eats and drinks judgment for himself . . ." Here, something about the body of the Lord would follow, but that she could not remember at all anymore.

And now Jóska appeared by the house. He was wearing only swimming trunks, and he was muscular, the sun glittering on his tanned skin. His neck was taut, and he was stepping carefully, because he was carrying something heavy that could not be seen for the branches of the pine trees. Now his head also disappeared behind the dark green branches; then he stepped out from behind the trees and could be seen in full: he was approaching the pigsty with the slop pails. Then he disappeared behind the whitewashed slate-roofed neat little outhouse, reappeared below the window, and now she could see clearly the blue veins on his neck and arms, swelling hard and seeming to pulsate. And then the boy stepped into the pigsty.

Jucika counted the potatoes she had peeled, tried to guess whether they would be enough, and then took another one in her hand. I should have done the onions before, she thought. But where are the onions? She began to rummage in the drawers and on the shelves but did not find them. She opened the window, and the sounds of slop plopping into the trough and pigs squealing filled the kitchen. With his bare feet, Jóska was kicking the jostling animals.

"May the plague take your body, Zuleika! Hey, Ilonka, your eyes should flow out of their sockets, you rotten critter, you!"

He threw the pails into the corner and let the two animals get to the trough. They charged, squealing, their pink hides flashing under patches of mud and quivering with excitement; huffing and grunting, smacking and slurping, they gobbled the delicious slop voraciously, and their big, shaking, quivering bodies seemed visibly to grow. Jóska kicked them in the rump, but that was a sign of love. "Go on, gorge yourselves. Pigs," he said.

Jucika stepped away from the window and in the pantry she found both the oil and the onions. How stupid I am. She giggled to herself. This is where I should have looked for them in the first place. She looked around because a pantry too can reveal a great deal, but there was nothing besides dusty bottles of jam and various odds and ends on the upper shelves, old cardboard suitcases, lampshades, and books. From the pantry door she lobbed three onions onto the kitchen table; taking good aim, she threw a fourth one into the pigsty. The middle-size onion hit Jóska's back with a large thud. Jucika let out peals of laughter. Jóska felt his back with his fingers, picked up the onion, and stared oafishly at the girl. Jucika quickly swept the potato peels onto a piece of paper, made a small bundle of it, and threw that too into the neighbors' garden. "Catch!" she called out as she threw.

The boy opened the bundle and strewed the peels into the trough. The two pigs, Zuleika and Ilonka, began to struggle for the choice bits.

"Throw me back the onion."

The boy laughed and archly narrowed his eyes. "I will not," he said emphatically, as if speaking of a most vital matter.

This emphasis moved something in Jucika's soul. The onion that the boy was still holding in his fist gained a special importance.

"I'd rather give it to the pigs," the boy said tauntingly.

"Throw it back," said Jucika.

"I won't."

"Come on, I was just playing," said the girl.

The boy leaned against the plank wall of the sty, which was against the wire fence, and let his arm, swelling with muscles, hang over it. Jucika liked the game. And Jóska liked the girl framed in the window. He liked her so much that he blushed, and in his embarrassment he kept rubbing the pimples on his forehead with the onion.

"Please throw it back, I ask you very nicely. Don't be fresh." Jucika pleaded.

"Why did you throw it here then?"

"Just for fun."

"I'd rather give it to the pigs; I won't give it back." Without breaking the taunting and intimate contact of their eyes, the boy began to retreat toward the trough, and the girl began to peel another onion. "Shall I give it back or give it to the pigs?" asked the boy, winking toward the trough.

Jucika shrugged. At that instant the onion flew through the window and landed in the kitchen cabinet among the wineglasses.

Lady Klára stood up at the rattling and ringing noises, put out her cigarette in the ashtray, and headed for the kitchen. Before putting her hand on the doorknob, she changed her mind and went back to her favorite armchair by the window.

Jóska was guffawing under the window. Jucika leaped to the kitchen cabinet and closed its double doors; she dumped the shards of glass and the onions quickly into the garbage pail, then stopped and stood stiffly in the middle of the kitchen, listening for any noise of movement. She probably didn't hear, she thought. Standing like that, still listening, she noticed that water was trickling from the icebox. She slammed the icebox door shut and stepped to the window. With his upper body leaning over the fence, Jóska was laughing under the window.

"See what an idiot you are, look what you've done!" Jucika whispered, and sternly wrinkled her forehead. The boy's eyes, which usually hazed over with embarrassment or hesitant doltishness, were now happily afire. Behind him the pigs were competing over the empty trough, and farther away, in front of the house, Mrs. Kalher appeared. Casually pounding the faded pink pillows and eiderdown, she looked around, threw her head back and yelled, "Jóska!"

The boy was rocking on the fence and did not respond.

"Jóóska!" Mrs. Kalher warbled and gurgled even louder.

"Why don't you answer her?" Jucika whispered.

The boy grinned. "Let her yell."

"How can you talk like this about your mother?"

Jóska, surprised, wiped his forehead with his fist. "How am I talking about her?"

"Jóóóska!" The call came again, and Mrs. Kalher went back into the house.

The boy glanced back, took a few steps backward in the sty, kicked the pigs aside, and hurled himself over the fence, landed with a plop, and, losing his balance, knocked against the wall.

Jucika laughed. "You had it coming, didn't you?"

Jóska put his elbows on the windowsill and pulled up his shoulders. "Let's see you try doing the same thing!"

"Leave me alone," Jucika said. "I've got enough trouble already because of you."

Jóska, supporting himself on his arms, pushed his face farther into the kitchen. From close up, his deep-set blue eyes appeared to be slightly crossed. Cheekily he kept looking at Jucika, and to be even more comfortable, he rested his chin on his arm. "Because of me?" the boy asked, and squinted mischievously.

"That's right; because of you, I got it on the head for going bathing."

"Pay no mind to that, I think the old girl is cracked," said the boy.

Jucika did not respond. She pulled open the kitchen table drawer, and from under the strings and wires, pliers and hammers, cutlery, thumbtacks, and hobnails, pieces of leather, old newspapers, broken plates, and stuck-together pastry bags, she took out a cutting board for the onions.

"Ever since she moved here, she's been writing some book, but there ain't no book nowhere. My father asked in the bookstore about the book, but it wasn't there neither. The whole thing is just a lot of talk or she's a loony."

"How stupid can you get?" Jucika said, shaking her head. "Expecting the book to be in the store when she hasn't finished writing it?"

Jóska Kalher wrinkled his forehead and then blurted out triumphantly, but only in a whisper, "At night she walks around the garden in her nightgown. Mother says she even dances. She throws off the nightgown, dancing all naked. What d'you call that if not cracked in the head?"

She cut the onions in half, laid them on their flat side, and, holding her head high, began to slice them. It occurred to her that she could put on the oil; she went into the pantry, poured some oil into a pot, and returned to the table. The boy continued to stare at her arrogantly from the windowsill.

"You've got a pretty stupid stare, boy," she said.

The boy burst out laughing. "And you? What about you, girl?"

"If it's not too hard for you, please address me in formal terms."

"Do what?"

"I could be your mother, you know," said Jucika. No matter how high she held her face, tears began to roll from her eyes.

"How old are you then, girl?" asked the boy.

"I told you to address me formally, didn't I?"

"And you, you can call me boy, eh?"

"You're just a snot-nosed kid."

"Is that so? Then how come I got so many women I can't even count them on one finger?"

"You?"

"Yeah, me!"

"You said, you got enough women you can't count them on one finger," Jucika said, laughing with the tears streaming down her face.

The boy was confused. "On one hand . . ."

"One finger!"

"Don't believe me?"

"Oh, sure, women are falling all over your pimply mug, aren't they?"

The boy grinned and bit his lower lip with his healthy white teeth. "It's not my mug they're falling all over."

Jucika slammed down the knife, grabbed the two wings of the window, and shut them. The boy did not go away; he knocked on the glass. Jucika turned the window knob. Jóska pressed his face to the glass, his nose flattened out, his teeth sparkling. Jucika pretended to pay no attention to him. The hot oil sizzled in the pot. She hurled in the diced onions, looked for a wooden spoon and then for paprika, for a few seconds forgetting the boy in the window. She had to slice the potatoes quickly and at the same time keep an eye on the onions to make sure they softened and browned without burning, and also pour water into a pitcher to be used at the right time. The familiar yet new motions, since she didn't know where anything was to be found, kept her busy. When the white potato slices were simmering in the reddish liquid, she glanced toward the window, making it look as though by chance. The boy was not there.

Until the time she heard the high-pitched ringing noise, Lady Klára had written half of the new chapter. When she sat down again in her armchair to continue working, her thoughts had scattered, and the four pages she had covered with her angular letters now seemed to be meaningless and laughable. She read them again, and she was ashamed. She could not possibly let this out of her hand. Fie! Or maybe not fie? She lifted the four-hundred-page manuscript and felt that these last four pages destroyed everything that had come before them. Or was it the rest of the manuscript that would destroy these last four pages? Lady Klára had precise notions regarding the unity of a book's style. If until now she had not written about love, she could not do it now. But why couldn't she?

She was tossed on waves of conflicting emotions, and this was all the more painful because in one split second the entire book had become completely devoid of interest to her. On the one hand, she was bored with it, and on the other hand, she had the feeling she should be living rather than remembering. She ought to bathe in the Danube, lie in the sun, go somewhere, throw the furniture out the window, get to know someone and get married, climb up and swing on the chandelier, and then go into the kitchen and empty the plate of potatoes on Jucika's head.

Until now it was the little chores of life, cooking, cleaning, and shopping, that hindered her in her work.

Now the work was preventing her from living.

First, she lit up. Then, from a compartment of her desk she produced a bottle of sour cherry brandy, pulled out the cork, and took a long swig. She did not sit down again in the armchair but paced up and down and then took a few dance steps. The drink went to her head in a palpable rhythm.

"Mademoiselle, you have promised me this waltz," said Lady Klára. She stretched out her arm and began to spin. Her robe floated and spread out around her; the ashes from her cigarette fell to the (Persian) rug, and

she danced all the way to the Biedermeier couch and there she collapsed
on its striped silk cover. She pulled up one leg, the other was dangling
toward the floor, her robe opened, the cigarette fell from between her fingers, and in her thoughts she was whirling in a daze, in a grand ballroom;
then she was dancing at a folk festival where all the jewelry had disappeared, the music was loud, and the dust was flying in golden little
clouds . . .

The potatoes seasoned with paprika were sizzling in the pot. Jucika
was slicing the cucumbers. There was silence in the kitchen. On the windowpane two flies were chasing each other; later they mated. Jucika
found a tray and the vinegar, prepared the dressing for the cucumber
salad, sprinkled pepper and paprika on top, and then sat down on the
kitchen stool. She listened to the sizzling potatoes, thinking of nothing at
all. Except that she felt bad. This sort of ill feeling, depressing and making her chest feel tight, often took hold of her. Signs of melancholia
appeared. On her face, her nose grew more pointed, her lips narrowed to
a thin line, her jaw jutted sharply forward, making her face look nearly
square. And she saw a row of images that she hated. And she was also getting hungry. She heaved a sigh and stood up. She set the table. She
cleared away the broken glass from the kitchen cabinet and took the lid
off the pot. She poked the potatoes with a fork, but they were not yet soft
enough. She walked into the hallway and stopped before the glass door to
the study. No noise was coming from within. In the garden she picked a
few flowers, stopped by the study again to listen, but there was silence inside. She put the flowers in an old chipped vase, which she placed in the
middle of the set table.

"It's very nice like that," she mumbled to herself half aloud.

She checked the potatoes again; they were done. She transferred them
to a china tray, put the cucumber salad on the table, and knocked on the
glass door.

"Come in!"

Jucika opened the door. Lady Klára, disheveled and in a bad mood,
was sitting on the edge of the sofa.

"Well, what is it?"

"Lunch is ready, comrade," Jucika said.

"I'll be right there," Lady Klára said. "I must finish this line of
thought."

"But hurry up. Food's getting cold," Jucika said, and returned to the kitchen.

They ate without talking. We must mention this especially because there are different ways of eating without talking. These two women, facing each other across the table covered with a nylon tablecloth, were not simply eating but were, rather, having a meal, or to be more precise, they were performing some fancy maneuvers with knives, forks, and napkins.

They held their eating utensils lightly, with no scraping noise from the plates; they used their teeth and tongues to chew the food without champing or smacking their lips; the overall impression was of two people having a meal across the table from each other who had gone beyond the simple pleasure of food intake and were aiming with their utensils—though they served their utilitarian purpose as well—for a loftier pleasure, one stemming from their consciousness that humans are civilized beings, and that it was possible for someone to observe from on high those who eat greedily and, by rising above them, gain a double pleasure: the joy of looking down at others and the ethereal awareness, growing from this joy, that can turn potatoes seasoned with paprika into lobster salad or beef bourguignon. Erstwhile aristocrats always starve more elegantly than do erstwhile civil servants.

Where could she have learned to eat like this? Lady Klára wondered, and sent stealthy glances at Jucika across the table. Jucika's movements provided no explanation. She did not affectedly stick out her little finger, as snobs do, but she did not fail to tap the corners of her mouth lightly with her napkin each time she picked up or replaced her glass. She did not bite into the bread but broke off small pieces first; neither did she pretend that bread was only an insignificant or an embarrassing ancillary to the real food on the table. She did not hold herself stiffly, nor did she slouch over her plate; she did not lean against the table, nor was she too far from it. Lady Klára could not have behaved better (without of course doing it deliberately); after all, her entire childhood had meant an upbringing in a genteel environment that encouraged elegant manners and general refinement, all of which had become second nature to her.

And now she had found her match. From Jucika's behavior until this moment she could not have guessed that the girl's nihilism (as Lady Klára

had called it) was matched by an unconscious ability to accommodate
herself to new situations. Where could she have learned all this? Lady
Klára kept asking herself. But the two women said nothing. They ate
without talking.

Jucika concentrated on her actions. She immersed herself in her gestures. She worked her utensils as a self-taught artist would. She enjoyed
the fact that she was able to do instinctively what her partner was doing
as a result of her upbringing. Thus she stood on a higher rung of pleasure,
looking down on those from whom she had learned the gestures and
movements.

Lady Klára spoke first. Not wittingly, only sensing that this fine silence deserved a few words. "There was a time," she began, bringing carefully a bite of food on the tip of her fork close to her mouth, "when the
Kalhers would invite me for lunch on Sundays," she said, and, without
touching it to her lips, lifted the food from her fork, chewed it, and swallowed it; she put the fork down for a moment, touched the napkin to her
mouth, picked up the fork, and continued. "But I could oblige them only
a few times."

Jucika looked at Lady Klára and, with this reticent glance, let her interlocutor know that she was paying attention, waiting eagerly for every
word, and then, to give her look more emphasis she also spoke, saying,
"Really?"

Since in the statement meant as a question or the question meant as
a statement there was nothing intrusive, Lady Klára easily picked up
the line of conversation. "The Kalhers, my sweet, are among those
who worked their way quickly from poverty to affluence, but this step,
or I should say this new framework they are unable to fill with culture . . ."

Jucika was in a difficult situation. Her instincts were telling her to
roll on the thread of conversation at least by the length of a conjunction.
Tact and artistic sense of proportion required it. Time had to be made for
Lady Klára to chew her next bite of food. And her instincts not only gave
her the urge to act but helped her out. "Perhaps the next generation . . ."
she said ingeniously, and to add profundity to this statement, she lowered
her eyes for a second.

Although too short, the phrase was appropriate. Because of its brevity,
there followed a few moments of silence, with only the pigs snorting in

the neighbors' pigsty. Jucika glanced at the window and realized that the snorting was no accident. A man was standing in front of the sty, petting and rubbing the two animals' pink and muddy bodies.

"Oh, the next generation . . ." Lady Klára said, and the phrase brought Jucika's attention back to the conversation. "If only it were so simple. It takes centuries for a society to develop its own unique culture, and then it fits no other group."

Lady Klára was now plucking the strings of her favorite topic, which she felt to be so much her own that she expected no response. But Jucika continued with the conversational thread. Pensively, and nodding a few times, she looked at the ceiling. "This is true of the middle classes too . . . The bourgeoisie of the French Revolution is different from the bourgeoisie of French imperialism."

Lady Klára did not hide her amazement. She nodded vigorously. "Yes . . . yes. I'm referring to these historical analogies," she said, and with her fork pointed at her plate. "But to return to our original topic—" She interrupted herself to place a thin slice of potato into her mouth; taking advantage of this momentary pause, Jucika looked out the window again. The burly man by the pigsty slapped the rumps of the pigs and then disappeared behind the whitewashed door of the neat little outhouse.

Is that Mrs. Kalher's husband? Jucika would have liked to ask, but on the one hand, she felt it would have been inappropriate at the moment, and on the other hand, Lady Klára had swallowed her bite and returned to the original topic.

"The Kalhers," she said, "eat like . . . wild people. So after a few attempts I was compelled to excuse myself."

"Some cucumber salad?"

"No, thank you."

Kalher stepped out of the outhouse but did not close the door behind him; the wooden seat became visible from the kitchen. Jucika turned away; Lady Klára smiled at her kindly from across the table.

"You are a very thoughtful girl," she said, and placed her fork and knife parallel to and facing each other on the plate, and then glanced at the flowers. "And you cook very well."

"You mean to say you found it tasty?"

"I do; I have."

They smiled at each other. One last time they touched their napkins to their mouths and stood up.

The smiles slowly faded from their faces and stiffened into distorted grins around their mouths. Lady Klára was looking at the kitchen cabinet, Jucika out the window. In front of the pigsty, Mrs. Kalher was surveying the animals, and then she angrily slammed and bolted the door of the neat little outhouse. The two women in the kitchen looked at each other again, as surprised as if they were meeting for the first time. Jucika would have begun to clear the table, but at the artist's house she had learned that the table should not be touched while someone is still in the dining area. And Lady Klára was not about to leave; she may have wanted to say something. She was rifling through the pockets of her robe, probably for cigarettes.

"Well, then, I think I'll do the dishes now," Jucika said.

"Do you need help?"

"Oh, Auntie Klára, why would you want to do that? This is my job!" said Jucika.

"Well then, go ahead, do the dishes . . . What was broken this morning?"

"Just two glasses."

"Just two glasses?"

"Yes."

"What kind of glasses?"

"Wineglasses, I think."

Lady Klára said nothing and turned to go to her room. She stopped at the door because it bothered her to think that Jucika might consider the glasses a big deal—they were not, for glasses do break—but it was that she would always like to know when something broke in the house. So she wouldn't have to look for it. Because it's not a big thing when something breaks—lately everything had been falling out of her hands too—only she'd like to know about it, so she won't look for something in vain.

Lady Klára thought all this over and then said, "How did they break?"

"I knocked them down by accident. When I took out the plates."

"They're not with the plates."

"But that's when I knocked them down, by accident."

Now they smiled again. Lady Klára smiled to control her rising irritation. Not that there was something in the breaking of two (cut) glasses,
no. What irritated her was that Jucika seemed to take the matter a shade
too lightly. It was this taking the matter lightly that was important, not
the two glasses. It hadn't even occurred to her to report it. If she hadn't
been asked, she wouldn't have told. And should there have been a need
for those glasses, she, Lady Klára, would have looked for them in vain.

"Well, I didn't ask you because . . . These things happen," Lady Klára
said.

"They do." Jucika nodded helpfully.

Lady Klára gently bit down on her lip with her protruding upper
teeth and left the kitchen. "Come into my room later. We shall talk about
what else needs to be done."

Jucika nodded. She collected the plates and the cutlery, opened the
window, took off the tablecloth, and shook off the crumbs. Jóska was
hanging over the fence, his naked arms dangling.

"Fed yourselves, did you?"

"We ate, kid, had a meal."

"Ain't that the same thing?"

"It isn't. Now get lost."

The boy smiled impudently. There was a certain teenage uncleanliness
about his whole pimply face, but his large blue eyes sparkled with unambiguous charm. Jucika sensed that she wasn't sending the boy away
because his presence bothered her; in fact she liked his being around,
hanging over the fence and making eyes at her. She didn't even move
away from the window; in washing the dishes, she had a good excuse
to stay by it, and while dipping the dishes in the water and sloshing
them around, she could exchange glances with the boy. Jóska was playing the experienced seducer and Jucika the woman who could not be
seduced. This role-playing was manifest in that the seducer was attempting with a smile at the corner of his mouth to conceal his insurmountable uncertainty and eagerness for victory in face of the unknown, while
the woman who could not be seduced, with her reserved, immobile,
and all-observant, evaluating glance was masking the feeling that here
and now she has already surrendered.

"Why are you using the outhouse if you have a regular toilet?" asked
Jucika.

"Dad says our shit is the best thing for the lettuce—".

Jóska continued his explanation, but Jucika called out, "Why are you talking like that?"

For the first time the boy seemed to lose some of his confidence, and he pulled his arms back to his side of the fence.

"I don't want you to talk to me in ugly tones like that, kid!" Jucika said, and under her bony forehead she wrinkled her brows. The boy pulled up his shoulders and backed away toward the pigsty. "Your mother hasn't taught you any manners?"

The boy stepped back to the fence and grew red in the face. "Don't insult my mother."

"I didn't."

"I'll slap your mouth for you if you do . . ."

Jucika burst out laughing, dipped a pot in the rinse water, and slammed it on the windowsill. "Who was insulting your mother?"

"I'm telling you not to, 'cause I'll slap your mouth for you if you—"

"All right, that's enough. Now, get yourself out of here. Move!"

Jóska was getting redder and threw his arms across the fence again. "I slapped Söregi in the mouth so hard he woke up in the hospital. Because he cursed my mother. Nobody's gonna curse my mother, 'cause anybody who does will get his mouth slapped and will wake up in the hospital like Söregi with his kidneys all messed up."

Jucika took the pot off the sill and slammed the window shut.

When she finished washing the dishes and wiped away the last drops of water on the floor, she stopped in the middle of the kitchen and looked around. Sleepy flies were buzzing between the walls and on the windows. There was silence in the house. For other people, evening signals the end of the day; for Jucika, this afternoon calm was the time when one asked oneself what had been done, what should be done, and what it was that one must still do? And these were desolately empty moments—always in the kitchen, in the company of the wet sparkling slate surfaces, the tile floor drying in spots, isolated from the spaces where people were resting or living their alien and in a certain sense unapproachable lives. It was only in the rarest of cases that Jucika posed questions to herself and formulated answers that hinted at plans or at the possibility of goals to be achieved, that she formulated something precisely, she relied rather on her feelings, and because her sense organs functioned well and her memories were also accurate, plans and decisions appeared to her in the form of concrete thoughts only in extreme situations, summarizing, as it were, what she had been weighing with her sense organs for months or even years. For this reason, people usually thought of Jucika as a creature of instincts who did not know, only felt, what she did, who let herself be swept along by the current of life and could not plant her feet firmly on the ground. And this (according to Mrs. Viczmándy) showed itself in Jucika's face, in the meek, slightly amazed bovine look (to use Mrs. Viczmándy's words) with which she sized up objects and people around her. They believed her to be a person who put herself at the mercy of circumstances. And this sort of person (according to the artist) made the best servant.

Even now, standing hesitantly—in a cowlike fashion, really—in the middle of the kitchen, Jucika was not thinking of anything special, unless we consider the flash as a real thought, which she directed at putting the drawer of the kitchen table in order. In the very same instant, on the basis of a single day's experience, she weighed the similarities and differences between this place and her previous places of employment. She sensed that here for some reason or other, she would be freer, less constrained to force her personality within narrower limits, but she also sensed that because of the greater freedom, the pent-up emotions inside her, and the unpredictable duality of the old woman, the dramatic turn would come much sooner. Jucika's relationships always ended with a dramatic turn.

Lady Klára had been standing in the middle of her study for a few minutes. She was looking at the manuscript pile from a distance. Everything she desired or would want to desire was here, within reach: a window giving on the slowly rolling river, silence, cleanliness, and a person to serve her. She had desired this state for so long, and she had feared satisfying it ever since the desire had been born. When she did not force her thoughts into the limits of her own principles, she could think of these planned moments, when she would be left only with Zoltán and her work, as if beyond her principles the blue waters of complete spiritual freedom, free of the body, awaited her. And in fact these were the waters of total freedom. Still, she felt that her little boat was rocking slightly under her. The effect of alcohol had worn off, leaving behind a bitter sense of shame, the kind felt only by very conscious people when they think back on a state in which they were deprived of their self-possession. It was the kind of shame felt only by very conscious people who try to curb their emotions with their conscience, stifle their secret, sometimes very dark, desires. And in Lady Klára, this sense of shame was coupled with another strange, not very new, only forgotten feeling. Perhaps she experienced it first when as a little girl she and her younger sister were dressed by Miss Papanek. Every morning Miss Papanek would squat before them, and they would stick their feet into her lap, allowing her to lace their high-quarter shoes. But it is also possible that she had felt nothing like shame then because this everyday movement had to be natural; it is also possible that her experiences later in life rearranged her memories and gave this innocent scene special significance. Oh, it was not the image, only its mood and atmosphere, that occurred to her now, the guilt feeling carried for so long, all of it expressing itself in insuperable nervousness. As if she, whose shoes in her childhood were laced by Miss Papanek, had to be more careful than anyone else; as if regarding Jucika she had something to pay back, and if not to pay back, she had to understand or do something, to overcome the shame and guilt and to accept the role that this situation had created for her, to calm herself, and to exploit the freedom, or to think hard about the freedom that Jucika would create for her, to give it serious thought, and to gain insight into the person she did not know but who, by some unknown law, was ordered to be at her side, to wash her laundry and scrub the tub after her bath. Here, around the tub, was where Lady Klára's thoughts came to a temporary rest, and she was surprised how thoroughly she could humiliate herself by using the humiliation of a stranger, and how the lashes of humility she meted out to herself had to be much harsher than those that Jucika could possibly have felt—if she felt anything at all—while scrubbing the tub. Lady Klára went so far in her self-torture that it did not occur to her that Jucika worked for a wage in a position designated for her by society; this did not occur to her, only her feeling of being privileged, which grew to gigantic proportions; and compared with her seemingly infinite lonely freedom, everything appeared to be slavery, which, by the way, is the natural and regular provider of freedom. And in this heightened state of hers, exacerbated by self-torture, the pile of manuscript on the bentwood table meant nothing to Lady Klára; she felt there was nothing she could do with the time that had been freed from shopping, cooking, dishwashing, and doing the laundry, for this freed-up time was now being weighed down by another burden, the burden of another human being.

If only this other human being were quiet, accommodating, and noiseless. After all, if she wanted to, she could be quiet, accommodating, and noiseless. But she was an unrestrained, noisy, and bony person. Even at the bottom of her noiselessness something was rumbling. Maybe if she were translucent and unnoticeable . . .

The more Lady Klára immersed herself in her thoughts, the more she felt compelled to make a decision. It was the second time within a day that she had felt this. To flee from something she did not want to acknowledge, something that could mean her end, could destroy the world she had built on her own notions or would drag her down somewhere where she would have to accept a communality she did not desire. She had to turn back, to flee. But how?

She lit up, though she should not be smoking this much, and lowered herself to the edge of the Biedermeier couch. As she looked around in the room that showed her its more than usually disorderly appearance, she was seized with hatred and desperation. Hatred directed at every power and order that had been upsetting her life. Against Mrs. Viczmándy, whom she had always detested, who was always hanging around her neck, who . . .

Where had she been at the time of the arrest, when the police had to be dealt with, where had she been then? Who knew her then at all? Today she was everywhere. And now it turned out that she had been a member of the party forever; now they were going to exchange her apartment for a villa for her. When Zoltán asked if he could keep a few of his books at her place, well, fine . . . They happened not to be at home—by chance. Zoltán had to carry the books back, he with his scoliosis. And what sort of thing was this anyway? I was good enough to share the trouble of the arrest and dealing with the police, and now I am being urged to write my memoirs. I should write about the things they are doing nowadays, once again . . . If Zoltán were here, what would he have to say about this? He never imagined it would be like this . . . That's not how he had imagined it! My God, how did we imagine it? We imagined that everybody would be equal. If only he were here . . . God, how did we imagine it? Some other way. What did we think about life? About our life? About my life and his. They spread a net over you; they were secure in their fortified positions; they handed out villas and decorations, but nobody asked, Klára, is this the way you imagined it? I know what they're doing. Do I ever! The Viczmándys . . .

Lady Klára was breathing heavily.

And as if with a calculation wrapped in benevolence, they had foisted the girl on her so that she'd become part of something that was alien to her. Alien? Not really; she had asked for it, dropped hints, and then referred to it openly: how good it would be to be free of all the unpleasant burdens. And there were further questions. Unpleasant burden? Yes. Because for her, beyond sixty, to walk a kilometer and a half in the burning sun or in a snowfall to the People's Store was a burden, and yet it was not, because now she was thinking of the hours of long and sometimes difficult walking as a time of freedom that would never return. And not even the cigarette that at other times she smoked so majestically would cool the heat of hatred and desperation. Her hatred was directed not only against her (otherwise rather loose) circle of friends but also against herself—hatred spilling into shame—because this fretting, along with the mountain of questions, was something new for Lady Klára, a long-forgotten feeling that crossed the boundaries of her principles, which she had thought to be so solid. She laid great store by her principles, in the honesty and purity of her principles.

She put out the cigarette, which she had smoked to her fingernail, and was pressing the butt violently against the wall of the ashtray when Jucika knocked.

"Yes."

Jucika entered cautiously, did not quite close the glass door behind her. There was a smile on her bony face, and she stopped in the middle of the (Persian) rug. The expression of hatred had not left Lady Klára's face, she just stared at the girl without seeing her, and Jucika looked at Lady Klára with surprise, the smile vanishing from her face.

"I've come only to talk about what else needs to be done, as you said."

"What?"

"You said earlier . . ."

"What needs to be done . . ."

"Yes. As Auntie Klára said earlier."

This "Auntie Klára" was out of place now. "Please sit down." The
voice, so pliant at other times, now seemed stuck roughly in the air, and
Lady Klára quickly sent a pacifying smile after it, which made Jucika
sense even more emphatically that something was amiss.

She did not even sit down. But Lady Klára did not notice this.

"I should like you to leave."

Jucika's hands, as if she were standing at attention, pressed themselves
against her thighs.

"It would be best for both of us." Lady Klára continued.

A long silence followed. They were looking at each other, a meek and
open countenance locking into a maniacally determined cold countenance. The sentence, supported by an additional one, had been pronounced. There was no turning back. Something like a grimace flitted
across Jucika's face; she lowered her head and raised her skirt a little. The
movement seemed almost like an interrupted curtsy.

"I would pay for the glasses," she said.

Lady Klára's face contorted and turned raspberry red for a second. She
jumped up from her chair. "That is not what I was talking about!" she
yelled, beside herself.

Jucika's glance brushed the old woman's face, and perhaps she really
understood that they were not talking about the glasses.

"I don't . . . understand," she moaned softly, haltingly.

Lady Klára flew across the room, slammed the door shut, and propped
her back firmly against it. This calmed her down. Jucika turned around
in the middle of the rug.

"I'm . . . sorry," said Lady Klára, also softly and haltingly.

"I don't know . . . did I cause some trouble?"

"Oh, no . . . you caused no trouble."

Jucika took a step on the rug toward Lady Klára. They were quiet.
Lady Klára felt a dreadful fatigue, but in her brain her own scream was
still raging. She would have loved to disappear from this room, but she
would have also liked to take control of her weakness. When she finally
managed to open her mouth, her voice was once again cold and rough,
but this was a coldness and roughness that could originate not in hatred
but only in desperation. "I ask you that if you can, please forget what I
said before."

Another long silence followed.

"If you can."
"Yes."

Why did she kill herself? She grabbed the knife, found the spot where the heart beat, made the opening above her beautiful breast, and the blood was already flowing, her eyes rolled up . . . Why did she do it? Who was this woman?

Jucika was sitting on the sofa in her room, which even in summer exuded the cool and musty air of the earth; she was looking at the reproduction hanging on the wall. The death of this peculiar woman, however hard the painter must have tried, caused no dramatic effect. Perhaps because the eyes turned skyward, the densely pleated crimson tiffany parted over the full breast, and in an odd, almost disturbing disharmony with the oozing blood, the gaping gash in the creamy skin and the glittering steel of the knife's blade were all so precisely dramatic, perhaps this precision put an end to the drama. The death unfolding before our eyes was nothing but a very theatrical scene. Jucika's eyes gradually grew used to the shapes and colors in the painting, so much so that the old frame slowly disappeared and the coarse whitewashed wall faded away; her eyes absorbed the frameless picture so thoroughly that the painted woman turned into a three-dimensional reality inside the tiny room; that is where she thrust the real blade into her heart, an act Jucika felt she had no strength to prevent. All she did was grasp the handle of the shopping basket lying next to her on the floor and keep squeezing it. Her gaze wandered past even the suicide, the woman who had become real, blotting out the imagination that had been born of imagination, leaving only a spot on the bare expanse of the wall with shapeless planes and colors; she was still staring at a single point. Her usually wide eyes now narrowed to a slit through which the nearly reified pain and desperation seemed to squeeze out. Jucika was crying. Jucika cried, but she did not drown in her tears when the world became blurry before her, when the saintly woman who for some reason had killed herself disappeared and Jucika was left alone with her own physical being. Everything cleared up for her although for only a few seconds; she was consciously aware, in well-formulated terms, of the difference between her inherent sensitive longing for freedom and her present situation. Preoccupied by her past and her present situation, she was unable to see goals or solutions. This did not make her sorry for herself or others; she felt only an impotent rage that, for the first time in her adult life, plunged her into the depths of an insoluble problem. The feeling lasted only for seconds, but the seconds penetrated deep into her blood, were absorbed by her nervous system and ravaged half of her being, her uninhibited openness, with an invisible power. And when the reproduction on the wall emerged from the white dimness, it was a different person who saw the hollowed-out holy tragedy. Perhaps the eyes were less meek and more reserved; Jucika's imagination ceased to gambol. With instinctive gestures she wiped the tears from her eyes and stood up. Her gaze wandered to the tiny window; clusters of morning glories, their petals closed, were peeking at her. Outside, the early summer sun was shining brightly.

Jucika got up and stepped out into the garden with the empty basket. The pebbles crunched under her feet; listening to this noise, she made her way to the gate. There she stopped. Now she knew what she had to do. She sensed this in the calm that came from holding the basket and from the even steps with which she had covered the short distance, perhaps in the calm emanating from her surroundings. She felt precisely, and without regret, that something in her life had come to an end. With a hitherto unseen clarity, her little boy came to stand before her, and with a hitherto never-felt clarity, she understood that she was a mother. She had not realized this even while carrying her shameful burden in her belly, because she had paid no attention to the shame or the burden, not even after the terrible hours of labor that freed her of the burden, because even then she concentrated on regaining her own freedom. It seemed that years had to go by before she could murmur to herself, I am a mother, a mother. And she already saw little Lacika roaming about, running up and down, chasing a ball, digging out snails in this garden, as Lady Klára had described it to her. She smiled happily, and the wide-open meekness in her eyes vanished even further, making room finally for a pure conscious joy. Cradling the basket in a womanly fashion, she stepped out on the street.

When she shut the lattice gate behind her, from the stone fence of the neighboring garden someone jumped down next to her. Jucika stopped for a moment but was not surprised and did not cry out; her inner calm was protecting her. Although they had usually communicated across the fence, Jucika judged that the boy was now approaching her with his other face. She moved on. Jóska kept up with her, but almost on the other side of the street, without looking at her. They walked like this, without a word, for a long time, casting occasional side glances at each other, Jucika with a cheerful calm, Jóska with a dark and offended determination. The shady little street turned suddenly into a wide and treeless highway. Cars and trucks went whizzing by them with their usual noise. The traffic forced them closer to each other and ended the intimacy of their earlier ambling. Somebody had to say something.

"Are you going shopping?" Jóska asked awkwardly, without raising his eyes to the girl.

"Yes."

"May I accompany you?"

Jucika smiled. "It's a fine time to ask, isn't it?"

Her smile and captious question made the boy's pimply face take on a darker expression. He would not say anything for a long time. When the silence stretched too long, it was Jucika who broke it. "How old are you?"

"Twenty," the boy answered after taking some time to think.

"Twenty?"

"You don't believe me?"

"Why wouldn't I believe it?"

"And how old are you?"

"It's not proper to ask a woman that question."

Now the boy's thick neck moved a little, and as if resisting an inner force, he turned his head toward Jucika. He blinked, confused. "Did I insult you?"

"Not at all. I am past twenty-six."

"Twenty-six?"

"I said 'past' . . ."

Again they walked without talking. Although he did not fall behind the girl, Jóska's progress was like that of a beaten dog trailing after its master, maybe because of the way he held his body. He was wearing bleached cotton pants; hunching his back, he kept his fists in his pockets and walked with his legs loosely turned outward.

"Aren't you hot?" he asked.

"No, I'm not."

"It's damn—the sun is very strong, isn't it?"

"Strong enough."

"I can take the heat. I'm just asking because maybe I should take the basket."

Jucika looked at the boy, her eyes met the pair of light blue eyes swimming in confusion, and she merely shook her head that she needed no help, thank you, and the faint smile did not leave the corners of her mouth.

"But I could carry it on the way back?"

For Jucika the whole thing was becoming strange, and she did not feel like answering this question either, because she had no answer, and then a very strange sentence left her lips: "That would be very kind of you."

It sounded as if she were making fun of him, but she had no such intention; on the contrary, she was touched by the offer. Still, the mistaken tone of the sentence caused—though something had brought them a little closer—another period of silence. Later Jóska said hello to a man walking in the opposite direction on the other side of the road, and he blushed. When out of hearing, Jucika lowered her voice to a confidential level and asked, "Who was that?"

"My principal."

"What kind of principal?"

"In high school he was—"

"You went to high school?"

"Yes."

"And what do you do now?"

"Now?"

Jucika nodded twice, signaling that she was very interested in knowing what the young man did now, but Jóska, wrinkling his forehead, began to stammer. "Now . . . actually . . . well, actually now it's . . . I'm on leave."

"On leave?"

"Yes."

Jucika asked no further questions, but Jóska kept on thinking about his answer. "Actually, what I do is a secret."

Without too much credulity, Jucika's eyebrows began to rise, but Jóska was already speaking.

"Actually, I'm not supposed to talk about it because it may cause a lot of trouble, and I can't even tell my parents about it, because of the oath I had to swear, and that oath, that was a very special oath." He looked at Jucika.

"I don't want to get you into trouble," the girl said, with a shade of mockery in her tone, which the boy failed to notice.

"Of course I'm not afraid of anything, but I shouldn't tell . . . I trust you, so if you want me to, I could tell you . . . if you won't pass it on."

Jucika shrugged, and as she watched the boy, the wide-eyed meekness stole back into her face.

"You won't pass it on to nobody?"

"Why would I?"

"My father says women are blabbermouths, every one of 'em."

Jucika turned away, offended.

"Did I offend you?"

Jucika shrugged again and burst out laughing. "Now, even if you told me, I wouldn't believe it."

"You're just saying that so I'd tell you anyway," he said, and fell silent. Then, blinking slyly, he added, "Don't worry. We were trained good how to spot the methods spies use to squeeze information out of a person."

A strange tension set in. The air of suspicion. An atmosphere that makes one curious but also fearful of one's own curiosity. Spies. Methods. Maybe because of the strange sound of these words.

"I don't want to squeeze anything out of you," said Jucika with an ungratified curiosity at the depth of her proud denial.

"Then I'd rather not tell you."

"Suit yourself."

They walked on without a word. No car passed; the empty sun-drenched highway crossed the bare meadow that stretched between the holiday center and the village. With their every step, the dense afternoon heat seemed to quiver around their bodies, and the vibration made the air visible. Their faces were turning red; the boy's big ears took on a purple hue, and sweat slowly poured from his forehead. A dull stupor took hold of them, and in this dull stupor they traipsed along, alone on the empty road. They needed to talk, and Jóska, with a parched throat and raspy voice said, "I don't want you to think something about me that—"

Jucika gave him a lazy look; Jóska turned away. "The guys in high school always made fun of me, and like . . . But they were just showin' off, only their mouths was bigger, that's all . . . That my mug is full of pimples, and they said that was because . . ."

Jucika's eyes narrowed as she tried to figure things out. She did not understand the words, but from the way the boy was talking she thought she should feel sorry for him.

"I don't want you to think something about me like what I said this morning. I only said that because I got a big mouth, 'cause otherwise . . ."

Jóska halted and looked long at the girl's arm around the basket. Then his gaze crawled up between her breasts to her mouth; it stopped there, not having the courage to continue on. Jucika watched the boy's eyes, the sun-bleached fast-fluttering lashes, and felt something that frightened her; she felt an attraction similar to what she had already felt for this much younger fellow earlier in the day, only now it was deeper, and she could hardly wait for the boy to finish the sentence so she could make the move she had been longing to make.

"Why don't we sit down for a bit?" the boy asked.

Jucika took a step back and, as quickly as if executing a command, sat down on a milestone. Jóska pulled his hands out of his pockets, looked at them, put them back in; there was something on the tip of his tongue, but he was only sighing, he did not dare say it. He lowered himself next to Jucika, against the girl's feet in the dust-covered grass, and again he took his fists out, plucked at the grass, and while slapping the ground with his palm and with his fingers mowed the puny roadside weeds, he finally blurted it out. "They called me Little Virgin." The sentence could not have reached Jucika's brain before the boy quickly added, "But they liked me because I wasn't so macho, and I wasn't really angry because . . . but that's what they called me."

Jucika looked at the boy's neck, at the two pulsing little veins that protruded in manly fashion from the smooth, suntanned skin, and she finally made the move she had so desired to make, stroking the boy's head once, then twice, and her palm rested for a moment on the back of his neck. "You're still a kid," she said, pronouncing the words gently.

Jóska pulled away and did not look at her, as Jucika would have expected after she had stroked his head; he did not look up at her eagerly, but that made the whole thing even nicer. They sat like that for another minute, and then Jucika stood.

"It is really hot," she said, but the boy did not move. "Let's go, or I'll catch it."

Now Jóska got up too, their eyes locked for an instant, frightened and alarmed, and then they let each other escape. They started off. Jucika did not see that Jóska had changed again; thrusting his fists into his pockets and slouching his back, he regained that stiff, hunted posture that contrasted with his usually careless gait. And his tone also changed. "I just wanted to tell you, because lots of time passed since then, and I was in the fighting too . . ."

Jucika looked at him surprised. "You were in the fighting?"

"I don't like to talk about that. You might think I'm bragging, but I got wounded. If you want me to, I can show you."

Jucika turned sad. She stopped listening, did not comprehend the words, was only sorry that it was over, that it was again a pimply adolescent walking along with her, with whom she had nothing in the world to do, and he might be lying too.

But for Jucika this was only an intimation. How could it have been anything else? How could she have suspected lies to follow so much honesty?

But whoever has a chance to taste what is good will strive for it again, even if at the cost of an occasional lie. Jucika did not think this all through; she was acting instinctively when in her voice she hinted at her concerned curiosity. "You were wounded?"

"Yes. In two places too."

"Where?"

"In my thigh and also got a bullet in my lungs."

"But how?"

"I don't like to talk about it because you'd think I'm bragging. Maybe I look like a kid, but I was fighting along with my father against the rebels in the Corvin Lane."

"Really?"

"Yes."

"Because my father was a captain then, and my mother worried about him and she sent me over with a chicken, but I understood right away what was going on and we fought together, so that he was promoted to major and me, that's when I got the secret mission—"

The boy stopped and knitted his brow, looking at the girl seriously as if to test whether she could be trusted, and then he nodded because he had made his decision, and still scrutinizing the girl's face, he continued. "And after that they took me into the police force as an interrogating lieutenant, and I said it was a secret because other people shouldn't know about it. I'm telling this only to you."

She was chain-smoking, the room filled with the smell of the butts. She felt her heart grow heavy, and from time to time the numbing sensation of weakness coursed through her limbs. These were the best moments, when her brain disconnected and all her fears were concentrated on her own physical state. Good God! I am ruining myself, she thought, and quickly put out the cigarette, only to light another a moment later.

She was standing by the window without looking out; it is possible to stand like that in front of a window . . . Maybe it's because of this heat wave, she wondered, but her brain, used to some kind of orderliness, would not tolerate this momentary excuse; she knew that from the moment Jucika had arrived her life had switched to another order, had become helplessly entangled, had developed knots, and then the knots had come undone, and with the loose threads her life was becoming entwined in the life of another person whose character, consisting of strange contradictions fluttering among humility, audacity, coarseness, and refinement, was holding her captive, and she could not find the key to this character or to this situation, the key that she believed comes with every character and situation. As her thoughts were circling Jucika's character, the self-tormenting questions arose again, but this time without the theatrical rant that had accompanied them half an hour earlier, going beyond all appearances, beyond all the played roles, beyond the strange mesh of honest and dishonest poses; the questions that faced her in their stark simplicity were, And who am I? What am I in her eyes?

She tried to fit together the mosaics of the last hours, and it seemed to her that she could not remember anything. She could not remember anything separately, not a single moment, since not a memorable second had occurred between them on the basis of which the essence of their relationship could methodically have been defined. And here Lady Klára's thoughts of necessity came to a sudden halt because despite her many good qualities, there was one thing she could not do, for lack of an ability that is given to only a chosen few—namely, both to be in a relationship and at the same time to see and define oneself from the outside with the eyes of the partner, practically doubling one's own *self* and rising above oneself, thereby also defining the other person. And since her judgments, of necessity, always originated within her, without any control of a doubled *self*, we can catch the exact moment when her thoughts took the wrong turn—for example, now. For example, she should have seen clearly (if her thoughts had shifted to an unusual path in order to define her relationship with a servant) that her relationship with Jucika was indefinable precisely because it was completely unusual, because it lacked the most essential of socially accepted norms found in similar relationships: obligatory indifference. Lady Klára felt only the unusualness, which measured against social norms was embarrassing and irritating for someone who cannot discover the new in what was unusual or, having discovered the new, cannot rejoice in it. If Lady Klára had been able to take this step, she would not have fled from the unusual; on the contrary, she would have eagerly, albeit carefully, embraced it; she would have been glad for herself, for she would have been discovering herself, and since joy would have come to her in thinking of another human being, she would have also realized that joy and happiness could originate only from her and only in this way. This could have been the first step on a new path, on the path of the unusual.

But she did not take the step. Maybe she was too old and too tired. Maybe she could not step out of herself and was sensitive enough only to defend herself. Maybe she avoided the only certain solution because since her situation was stable, she was not afraid enough to understand that she had to take stock of her personal position lest she be forced into an obstinate self-defense, which is equal to self-elimination. Maybe.

She was growing uncertain. She felt sorry for herself.

She went to sleep in the other room.

It was a dazed, escapelike sleep. She was startled at the opening of the door, and the whole thing began all over again.

"Is that you?"

"Oh, I didn't know you were asleep."

The sentence rang false.

"Come on in . . . I only nodded off a little."

Although obviously this was not true either, Jucika put the basket in the middle of the rug and lowered herself next to Lady Klára on the bed. Lady Klára moved a little farther in.

"Why didn't you tell me not to talk to Jóska Kalher in the familiar form?"

"Why wouldn't you?"

"I didn't know anything about him."

"You didn't?"

"How would I have known—"

"Known what?"

Worried, Jucika lowered her head. Lady Klára, apprehensive about everything that had to do with Jucika, shook off her sleep-induced daze, propped herself up on an elbow, and instinctively went on the attack.

"I hope you're not planning to go into the business of seducing minors," she said half-jokingly but not without some mockery and sternness.

"I'm not," Jucika said curtly, and the smiling bashfulness vanished from her face. She stood up and took hold of the basket handle.

Lady Klára did not want to notice she had offended her. "Did you get everything I asked for?" she asked quickly.

"Yes."

"Then please prepare supper."

"Yes."

"And please bring it in. I shall eat in my study."

"Yes."

When the girl left, Lady Klára lifted a French novel from her night table, felt her face while standing before the bathroom mirror, and then called out to the kitchen, "Jutka!"

"Yes . . ."

"Take an armchair for me and put it under the chestnut tree . . . if you please."

Jucika looked into the bathroom; Lady Klára was patting cream into the wrinkles under her eyes.

"Which one?"

"The one from the hallway."

"All right."

Lady Klára left off examining her face and followed the girl. Jucika placed the armchair under the chestnut tree; Lady Klára sat in it, crossed her legs, and opened the book.

"And make me a lemonade."

"Yes."

"Without sugar."

"Without sugar?"

"Yes."

In a few minutes Jucika appeared with the lemonade.

"Please bring out the little table from the hallway, and a tray too, to put under the glass. I wouldn't want to see the furniture ruined."

Lady Klára began to read. When the girl reappeared again, carrying the small three-legged table in one hand and balancing the drink on the tray with the other, Lady Klára did not look at her. Jucika carefully arranged everything around her and without a word returned to the house. Only the pebbles made creaky noises under her feet.

When she disappeared, Lady Klára looked up from the book. A branch of the chestnut tree was bent almost to the ground, and its leaves were rustling in a solitary breeze. Lady Klára long observed this peculiar phenomenon and then threw the book down on the small table, stood, took a step, and put her palm up in the current of the breeze. The leaves slowly came to rest, and the breeze, the cause of so much movement only a moment before, turned into a gentle stroke on the outside of her hand. She squatted next to the bent-down branch, pulled it aside, stretched out her arm again, and watched the dying and reviving movements.

Beyond the chestnut tree, a stretch of grassy lawn was bordered by shrubs. From somewhere in the shrubs she heard exploding, suppressed bursts of laughter. As if following her original purpose for standing up, Lady Klára bent down, picked up a pebble, and quickly sat back down in her armchair.

Later, as if by chance, she looked in the direction of the shrubs, but nothing was moving there.

About a half hour went by like this, but the book did not hold her attention; she had to go over pages she had already read because her mind wandered in too many directions. Not that she was nervous; only this quiet, this calm around her was so strange; strange, because it did not seem real. She knew she should not have squatted down by the leaves, but she would have liked to do it again because the breeze had not changed direction, and for some reason this little movement of the branch was the only thing that contradicted the silence around her. It did not irritate her, yet she felt an urge to put a stop to it, but she also felt that from various directions, and continually, eyes were watching her, following her every move and forming judgments about her, judgments that included her supposed hatred for the stranger busying herself in the kitchen. And because she felt that judgmental pairs of eyes were trained on her, that people were hiding behind the shrubbery and trees waiting for a moment when they could proclaim their mocking views in some scathing manner, for the time being she decided not to carry out her plan.

She appeared to be reading. The boom of the afternoon ship on the river came as a good excuse; she could look up. Only a few steps from her feet a chestnut leaf was quivering. But she gave it only a cursory glance and looked around the garden.

Everything was still. Tired and overcome by the afternoon heat, leaves were drooping on their stems. Somewhere children were squealing. Maybe they were just jumping into the waves created by the ship's wake. But that was far away. All around her the colorful garden was resting, silent and motionless. Lady Klára did not accept this silence, and in the corner of her eye the chestnut leaf kept quivering; slowly she was being overtaken by fear mixed with irritation, and she felt that it was only a matter of seconds before she must act.

"*Ses jambes étaient molles et rouges de froid. Lorette n'avait pas—*" she read, then quickly rose, stepped over to the bent-down branch, and tore off the quivering leaf.

When she sat back down, she looked around with satisfaction. The lonely current of the breeze no longer played with the branch. And the observing eyes seemed to have disappeared too.

"Please make my bed."

"Yes."

Lady Klára began to eat.

"If you do the dishes, we are done, for today."

"I'd like to rearrange the drawer."

This overly humble tone grated on Lady Klára's ears. "What drawer?"

"In the kitchen."

"Oh, yes . . . That can wait till tomorrow. You couldn't get yogurt?"

"No."

"Then starting tomorrow, you'll have to do the shopping in the morning."

"Yes."

"If you want something to read, just pick a book from the shelf."

"Thank you."

Since Lady Klára said nothing more, Jucika began to make the bed in the adjacent room. Although it was growing dark, they did not turn on the lights. Lady Klára ate dutifully, without appetite. In the neighboring house Kalher was yelling loudly, calling his son, and through the windows mosquitoes were swarming into the room. Stopping here and there between the walls, they let out their high-pitched buzzing and from time to time, as if on some command, would take off for Lady Klára's neck and bare arms, whereupon Lady Klára would put down her fork and knife, wait until the mosquitoes settled down, and then slap them hard. The ones with bellies already filled left bloody little splotches behind; Lady Klára wiped off the stains and continued eating. But even the noises, the slapping, the busy activity during the meal could not hold her attention. She was sitting with her back to the other room, and behind her the girl was making her own little noises. A living question mark in her life. She knew that this day had made her confront something in whose labyrinth she had lost her way, and she had no remedy for the situation. Maybe time would help, the getting used to it. She heard whispering under the window.

"Jucika." And again, louder: "Jucika."

She put down her knife and fork and listened. The whispering was repeated. Jucika must have leaned out the window in the other room because Lady Klára heard her whisper back, "Right away . . . Wait a bit!"

Lady Klára stared vacantly in the air. What an idiot I am! she thought, and from that moment on she felt relieved, as if this whispering had clarified for her everything that in retrospect made all her doubts senseless. Well, I am one big idiot, she thought now, quietly happy. Is there anything in the world that bothers this girl? She starts up with the first man she meets . . . If he were a man at least . . . With the first pair of pants . . . And here I am, debating with myself about freedom and all sorts of nonsense . . . If only it were true, if it could be true that we are equal . . . But it's not true . . . It simply is not true. In her joy she almost burst out laughing.

Jucika was standing before her. "May I take this away, comrade?"

She looked up, smiling at the girl. "Just leave it, go ahead, go. I heard them calling you."

Jucika did not smile. "Who said I . . . I won't go. I'll do the dishes first."

Lady Klára rose and firmly pushed the girl out of the room. "And I am telling you to go. Go!"

When she was alone, she bolted the doors and sat in the armchair by the window. Outside, the trees were hidden in the dimness, and the sky was calm and clear. The earth, freed of the great heat, was taking a deep breath. Tomorrow we must water the garden, Lady Klára thought, and felt that everything had been solved.

"Jóóóska!" Mrs. Kalher's voice slashed the dark silence of nature.

Of course Jóska did not respond because he was sitting on the couch in Jucika's room.

Mrs. Kalher yelled again, and from the third or fourth house over received an answer in a female voice as sharp as her own. "What are you yelling for all the time? How can anybody get any rest around here?!"

After a few moments of silence Mrs. Kalher cheerfully let out her voice again. "Jóóóska!"

"Are you deaf, you dumb ox?"

Mrs. Kalher replied immediately. "Your grandma is a dumb ox, you hear? And if you can't keep your trap shut, I'll sit on it for you!"

"You'll sit on the shithouse, you with your huge ass," came the response from three or four houses away, and the dialogue would have continued, but Mr. Kalher appeared on the scene, and it was his deep, restrained voice that was now heard.

"Shut up!"

"Let go of my arm! Watch who you're picking on . . ."

"Shut the hell up and get inside the house, now!"

"Is it my fault that your shitty son   "

"Inside, I said; get while the getting's good."

Suddenly everything was quiet. A door slammed. The third or fourth neighbor must also have heard the couple's verbal battle, but she seemed to have some of her own fury left over because she yelled into the velvety darkness, "The devil take her, her and her kind! Can't I get some rest here anymore, not even that?" Her voice was rising higher and higher. "A body works all day long, working like a dog, and then what? No rest, not even that!"

Either she got bored, or the third or fourth neighbor whisked her into the house too. But the question kept echoing in the air for a long time. The mountains reverberated with it.

Jucika walked into her room. The ceiling was so low that willy-nilly she had to sit down next to Jóska on the couch.

"Good evening, Jucika!"

"Good evening, Jóska!"

"I thought I'd invite you to the dance."

"There is dancing here?"

"Yes. In the Mermaid."

They looked at each other.

"The problem is I can't dance."

"I'll teach you."

"And I'm pretty tired too."

The light went on upstairs, and in the light reflecting from the trees through the tiny windows they could see better in the small room. Jóska was tugging his tie under his Adam's apple.

"You're tired?"

"But I don't mind going over to your house."

"They're in bed already," said Jóska, and pressed his clasped hands between his knees. "Father gets up very early; he's on duty."

"And you?"

"I'm still on holiday . . . for a long time!"

Jucika sighed. She did not really know why. But her breast was full of anxiety, and she felt that with the boy next to her she might be free of it. She would have liked to sigh some more, even deeper, but she thought it would be inappropriate. "Then let's go for a walk," she said.

The boy did not answer. He was pressing his fists between his knees;

his eyes were scanning the floor. He seemed on the verge of saying something. Jucika looked at the boy, his face and neck, his slightly outgrown dark blue suit, the tip of the shirt collar that had slipped over the jacket's lapel, the badly knotted tie. Above their head some strange little noise began, as if Lady Klára were pacing up and down in the apartment. "This is where you sleep?" the boy asked.

"Yes."

They were quiet again, and then the boy squeezed another question out of himself. "And you won't be afraid to be alone?"

"What would I be afraid of?"

As if he had reached his goal, the boy's eyes lit up, and the whispered words began to flow from his lips. "Because if you're afraid, Jucika, just tell me, I can lie down here in front of the doorstep and spend the whole night . . . Because I'd protect you from everything!"

"Protect me?" Jucika laughed.

"You don't believe me?"

"I do."

They were getting too close to each other, and they both felt it; simultaneously they turned their heads away. Up in the apartment the movement had turned into definable noises. Jucika looked up at the ceiling and suddenly felt very tired. She adjusted the skirt over her knees and glanced at Jóska. "It's late."

"No, it's not!" said the boy, alarmed. "It's not even nine o'clock. It just gets dark early. And will you come dancing with me tomorrow?"

"I will."

"And you're not angry with me?"

"Why would I be?"

"Because of the thing this morning . . . That situation . . . that was still in high school. That I beat up Söregi because he was cussing my mother. And that's the one thing that makes me real mad, that's for sure." Jóska put his elbows on his knees and leaned very close to Jucika; it was obvious he did not feel like leaving; he wanted to talk. "Söregi was the chemistry teacher, and they took him to the hospital with a messed-up kidney, which I didn't want, but he shouldn't have cursed my mother; the whole thing turned into a holy mess."

"A teacher? You beat up a teacher?"

"I did."

"I beat up a girl once in the UWY. Back in Mágocs."

"Where is that?"

"You don't know?"

"No."

"That's where I'm from, Mágocs."

"And——" The boy wanted to ask something else but stifled the words. Above their heads the noises were becoming uniform frictions.

"What is she doing?"

"Who?"

"The old woman."

Jucika shrugged her shoulders and stood up. Jóska stood up too. They stood facing each other, but they could not straighten their heads in the low-ceilinged space.

"And haven't you got married yet?"

"No, I haven't."

"And don't you have a fiancé?"

"I don't."

Jucika smiled in the dark. It was uncomfortable to stand like that, but the boy was not moving. "So then, you'll be sleeping here in front of the doorstep?" Jucika asked tauntingly.

"You don't believe I'd do it? Like this, in my suit. Don't believe me?"

"I do. You're a very good boy, Jóska."

"Really?"

"Yes, I can see that."

Jóska, in the dark, stretched out his arm, found Jucika's hand, bent down, kissed it, and jumped out the door. Jucika looked after him but could not see him; he vanished among the dark trees, she only heard the pebbles crunch under his steps. And then the garden gate slammed shut loudly.

It was quiet, but Lady Klára upstairs kept walking back and forth. Jucika sighed, closed and locked the wooden door, and made her bed. She hung her clothes in the closet and lay down. She was staring at the ceiling and listening to the little noises when there was a knock on the door.

"Who is it?" she whispered, frightened.

"It's me . . . Are you in bed?"

"Yes."

"Just want to ask if you're afraid?"

"I'm not."

"You sure?"

Jucika sat up, lowered her legs off the couch. "Sure."

The boy kept quiet for a long time.

"Just want to ask if for sure you come dancing with me tomorrow?"

"For sure," the girl whispered.

"Should I look through the window?"

"Oh, no, don't!"

"Then I'll tell you something tomorrow. All right?"

"All right."

Jucika, without knowing why, felt for her shoes with her feet and slipped into them. Pressing the cover to her chest, she edged closer to the door and waited. She waited to see if the boy would look through the window. But the boy beyond the door was quiet and motionless. They stayed like this for minutes, waiting for each other's words. And then Jucika heard even, receding steps.

Lady Klára was free of her moral burden and in her happiness could not stay still. She filled the bucket with water to wash the floor, then changed her mind and left it in the middle of the kitchen and went into her study. First things first. She emptied the ashtrays. Then she also washed the ashtrays. She was still not satisfied. Around the small table where she had had her supper, there were crumbs on the floor and even on the (Persian) rug. First of all, she made her bed, and then, wetting a small hand broom, she swept up the crumbs into the dustpan. But she noticed that the rubbish bin was full. She unbolted the door, turned the key in the lock, and took the bin into the garden. Carefully feeling each step with her feet, she made her way down the stairs. When she passed the bent-down branches of the chestnut tree, she was greeted by the moonlit night. A figure was standing in front of Jucika's door. Lady Klára stiffened. The figure was not moving. The bin was shaking in her hand. She would be robbed; she had left the door open behind her. This was her first thought, as if it were more important than her life.

"Just want to ask if for sure you come dancing with me tomorrow?"

Lady Klára could not make out the girl's reply, maybe because the whole thing was so unexpected. She would have probably thought it more natural if the figure had moved, jumped on her, and knocked her out.

"Should I look through the window?"

Now she recognized the voice, and she smiled. She took a step back, up on the stairs, and the chestnut tree again concealed the moon and the dark figure of the boy. You little scoundrel, thought Lady Klára, and I even gave you money for ice cream!

"Then I'll tell you something tomorrow. All right?"

Lady Klára was all ears. She was so curious to hear the response that she stepped down again, putting the chestnut tree's foliage behind her again. But she did not hear the answer, and the boy said nothing more either, just kept standing motionless by the door. And Lady Klára was seized by an unrestrained ticklish feeling because she would have liked to see the wooden door open and then close; standing there on the steps with the rubbish bin in her hand, with her white hair, she seemed like a teenage girl whose eyes widen and ears grow long as she sets out to discover her parents' love life. But no matter how eagerly she listened nothing happened. The figure in front of the door waited quietly, then left. And Lady Klára came to her senses. She sighed. Very nicely and properly. As someone who had been deprived of something, which made her a little sad but not angry. She waited a little, and then she too headed for the gate. She opened it carefully; maybe the boy was still standing there; her last hope was to surprise him there, but the street was empty. She put the bin outside; taking long deep breaths in the fresh air and delighting in the contours of trees and shrubs in the cold moonlight, she returned to the house. She walked from room to room, turning on lights and stopping from time to time. In a strange apartment, among indifferent objects, she was alone. But she remembered the bucket. She had left it in the middle of the kitchen. She went into the kitchen. She put an apron over her robe, opened all the windows, set up the vacuum cleaner, then changed her mind, put the bedding back into the commode drawers and dragged into the room all the cleaning equipment, rags, push broom, dustpan, the buffer for polishing, even the floor wax; she lifted the armchairs, the regular chairs, and tables off the rug, put things in order on the shelves; on her writing stand everything was filthy, grimy; she should wash the doors too; she plugged in the vacuum cleaner and feverishly began to free the rugs of dust. She was enjoying this furious yet cheerful work, the large—and mostly senseless—movements, and did not hear someone knocking on the hallway door. The knocking grew louder.

She carefully placed the cleaning head on the rug and turned off the machine. Suddenly her good mood was gone; silence ruled in the disorderly apartment. The knocking was repeated. Lady Klára started with careful steps toward the hallway. Luckily the glass-paned door was open; she did not have to make any noise.

"Who is it?" she asked, fearful.

"It's me, Auntie Klára, please open up."

Lady Klára still did not dare go close to the door.

"Is that you?"

"Yes."

She felt a fleeting irritation, but her thoughtful calm returned, and she pulled the bolt aside, unhooked the chain, and turned the key.

Jucika, tousled and blinking, was standing in the door, pressing her quilt, sheet, and pillow awkwardly against her body.

"You gave me a scare." Lady Klára laughed. In that first moment she did not understand why Jucika was holding on to her bedding.

"Auntie Klára, somebody is in the garden."

"In the garden?"

The girl stepped into the hallway and as if trying to get away from someone cast a fearful glance back into the darkness.

"What are you talking about? It was me, taking out the rubbish."

Jucika looked suspiciously into Lady Klára's shiftily blinking eyes and in her confusion let her bedding slide into a cane-bottomed armchair. "If she was," she thought, "maybe Jóska . . ."

"It was me you must have heard," said Lady Klára, still smiling, and leaving the girl with her doubts, she started up the vacuum cleaner again.

Jucika leaned against the glass-paned door and watched the old woman's fluttering white hair.

"I would have done the cleaning."

Lady Klára kicked aside a chair, making it spin on the slippery floor; the smile did not disappear from her face, and she did not even look at the girl.

"Why haven't you gone to sleep?" Jucika asked in a loud voice.

"I wasn't sleepy."

"Oh."

Lady Klára worked the booming cleaner.

"I would have done it in the morning."

"Everything is so filthy, and I mean, really filthy."

"Do you need help?"

"Oh, no, go ahead, go to bed."

And they looked at each other again. Jucika turned away, embarrassed. Lady Klára smartly rolled up the rug, slapped the huge cylinder under her arm, and heaved it out into the hallway.

"This is too hard for Auntie Klára."

"I've been doing it forever."

There was no edge to the sentence, but Jucika still looked with suspicion and distrust at the uncertain features of the old woman's time-ravaged face. Lady Klára paid no attention to her. Maybe it was these femininely simple movements that returned her confidence; Jucika pushed herself away from the door, without a word dragged the vacuum cleaner into the other room, and, as furiously as she had seen Lady Klára do it, attacked the other rug. They continued their dialogue over the noise and the changing distance between them.

"Aren't you sleepy?"

"Not at all. You know, in the artist's house life always began around this time. During the day he and his wife were like sleepy flies, at night like lizards. The comings and goings there, and you have no idea what kinds of things happened."

"What are you saying?"

"I said, the kinds of things that happened there—"

"What kinds of things?"

"One time— Should I vacuum the couch too?"

"Yes."

"I always went to sleep by twelve o'clock. At two in the morning the artist's wife woke me up that I should go in right away, there was some kind of trouble."

Lady Klára swept the dirt toward the door, the better to hear the story.

"I grab my clothes, go downstairs to the dayroom, but by then it was kind of strange because the artist's wife, when I left my room, she sneaked in with Kálmán behind her."

"Who is Kálmán?"

"Wait!"

Lady Klára leaned the broom against the doorpost and put her hands on her hips.

Jucika continued while bending over the vacuum cleaner. "So I'm running into the whatchamacallit, because nobody was supposed to call it the salon, only the dayroom, but it was night then . . . and just imagine, the way I was, my hair a mess, because when there's trouble, you just run . . . and I stop in the dayroom. Lots of people. About twenty of them. And I just look and look, wondering what's wrong . . . They looked at me and started to laugh. 'I don't know what you're laughing at,' I said to them, but that made them laugh even harder."

Lady Klára burst into laughter herself. "I can imagine how you must have looked to them."

"That's nothing. I had only one shoe on. My right shoe on my left foot, and my housedress was on inside out."

Lady Klára was supporting her belly with her outstretched palms; her whole body was shaking with laughter.

"That's nothing," said Jucika, straightening up, her eyes sparkling with joy. "Because I'm running back to my room to tell the artist's wife that they shouldn't do things like that to me, and those people are running after me, and they are screaming and yelling, and I am trying to get away, rushing to my room. I push down the door handle, closed."

Lady Klára wiped the tears from her eyes. "Closed."

"That's right. And it was quiet, like now, in the kitchen, because the whole company was there, watching why the door was locked. And one of them was rotten enough to ask, 'Where's Zita? And where did Kálmán disappear to?' "

Lady Klára advanced all the way to the couch, and Jucika pulled the vacuum cleaner tube close.

"So they locked themselves in?"

"They did."

"And would not come out?"

"They came out at dawn."

"And what did the artist have to say to all this?"

"What could he say? He was so old I had to put him in the tub. And Zita was twenty-eight. But that's nothing."

Lady Klára first giggled, then laughed and lowered herself to the edge of the couch. "That's nothing?"

"You can't imagine what kind of people are going around in this world. Terrible. And I got sick, I mean, really sick of the whole thing. Believe me." Jucika became pensive; Lady Klára followed the girl's gaze, gluing her own gaze to the girl's as it swept the walls, the floor, and the ceiling. "Believe me, the kinds of things, and I mean, such weird things . . . that happened. I don't know. One time, for example, I was cleaning and the artist was dozing in his chair—"

"Unplug it."

Without losing the thread of her memories, Jucika unplugged the vacuum cleaner and continued quietly. "—because at night, I don't even know what was happening then, because there was always something about Zita, and the artist looks up and says . . . He had such big, sad eyes that sometimes I felt very sorry for him; he disgusted me only when I had to put him in the tub . . . He calls me over. 'Jutka, come over here.' I go to him. 'Sit here, on the armrest.' I sat there. 'Yes, sir.' He put his arms around my waist and pulled me down to his lap. 'Oh,' I said, 'but I'd be heavy like this for you,' because I wanted to avoid things with a joke . . . He says, 'Don't be afraid of me, Jutka.' All right, I thought, if that makes him feel good, all right, I don't mind, it's all the same to me, because I feel sorry for him. And then, while we keep sitting like this, he says—"

Jucika looked at Lady Klára, and the excitement made the corner of her mouth tremble. In the momentary silence she too lowered herself to the couch. Lady Klára's curious gaze followed her there, and they looked at each other.

"Suddenly he says, 'Do you know, Jutka, what the best thing is that's left for me in this world?' 'I don't know, sir.' 'Well, Jutka, the only thing that's still good for me is when I can take a big shit.' " And as Jucika pronounced the last word, she threw her head back and shook with silent laughter.

Lady Klára grabbed her because she saw that this silent shaking was not laughter but something strange, and Jucika's neck was craned backward; Lady Klára could not see her face, saw only that the whole thing was very peculiar, and with both her hands she reached out and grasped Jucika's head, but Jucika's whole body was straining backward. "Come now, calm down, what's with you?" Lady Klára said, and the girl's head obeyed the voice and the touch of the two palms, and Lady Klára saw that tears were streaming from Jucika's eyes, but she had no chance to say anything because Jucika sprang up and with a single movement wiped the tears from her eyes; as she drew her hand past her face, another face appeared, smiling again. "Don't get scared. It's nothing, already gone."

"Jucika—"

"Nothing, it's nothing. Listen, I'll tell you that other—" She got stuck.

"We'll finish up tomorrow," said Lady Klára later, quietly.

She stood, and the two of them pushed the furniture back to their former positions—more or less.

"Have you had any supper?" Lady Klára asked.

"I'm so mad at myself," Jucika said.

"Aren't you hungry?"

"I shouldn't have told you this."

"All right. Will you make my bed again, and in the meantime, I'll make you something to eat. You like bacon and eggs?"

"Yes, Auntie Klára—"

But Lady Klára did not let the girl finish the sentence; she left for the kitchen, sliced some bacon and some bread, and all the while kept repeating to herself, Life is rotten. Life is so very rotten. It's a rotten life. And she flooded the curling slices of bacon in the pan with eggs; in an almost rough tone she called out, "Come on, what's holding you up?"

Jucika yelled back. "Can I turn on the radio, Auntie Klára?"

"Turn it on."

Jucika turned on the radio and made her appearance in the kitchen. "They usually have dance music around this time."

"Really? I hardly ever listen to it."

The radio warmed up slowly, and the rooms filled with music. They were eating. As Lady Klára watched the girl's bony face and her jutting chin as she gently chewed her food, something occurred to her. "Do you know how to dance, Jucika?"

"I do. And I'm so glad you don't call me Jutka."

"And do you like dancing?" asked Lady Klára with a cunning smile.

"I do," answered the girl with a meek look.

"In the Mermaid there is dancing every night. I could take you there once if you want me to," Lady Klára said in an innocent tone. "Maybe even tomorrow, if you feel like it."

Jucika's brow darkened. Lady Klára retreated immediately

"Well, how do you like the omelet I made?"

"Delicious."

"Would you like some more?"

"Yes."

Jucika sent another distrustful glance toward Lady Klára but saw no sign to indicate that the old woman had overheard her conversation with the boy.

"I don't remember when I had such a tasty meal. You know, in the Viczmándy house they cooked really good, but it wasn't for me. All that bloody meat, all the time . . ."

"Mrs. Viczmándy was raised in Paris—"

"Really?"

"She didn't talk about it? She is very proud of it. By nuns."

"Nuns? May I say something?"

"Go ahead."

"There is a nun in Mágocs who was defrocked, as they say, when the convents were closed. Ever since then all she does is take off her 'frock.' "

They laughed. The radio was blaring.

"Making up for lost time," said Lady Klára.

Jucika brought her hand before her mouth. And then they heard the sharp voice of the neighbor three or four houses away yelling something. Jucika left the table and leaned out the window.

"Why are you blasting with the radio?" screamed the woman three or four houses away.

"What's she saying?"

"Why are we blasting with the radio?"

Lady Klára leaned out the window, signaling with her hand that everything was all right.

"Can't you heeear?"

"Should I answer her?"

"Go ahead."

Jucika stuck her head forward and screamed back, "Can't hear you! Speak a little louder!"

They collapsed with laughter on their chairs and then quickly leaned out the window again to hear the response.

"A body works all day long, working like a dog, and then what? No rest, not even that!" came the response, and then there was silence. The question echoed in the air for a long time.

"Well, go turn it off," Lady Klára said, still laughing, and followed the girl, still laughing. "Even if there is not a sound in the whole neighborhood, she has to yell. She does it every evening."

"Every evening?" Jucika asked as she turned off the radio.

"Sometimes at the crack of dawn."

"At dawn too?"

Now the smile left Lady Klára's face. "Well, shall we go to bed? It's getting late, though I'm not sleepy."

Jucika hugged the radio with both arms and lowered her head. She was silent for a long time. "Auntie Klára, can I ask something of you?"

Lady Klára knitted her brow, ready for a request.

"And it's only for tonight . . ."

"What?"

"Could I sleep here? I was so afraid down there. And I'm afraid to go back down."

"But . . . where? You don't mean to sleep with me, do you?"

"I can sleep over there, on that—"

Lady Klára spread out the fingers of one hand and with the other bent the fingers one at a time, in turn. She was immersed in this little activity. Should the girl sleep on the sofa? Maybe in the other room?

"Well, all right, if it isn't uncomfortable," she said hesitantly.

She moved into my own apartment, Lady Klára was thinking after they turned out the light. Jucika was tossing on the couch, and she had forgotten to close the door between the rooms. In fact nothing separated them, and if this fact impressed Jucika, it downright bothered Lady Klára. After all, Jucika was a stranger. Lady Klára did not have to listen to a stranger's tossing on the couch. But she would neither ask Jucika to close the door nor get up herself to close it. She felt that such a request, in words or in movement, would spoil their relationship, which was being restored very nicely. She began to make evasive little movements. She adjusted her pillows, straightened her sheet, and then closed her eyes and tried hard to think of something else, something that would put her to sleep, but this something simply refused to come to her. Scraps, images, and thoughts hovered before her in the dark, and though the day had exhausted her physically and mentally, sleep would bring no relief. She opened her eyes and decided to take an inventory of the furniture. The moon was shining through the window, and its light seemed chilling to her, as if she were sitting at the bottom of a dark well from which there was no escape. She had felt the tormenting effect of this light on another occasion when it was more powerful and she had to pull a pillow over her head or turn on all the lights to make the contours of objects friendly again. Now she would have wanted Jucika to stir, but Jucika did not.

Later, however, as if wandering about in another, warmer world, Jucika quietly addressed Lady Klára from the other room. "Auntie Klára never had any children?"

Lady Klára clutched at the question and would have liked to give a quick, long answer, but the distance she had created kept her from doing so.

"Two sons," she said after a long while.

"And they never visit?"

"One of my sons is dead. My other son defected." It was quiet again, and Lady Klára propped herself up on her elbow, but the moonlight was no longer bothering her. "He defected together with the Romsauers' boy. Maybe you know the Romsauers; they often go to the Viczmándys'.."

"Yes."

They fell silent again.

"Then you are all alone."

"Well, yes."

"And the Romsauers are big Communists."

This sentence sounded strange and irritating. "What do you mean by that?"

Jucika thought about what she meant by that. The sound of a passing ship came from the river. "Ships go at this time of the night?"

"It's the produce steamer."

Jucika would have liked to ask what a produce steamer was, but she suddenly remembered what she had meant before. "We had a party secretary in Mágocs. He was appointed right away because when the people's republic was declared at our place too, the police beat him up so bad that one of his legs didn't heal good, and when the Communist regime came, people said that who else could be the party secretary if not lame Uncle Gergő. He had three sons. The oldest set up the farmers' cooperative, that was Dezső, and when he stole enough on the job, they trained the middle son to take over, and the youngest became a priest. Who would have thought?"

Jucika was speaking as calmly and nicely as if she were telling a fairy tale, and Lady Klára began to feel drowsy.

"Uncle Gergő, when they dismissed him because of his youngest son, he went almost crazy, and he couldn't stay because when they announced the revolution, he stood at the head of it, but the trouble was the people wanted to hang his son Dezső, but he sent Dezső a message, but the people found out and then they got mad at him, and in the middle of the night they chased him out of his house, and if his youngest son, the priest, didn't come after him, they would have run him through with pitchforks." Jucika stopped.

"Are you religious?"

"I don't believe in God, but sometimes I try to imagine how the whole thing works."

They both thought about that now while staring into the night. Later Lady Klára said, "I feel a draft. I'll go close the door," and she made a move.

"Leave it, Aunt Klára, I'll do it."

Lady Klára relaxed and fell asleep.

Jucika was sleeping with her head on the elevated part of the Biedermeier sofa. And opposite the loudly wheezing girl a face appeared in the open window, blocking out the moon.

The head rose higher, and two hard elbows thumped on the windowsill, so the naked shoulders appeared too, the body rose even higher and, having lost contact with the ground, dangled there. From the distance, with short interruptions, music was heard; maybe the Mermaid was still open. Skin grazed against the rough wall of the house, and then, like a cat, he jumped into the room, lost his balance, and went sprawling on the thick (Persian) rug. He stayed there for a long time, listening; the moon shone on his face while he blinked, looking about him like a thief, but nothing stirred. Jucika wheezed evenly as she slept, and there was no noise coming from the adjacent room.

Without rising, he crawled toward the sofa. The floor creaked, he froze and then carefully looked around again; Jucika's face was pale like a dead woman's and seemed very far away from him. He did not dare continue, but when his arm grew tired, he made another move; the floor creaked again, echoing through the entire room. Jucika whimpered; strange sounds came from the sofa's springs. Jucika turned away, showing him her back; the boy used the moment to move quickly away from the creaky spot. When he reached the sofa, as if having completed a job successfully, he lay on his back, put his clasped hands under his head, and, staring into the grinning face of the moon, let out a deep sigh. Somewhere in the depths of the room's darkness, the old alarm clock began to rattle as though spurred into activity by an invisible force; it struck once and then slowly, stretching out the seconds, began to tick. Jóska turned only his eyes in the sound's direction. The clock was growing wild, coughing and rattling as it swallowed the seconds, violating its own laws and then, as could be expected, ran out of steam, running after time with ever-increasing difficulty until, with an apathetic calm resigning itself to its fate, it stopped and, as if it had never existed, blended into the dark silence. The boy waited awhile longer and then, as if doing a stomach exercise, sat up. His head was on a level with Jucika's back. Closing and opening wide his eyes, he scrutinized her naked back—only from the waist down was she covered—and while doing it, he also nervously scratched his toes. A few minutes went by like this, though they seemed like hours to him, and then his hand began to move toward her hipbone, but it got only as far as the sheet hanging from her body; he quickly grasped and gathered the edge of the sheet into his fist, slid closer to her, and in that instant the sofa's springs began to creak again as with a full turn, Jucika flipped herself onto her stomach. The boy was very close to her, his eyes ran all over her body under the cover, felt her breath on his mouth, her voice in his ears, and with a single outstretched finger he wanted to touch the girl's naked arm, but the alarm clock ticked again . . . A few millimeters from the warm skin the finger remained suspended in the air, and the boy's mouth opened as if to curse. He lowered his hand and tried the same movement with the other hand. And now nothing disturbed him; now he felt the girl's breath on his finger, but Jucika did not stir. He bent close to her, sliding his hand along the sheet. He fairly glued his mouth to the girl's ear. What left his throat was more like hot air than a sound. "Jucika."

No response. His patience was running out, and he would have liked to take the small ear into his mouth, and the novelty of this idea took hold of him so powerfully that he had to do something to counter it, not to cause any trouble; he was sure that giving in to his urge would cause trouble. He grasped the edge of the sheet and pulled at it. The girl did not move. Now his breath stopped. He took the sheet into his fist and pulled again, this time as if he meant to yank the girl to the floor. Jucika sprang up and with wide eyes stared out into the garden.

"Jucika," whispered the boy, the sheet still in his fist.

"Jóska! How did you get in here?" the girl said aloud, and as the sentence left her throat and reverberated among the furniture filling the room, it woke her up; she drew her hand in front of her mouth.

The boy was coiled up by the sofa, his face out of sight; he was a dark ball; only on the back of his neck, as though on the edge of a knife, was there a glimmer of hard light. Biting her nails, Jucika leaned close to him and whispered her question again, "How did you get in here, Jóska?"

The boy looked up at her, the moon obliterating his pimples, his entire face writhing between fear and will. His mouth opened, then closed again, as if in the grip of some illness, and then pushing the sound ahead of him, he kept repeating Jucika's name, and his head dropped to his chest.

Jucika pressed the cover to herself and withdrew to the corner of the sofa.

"Jucika . . ."

"What do you want from me?" the girl asked, almost crying.

The boy's arms reached out toward the girl, and the girl, as though she still had a chance to escape, retreated farther from him.

"What do you want? What do you want?" she whispered, almost crazed, and when the boy's arm reached her, she leaned forward, took aim at the face, and slapped him. The sound of the slap filled the room and probably spilled into the other room too. Jóska clamped his hand on his ears and curled up again. Jucika went on the attack, grasping the boy's arm. "You want me to . . . call for help? Right this minute? What . . . d'you want?" She tipped up his head and again saw his face writhing between fear and uncontrollable will.

"Jucika—"

Jucika bit her lips and slid back into the corner.

"Jucika, Jucika."

"What—"

"Jucika, all I want to say is . . . all I . . . Jucika . . . Jucika . . ."

The girl moved.

"Jucika . . . Jucika . . . I just . . . It's not true, the whole thing is—"

She leaned closer because she thought she misunderstood what he had said or that she was dreaming.

"Jucika, the whole thing . . . is not true."

"What?"

"Nothing." The boy's mouth, all white now, was trembling. "What I said to you." He was stuttering.

"I don't know," the girl whispered, her whole body turning in curved amazement.

"Don't you remember what I told you? All that . . . is not true."

In Jucika's breast the cramp of fear suddenly turned to tenderness. Her eyes closed. And that seemed to give the boy some encouragement.

"Jucika, it's not true," he said, and took a deep breath. "I am not a policeman." He laid his head on the edge of the sofa. Neither of them said anything. The silence calmed them both.

Jucika raised her lids, and a gentle, painful smile crossed her face; her hand set off toward the boy; her whole body slid farther down on the sofa; with her other hand she touched the boy's face, their breaths united in a quick rhythmic panting, and Jucika felt that the boy's body was filling up with trembling and this trembling crossed over into her body too, and she let her arm slide over his shoulder while she was still sitting with the painful smile on her face, and the boy with a fearful tremor on his face, but all this they no longer saw, and their lips still made no contact; only their rhythmic breathing was united, and the heat was spreading in their faces. Jucika slipped farther down on the (Biedermeier) sofa, her body turning toward the boy and arching outward, and in a fraction of a second they touched each other's parched lips with the tips of their tongues. In their clinking teeth, in the cool depths of the palates a world opened up that protected them, for it enveloped them both. This world existed only because of the two of them, and the girl's slippery lips glided up to the boy's nose, touched his eyelids and hard neck; the cover slipped off, and from under it the heat of a human body invaded the boy's senses, and he remembered that he had forgotten to close the chicken coop. He stood up, but the memory of the chicken coop lasted only a moment. The girl was there, wide open, before him, white, and he was standing above her, his legs rubbery, and Jucika looked up at him, her two arms moving, grasping his waist; she pulled him down on top of her, the springs of the sofa creaked disagreeably, but neither of them thought of the danger inherent in the creaking. Only the beauty of completeness was marred by the creaking. They clung to each other, holding on with arms, thighs, and waists, squeezing each other's backs, and again their lips mingled in hot breaths; they turned over, and now the boy felt her breasts as if for the first time as they lightly pressed against his skin, and they turned over again; Jucika's fingers slithered quickly over the boy's body, coming to rest on the elastic of his pants, the boy's lips closed, his body slackening, and now he rested on the girl with all his weight, but she did not mind, she was kissing him and trying to free him from the only piece of clothing that still separated them, she was furious at this article of clothing, the boy's muscles were overtaken by a soft trembling, and he slid off the sofa.

And the world they had conjured up fell silent. A room. The moon looking in through the window. Dogs barking. And another room next to this one.

They sobered up.

Jucika yanked the cover over her and above the boy's shoulder glanced at the door. She propped herself up on her elbows. There was silence in the adjacent room.

She took hold of the boy's head and looked into his face. Lips pressed hard together, eyes shut tight. "What have you done to me?" the girl whispered.

"Who, me?"

"Oh, you."

They looked at each other, and then the boy closed his eyes again.

"I knew it," she whispered. "I knew it."

"What?"

He looked at the girl with wide, frightened eyes, and Jucika smiled, gently and cheerfully, slid closer to him, hooked her hands into the elastic band of his pants and pulled them off. The boy did not move.

"There, like this," said Jucika, and the boy, without rising, slipped out of the pants that remained on the floor while he, kneeling, pressed the girl's head to his breast and their world came to life again; Jucika's mouth glided over the boy's chest and neck as if calling, alluring him; her body was sliding farther in toward the wall on the creaking Biedermeier sofa, and the boy followed her, and then they did not even know how they wound up next to each other again; their bodies intertwined, simply and with no obstacles.

The boy adroitly leaped onto the windowsill. Jucika, curled up in the corner of the sofa, watched him. But then Jóska did not jump into the garden and instead leaped silently back into the room.

"Didn't I tell you she was loony?"

"Who?"

"The old woman."

Jucika wrapped her body in the cover, and the two of them cautiously sneaked up to the window. Lady Klára was standing outside, motionless, in her nightgown, with her back to them, her arms folded under her breast, staring at the moon.

"I'd have the right . . . yes; I do have the right . . ." She must have said it ten or twenty times. When this expression had surfaced from the depths of her agitated thoughts, she welcomed it, but the expression, like everything else, lost its meaning in the constant repetition. And she could not go on; she could not define what it was she would have a right to do. She kept forcing it, "I'd have the right . . ." And then this too, like all the other thoughts, floated away in the reddish fog of pulsating fury.

Slowly the moon had disappeared, and she was still sitting huddled up on the edge of her bed, staring in front of her at the single pattern of the rug, curling the soles of her feet.

Whenever the fever that had urged her to search for her rights subsided for a little while, she felt only her own gray desolation, and each time it happened—as if to verify her alarm—she ran her hands over her old body.

That is how she was spending the night.

And then, while sitting up, she dozed off.

But at dawn, without sinking into full sleep, she started up. She did not want to forget what they had done to her. She wanted to keep her fury alive, boiling.

But she could not. She was no longer thinking of Jucika or of the boy next door; the slowly vanishing night cleared away her unformulated rights and plans for revenge. She was left only with her fatigued emptiness.

When the disk of the sun emerged from the vapors hovering over the river, she thought of how after having lived here for ten years, she had never seen the sunrise. She luxuriated in the sight for a long time. Like a Turner, she thought, and realized she was cold. She put on her robe and her slippers, blew her nose, and went into the kitchen to make herself tea.

It was still dark in the kitchen; she had to turn on the light. She walked around the bucketful of water and put on water for the tea. She sat down at the table and buried her head in her hands. Her gray hair was tousled, her face worn; there were blue rings under her eyes.

"Oh, well." That was all she said, nothing more, but her whole life was compressed in these words, everything she had felt all along but did not know; everything caught in her brain as intimations that she had been ripping out, chasing away. She had chased them away so she could live. But now she also knew that she would not continue her book. She would burn it, tear it up, or lock it up. So that nobody would ever! Or maybe she'd burn it, after all. ". . . We accepted it with full enthusiasm because we understood that one must subordinate one's desires and interests—" Once this may have meant something, but not anymore. She would be left alone in her house, in her own house. And she could no longer summon Zoltán to be with her, by her side. Because Zoltán was gone forever.

She prepared the tea and then forgot about it; she had to reheat it.

The further she got in her thinking, the more she felt she needed Jucika, though she did not formulate this clearly. She only knew she was no longer angry. No matter what the girl did. But Lady Klára was frightened. Except for her own self, there was nothing else in the world anymore.

She kept stirring the tea until it got cold again; in the meantime, the kitchen had become bright, but she did not turn off the light. She stared at the bucket in the middle of the floor.

Later she heard Jucika leave the room, open the hallway door, and undo the different locks, and these careful little noises made her feel an excitement, a curiosity, and a desire to tell Jucika that she would forgive her. But she did not move.

Perhaps a half hour went by.

Then the hallway door creaked, followed by the other doors, and finally Jucika, with her nice lacquered suitcase in her hand, appeared in the kitchen doorway.

They looked at each other and said nothing.

Then they turned away their heads.

"Well, I'm leaving, anyway," said Jucika.

Silence.

"All right," Lady Klára said.

Jucika turned around and walked out. She closed the hallway door behind her. Lady Klára still did not move, though she would have liked to; to run after her. But she felt this was impossible.

She stirred the tea again. But she did not drink it. She put the cup back on the table and stood up. With quick steps she crossed the hallway and walked out into the garden. Dewdrops were trembling on the leaves, birds were singing, but the summer dawn meant nothing to her anymore. She hastened along the pebble path, her unbuttoned robe fluttering around her, occasionally getting wrapped around her legs. All she wanted was to say goodbye. She opened the gate, almost knocking over the rubbish bin; she looked to the right, then to the left, but only the morning light, breaking through the foliage, was playing on the pavement.

First published as "Klára asszony háza" in *Kulcskereső játék* (Budapest: Szépirodalmi Könyvkiadó, 1969).

Melancholy

Mélabú (May-luh-boo)

Even among our phonetically most beautiful words this is one of the finest.

The first syllable lacks all aggression yet cleaves its way sharply into space, only to be blunted by the second syllable, allowing the tension of sharpness and bluntness, as a unit, to burst like a rainbow-hued bubble on the first consonant of the third syllable and the resulting hollow emptiness to resound long and deep at the end of the word.

It is an emptiness that addresses space in this open-ended word, demanding an enormous space for itself, the largest of all unimaginable spaces.

Insofar as death is the imaginable phenomenon of life, we might say that the phenomena of the world are survivable and comprehensible. For if we say "table," the word will demand a space as large as our table is; "cathedral" a space as large as the most imposing cathedral of our imagination or experience; and "God" no more than what man demands for himself.

However, when the bubble created by the tension of human forces bursts and we wish to name the resulting lack, our word longs to be in an infinity, to be immeasurable by imagination or experience.

This is where every word is headed. No word has ever entered this realm.

Caspar David Friedrich has a painting that allows us, silently, to look into the secret space.

At first glance, it appears to be what it is and nothing else, a moonlit seascape. Nature's space is neither beautiful nor ugly; it is modest and unassuming. In the foreground, stones are strewn on a beach gently sloping toward the water. Yes, there are places like this, we say to ourselves, reinforcing the painter's experience with our experience or imagination. There are no brilliantly cresting waves; at this hour the water is completely dark. Above the horizon the sky is clear, though heavy clouds, swirling into themselves, are tarrying in the firmament; the light emanating from the upper rim of the full moon can barely be made out behind the dense, threateningly rolling masses. We cannot have more light than what we are receiving. The sky is above, the earth below, and between them the sea. The world is spread out before us in its reassuring orderliness; this is how we have come to know it.

A more restfully neutral communication than this simply does not exist. The unassuming quality of the sight is confirmed by the night. The eye cannot see at night, for it is dark.

Yet there is someone here who sees the night.

This peculiar, almost thrilling sensation of being able to see, unassumingly, is what makes the night-watching visitor feel he is not alone. There, where one assumes the shore is under deeper water, glimmers a tiny light, an orange-colored fire, no larger than a dot, that casts dimly reflecting yellow stripes of light between the rocks. Two, maybe three people sit on one rock. Men. One of them reaches into a curling plume of smoke with his stick; another simply crouches next to him and looks away from the water; the third, if there is a third one at all, has his back toward us and is staring into the impenetrable darkness of the open sea. Shipwrecked men. In the light of their fire, we can vaguely make out their small bark tipped on its side, a tiny pennant dangling from its mast, which is tilted at an angle toward the sky. The flag is probably red. There must be no wind; the current of air barely changes the flag's angle, though it seems to be curling slightly upward. This imperceptible movement indicates that the rising air is moving from the sea inland.

We look into the picture, and similarly, the picture sends its breath toward us.

One man watching the fire is blinded by the smoke, the second one watches only the dry land, which of course cannot be seen from there, and the third is dazzled by the emptiness of the water glittering on the horizon; there are those who look but cannot see, and there is someone who sees this. They are similar in their ability to see but different in their modes of seeing.

And we, who are looking at this painting, alternate between looking out of the picture—from the viewpoint of the three shipwrecked men, at the one who sees this night—and, while locked in our own night, looking into the picture at the three men; but to see them really, we must lean very close, though there is someone who does not lean close.

Heinrich von Kleist wrote of Caspar David Friedrich's way of seeing that it is of a person "whose eyelids have been removed." No matter how we look at the painting, we find ourselves blinking, unavoidably; we use the blinking to make distinctions, and therefore we must identify with the people Friedrich painted, leaning in close, or, pulling back from the painting, with the things he painted. Like the unfortunate shipwrecked men, we too can comprehend only in its details what someone else sees, unblinking, as a whole. Watching the three men's fate, we are the audience of our own fate, though there is someone who sees the whole; we cannot be both close and far at the same time, just as the one who is simultaneously both inside and outside can only be the creator of the world. An unblinking vision means that nothing can separate one moment from the next, and a timeless night means that there is no night.

And indeed there is no night in this painting. Everything is too light and colorful for it to be a regular night. It is the illusion of night that we have called night. It turns out that what at first glance the eyes accepted as an unassuming, dark, and almost too familiar moonlit seascape is but an allegory of feelings concerning the night, infinity, emptiness, and lack. The feeling is born not from what there is but from its illusion. What I see is not the painted view, but—as happens when I see a view like this or similar to this, I am absorbed in the viewing of my thoroughly familiar yet inexpressible feeling.

We all are familiar with the fairy tales in which the smallest of the three wandering brothers, or the little girl untouched by life's tribulations, or the little prince cast out of his castle reaches an enormous dark and impenetrable forest. There may have been an entrance to this forest once, but there is good reason to fear that there is no exit. Dry branches crackle; owls screech from the foliage. Will-o'-the-wisps flicker in the hollows of decaying stumps. And the little person wandering about in this blind night thinks it is a splendid brilliance when discovering a faint light among the trees.

In the ominous darkness, light calls everyone; from the ominous light, everyone repairs to the calming darkness.

Maybe that is where the iron-nosed witch is concocting her miasmal poisons in the light of her flickering lantern, maybe this is the den of an evil spirit, and it is also possible that among smoky candles, and with their hands bloody up to the elbows, robbers are counting their gold thalers; still, we must approach. We are shelter seekers.

Alone or with a partner, we stand in the dark night while a lit-up train races by, taking its light with it, and the clatter of the wheels slowly vanishes. If only we were hurtling toward a destination where we might safely arrive and not standing here, motionless and mesmerized. If only, in the small-print maze of the real estate classified section, we could find an apartment that has only advantages and no disadvantages. Or think of being in the totally unfamiliar street of a foreign city, thickly covered with snow, and suddenly a lit-up window forces you to halt; the thin curtains are half drawn, and inside, in the warmth, in the soft light of a shaded lamp, someone is sitting in a room furnished in exquisite taste; nowhere else could I imagine my life to be more perfect.

The wish is great, the desire is strong, and the light of hope is small and flickers always in the distance.

A person who cannot but surrender unconditionally to this roaming-in-the-dark-and-longing-for-light feeling we usually call a melancholic person, and we call this condition melancholy.

The color of this mental state is black; its season is autumn; its hours are nocturnal, its climate northern. There are many words for melancholy—"weltschmerz," "gloominess," "melancholia"—and it has many definitions: morbidly despondent, abnormally dispirited, a persistent mood of dejection, loss of stamina, feelings of lack, emptiness, apathy. We usually refer to it with the modern word "depression," which, in geography, refers to the part of dry land that is below sea level; in astronomy, to negative height that is the height of a star below the horizon; and in meteorology, to an area of low barometric pressure.

There can be no doubt that in Friedrich's painting we are at the North Sea, the air is coming in from the North Pole, and we are looking at a territory of low pressure with the air current moving upward. Probably after a storm. Both above and below, the wind has stopped raging. The elements have measured themselves against one another, but the land has remained land, the water water, and the sky sky. And now they each may subside, for they have found the golden mean necessary for keeping their independence. The fire is burning.

And if there had been no storm, after all, then the tide is now low. The three men's vessel hit bottom on a shoal and the low tide siphoned the water from under them; there are no signs of damage to the bark. And so it is also possible that the man spying the dark horizon is in fact waiting for the high tide.

Melancholy is remembrance. If there was a storm, there will be one again. If there was a low tide, there will be a high tide. A melancholic person does not keep an eye on what is happening now but waits for what is not there now. With his mind he clings to the predictable, though remembrance of the unpredictable has already sprung a leak in the confidence he had in his common sense; he fears what is not, therefore is anxious about what he is waiting for. He knows that what does not exist now might come to exist and would squeeze out what after all does exist or is happening now. Yet what there is now is uncertain, for it may turn into anything, but it is more certain than what it might turn into, for one realized possibility is more certain than countless unrealized possibilities. What there is, is definitely life, and one may be deprived of it by what is yet to come; only what is yet to come hides the death of the now. That may not be a problem, according to my feelings, because it would also mean the dissolution of my torments, but my mind would consider this as no problem only if I knew what would follow the torments of the mutable certainties in my permanent uncertainty, what sort of possibility extinguishes both the uncertainties of the mind and the certainties of feelings. If this is unknown to me, everything I can count on as either certainty or uncertainty loses its value. Neither waiting nor not waiting makes any sense. This is how the melancholic person winds up on the outside of what he is inside. This is how what could be useful becomes useless.

What for the viewer of the painting is the flickering little fire of hope, for the ones in the painting is the practical precondition of survival. And since no man can be both viewer of and participant in the same picture, the fire means light in the one case and warmth in the other. Whoever enters the warm room of his desires must look out and see the darkness where earlier he felt cold; gratifying one's desire both causes pleasure and spurs one on to further pleasure, for we never attain what we pursue, or for the same effort, we may be thrust into hopelessness. All by ourselves we can never light the fire of our hope; we are allowed to light a fire only to warm our numb limbs; that is how our means turns into a goal for others, and the means of others becomes hope for us. Either there is or there isn't hope. It is impossible to know where death is; its purview is unimaginable. But in the space between these seemingly extreme possibilities, human thinking ceases.

We are looking at a painting, and we cannot even know how these men lit a fire on the rock protruding from the water. In such a small bark there would have been no room to store enough fuel to keep such a calmly flaring fire going. Nor is it likely that they collected twigs and branches, for if they had decided to cross the shallow water, why did they not lay a fire on land? Neither proposition seems to be true. If the reason they did not light the fire onshore is that they waited for the high tide, who brought them the firewood? They do not sit as if they had any intention of making a move. Or rather, one of them reaches into the smoke with his stick, but why reach into a fire if not from absentmindedness? With a stick one can poke at embers, but if it is a spit, no one in his right mind would hold it to toast bread or meat in the smoke. These are very simple questions. Or maybe the men were hurled against the rock by the storm, only we cannot see the damage, and they are burning the bark's damaged staves and ribs. But then it would make sense to leave the crashed bark to its fate and seek shelter onshore rather than sit in the water and feed a fire that the first wave can put out. Although we see them and scan the night, regarding these men's fate we are as blind as they are.

If unblinking seeing means that there is separation from one second to the next, the unblinking seer can be neither inspired nor tormented by a sense of fate; this is all he knows.

As opposed to this, a melancholic person, no matter where he starts, will end up exactly where he started: in the tormenting darkness of his fate. He looks into the darkness and is not surprised that he sees nothing. He cannot explain the fate of others by means of his own, nor, seeing of the fate of others, can he explain his own, because his explanation lacks this unblinking seeing. Realization of this lack turns into premonition of death. But it is precisely the sensing of things that demonstrates that a sensation can never be identical to the thing it refers to or to the thing from which it originates. If I say of something that it is hard, cold, and sharp, I may be referring to a stone, but I can feel hardness, coldness, and sharpness about a piece of iron too.

Sensation is the only certainty that thinking about things and about the relationship among things can have a grasp on; yet in relation to the whole about which the thinking is concerned, thinking itself remains uncertain. Premonition is even more uncertain. Premonition is a remembrance of old sensations directed at something that may come to pass as a possible sensation, in case the future is similar to the past and my senses make no mistakes about that past. Thus a premonition of death, fear of death, or longing for death not only fails to carry one closer to the actual sensation of death but is one of the strongest feelings one can have about life. It is not the cessation of what I sense to be life but its reinforcement.

When observing an ant carrying a blade of grass, one has a weaker feeling of the situation than one does when one is carrying a beam oneself, when one has no image at all of the picture of the world because it is blotted out by feeling the beam's weight. Perhaps in thinking about death, one tries to define the weight of something that has no measurable expressible unit of weight, volume, or time. Can we form a picture of something that has no unit of measurement? Can we imagine something of which at the same time we cannot form a picture?

Whenever we are faced with this, we still have words, and then we usually speak of absurdities. Or if the magnitude of absurdity is greater than our picture-forming ability, we talk of nothing, though the words turn it into something. Ironically, it is exactly the thinking about something that I should obliterate in myself so as to become the kind of nothing—fateless, ignorant of past and future, uncharted by known geographic zones, unblinkingly seeing—that, tormented by defective knowledge and unreliable sensations, I do not wish to become.

This is how the melancholic person reaches the thought of suicide.

Before relating what I think about the melancholy I've been hoping to approach, I should like to refer to two works from which I have gained much information and even more knowledge. One is a book, the other a painting.

László Foldényi wrote a book, *Melancholy*, in which, surveying the subject as one of cultural history, he comes to the following conclusion.* Depending on a given historical period's notions about the individual's relationship to the universe, melancholy, as a condition as well as a sensation, has been variously considered as being a form of being possessed by the devil; as the mark of being one of a chosen few; as a sign of lunacy; or as a way of experiencing life that might affect anyone. At different times it has been thought to be an incurable or a curable illness or at least one that should be treated. How can all the above be lumped together? Földényi, who may himself be a practicing melancholic, makes great mental efforts not to negate the claims of one period of our cultural history as against those of another; rather, with contradictory though interrelated truths he surrounds the dead space where, in a mentally sound condition, we cannot hope for an answer, though we could have never asked the question without that hope. When one reads this book, the image arises of being in a dead space but besieged by a desire to know. because regarding the different cultural tools and methods of analysis, the author is in no hurry to make judgments. He does not consider the science of alchemy inferior to religious ecstasy, does not place neurological explanations above those of astrology or see medical recommendations for healing as more important than poetry's call for help or philosophy's fine pronouncements. To draw a parallel, his book provides a realization similar to the one that modern astronomy reaches about black holes.

Whoever reads this book will feel more precisely what melancholy is but will understand it less. This is natural, since the most characteristic trait of melancholy is the sensation of a void of knowledge or an awareness of a void of sensation. There is awareness in conformity with sensation and likewise sensation in conformity with awareness. But since sensation and awareness are two different things, we must admit that we may have feelings about which we are unaware and awareness independent of feeling. It is possible, then, to think in conformity with feelings and to feel in conformity with awareness, but awareness and feeling cannot be each other's lighthouse. One may have an image of the other but not words, and if it has words, it cannot form an image of it.

---

*Melankólia (Budapest: Magvető, 1984).

The painting I should like to refer to is one by the great romantic Georg Friedrich Kersting depicting the great melancholic Caspar David Friedrich working in his atelier. The studio is small; the cell of a monk in the church's strictest order could not be more clean or stark. This should not mean of course that the sight is cheerless. There are three objects in the room: a table, a chair, and an easel. It is not by chance that we usually consider a triple association holy. The three objects are placed at convenient distances from one another, as required by the painter's work. The rest of the space is empty. In the wall on the left is a button-operated door; the bare floor is striped lengthwise by gaps between the wooden slats; the blankness of the ceiling is emphasized by light reflected from the window.

We should have no explanation for this reflected light if we were unaware of the sepia drawings in which Friedrich himself twice recorded the windows of his studio near Dresden shortly after he moved in. In one, he put the window on the right; in the other, the window is on the left. In both pictures the windows are wide open, giving on to a broad, lazily rolling river and the poplar-lined shore on the far side. Under the window on the right, a bark is tied up; under the one on the left, rowboats and tugs are floating on the gentle water under a sparsely clouded summer sky.

Now we can understand Kersting's painting. Friedrich's atelier is made visible not by direct light but by reflected light bouncing off the surface of the Elbe. During the six years after his arrival, Friedrich, dissatisfied with direct light sources, completely changed the light conditions of the place. He had the right window walled up, of the left window only a square, divided by a cross, was retained; the lower third of the window was boarded up. This is how he managed to filter out the reflected light from all direct light and to turn a formerly cheerful, evenly bright room into an almost dark box receiving from above only a reflected light coming from below.

If he sits down, he cannot see out the window. Even if he stands up, he can see only the far side of the river. Through the cross-divided remainder of the window we can see nothing but the tip of the mountain blending into the perspective of the sky.

In Kersting's painting the painter sits on his chair, leaning forward, and, with his brush, just touching the canvas on the easel. From the surface of the river, light is cast on the ceiling and from there to the canvas. The painter in fact is sitting not in a room but in a camera obscura created by the room. On the canvas, dazzling in the reflected light, we can make out something of the work in progress; he is painting one of his extremely emotional landscapes. On the table we can see an open box of paints, three different-size bottles of thinner, and two rectangular objects; the latter two may be smaller boxes of paint. It's probably cold, or at least cool, because Caspar David Friedrich is amply dressed. Warm items of clothing stuff his coat nearly full; they are folded in soft sausages on his arms and around his waist. He wears comfortably worn-out cloth slippers.

I cannot emphasize the importance of the fact that the natural light has been deflected thrice, transformed thrice, before reaching his eyes: first, on the surface of the river, then on the ceiling, and finally on the paint freshly applied to the canvas. Caspar David Friedrich must see through these alterations to see as natural the light he is creating at the moment. He is looking through his own blindness to an imaginary picture. His face is swollen; his beard and hair are unkempt; his countenance is obsessed.

There are three different openings in the wall. There are three different pieces of furniture. There are three boxes of paint. There are three bottles of thinner. On the wall of the empty recess in the blank window hangs a palette, and on the wall between the two window arches similarly hangs a second palette; the third palette is in the painter's hand. In the same hand he also holds four brushes while he is touching the fifth to the canvas. And on the wall between the windows are three rulers: a straight one, a set square, and a T-square.

But there is only one man.

And there is someone else here, the person who sees the man.

They are similar in their ability to see. Still, they differ in the mode of their seeing. Although Kersting sees through his friend's maneuvers about the light, because of the peculiar condition of visibility he can barely see the result of these maneuvers, the picture itself. And we can rely only on our own maneuvers to know where on earth the light comes from in which the two friends are engaged in their similar activities. The invisible Kersting is in the same position at his chair as Caspar David Friedrich is, as Kersting shows him. Friedrich can overcome the dazzle from the canvas, and Kersting can see through it, meaning that Friedrich has his own dazzle and Kersting accommodates himself to it. This is how their modes of seeing differ.

Kersting sees what he sees, and thus, with his seeing, he returns to where he started. In contrast, Friedrich, seeing through his own dazzle, does not return to the point of origin, for then he would have to return, via three intermediary deflections, to the reflecting surface of the Elbe River; however, progressing on this intermediate route, he sees a picture in the common light that in these circumstances no one else can see. Kersting is copying a picture, Friedrich is creating one; he sees it in his imagination, while his friend sees it to some extent, and we barely make out the work being created in the dazzle of the trinity. We may have a sense of the trinity at the depth of things, but out of this holy trinity the mind is capable of grasping only two members, for we don't know whether the seer's viewpoint, the third thing, is a pole, a dazzle, or the third dimension of a flat surface.

In the painting we see Friedrich but not Kersting, though what makes the picture a picture is that we can see the sense of friendship that, according to Kersting, binds them together. That is why I stated so categorically that what I see is not the painted view, but as it happens when I see a real view like this one or similar to it, I am absorbed in the viewing of my thoroughly familiar yet inexpressible feeling. In this case, I am absorbed in the viewing of friendship, though I can see only the illusion of the two men's friendship.

And this holds true for the two men as well. They cannot see me at all, nor can they imagine me, for they have no awareness of my existence in their affairs, yet since my awareness of them comes from a painting shaped in conformity with their feelings, it would be impossible to claim we have nothing to do with one another. That is why I have stated so categorically that there is a feeling of which there is no awareness and awareness that has nothing to do with feeling.

Sometimes the death of human thinking, sometimes the death of human feeling stand between these two different possibilities. They probably find their deaths in each other, and therefore only with the gesture of creation can one see through the dazzle of feeling or thinking; however, one cannot see through both at the same time, just as one cannot see through death, which separates these two concepts.

Ever since I noticed the three rulers hanging on the wall, I cannot help thinking that in designing the painting that at first glance I took to be a moonlit seascape, Friedrich was guided by the same sense of proportion with which his friend designed his. For if Kersting had seen his friend's activity through the dazzle and therefore possessed the proportion conforming to the seeing of the friend, then the work in progress on the canvas, which is barely visible to us, must have at least similar proportions. If the two artists had no feelings of each other, in conformity with awareness, we would not be aware of the intimate feeling of friendship that radiates from the painting.

Friedrich's picture is divided in two by a single ruler-drawn line; the sky is above, the earth below. At first glance everyone would say the earth takes up more space than the sky. But if we measured the spaces we would see that it's exactly the other way around: the space taken up by the earth may seem larger, but our measuring tape shows that the sky takes up the larger area, the proportion of the spaces being five to three. This illusion is not a deception, of course, but the accepted proportion of the displacement of our awareness and feeling—neither verifiable with the other—about the world. We think of the whole from the viewpoint of the parts, for compared with other parts, we ourselves are the whole. More correctly, like a babbling person unaware of what he is saying, we speak now according to our awareness, now according to our feelings, now as the whole speaking of the parts, now as a part about the whole. That is not what Friedrich does; with his inverted measures he speaks at once according to his awareness and his feelings, and the reality of an illusion thus formed alludes to a supposed reality beyond illusion, in which it is not the measure of the part that determines the whole and not the measure of the whole that determines the parts; either both or neither of them are active.

And if, having enriched myself with this realization, I step farther back to take another look at the picture, I am rewarded with another realization. I do not see it differently from how I did at first glance. To my eyes, the dividing line still gives more space to the earth and less to the sky, though I know well it is the other way around. This is the kind of situation in which people usually say that one cannot fool one's feelings or that it's no use knowing something if you don't feel it.

At the horizon, the uniform darkness of the water meets the light-suffused emptiness of the sky. The horizon is the kind of meeting point that separates. It is the illusion of a meeting of two apparently different elements. For ourselves, we supplement this illusion with the knowledge that the world is round—that is to say, what seems flat is really curved and what seems like a line is really a surface. Friedrich is not busy with the awareness of the curve but stays with what seems like a straight line, so we must look for the picture's perspective not according to knowledge but according to illusion. In the geometrical center of the picture, by the way, I can see nothing. I am immersed in viewing the stones strewn on the shore and the swirling dark clouds above, because that is where I am trying to find an answer to the question of what will happen to the shipwrecked men. And in asking this question, I must also ask about what happened before. For this reason the nothing in the geometrical center of the picture will gain the largest perspective. I am looking at things, but in fact my eyes are staring at the void at the intersection of the picture's diagonals. This is the lack of response. Or the hope of response. Which also leads to the death of thinking, which in turn leads to thinking of death.

In Friedrich's painting heaven and earth are reflected in each other. Below, on earth, on the right side, the stones are piled similarly to the banking clouds in the sky, on the left side. I know that things of different qualities cannot be mirror images of each other, yet the sky's blackening blue conjures the green from the brown of the earth, and similarly, the earth turns the sky's black brown. Under the upper rim of the sky the cold light of the moon and under the upper rim of the earth the warm light of the fire provide illumination; the former illuminates the whole picture but not itself, while the latter illuminates only itself and not the whole picture. The warm flame of the fire is lost in the cold of the whole, but in the moonlight illuminating the whole our viewing itself becomes lost; we cannot see into the cold white, just as we cannot see into the black, which we sense is warmer. At most we know that the moon, giving light to the whole, borrows its own cold light from the warm light of the sun. The painting's most profound perspective therefore is to be sought not in darkness and light, not in day or night, not in cold or warmth, not in knowledge or sensation, not on earth or in the sky, but at the point where Friedrich, with his rulers, put nothing in among the illusions of these extreme possibilities.

At no place else does he paint so uniformly empty a blue as here in the geometrical center of the picture. Ostensibly, in the cold night we warm our numb hands by the fire, but in reality we are communicating with a lack of hope. Just as illness is the lack of health, so night is the lack of day. The idea of time includes both night and day, but in the realm of death there is no room for either sickness or health. According to our awareness, we feel the death of our thinking, as the shipwrecked men feel what kind of fate threatens them though they cannot picture it. According to their feelings, they can only warm themselves, but then they form an image of the cold, indifferent night. The mast of their stranded bark resting on its side follows the diagonal of the picture and rises into the space in which neither our awareness nor our sensations have any more questions or answers regarding one another. Navigation's blood-red flag dangles in the blue space.

The painting has two centers. One provides the illusion of a central point according to the psychology of feeling; the other supplies the reality of the same point according to the geometry of awareness. The two centers are fairly far apart and can be related to each other only by the existence of a third point outside the picture, from which we view the two centers in their respective isolation. And since we do not have the ability to see unblinkingly, our view inevitably slides back and forth between the two points.

Thus the unblinking seer admits us to his view but does not grant us the ability to see unblinkingly. At most we might be aware that it is possible to see in a way that we can't or sense how we might speak of it if only we had the words; this is melancholy itself.

Melancholy is usually referred to as a mental condition, yet I say that it is not a condition but an activity: the spirit's work in the soul or the soul's work in the spirit.

And I quickly acknowledge that this may sound incomprehensible. Until now I have been writing of awareness in conformity with sensation and sensation in conformity with awareness, and I have also distinguished this from sensation that goes with no awareness and awareness that has nothing to do with any sensation. But I have said nothing about the spirit or the soul, and it is not clear what I mean by these words.

Sensation creates pictures; awareness creates concepts.

A melancholic person's activity aims to correlate the pictures of his sensations with the concepts of his awareness, to explain one with the other. This activity creates the dead space, the awareness of the void of knowledge, and in this sense it is a very lively space.

In it, the subject of awareness without sensation is what we usually call spirit, while the subject of sensation without awareness is what we call soul.

I can identify with either, but not with both at the same time; thus I am apparently back where I started. With the concept of spirit I have named the whole of space from the viewpoint of the parts. But in fact I am not where I started because whether I identify myself with the subject of awareness without sensation or that of sensation without awareness, I reach a space of unknown nature that can contain both without being identical to or different from them.

If the world has not two but four principles that cannot be deduced from one another—just as the number of distinctive elements is not limited to two—then birth and death, for example, cannot be two different things but the two sides of the same thing. The question is of course, Two sides of what? Most probably that of a two-dimensional plane, for the defining characteristic of a plane is that it is identical to neither of its sides, but that means it cannot be different from them either.

Then there is this question. Which or what sort of dimension of the space of unknown nature is this two-dimensional plane that with a casual shrug or deep sigh, we usually call life?

And when after this vacillation and dubious deliberation we return to Caspar David Friedrich's painting, we shall be easily convinced that the painted surface has not two but three central points. The mass of clouds is like the pile of stones on the ground; the two are related on the diagonal and reflect each other as the colors of the sky and earth indissolubly reflect one another in the common light, though they are of different quality and therefore cannot be identical. And if as a result of my feelings for the shipwrecked men, I perceive the landmass as larger, though it is smaller, then the apparently smaller-surfaced but known-to-be-larger sky must also possess its own illusion in conformity with awareness. The balance needed for the mutual mirroring of appearances is created by the billows of rising clouds that almost completely cover the shining moon; an intimately familiar bearded face emerges from them. The face floats and hovers alongside, going in the same direction, but without intending to float away with them.

The illusion of awareness is exactly the opposite of the illusion of sensation.

Although I had not noticed this face at my first encounter with the painting, once I did I could no longer think of it as a cloud.

Round and ancient is this face with its pug nose, puffy and fraying cheeks; the open mouth leads to a dark hollow, as do the eye sockets, probably hiding a blind look or the lack of eyeballs. It is not looking at us, it sees air, and if it is shouting, it is shouting not to us but to the air. The mouth's dark hollow would indicate a sufferer, while the eye sockets' soft depth suggests a cheerful disposition; the face might be kindly or evil. And we may call him a friendly acquaintance because he reminds us of different faces in our imagination and experience.

The frightful Gorgon comes first to mind and lastly the merciful God of the Christians. With its evil and benevolent, cheerful and suffering look, the face also conjures up human visages; Socrates' flat-nosed, bearded, porcine head as sculpted by Silanion, for example, or the lunatic face Caspar David Friedrich drew in chalk of himself; and in our memories we also have a glimmer of Homer's all-seeing blind countenance.

Cultural memories, sailing on the waters of comparisons and distinctions, finally run aground on the shoal of the illusion of knowledge, and in the ancient face we tend to recognize that of Proteus. The godhead of the deep sea is in the heavens just as the godhead of the earth is in the void. Clouds put a face on the invisible air; fire gives the earth warmth that water can extinguish at any moment. According to sensation, this is happening by the fire; according to knowledge, in the void that is birth on one side and death on the other, cold on one side and warm on the other; on the one side night and the other day; sensation on one side, knowledge on the other; fire and water, air and the earth.

Having arrived in this space of unknown nature, we must distinguish between things that do and don't belong here, because we may speak in this way of dimensions of existence, but not of the dimensions of nonexistence. For example, we ought to modify the popular idea that death and nonexistence are as identical as birth and existence are. It is more likely that birth and death belong to the dimension of existence while spirit and soul belong to that of nonexistence. These two planes, located within each other, form a space that cannot be identical with the dimension of either, nor be different from them either.

Of necessity, the melancholic person, thinking of the plane of birth and death—of existence—winds up in this three-dimensional space of unknown nature, because only by thinking of the plane of spirit and soul, not of existence, can he reach the plane he meant to think about, that of existence, which is birth and death. Now he thinks about existence from the standpoint of nonexistence, now about nonexistence from the standpoint of existence, but he cannot do both simultaneously.

If nothing else, we have managed to say the following about the nature of this space: it has two sides and, consequently, three dimensions. In the same sense we must modify what has been said about the activity of the melancholic person. It is true that it is the spirit's work within the soul or the soul's work within the spirit, and in both cases directed at existence, but since the melancholic person deals with existence from the standpoint of nonexistence, it must also be true that his activity is the work of birth with death, or death with birth, in which case the activity is directed at nonexistence, since the melancholic person deals with nonexistence from the standpoint of existence. And from personal experience everyone knows that activity has only two possibilities, creation or destruction. An activity dealing with existence will destroy, while one dealing with nonexistence will create; activity can never be directed at itself.

Where does Proteus fit into this apparent order, in the dimension of existence or nonexistence? Where can we fit in the four elements, if sometimes their existence and sometimes their nonexistence are a condition of the others' existence? Where can I assign a place to the concept of nothing if according to its meaning, it belongs among the nonexistent, but according to its character, among existing things?

Before trying to answer these difficult questions, following the words of the classicist Károly Kerényi, let us follow Homer's tale about Proteus.

Proteus is one of three godheads, Kerényi tells us, whom Homer refers to as *halios gerón*, an old man of the sea. Although we have no exact information about his birth, the meaning of his name suggests that he may be among the descendants of the primary beings Kronos and Rea.

At the time of Homer's story, Menelaus, son of Atreus, the blond hero whose ships neither wind nor water will convey farther, has been tarrying for twenty days on the island of Pharos. He started out from Egypt, and his "clean hull" progressed swiftly all day with "a brisk land breeze," until it ran aground on the island's sandy shore. And when in his distress Menelaus wanders away from his men, who "were off with fish hooks, angling on the shore," Eidothea comes to his aid and reveals to him what he must do in his dire situation.

> " 'I'll put it for you clearly as may be, friend.
> *The Ancient of the Salt Sea haunts this place,*
> *immortal Proteus of Egypt; all the deeps*
> *are known to him; he serves under Poseidon,*

and is, they say, my father.
If you could take him by surprise and hold him,
he'd give you course and distance for your sailing
homeward across the cold fish-breeding sea.
And should you wish it, noble friend, he'd tell you
All that occurred at home, both good and evil,
while you were gone so long and hard a journey.' "

This is how the wily divine woman spills her father's secret to the mortal
man she likes.

However, the hero Menelaus knows that it would be difficult for a
mortal to overcome a god with his bare hands, and when he inquires further on how to ambush Proteus, the artful Eidothea quickly replies,

" 'I'll tell you this, too, clearly as may be.
When the sun hangs at high noon in heaven,
the Ancient glides ashore under the Westwind,
hidden by shivering glooms on the clear water,
and rests in caverns hollowed by the sea.
There flippered seals, brine children, shining come
from silvery foam in crowds to lie around him,
exhaling rankness from the deep sea floor.
Tomorrow dawn I'll take you to those caves
and bed you down there. Choose three officers
for company—brave men they had better be—
the old one has strange powers, I must tell you.
He goes amid the seals to check their number,
and when he sees them all, and counts them all,
he lies down like a shepherd with his flock.
Here is your opportunity: at this point
gather yourselves, with all your heart and strength,
and tackle him before he bursts away.
He'll make you fight—for he can take the forms
of all the beasts, and water, and blinding fire;
but you must hold on, even so, and crush him
until he breaks the silence. When he does,
he will be in that shape you saw asleep.

> *Relax your grip, then, set the Ancient free,*
> *and put your questions, hero:*
> *Who is the god so hostile to you,*
> *and how will you go home on the fish-cold sea.' "*

And that is how it happens. Kerényi continues: Proteus changes himself into a lion, then a snake and a leopard and a wild boar; the next moment he becomes running water and a moment later a tree; in the end he tells the truth about everything he has been asked.

Whoever is curious about his own fate must wrestle to the ground not only the lion, the leopard, the boar, and the snake but also the tree and the water. The use of force, aimed at satisfying curiosity about fate, cannot heed the many unpredictable alterations of shape and form, because keeping an unbreakable grip on them still means wrestling with only one godhead. This is how many figures become one in the hands of the active mortal. But to succeed in such an ambush, a divine being must help a mere mortal; without divine help no mortal could grasp fire or a lion with only his bare hands. As for the deity trapped by another deity, he tries to resolve the situation by referring the seemingly victorious mortal to the official purview of a third deity. The promised truth is always more than what can be obtained by force; though with the aid of godheads we may overcome one deity, there are many deities.

This is how Proteus ends his exchange with Menelaus, after his ambush, and when Menelaus asks him how he will get home:

> " *'You should have paid*
> *honor to Zeus and other gods, performing*
> *a proper sacrifice before embarking:*
> *that was your short way home on the winedark sea.*
> *You may not see your friends, your own fine house,*
> *or enter your own land again,*
> *unless you first remount the Nile in flood*
> *and pay your hecatomb to the gods of heaven.*
> *Then, and then only,*
> *the gods will grant the passage you desire.'*
>
> *Ah, how my heart sank, hearing this—*
> *hearing him send me back on the cloudy sea*

in my own track, the long hard way of Egypt.
Nevertheless, I answered him and said:

'Ancient, I shall do as you command.
But tell me, now, the others—
had they a safe return, all those Akhaians
who stayed behind when Nestor and I left Troy?
Or were there any lost at sea—what bitterness!—
any who died in camp, after the war?'

To this he said:
                          'For you to know these things
goes beyond all necessity, Meneláos.
Why must you ask?—you should not know my mind,
and you will grieve to learn it, I can tell you.' "

Menelaus may learn from Proteus the fate of the men he left behind, whether his eyes fill with tears or remain dry, but he cannot draw conclusions about his own future from that part of the past.

We are shelter seekers. We move from here to there, from there to here, from the darkness into light, from the light into darkness. Either there is hope or there is no hope.

Action, which means choosing one of many possibilities, necessarily puts an equation mark between the one and the many, though the two sides can never be equal. Every action obviates all other possibilities in the interest of the chosen one. It cannot be otherwise. To avoid the one possibility in the interest of the many others is not action at all. Also, the act expressed in the one chosen possibility may be of two kinds, destructive or constructive, depending on whether it is directed at existence or nonexistence, but it cannot be both at the same time; therefore in the interest of one I would avoid the other. And avoidance requires sacrifice, because there will be damage, to the completeness that is nevertheless present—according to my knowledge in my feelings and according to my feelings in my knowledge—the entirety of the three-dimensional space of spirit and soul, feeling and knowledge.

A shelter seeker must keep returning to where he started. From a state of action he will fall back to a state in which he has no opportunity to act and must acknowledge the validity of the space in which the one and the many, the looking and acting, chaos and order are not equal but are simply two sides of the same thing. In this state he will see order from the viewpoint of chaos, or chaos from the viewpoint of order, and once again he will choose one out of many or many instead of one. He will either act or not act.

This return, executed at the command of Proteus, is the cardinal point of melancholy.

Since action is the forgetting of the many in the interest of one possibility, an adjustment made in the interest of the many cannot be but a remembrance. And the reverse is also true: since action leads to experiencing the one possibility, the means of adjustment cannot be anything but imagining the many possibilities that lie outside experience.

And the plane whose one side is forgetting and the other remembrance, which is experience on one side and imagination on the other, avoidance on one side and sacrifice on the other, but which we cannot equate with the plane of birth or death, soul and spirit, which we therefore cannot assign to the dimension either of existence or of nonexistence though it has strong bonds to both—this is what the ancients usually called myths and modern thinkers refer to as civilization.

Menelaus can realize his fate as his one possible future only if from the present of avoidance he returns to where he started, to the present of the single past still pregnant with many possibilities.

From the standpoint of the gods, therefore, while sacrifice may prevent avoidance, one can imagine a kind of human action that includes both the road leading from the many to the singular and the return journey from the one to the many; we are then dealing with something that is neither action nor nonaction. This two-way movement, whether action or nonaction, must be performed by everyone, and indeed everyone rightly does it. When one acts, one moves on the plane of experience and forgetting; if one does not act, one moves on the plane of remembrance and imagination. Although one cannot do both simultaneously—for remembrance cannot do without forgetting or imagination without experiencing—at different times one can move in either direction.

There is no action that does not result in an omission, and there is no omission that does not demand its own sacrifice. Melancholy is the sacrifice that fits all action. From the standpoint of action, the greatest omission or avoidance is nonaction. And melancholy is a kind of nonaction directed exclusively at action; because of this directionality, it must be qualified, after all, as an action. Melancholy is the only sacrifice pleasing to the gods that may prevent omission, even though it is a result of it.

Using analogies, we may say that remembrance is like fire, forgetting is like water, experience is like the earth, imagination is like the air. Just as nature has four basic elements, so does civilization. According to their measurable relationships to one another, these basic elements, like those in nature, form not two planes but only one, now that of remembrance and imagination, now that of forgetting and experience.

It is on this plane that melancholic man moves in the space of unknown nature.

These two related planes, which we might call the independent dimension of civilization, operate similarly to the pairs of birth and death, soul and spirit, which we also consider an independent dimension. But despite the similarities, we cannot claim that the dimension of civilization is identical with the dimension of either existence or nonexistence. The most we can claim is that in the space of existence's and nonexistence's dimensions, civilization gives us a third dimension that we have not been unable to name, though we have given it a numerical designation. If action moves on the plane of forgetting and experience, then it is directed at nonexistence, will be destructive, and in this sense leads to omission; if it moves on the plane of remembrance and imagination, it is directed at existence, will be constructive, and too will lead to omission. Both actions have in common that they demand their own sacrifice. This is how we can speak, from the standpoint of civilization's dimension, of events taking place in the two other dimensions.

If this is so, how and by what means can civilization be evaluated? That is the melancholic's question. For if he looks at civilization from the standpoint of something, he will see it as nothing, and from the standpoint of nothing, he will consider it something, but there is not much he can do with such conclusions. It is the same with a triangle whose individual angles cannot know the sum total of the three angles; a fourth viewpoint must be sought from which to judge the validity of what the part claims—of the whole of the space of unknown nature.

And we have no other choice either. We must return to where we started.

After so much vacillating and dubious deliberation, it is now clear that Caspar David Friedrich's painting, despite all our former claims, has not one, not two, not three, but four central points.

The first offers the illusion of the center according to the psychology of feelings; the second offers the reality of the center according to the geometry of knowledge. While the first initiates us into the world of something, characterized by birth and death, the second leads into the world of nothing, characterized by activities of the soul and spirit; but all this can be expressed only when viewed from the third central point. We have called it civilization and can equate it neither with something nor with nothing, since from the standpoint of the former, it behaves as nothing, from that of the latter, it behaves as something, it is a third dimension, resulting from the relationship between these two planes. If, however, it behaves like an independent plane, then the three planes, located within one another, must form a four-dimensional space that cannot be identical with the dimensions of the first, second, or third and cannot be different from them either.

If civilization is the third dimension, containing the relationships between the one and the many, illusion and reality, existence and nonexistence, then melancholy must belong to a dimension that partakes of, but is not identical with, all three dimensions. It behaves as an independent whole, but only if it judges actions solely from the standpoint of the plane at which the action is directed.

If action moves in the plane of forgetting and experience and is consequently directed at reality, at nothing, at the many, and at nonexistence, it is destructive, in which case civilization will refer to illusion, to the something, to the one, to existence, and to constructiveness, and it will name the nature of omission and designate the sacrifice appropriate to the means and scale of destruction.

While behaving as the third dimension superior to the other two, and acting as some independent and impartial supervisor, civilization acts now destructively, now constructively. That is to say, in each case it is guilty of omissions.

In Friedrich's painting Proteus is looking out of the picture with a blind countenance.

In Friedrich's painting, one shipwrecked man is looking at the fire, blinded by the smoke; a second man looks at the dry land that cannot be seen from where he is; a third is dazzled by the void of the water glittering at the rim of the horizon.

Proteus is looking out of a three-dimensional surface.

The fourth central point of Friedrich's painting lies outside it.

Proteus is looking at a plane of which he has knowledge; we, on the other hand, are inside this plane because it is located where the fourth central point of Friedrich's is: outside the picture.

While standing at the picture's fourth central point and certain that the world is three-dimensional, we look at the two-dimensional plane of the painting; the picture of a three-dimensional world looks back at us from its two-dimensional plane of which *we* must be its missing third dimension.

The illusion of the picture's space being two-dimensional behaves toward the three-dimensional reality of our own space as the reality of the four-dimensional space behaves toward the illusion of Proteus's three-dimensional space.

If this were not so, Friedrich could not have painted his melancholic picture, for the three-dimensional world can lose its third dimension only if we observe the illusion of the three dimensions from the reality of a fourth dimension.

Proteus cannot know anything else of a world of which he has no picture other than what Friedrich senses of a world of which he does have a picture.

If the cosmologists are right and the world is the three-dimensional plane of a four-dimensional formation, and Poincaré did not err when he said that the nature of a multi-dimensional formation cannot differ from that of the space we know to be three-dimensional, then it follows that we should nurture and protect not the person who senses this very significant difference as a similarity but the one who lacks this sensation. Such a person is the politician—and so is the lover.

Let us speak then of politics; let us speak of love.

First published as "Mélabú" in *Játéktér* (Budapest: Szépirodalmi Könyvkiadó, 1988).

Vivisection

The model moves behind the folding screen. She steps out of her skirt, slips out of her blouse, takes off her brassiere, pulls off her underpants. She comes out and stops between the desk and the rocking chair.

Worn-out loafers on her feet, cheap medallion on a chain around her neck. They have not decided on the pose; she is ungainly. The diffused light produces no contrasts; everything is clearly visible on the body. The sun has left negative imprints from her pants and bra. On her belly the stigma of an appendix operation. Her pubic hair is thin. Her breasts are strongly diverging but flaccid. Her hands are ruddy and puffy. Her bottom is shapeless. She is ashamed of her feet, but she has to kick off her loafers. She is flat-footed; calluses on both heels.

The categories of beauty and ugliness cannot be applied to her. Raw. Only the medallion between her breasts can be defined because *it* is made of material. The body is defenseless and fallible. Existing, alive. But that trinket *is* more alive than she is. She has to take it off. Let her be completely naked.

My friend S. sets her up, finding the least favorable pose; he could have just as easily found the most favorable one.

What intrigues me most are these few moments—the no-man's-land between being fully dressed and assuming the poses of nakedness; what lies between the *not yet* and the *already not*; the vibrating dead spots of history. Only the rare moments without posing offer some certainty in the universal uncertainty. Perhaps.

Now we are talking about me; from the sense of universal uncertainty comes an all-pervasive distrust. Of people, objects, and phenomena.

Searching to understand people, objects, and phenomena, looking for some explanation, I reach several definitions, all of them logically correct. But what sort of definition whose variations, if not its opposites, are endlessly verifiable? If I apply the necessary strictness to my own observations, and if I compare this relatively broad intellectual/emotional domain with a described detail, I uncover the description's contingency: the distortion.

The model does not go behind a folding screen. In this studio there is no screen.

Her undressing? Probably a characteristically varying series of movements, momentary results of defined physical and mental functioning. I know nothing about her. I am not familiar with the distinguishing signs. The model herself I have known for only ten minutes. My description is therefore but an ungenerous generalization, based on incomplete information, of the process of undressing.

But what if I knew the model? I cannot lift her out of the generality of *model*. What if I started with a possible acquaintanceship? If I widen my knowledge beyond a certain limit—where is that limit?—she ceases to be a model; she would be beyond the limits of description, she would become *somebody* for me, the person that she is. What if I invented what I do not know? Knowledge replaced by invention would also mean *emphasizing*, generalizing.

It seems I am flailing uselessly. Instead of facts, a pattern is left.

But the facts of distortion are also facts.

The model did not wear a skirt and a blouse but a sleeveless summer dress. I changed the details for stylistic reasons. I thought that with the verbs *"steps out of," "slips out of," "takes off," "pulls off,"* I would give the sentence a rhythm that referred to the similarities and differences of the various activities. Since it was the rhythm of the second sentence, this seemed very important to me.

And the naked model does not move to stand between the desk and the rocking chair. In that studio there is a desk and a rocking chair, except that at the moment, the rocking chair is not there. I arranged the image afterward. I thought that the body would be more palpable between these objects. Because my original goal—if I had one—would have been to evoke this thought: the disharmony between the naked human body and the objects in the environment—in human-centric thinking— may lead to a tragic realization that the object is more permanent and stable in this world than the living body, less vulnerable and more describable.

The naked body, with elements of the material world hanging off it and being the pliable continuation of this world, wipes out this disharmony, establishes a transition between the two worlds, and evokes the feeling of invulnerability. Henri Bergson says, "It does not occur to us to pit the covering's stiff helplessness against the covered body's living flexibility." The vulnerability and tragedy of the naked body might not be conspicuous in a natural environment, but they are so here between the desk and the rocking chair. Thus I meant the rocking chair to be a symbol, the unstable partner of the stable desk.

I shall start again, trying to recall the scene more accurately.

"Should I take off my shoes?" she asked. The silence made the answer obvious. She blushed and kicked her shoes into a corner. Only the medallion remained, hanging around her neck like a foreign body. A few moments passed. She stopped blushing and also left off awkwardly mauling one foot with the other. But she did not kick the shoes into the corner of the studio. I just invented this fact because I don't remember whether she bent down or not. How did she take them off then? She could have simply stepped out of them. But then how did the shoes wind up next to the stove? They did not.

Yes. She was not yet in front of the desk when she asked, "Should I take off my shoes?" but was standing under the large sketch of the sgraffito designed for the school at Patak. And she blushed. He did not answer her. She stepped out of her shoes. With one foot she trod, pressed, and mauled the other. "I've got corns," she said. My friend S., attentively narrowing the corners of his eyes, replied, "Other people do too," and pointed with his hand that she should go *that way*. The model obediently and hesitantly stopped in front of the desk.

And then I waited to see what would happen with the medallion. The shoes, one neatly next to the other, remained under the Patak sgraffito sketch. This is almost uncertain. She flipped the medallion behind her back but did not take it off. With this movement she completed the process of undressing, and if I remember correctly, shortly afterward, she was told what pose to take up. As for me, nothing whatever occurred to me about this whole matter of the relationship between objects and the human body. Maybe it happened a little later.

Desk instead of shoes, rocking chair instead of medallion, is what I say now. But it's all too nice and logical to be true.

She had never had an operation on her stomach. I should say I invented the appendix operation because I thought it tasteless to write something like "On the model's waist one could see traces left by the elastic band of her undies." But I don't know if one could really see them. Usually one can. The well-composed description of the appendix stigma was meant to emphasize the rawness of the image. But the image is raw enough without traces of underpants or stigma of an operation. The flat-footedness is true. The two calluses on her heels are my inventions. She did say she had corns, but her toes were knobby. Looking for motives, I believe this is what happened: she said corns instead of calluses because she thought the former were more delicate than the latter, and I pushed those calluses from her foot or toes to her heels because I wanted to avoid repeating the same words (foot or toes). Both the transparent mincing of words (on her part) and the strict adherence to a certain, probably conservative notion of style (on my part) were detrimental to the truth.

What is surprising to me is that approaching a goal of so little importance can lead to such a distortion of reality! And the list could go on. But just as with reality, we can uncover only the details of reality's distortion.

Behind the deliberately twisted facts more and more monkey faces of distortion are grinning back at us.

I wrote: her pubic hair is thin. I can emphatically state: the hair in the model's pubic area was not thin.

When she came out from behind the makeshift folding screen, a piece of fabric stretched over a so-called canvas stretcher that was leaning against one of the studio's open doors, she immediately surprised me with the large size of her mons veneris. I did not mention this in my description. I could not decide whether the size of this area in her body deviated from the average. It seemed to me to be larger, but I am not sure. Therefore I substituted the missing uncertainty with an invented certainty. I don't recall whether her hands were ruddy and puffed. I don't remember her hands at all.

I am trying to remember.

When she came into the studio and sat down on the podium a few meters away (about a meter and a half, but it could have been more, or less), I offered her a cigarette. That means that I should remember her hands; after all, I did hold out the cigarette to her. And she? Did she accept it? Did she light up? I don't remember.

I probably did not offer her a light. If I did, I should recall a close-up of her face. I get up, draw the match across the matchbox's phosphorus surface, and lean closer with the flame. I did not get up, did not draw the match across the matchbox's phosphorus surface, and did not lean closer with the flame. I have not a single picture of her face from close up. I did not offer her a light.

From the moment of her entrance until her assumption of the modeling pose, I had been sitting on the podium. Actually, I did get up once. The drawing board for *The Girl with the Interesting Face* slipped off the easel, and I picked it up. The board knocked over the metal box in which my friend keeps his graphite and charcoal. I believe he picked up the board and I the metal box.

As it happens, it is also not true that my friend S. was preparing to paint the girl. He was setting her up for his students. Two boys and *the girl with the interesting face.*

I did offer her a cigarette. Even if I gave her no light, she could have lit it with her own lighter or with her own matches. It seems she had no bag with her. I send her back to the place of her appearance, in front of the open wing of the door where later S. leaned the canvas stretcher frame, which I later called a folding screen. There she stands, but I still can't decide whether or not she had a handbag or shopping bag or something women usually carry with them. I do recall shoulders protruding from the sleeveless, overlaundered print dress; they were round. Her hands I don't remember. There were no introductions; I did not hold her hand. I did not give her a light. I cannot see the characteristic or uncharacteristic hand gesture with which she held the cigarette. She probably does not smoke. And she did not even accept the cigarette when I offered it. The single *wrist* action I can recall: she flips the medallion behind her back. It is a heedless undertaking to pass judgment on an unfamiliar hand. It is possible, though, that I was not mistaken, and her hands were indeed ruddy and puffy. That is what her legs were like. Thick ankles, strong reddish shins and calves, pale thighs, tanned arms, the impression being that this faded sleeveless print dress is what she always wears.

Therefore there is not a trace of sunbathing in a two-piece bathing suit. On the contrary, the sun left only occasional little spots on her skin. *The sun has left negative imprints from her pants and bra.* This is nothing but a pleasant little stylistic turn.

And finally, S. did not set up the model; she did it on her own. "Is it all right like this?" "Yes! A bit more like that!" "Like this, all right?" "All right." The pose is not favorable and it is not unfavorable; simply a pose. That is how she has to stand for forty minutes.

And almost every other element of the description may be refuted as well. And the refutation may also be refuted.

The ambiguity of facts is unavoidable if we destroy our tamed images, our thoughts sent out on restricted tracks or shunted off to dead-end sidings, and if we try to clarify the relationship between the distorted and the distorter.

The model again appeared in the doorway. There is a key in her hand, on a ring.

First published as "Élveboncolás" in *Leírás* (Budapest: Szépirodalmi Könyvkiadó, 1979).

A Tale of Fire and Knowledge

One hot summer evening unknown perpetrators, in unknown circumstances and with unknown intentions, set fire to the four corners of Hungary. What we know is that fire broke out at Ágfalva in the west, at Tiszabecs in the east, at Nógrádszakáll in the north, and at Kübekház in the south. Aflame were harvested fields, ablaze arid meadows, and sometime after midnight fire reached the first village houses. A most gentle and innocent breeze, blowing from the west at Ágfalva, from the east at Tiszabecs, from the north at Nógrádszakáll, and from the south at Kübekház, was bending and swaying the flames toward the interior of the country. Budapest, unaware, was sound asleep.

It was reported, as the seventh item in the morning news, that in the eastern, western, northern, and southern counties large-scale fire drills were being conducted since early dawn; this insignificant little piece of alarming news let every Hungarian know that the occurrence was indeed significant.

Although everyone knew the news did not mean what it meant, as a public they all pretended not to know what it meant. In the Hungarian vernacular of the time, "significant" meant "insignificant," for example, and "insignificant" stood for "significant," but since words had not completely lost their original meaning, there could be no consensus on just what they really meant. Silent agreement could therefore extend only to what a nonexistent general agreement could *not* mean.

If by some turn of good fortune the words lost their original meanings, they would acquire new ones, but this in turn was unimaginable without making individual knowledge public, without a new general agreement. As a result, every word of the language—now according to people's individual knowledge, now according to their common ignorance—meant something other than what it once had meant, and people had to look for the word's meaning by alternately considering the speaker's situation and the word's new meaning relative to its original one. And if the word had seemingly become meaningless, because neither its sense nor the speaker's situation was credible, then this absurdity had a deeper meaning, as if it meant something. In the language of the Hungarians, words with noncredible meaning referred to a profound human collectivity that Hungarians were forbidden to think about. When people who think in other languages think of nothing, they inevitably come up with something; those who think of nothing in Hungarian, however, have the following evidently impossible historical task: not to let anything come to mind when thinking of nothing or to allow, when thinking of something, nothing to come to mind that would lead their thinking to something.

Although this peculiar mode of using the language did not make communication simple, the basic rule was to avoid making individual knowledge collective, something in which Hungarians had great experience. In the last century and half of their history they learned that only collective ignorance could save them from individual folly. If they therefore did not share their individual knowledge among themselves, they could commit no collective folly that might get them into trouble with one another or with others. That is how they were thinking. Hard as it may seem to follow their logic, in the governance of their individual and collective lives it did not prove to be faulty. By dint of this common logic, which shut out collective knowledge, they remained Hungarian. So not only was their logic not useless for their survival, but it became the only and exclusive condition for it. However, what had proved to be a useful tool in a windstorm might not necessarily be useful in a conflagration.

On a ship in a storm the sails are usually lowered, but the wind can sometimes create circumstances in which it is best to raise them. But if fire breaks out on shipboard, in the struggle with the destructive flames it makes very little difference whether the sails are up or down.

Therefore the Hungarians' behavior, the logic of their way of thinking and use of language, had one feature we can call neither erroneous nor flawed but, rather, a drawback that is characteristic of everything ambiguous. When the avoidance of sharing individual knowledge became the basic rule of communication, because only by clinging obsessively to this tacit agreement could Hungarians preserve the national collective, it also had an inevitable consequence for individuals. Every Hungarian assumed that what he or she knew was also known to everyone else, though no one could define what it was that was known or not known. However, being in a constant, mutual need of assumptions and searching for the meaning of words by bypassing their meaning, they collectively could know only that they were compelled to make assumptions about matters of which they had no individual knowledge, or rather, individually they could not know what they did not know collectively.

Nevertheless, in this delicate situation, the country's population remained united in that no one hurried to put out any fires. In the absence of activity that unquestionably referred to the fire, they maintained their collectivity by thinking of the meaning of the fires. And who would doubt that thinking is an activity? As for what the fires meant, opinions differed, of course, but no exchange of opinions could take place because everyone rightfully assumed that everyone else knew that they did not mean what they meant. If the fires did not mean fire, then it was either superfluous to be concerned with them—because they could only be fires that didn't burn—or that one *should* be concerned with the burning question whether fire did not really mean water. Those who approached the question from the sense of the word had to think, inevitably, of water, and those who approached the question from the situation of the speaker were forbidden to think of fire. While the former thought that in reality a flood of unprecedented proportions was threatening the country, the latter thought that instead of putting out real fires, firefighters were igniting false ones. Because if one can talk about a fire that burns nothing, then for the same reason one can talk about a false fire that does burn things in its path and is no less dangerous than a conflagration, which in reality means a flood.

By the afternoon hours this collective avoidance of knowing about the significant danger had created an atmospheric tension, which in other languages to this very day is referred to as a tension of responsibility felt for the fate of the nation. Not so with the Hungarians of the time. Whatever their individual opinions, everyone felt the pungent smell of smoke, but even if they mentioned anything like that among themselves, collectively they opined that an unprecedented storm was in the offing—was not the sky becoming completely black?—though individually they knew that neither flood nor false fire could produce smoke, therefore no storm could result from them. The evening news program then gave a more detailed report of the events.

In the interest of better understanding these events, we too ought to say something more of the good women and upstanding men for whom reading aloud the news of public interest had become not simply an occupation but a way of life that involved body and soul. In those years Hungarians were becoming so equal in their thinking and behavior, and therefore in their outer appearance as well, that they could hardly distinguish between themselves and others. It was characteristic of them, for example, that they came into the world as adults, and since there was nothing to grow up to be, they remained children. Schools became unnecessary. As an adult everyone could teach anyone any subject because there was no one who would not remain a child; while as a child everyone could learn something from everything since there was no one who could become an adult. And if a person found him or herself without anyone around, he or she could use his or her own self for instructional purposes because it had become the common and inalienable peculiarity of every Hungarian that as a child no one was aware of what he or she might have known as an adult. Within this equality, however, certain self-sacrificing individuals, precisely in the interest of complete and perfect equality, had to remain more equal than the others.

We must qualify as unfair and misleading the irresponsible presupposition according to which these more equal individuals would have been the men and women who governed the country. In the current state of research and investigation, we have no evidence that any of these ever shared his or her knowledge with anyone. They did not do this among themselves or in connection with anyone else, and therefore the difference between inhabitants of the country who were well informed and those who were ill informed about public affairs was a mere formality. Inhabitants ill informed about public affairs, drawing precisely from their experience of being ill informed about public affairs, clung obsessively to the tacit agreement, which they had entered into for personal interest, that in no circumstance should any individual knowledge they had of things become collective knowledge. Inhabitants well informed about public affairs, considering themselves well informed about public affairs, clung obsessively to the tacit agreement, which they entered into for public interest, that only a collective not knowing of things could ensure the individual knowledge that no one should possess. The former pretended to have no individual knowledge of the matter, only collective nonknowledge, and the latter pretended that public not knowing was their individual knowledge. This was indeed logical. After all, if a person, through no fault of his or her own, is inexperienced in public affairs, how could he or she make individual knowledge part of the collective thinking? And if an equally faultless person is experienced in public affairs, on what basis could he or she not make the collective not knowing of things the basis of his or her individual thinking? In this regard, we may surely speak of the essential equality of those who govern and those who are governed. Those who govern could not limit the governed in the freedom of their individual knowledge, but neither could the governed limit those who govern in the freedom of their collective not knowing. In Hungary at the time everyone could act on whatever he or she didn't know, and publicly anyone could think of this anything he or she didn't think. And if Hungarians, with this noble and attractive unconsciousness, managed not to hurl their country into the chaos of utter destruction, it is because among them were individuals more equal than they. These individuals were none other than the news presenters.

Hungarian news presenters resembled every other Hungarian to a tee, but the moment they opened their mouths they differed from them in every way. They resembled all other Hungarians because they were no less successful in blending adult and child in themselves. But while an ordinary Hungarian at any given time could unload his or her views about the world to only a few others, news presenters were able to instruct, in addition to themselves, every other Hungarian, yet they differed from other Hungarians in that their instructional activity could have no effect. Unlike the rest of the population, who could interpret what they heard as they liked, news presenters had to pretend, whether they liked it or not, that they understood not a word of what they were telling the country. They were lively in teaching but despondent in learning because if they were the kind of person who could not understand a word of what they were saying—were not individuals—then they could most splendidly embody the collective not knowing that was the possession of every Hungarian. And if I can represent something commonly found in everyone, wouldn't that be enough for me individually to be enthusiastic?

As for teaching, no one could be more grown-up than the news presenters, for they instructed everyone, but no one could be more childlike either, for they learned nothing from their own words. If, however, they had pretended they understood what they were saying, then everyone could have seen they were crazy, for that would have meant they understood something that in reality was meaningless. So they did not pretend. And that was more than reason enough to make them despondent.

There was another reason for admitting no doubt about their unparalleled popularity. In those days Hungarians used only three words for speaking. Although they were taken from the realm of basic life functions, they had lost their original meanings. One word designated activity, another the object of the activity, and the third was a substitute for all possible adjectives and adverbs. We would not only violate common decency but burst the limits of a scholarly study if we said anything more about these three words. However, we cannot keep silent about the fact that while in everyday speech the news presenters as individuals used no other words than these, like everyone else, the moment they appeared before the public, they spoke a language no one else did. And this had multiple ramifications for every Hungarian. Mostly it meant that there existed a public language that did not exist, and it also reminded people that this language not only did exist but, by common consent obtainable through lucky coincidence, could exist.

On the hot summer evening when most of Hungary was in flames, it was the turn of a maternally sweet-voiced, particularly popular news presenter. It would be no exaggeration to say that even among the more equals dispersed among the equals, she was the most more equal. From her Hungarians had been informed about every single heartrendingly uplifting or woefully stormy event in the last century and a half of their history, and therefore the grateful inhabitants of the country could do nothing but lock her into their hearts. Her exceptional popularity was due to her exceptional mental endowment, which others desperately longed for but could not obtain and at best could only imitate. Schizophrenia split her personality not into two parts, as it did other, ordinary Hungarians, but into three. As a result, she not only could present, with full conviction and complete identification, a text of which she apparently understood not a word but with her well-placed accents was able to signal to her listeners, on the one hand, what they should understand, from their collective not-knowing position, by all those meaningless words, and, on the other hand, from the point of view of their individual knowledge, what they should not understand by things that, no matter how they looked at them, made no sense. This woman was a fountain of information, a soothsayer, and an oracle.

I must start with the dramatic announcement that she began in her cloudless voice that evening, addressing those who were still listening to her. While the irresistible charm of her mature womanhood brightened her face, she faltered and got stuck, as if she were drowning in one of those common words to which her glib tongue was so used. She knew well that her compatriots would understand more from words not uttered, because they would understand not only what a word did not mean but also what it meant in relation to the current situation. Right afterward—as if referring in advance, from the standpoint of individual knowledge, to the words expressing collective not knowing that would soon issue from her lips—sparkling with sarcasm, she looked daggers. Despite the rumors circulating, she said, about Hungary's being on fire, it can be categorically stated, on the basis of information obtained from the most reliable sources, that throughout the country life is going on in its usual, calm, and uninterrupted routine. No one has permitted him or herself to be taken in by rumors. The daily portions of meat are being prepared in every kitchen; every child is brushing the teddy bear's teeth, as he or she should; and the mechanical hearts of discos will soon begin to beat. She made these statements in a voice filled with tender sentiment, her eyes clouded over with real tears. "Those who do not believe it," she said challengingly, lifting her head with death-defying courage, "let them look around." She was playing it safe. Of course, in the Hungarian of those days, a challenge meant a statement, and therefore even Hungarians who were still in a situation in which they could have looked around did not do so. The beautiful woman said nothing more about the alleged fire drill, nor did she employ the usual hysterics of hostile news agencies to explain away the rumors that were spreading. With a smile disdaining all credulous souls, she intimated that one possible source might be a report that over the last few days, during completion of an annual inventory at the National Cartographic Institute, certain maps had indeed been set on fire at their four corners.

Then, however, she made an irreparable mistake. The sheet before her said that the long-obsolete maps of Hungary had been burned, but what she said aloud was that the maps of the long-obsolete country had been set on fire. Which in fact almost meant what in fact it meant.

In the hands of blazing Hungary's surviving inhabitants knives stopped moving, forks came to a standstill. The parsley-covered potatoes, the marinated pickles, and grilled chicken remained unprocessed in their open mouths. They all stared before them; everyone was silent by and for him or herself. And this made for a silence that, whatever anyone's opinion had been of the state of affairs until then, could not be not ignored. No word is more powerful than collective silence. Every Hungarian had to acknowledge this simultaneously, and because of this lucky coincidence, his or her knowledge of silence became collective as well. The windows were wide open.

Everyone could hear his or her own silence, which did not differ from the silence of the neighbors. Silence does not disturb silence. And since everyone had more than one neighbor, it was unavoidable not to feel the same silence in themselves as the silence they felt emanating from one another. One Hungarian's silence became the silence of another Hungarian. The silence became so collective that it was impossible to determine which silence belonged to whom, though everyone, invariably, belonged to him or herself.

In the depths of their silence, they all heard the blazes of the conflagration. Only sound can disturb silence. But no one said anything. Because from that moment on, luckily for all of us, no one knew anything else but what the others might also have been thinking.

While there is still water in the wells.

First published as "Mese a tűzről és a tudásról" in *Játéktér* (Budapest: Szépirodalmi Könyvkiadó, 1988).

Family Picture in Purple Dusk

When I get off the bus, I have to look around really well. The houses are so much alike in the narrow street that the odd-numbered side seems like the mirror image of the even-numbered one. I don't know the house number, but I guess I can trust my instincts, however confused they may be. I can get started now. I could look up and find the windows on the third floor. The two windows that face each other because that's the only way I can decide. I always have to cross the street, and in the meantime, the street seems to be switching its two halves, as if deliberately trying to confuse me, always urging me not to trust my senses; I must go to the other side of the street where in the third-floor window potted flowers are kept.

In the stairwell two elderly men are carrying a divan; their faces are red, they hold their breaths, and they are accompanied by a young girl. I have to flatten myself against the wall to let them by. I can smell the two men; the girl has no smell. I ring the bell.

My aunt, my mother's sister, is exactly seventy years old at the time of this visit, and it is as if she were not a real aunt. She is enormous and sits directly in front of the window in an armchair of red velvet upholstery; her back is to the window. That has been the place of the armchair for a very long time, at least as long as I can remember. And everything else is in its place too. My aunt makes me sit, as she does with all her visitors, on the uncomfortable straight-backed chair. Her crutches lean against the piano within easy reach of her arms or that of the polite visitor whose eyes follow my aunt's every little movement. I have never seen my aunt stand up.

The door is opened by Adél, the tiny neighbor (she is also some kind of relative), and as we cross the dark hallway without exchanging a word, we might look a lot alike.

In the soft red velvet of the armchair, immediately under my aunt's hand—her fingers only have to inch their way to the bend of the arm-rest—there is a bell button. A kind of alarm bell. For a variety of pur-poses. It rings downstairs, at the super's. But for greater safety, my aunt is not alone; Adél is also present, sitting by the glazed tile stove, crochet-ing. She starches the finished little lace baskets in sugared water and fills them up—and she does it very tastefully—with lace flowers and lace birds. The baskets are for sale, though two of the more successful ones are in the room, one in the glass cabinet, the other—as if a reminder of my aunt's glorious girlhood, looking like the mummy of a bouquet handed out at a gala concert—on top of the piano. Adél sits on a stool, and even when alone, she smiles maniacally with narrowed eyes buried in wrinkles. When my aunt nods to her, she begins to speak rapidly and incoherently, but with the same kind of nod she can also be silenced. And when she is not allowed to talk, her presence is no bother at all; she leans against the tile stove, makes herself even tinier than she is, and with her occasional smiling glances she can reach only the back of the visitor sitting opposite my aunt or catch my aunt's eye.

The backlight from the window—on overcast days more faintly and on brighter days more strongly—highlights my aunt's white hair done up in a heavy, braided crown, but the face always remains in the shadow. My aunt lives off her past. Not only is she the possessor of one of the highest decorations, received for the same reason that caused her paraly-sis, but she also receives a pension far above the average, and because of her excellent upbringing and education, she is still able to teach Latin, Greek, and German, and since she is also the custodian of the family inheritance, she might be considered almost rich. Halfway between the stove and the red velvet armchair, the pupil or visitor sitting on the straight-backed chair is inspected by two invisible pairs of eyes. But giv-ing steadfast attention and defying the strong backlight, the pupil or vis-itor might seek out the eyes by penetrating the shadow the head casts on itself and make out a hard, masculine face; a thin, colorless mouth that seems always in the process of pressing back a constantly renewing pain striving to form sounds, the pronounced mustache above the lips being the elderly burgeoning of the soft, youthful fuzz that could be so exciting above the lovely lips of a young woman, the powerfully arched hawk nose leading the pupil or visitor to the the hazy, bleached-out irises, tainted with the yellowed whites of the eyes that somehow manage to draw the aggressive face into the pleasant uncertainty of old-age dullness. My aunt is as motionless as if her entire body were paralyzed. Her countenance is elusive not only because of the dimness in the room. It has no sparkle, moves slowly, and avoids living bodies and sharp objects. In the air it feels good.

On the third floor of the house opposite, the lace curtain is drawn apart, but for a long time nothing happens.

I am looking at my aunt's hands on the red velvet of the armchair and am trying to gauge distances.

And then a man, wearing an undershirt, unexpectedly opens the window; pigeons take off lazily from the windowsill and from the blackened stucco figures of the facade and hover above the street; the man leans out, looks around, spits, and very quickly shuts the window.

Not a sound to be heard. There is silence in the room too, because as long as I am quiet, the women won't speak either. The crutches leaning against the piano are only an arm's length away. My aunt may not even be nearsighted; she never complains of any illness. "Well, here you are then; welcome!" she says in a satisfied tone as someone who had been waiting for me, as someone who is worried about me, yet here I am, healthy and well, stepping into the room. What if I just grabbed one of her crutches and broke it over her head? I am looking at my aunt's hands. One move would not be enough; with another I would have to aim the raised crutch at her head and then bring it down. In the pause not registered by the senses between the moves—and no cleverness can arrest this rhythm!—not only would Adél scream—though I could hope for her conspiratorial silence!—but my aunt's fingers would also press the alarm bell's button, unless fright would paralyze them. I stir my tea.

"But if not for money, then for what?" I ask.

Snow is falling slowly, in large flakes.

At my aunt's not only do I get good tea, and served with candied fruits like cherries, sour cherries, and apricots, even in the summer, but they also know how to set a table. However, I get no answer to my question. On the smoothly rolling little serving table that is also used by my aunt's pupils, on a golden yellow tablecloth is a crystal tray along with bone-colored china, two-pronged little forks with which to pierce and pick up the fruit, and other silverware.

"Would you like some buttered toast?" my aunt asks, and seems to be nodding.

"How simple it would be like that!" Adél speaks up. "Of course, so very simple! This I may not have told even Henrietta, it's so terrible, so humiliating to hear something like this, and certain things one prefers to bury forever, or at least one hopes to, isn't that right, Henrietta?"

She falls silent, and my aunt is motionless.

"I can't, I just can't keep it inside, please don't be angry with me, Henrietta, I will tell it anyway. When he said that just now, though his defense attorney would probably talk him out of it, if possible, if it would be helpful, since both the prosecution and the defense reached a dead end, now he would like to make a confession about his emotional life, and I haven't talked about this before because I'm afraid that if I did, I would distort his thoughts or his feelings and, if I shaped the facts to my own images, get myself entangled in the whole thing. I chose to think about them, quietly; no, I did not forget; on the contrary, I tried to make it more vivid, to fix it in my mind, but it's so shameful that in him—that's what he said—in his emotional life gentleness and death, cruelty and life are in a relationship as though an angel continually had to copulate with a devil, and the first time he felt something like this, he did not want to go into details of his memories about other, earlier things, when they were washing his mother, he had never seen anything more maddening since, the water-soaked washcloth left drops of water in the crooks and curves of the body, the body hair became dewy and showed more clearly than ever before the differences between the living and the dead, because no matter how the flesh had transformed itself so mysteriously, water is eternal, and here the relationship of simple and complex should be elaborated on, but by the right of having a last word he would request anyway that on death row, just before the last moments he might put his thoughts, the most abstract ones, on paper, but now he wants to remain on the level of sensual experience, with the memories, because when he realized that the body would not absorb these drops, the pores had forever locked the flesh into itself and they would no longer absorb any drops, as if death had greased the body, then, yes, that's when he felt it for the first time, even though he was only a child, or precisely because he was a child and did not really understand what he was feeling, a living body should be laid out like that! or what if they had laid him out like that, naked! and to dip into it with a knife, or if they had dipped the knife into him! like a salami, being sliced! to be able to feel the power over the transition that shapes the living into the dead and the dead into the living, because this is the power that can be sensed only as a transition, and if he would want to spice his words with some spiritual flavor, then he would see becoming God as also something possible, that's why the dissecting room left him cold, but that's why he was more attracted to the experiments, to vivisection; in the case of arthropods, for instance, those insignificant-looking animals, like the simple earthworm whose dissection is not a murder but a multiplication of life, therefore the divine disposal over its existence is free to be studied, although! if we're already talking about this! from a moral point of view, this too is murder, because the earthworm is a natural or divine creation only in its original, we might say, phylogenetic length! therefore, if we slice it up and thus multiply its life, we must still talk of an excitingly paradoxical form of murder, because the criterion of morality can never be the means or the end, morality cannot be revolutionary, the individual must be kept in mind, and we must, in an ascetic fashion, respect every living thing, but of course nobody can answer whether we should consider every organic growth as an individual? and it was quiet, until he mentioned the earthworm, but then the indignation exploded, people were stamping their feet, the judge himself thought this confession so delicate and so lacking in instructive value that he had the hall emptied, yet it was then that, allegedly, he told them that he, as opposed to the story his lawyer had invented, not only would have hated his victim but if love is a passion beyond all reason for any species or kind of living beings, then from that moment on he had been a little in love, and he begged them not to look for some depth-psychological explanation because although the resemblance to his mother had played a certain role, he was much more excited by the problem of controlling life, the transition and its phases, and if he was going to be hanged now, what will happen to him would be what every lover ardently desires most, but in his fear, because what he really wanted could be achieved only by a mutual death, this way, however, he soils life with his love, and his love with his life, but he did not want that; for him fear was only a merciful addition, a pleasure that sheds light on the psychology of transition and that, with the rubbing together of genitalia, cannot even be approached."

As if touching their bodies, my laughter runs into a strange silence. Adél lets the thread lazily unwind from her fingers and fall into her lap; she gathers her dark brown robe about her neck. She nestles against the tile stove; the stool creaks and grates against the tiles. My aunt is motionless, but she raises her head a little. And it seems that I may have been wrong to imagine their lives the way I had, based on their meaningless communications: puttering about all morning until lunchtime; arrival of the pupils; coffee and brioche after dusk; making the bed; Adél's departure with the sound of safety locks from the hallway; the ceiling filling up with the reflection of headlights of cars passing by on the street; the piano stretching comfortably in the darkness as night descends.

"Why are you laughing?" my aunt asks, and her voice grows hoarse.

"Was I laughing? No! Or maybe I was, because it caught me so unawares and maybe because it wasn't even true, though it seemed very funny and complete, and maybe you know why, but maybe Adél just made the whole thing up."

"Adél!" my aunt shouts.

Adél does not answer, but my aunt is not holding herself back; we must hear her little whistling noises.

"Look!" she says, maybe a shade louder than she meant to, but then she gets stuck, her body convulses briefly on the armchair's darkening velvet, and then she seems to change her mind about something and unexpectedly turns her head toward me, but I cannot see anything of her face, her hair is glowing. "You usually plan your visits for an hour and a half, and if my calculation is correct, you still have about ten minutes left. I am asking you very nicely to give me these ten minutes. I won't be longer than that. It would be a great gift, because I have no right to speak. That's why I keep quiet. I simply live. I want nothing more or less. I eat just enough to maintain this condition. And I feel nothing exceptional in my situation; everyone is the way I am, only they haven't drawn the necessary conclusions. They haven't reached the point where they would regret even what they shit out because that's nothing but squandering, matter wasted; that's why I try to do as little of it as possible. And anyone who, as young as you are now, gives up prudent cautiousness, which we may call practical resource management, which is to say, the way of sustaining life—and not only stuffs his stomach extravagantly full—I'm just watching you as you gobble up a whole plateful of candied fruit that I serve only as a courtesy—but also has his senses tickled to the point of vomiting, and unfortunately there are always reckless spirits ready to help! hetaerae! well, that person will leave this world like a dog. Fast and without a trace. Which in itself is not that deplorable. And that's why I don't have anything to say. I can't even fritter away these ten minutes with you. Go ahead, gorge yourself! There is one cherry left!"

I can feel that Adél is getting up behind me.

"You should really be murdered, Henrietta!"

Making little plaintive yet pleasurable moaning sounds, my aunt knocks herself against the back of the armchair. We all are silent for a long time.

"At last you have given yourself away, Adél!" says my aunt later. "I shall not ring the bell because you have involved everyone in your plans. Go ahead, all of you, beat me. But the crutches are not hard enough. The hatchet is always there, behind the stove. You tried to fool me, you said you'd use it to protect me, but I knew. I knew what it was for. Well, nephew, why don't you make your move? You've heard the story, haven't you? Though I must admit that for a number of years I really thought Adél was telling the truth because one night I was awakened by a terrible rumpus, but she has made up the whole thing just for you! When I asked her in the morning that's when she invented the story that some young man was living here, right above us, the same age as your nephew, Henrietta, and just like him, an orphan, and everybody thought of him as a very serious person, always says hello, has a very great scientific career before him, at such a young age he is already a doctor of physiological sciences, and if we were to tell this to your nephew, Henrietta, we might manage to scare him away and he'd flake off at last, he'd think we suspect him of plans to murder, because it seems useless to emphasize to these young gentlemen that we haven't got a red cent hidden under the pillows, don't waste your time, and don't waste money on confidence-inspiring carnations either, now, in the middle of winter, when it's twelve forints a piece, if he sees the silver with which we set the table out of courtesy, all right, Adél, and my feelings warmed toward Adél, this might work, she knows how it pains me that you, superfluously, eat up all my candied fruits, and drink my English tea by the bucketful, and you still haven't learned to speak German properly, even though you know how important that is for me. I attach great importance to that. But here nobody learns it properly. They just stutter or hem and haw because they're lazy and stupid. Where was I? Adél! I wanted to say something, but not this! Do you know what I wanted to say?"

The streetlights haven't come on yet, it is dark in the room, but the crutches don't turn into shadows, and the snow will probably stick to the ground. And soon I'll be able to get up.

"May I pour? It's probably not cold yet."

"Yes, please. Go ahead, Adél, pour, I'll drink it."

"Yes! I know what I wanted to say," my aunt says, and in Adél's hand the teapot spout knocks against the rim of my cup. "I still have another minute, don't I, Adél? I also give my lessons without wasting a minute. Every second must be filled with words. But now I am talking only because I sense in the wantonness of your laughter the force that will destroy you. But time must be used well. I am not afraid for Adél, she will last out her time, if I am careful and don't let her desires run free, but she will die soon anyway. I shall live longer because I am careful. I do not tickle myself. This bell button I can push anytime, and I don't think you've managed to get the super to be on your side; he wanted to be my lover, but I didn't give in because I knew that if his passion remained, I could make use of it. But you are one of the stupidest kinds of person. You are more stupid than Adél. You are afraid of fear; that's why you indulge in candied fruit the way you do, that's why you laugh so eagerly, and that's why you drink your tea to the last drop. You think that all your fantasies are thoughts, and you'd like to turn all your fantasies into action lest they gel into real thoughts. That's the reason you haven't got a single thought in your head. Which, of course, you don't miss. Your whole life is nothing but a delusive light, a fragrance, a hollow sound. Yet there is a perfect thought in which every detail and connection and even wholeness itself can be found."

My aunt stops talking, and I pierce the last cherry with the little two-pronged fork, lift the crystal tray out of the silver basket, and hold it out to her. I lean forward, hold the tray high and close to her so she will notice it. She smiles sadly, the smile making the line of her mouth swell, as supporting herself on the velvet of the armrest she makes an effort to stir herself in my direction. We see each other; in the snow's purple reflection everything is sharper.

"It's not that one last cherry that I begrudge you, silly boy. Eat it, swallow it! I like to see people eat. But I am scared. There you are, down the hatch! That's why I have this bell. Scared of you too. And of Adél too. Of everything and everybody. Always. Because no one has any limits, and I don't know what is happening or what else can still happen to me. I hate everybody. That's why I'm so glad that finally I am through with Adél. And if I were to ask you to be good to me—and I have never asked you for anything, ever, and we are now past the secret's disclosure— would you consent?"

She has to shift the weight of her body so she could stroke my face with her ringed fingers. "I know you don't want to kill, only to play! Have you thought about that? Answer me that, just that!"

"Don't torture yourself!" I whisper.

My breath drowns her face, her mouth opens as if for a kiss, but she cannot strain her body toward me for so long; she slumps back into the dimness. And there she bursts into laughter.

I have to wait for a long time.

When the streetlights go on and their blue beams fill out the space between the furniture, I stand up. My aunt seems to be asleep. And I would have liked to take a look at the picture. The picture is in the casket; the casket is in the middle drawer of the commode, under the sheets. My aunt keeps the keys to the commode and the casket in an old velvet purse crocheted with silk thread, in the other room, under the divan.

When the casket is opened so I can see the picture, it is as if I were seeing myself in the picture; my face is serious, though I am not in my own clothes but in some costume for a masked ball! and a lady is sitting before me in an armchair, holding in her lap the purse in which the key leading to her world is now kept; although she resembles both my mother and my aunt, she is too strange to be my mother or my aunt, or maybe she is too familiar; one of my hands sinks leisurely into my pocket, the other I rest on the back of the armchair, and I would only have to stretch out my ring finger to touch the lady's neck; thus, when the casket is opened, for an instant I can also see my grandmother's jewels. In the picture I have a nice thick dark mustache, highlighting my stern lips, but my eyes are gentle. I look approximately the way I really am. And in a few months I shall be the same age my grandfather was then, because the photo could not have been taken much before that time.

I plant my hand on the velvet of the armchair, next to my aunt's hand, bend over, and kiss her forehead. Adél too gets up from her stool.

It is as though this door would never have to be opened again.

"If you come again in the spring, I might continue. But maybe you should bring potted hyacinths or Italian violets. Something that keeps," Adél whispers in the hallway before I kiss her too on the forehead.

First published as "Családi kép, lila alkonyatban" in *Leírás* (Budapest: Szépirodalmi Könyvkiadó, 1979).

Our Poor, Poor Sascha Anderson

1

When I was a student in journalism school and we were discussing court reporting, Aladár Ritter sent us to an ongoing trial. It was a violent, bloody case that had stirred up public opinion. People were practically hanging off the rafters. They wanted to see what a trapped animal looked like. They were rumbling, they were booing, they yelled and interrupted; the presiding judge could barely calm their frenzy. It was easy to prove that the accused had pretended to be a diplomat, had seduced and raped very beautiful girls and then killed them. Sometimes he did it in the reverse order: first he killed them and then he raped them. All this was ample reason for the public indignation, because a normal person would not do such a thing. The writer Endre Fejes may have been at the trial because not much later he wrote a short story based on this case; a movie was made of the story, and the leading role was played by a handsome, very clever young actor. But this bloodsucking animal, which the audience would have liked to pounce on and with tooth and nail tear into tiny pieces, was neither good-looking nor clever; he was not even cunning. He gave the impression of being a messed-up kid; he had stayed too short, was on the ugly side of plump, with a face covered with giant pimples, and he stuttered. The audience may have been irked also by the judge, who ordered the courtroom cleared whenever the most exciting details were reached. That stemmed from the nature of the thing. It was quite permissible to speak in public about how and what he had cut with his razor, but not when and how he had taken out his prick. When we were let back into the courtroom, we would hear only whether it was a cutlet or noodles that was found in the victim's stomach during the autopsy. There are knowable things, and there are things unknowable. Of the things unknowable, everyone can fantasize freely and commit his or her own obscenities. Afterward, of course, everyone can freely condemn such acts.

The behavior of the presiding judge was also very interesting. He was a completely apathetic man, yet from time to time he would yell like a madman, though one could see that on hearing a clumsy lie, he made an effort to work himself into a rage. It was as if these attacks were brought on not by the injuries done to his moral sense but by his excellent psychological insight that this was the way to gratify the hysterics of the audience.

Sascha Anderson's moral offense could most likely be established in such a way. But even then I was more interested in the secret ensemble performance of the hysterical audience and the indifferent administrator of justice, of the accuser and the accused, of the judge and the victim. I would have immediately become a court reporter if that secret drama had not interested me more. I would have worked tirelessly to make sure that such a miserable creature could not commit such heinous crimes, and I would have been glad to protect very beautiful girls so they would not become victims of such a miserable tempter. But since I could do neither of these things—out of not merely moral but mainly aesthetic considerations—I did not want to submit either to the sanguinary hysteria of the audience or to the calculating apathy of the judicial system.

Wolf Biermann is probably right: Sascha Anderson is a shithead.*

---

*Wolf Biermann, son of a Jewish Communist dockworker in Hamburg who died at Auschwitz, was born in 1936 and in 1953 moved to East Germany, where he became a leading figure in East Berlin's theatrical and musical life. Though he was a committed socialist, his nonconformism repeatedly troubled the East German regime; in 1965 it declared him an enemy of the state and forbade him to publish his music or perform in public. In 1976, while he was on tour in West Germany, the regime stripped him of his citizenship for "slandering our socialist state," and Biermann remained in his native city. In East Germany in the 1980s there evolved a new generation of dissident singers and writers, among them the poet and filmmaker Sascha Anderson, born in 1953, a popular figure among the artists in the Prenzlauer Berg group in East Berlin. In October 1991, in a televised speech given when he was awarded a major prize, Biermann denounced Anderson as a Stasi informant. The accuracy of his charge was confirmed in early 1992, when shredded Stasi files (scanned and read thanks to a new technology) confirmed that Anderson had for years reported in detail to the East German secret police about his colleagues, friends, and first wife —Editor.

And Jürgen Fuchs's claim can probably be documented: Sascha Anderson did malign, betray, and squeal on his friends.* Still, I would be the last person to speak unequivocally of his guilt. And I say this not out of Christian charity. Nor would I not evade the unambiguous verdict on the basis of some moral relativism. On the contrary, if I had not seen the connections between the audience's hysteria and the judiciary's apathy, between the greatly disturbed libidos of very beautiful girls and the irreversible deeds of that stuttering, pimply, ugly creature, then I fear I should have nothing to contribute to establishing a morality on the basis of which one might actually administer justice. To put it simply, in this case I too would be lost, and in all probability would contribute, with my ignorance, unsuspecting hysteria, and deliberate indifference, to letting other people fall by the wayside.

2

In a fairly low-key sentence, Sascha Anderson has alluded to the fact that his interrogators thrashed his kidneys with keys, each interrogator using his own bunch. At his first interrogation, he says, he was twenty years old. He did not understand what was happening. His kidneys hurt. All he wanted was to get out of there. Béla Szász's kidneys were also thrashed; he did not understand much of what was happening, and he too could not have wanted anything but to get out of there.† One man may be ready to pay the price of exit; another may not. One says I can't stand it; the other says I'd rather drop dead. And when I imagine a situation like that, my moral sense suggests that one ought to choose death. But when one does not think with the head of a youngster and has had some experience of

---

*Jürgen Fuchs (1950–99), another East German writer and civil rights activist, had been imprisoned in 1976 for having organized a petition in support of Biermann; in 1977, when he was released, he moved to West Germany and in 1991 joined in Biermann's denunciation of Anderson—Editor.

†Béla Szász (1910–99), editor, filmmaker, and writer, was arrested in 1949 along with many others rounded up at the time of the "show trial" of László Rajk, then Hungary's minister of foreign affairs; Rajk broke under torture and admitted to the false charges against him of conspiring against the Hungarian state. Szász was sentenced to ten years' imprisonment but released in 1954; he immigrated to Britain in 1957—Editor.

pain and pleasure, one knows that one's moral exigencies may not help solve this thorny problem. Although I have no doubt that it is better to die as a hero than to live as a moral corpse, I cannot know whether in such a situation I could pay the price demanded of me. Unless I wind up in a situation like that, I cannot tell what sort of person I am.

The writer István Eörsi,* for example, tells us that he began to grin. But he could not have known in advance that he would grin; on the contrary, it was precisely in that completely impossible, unanticipated grin, not found in any collection of moral precepts, that he was able to discover a hitherto unknown means by which he could preserve his human integrity in even such an extreme emergency. I am full of admiration for anyone with such means, but I can't know if I would have them. I could easily decide to be a scoundrel, I could also strive not to become one, yet I cannot have advance knowledge of how I might endure mental humiliation and bodily harm, or whether I would find some means with which to defend at least my own conscience. In a state of emergency, the comrades-in-arms will shoot a traitor because they must make themselves accept the situation. But they gain from this action proof only of their intentions, not of their character.

In his book *Remembering the Good Old Times*, Eörsi tells us that while thousands of arrested people were in jail, some grinning, some with clenched teeth, and some as simple stool pigeons, and while people were executed by hanging and by firing squad, eminent Hungarian writers and thinkers of their own free will signed a paper in which they demanded

---

*István Eörsi (1931–2005) was arrested in December 1956 and charged with "incitement" against the state; like others at the time, he was tortured while awaiting trial. Budapest was then an embattled city: mass anti-Soviet demonstrations in October had developed into a full-scale revolt against the Mátyás Rákosi regime of hard-line Communists, with citizens battling Soviet troops and the hated state security police; during those weeks of rebellion thousands of political prisoners were freed, and the Central Committee elected the popular Imre Nagy as prime minister. In his efforts to dismantle the one-party state, and encouraged by an apparent promise of help, Nagy appealed to the UN and western governments for protection, which was not forthcoming. Then, on November 4, a thousand tanks were deployed to the city, leaving a good part of Budapest in ruins; in the ensuing brutal confrontation, some thirty thousand people were killed in Budapest alone, and about two hundred thousand Hungarians sought political asylum in the west. Over the next five years thousands were executed or imprisoned by the Soviet puppet regime headed by János Kádár. Eörsi was sentenced to five years' imprisonment, later raised to eight years, and freed in a 1960 amnesty—Editor.

that the United Nations take the question of Hungary off its agenda because "the revolutionary workers/peasants government's conduct and its
calling on Soviet troops for assistance averted the ever increasing danger
of a bloody counter-revolution." I may countenance Eörsi's naming each
of the 174 signatories, but I cannot let myself do such a thing. The most
I can do is to wonder what induced these eminent people to sign such a
horrible document. And if I think about it, I cannot but recall that in
September 1957, perhaps at the very moment these eminent people
signed the horrible document, I joined the Young Communist League.

What really happened? I joined of my own free will; no one forced
me. If I did not want to strain my memory further, I could quickly add
that I was fifteen years old at the time. I could also add that a few months
later I announced my resignation, and in very aggressive terms. Was I ignorant of the arrests and the executions? It would be absurd to make such
an excuse, and my age was also not an extenuating circumstance. A few
months earlier, while enthusiastic about the revolution, I was not even fifteen. Could I have been afraid? No. Or should I say that I joined the
league because I was frightened by the enormity of the catastrophe that
the suppression of the revolution meant to my socialist or communist
ideas? That would be much closer to the truth. Because during the days
of the revolution it was not with socialist or communist ideas that I had
to settle accounts—that was still far in the future—but with the dictatorial implementation of them. And I remained a member until May 1958,
when I realized that in reality the purpose of the league was to help reor-
ganize that same dictatorial authority. With my current thinking, I can
follow the inner logic of my story, at least up to this point. The inner
conflict occurred later, when I was helplessly dashing now to this side,
now to the other; now I would think I should be defending the antidicta-
torial revolution, now the conceptions of socialism or communism. I once
again was a member of the league, from 1959 to about 1961, and I dared
not announce it when I decided to resign; holding my tongue, I quietly
withdrew. The two sides of my conflict were irreconcilable. Yet despite or
because of this, all the way to August 21, 1968, I hoped that socialism
could be reformed because it did not necessarily have to lead to dictatorship. Oh, how I hoped!

If on the basis of my later experiences and with hindsight, I were
looking not for the inner logic of the story but for extenuating circumstances, I would have to obscure events in my own life, and the collective

memory would be the poorer for it. I cannot wish for that. So there can be no reason to hide the story of my own lapses behind the moral demands of others to excuse them with the lapses of others.

When, in an official speech, Wolf Biermann calls Sascha Anderson a shithead and a Stasi informer, he defines both his own and Sascha Anderson's position, which in my eyes does not make Biermann wiser or more honest, but that is their business; let them fight it out. But I do find something irregular about Jürgen Fuchs's searching the newly opened Stasi archives for material documenting the activities of Sascha Anderson as an agent because the way I see it, this would be the task not of the injured party but of the police, the public prosecutor, and the courts. And if they have no legal authorization for such a search, then we are probably dealing with a moral question. In moral questions, however, I have authorizations that apply only to me. I have no authority to look for juicier, perhaps milder adjectives or to unearth more irrefutable, perhaps exculpatory evidence.

3

There are all kinds of people: honest, like Wolf Biermann and Jürgen Fuchs, and dishonest, like Sascha Anderson. We all have our own established and necessary moral judgments. We wouldn't like to be in the same category with people like Sascha Anderson.

But when moral judgment is put to the test, when one is up against it, it is partly very simple and partly brutal. It touches on personal integrity, and to protect that integrity, one responds vehemently, either by wriggling away or by rebelling.

And the bosses of these secret services are very brutal people, though their brutality most likely is not due to insensitivity. It must be due to their knowing something that we, sitting in our armchairs, are unwilling to acknowledge. When they need insensitivity, they hire an indifferent, hard-knuckled thug. In other cases they might hire a fine seductress, a desirable and beautiful woman, a man full of promises, or perhaps, in yet another case, a sharpshooter. Theoretically the chief of a secret service has as much psychological knowledge and mental sensitivity as a Shakespeare or Chekhov. He leaves it up to the politicians to answer the question, On behalf of what ideological concept do we act? Ideological concepts might disturb his sensitivity. For ideologies always strive to reshape societies, to make them into this kind or that kind but anyway something different from what they are, and he must deal with the very people who promote these ideologies. That is what he must remain sensitive to; that is his job.

Thus the chief of a well-functioning secret service is the worldly custodian of a very dark and constant knowledge: that we, humans, all are brutal monsters. Some do and some don't feel good about being monsters, but the mere not feeling good about it is no proof that one isn't a monster. And secret-service chiefs are mostly entirely right about this. Human history may be depicted as the story of ennoblement and improvement, but there still remains a difference between the Peloponnesian War and World War II, the latter having been more devastating. *They* have no use for such historical evidence. I am both the most profound and the most obvious evidence of their dark and constant knowledge. Although what I am after—like a Shakespeare or Chekhov—is to offer up this dark knowledge of mine in a cathartic or an ironic form, not to consider my own or anyone else's brutality or suffering as a constant, *they* make me pay the price for their actions. Maybe I shall never betray my friend, but I shall pay the price when someone else does. If I took it into my head not to pay, *they*, to the accompaniment of my fellowmen's hysterical approval, would exact the necessary sum from me. The dark and constant knowledge of the secret services is maintained not by dime-a-dozen rotten little informers, easily swayed careerists, or other moral nonentities, but by me.

For the chief of a well-functioning secret service, the hour of truth strikes when he can prove that people who consider themselves principled beings are in reality weak, cowardly, selfish, greedy, libertine, and depraved worms, and he makes me pay for the secretly executed proof-gathering procedure meant to prove him right—I, who also consider myself a principled being. With their accumulated information, these chiefs really gain strength when I hear, softly, the hour of darkness begin to strike. They don't give a shit about ideological implications and explications while they offer their services to states of every ideological stripe and even obtain, through the good offices of governments, the absolution of established religious institutions. In this sense there is no moral difference between the now dissolved Unit III/3, the Hungarian Interior Ministry's counterintelligence department, established to keep an eye on the country's "internal enemies" as France's still and functioning Deuxième Bureau, between East Germany's dismantled Stasi and West Germany's Bundesnachrichtendienst, and similarly, we can find only an ideological difference among the exposed agents of these different secret services. An Ignác Martinovics or a Sascha Anderson can always be found—and exposed. In the eighteenth century, Martinovics organized a secret republican society in Hungary to overthrow the Austrian Empire, and then, even more secretly, he exposed his own conspiracy. Sascha Anderson turned against the socialist state while secretly exposing his own opposition to it and also the members of the group he had legendarily organized and led so well. Now it was his turn to be exposed. Martinovics had to wait two centuries to be exposed. At worst, we won't name any streets or squares after Sascha Anderson. But the exposure of these two men, the shattering of their legends, gives us little hope for moral improvement. At best, we have had an insight into the motivations of the systems maintained with our moral and financial backing.

I do not believe that as a result of these exposures any secret service would look for new means, perchance to effect moral improvement in its operational methods. There is nothing new in the methods of exposure; they only increase and strengthen the secret services' dark and constant knowledge. An unequivocal moral judgment would have some basis if not only Bärbel Bohley but Katharina Blum* were allowed to peruse their files. If the latter could, she would probably find some astonishing things, certainly the name of a very good friend. The name of this friend wouldn't interest me in the least, but if Sascha Anderson didn't have to stand here all alone, we would grow weary of the finger-pointing hysteria and gain a deeper insight into ourselves, into what the era of "peaceful coexistence" meant in our lives. However, if we cavalierly forget Heinrich Böll's demands for cathartic resolution and, on looking at Bohley's files it doesn't even occur to us to muse on the no less interesting files of Katharina Blum, suddenly the lesson of the story is that the stronger dog always gets to mount the bitch. Which is true, but as a moral or historical lesson it has never worked.

Certain files and certain people are now prey to public scrutiny, and

---

*Katharina Blum is the besieged heroine of the German writer Heinrich Böll's novel *The Lost Honor of Katharina Blum* (1974)—Editor.

this too is part of a passive response to the situation: now everyone has a chance to be astounded at how despicable other people are. And that's all right with us; we can shriek, lament, scream for compensation and gratify ourselves. But of course in the meantime, the state must be maintained, the secret service must continue to work, because otherwise peoples and nations would fall on one another and we could not keep up even the semblance of man's not being nature's error, of his being a common, brutal monster.

This semblance has both a price and a method. And the secret-service chiefs are wise men. According to them, it is no big problem if it occurs to me, for example, to look for functional mistakes within these large systems. They know there are always people who, in summarizing their intuitions, manufacture ever new ideologies whose goal is the moral improvement of the human race. They will regard as hostile these newer ideologies, which of course could be old ones too, as long as it is in their interest to support the ideologies involved in maintaining the existing systems. If, for example, it occurred to me—as a result of lessons learned from the former era's terrible moral devastations—that along with international control over weapons reduction and disarmament programs we ought to begin to consider dismantling the world's major secret services, I would not only declare myself a dreamer but be opening my own new dossier with them.

They also know that certain characters are simply destructive. These characters must be either neutralized or not acknowledged at all. Again I think of Béla Szász or István Eörsi. But also of Heinrich Böll. When Szász got his first obligatory slap on the face, he instinctively, without assessing the balance of power, slapped the face of the person who had slapped him. And István Eörsi began to grin. According to the spies' dark and constant knowledge, this kind of response does not exist, and if it does not, it cannot be allowed to exist, either. But from prisoners' reports we know about, we have intimations that others, too, demonstrated similar reflexes but were kept from reporting them. This too is figured into the overall account, for although the dead—and also the survivors' reports—keep alive our sense of morality, they fly in the face of the claim that man is a brutal monster. Yet neither the reports nor the memories of the dead can assure us of the morality of our own behavior.

4

Let us imagine a world in which it would be possible to separate good and evil on the basis of certain criteria. I understand the wish to do this because I too imagine such a world. But for some reason, and this may be an incurable occupational illness, I prefer to see things in their contexts, and then it becomes fairly difficult to separate the wheat from the chaff.

The Hungarian writer and publicist Rudolf Ungváry has a debatable but fairly useful formula for gauging at least the differences among different regimes. He says that a communist regime is worse than a fascist one because communist ideology promises a universal good while fascist ideology promises the good only to citizens of one nation and evil to all the rest. Hearing the communist line, we are confused—after all, what is there to say when someone is looking out for everyone's good?—whereas everyone knows what to do when hearing the fascist one.

Hearing the fascist ideology, every other nation, including that of reasonable Germans, has to admit it would not work, and not only because fascism cannot really be accomplished, but also because its ideology does not offer any cultural or moral handhold even to preferred members of society; it claims that even they are only animals, though stronger ones. If my starting point is the dark and constant knowledge that all humans are brutal monsters, then this is a logical argument. But in no way, and not in any of its parts, does it satisfy the concepts that Europeans, being aware of their own brutality, have developed, over several thousand years, as their moral and aesthetic standards. Therefore, in the name of a civilization's millennia-old struggle for a universal human image and morality, one can say no to this ideology. It would be folly to forget that in 1932 twenty-two million Germans said no to it, that not only non-Germans but these Germans too wanted nothing to do with this kind of German bliss. Thus one can say that anyone who accepts such an ideology or even merely collaborates with it is an agent of evil. I must struggle against people like that, against an ideology like that, not because I am or am not a German, but because I am a human being. And if this is so, then I must train my weapon on the more militant representatives of this ideology and shoot them like mad dogs.

Communist ideology is much less transparent. It is difficult to struggle against something that purports to act on behalf of the universal good and claims that although at the moment the good may not be completely good, it will be if you too join the alliance of those striving for it, and it will be good not only for you but for everyone. Communist ideology struck one of the most sensitive nerve endings of European civilization. The civilization may still be evil, but we would like it to be good. Yet we see this goal is not reachable through Greek, Jewish, or Christian ideals of personal improvement; they have led nowhere. We would like to do away with the structures and institutions that have forced you and me to be evil or lured us into the service of evil. The most one can say against such a notion is that I will join no alliance because I leave it to my church to decide what I should consider good or evil or that I have more faith in the life force of existing cultural traditions than in the consequences of breaking up their structures and institutions. The democratic approach would be, at best, to say that one cannot go down such a dangerous road, but so long as you do not endanger my structures and institutions, you can do what you wish—to yourself.

Nowadays, to conceal our confusions, we try to forget these differences, and it seems chic to equate fascist and communist ideologies in statistical terms, to say that here this many people were cruelly destroyed and there that many. Someone partial to the ideologies of national self-interest could say, on the basis of such statistical maneuvering, that communism is the supreme evil, while someone partial to the ideals of human equality would claim the title for fascism. The data are gruesome on both sides and available for all to see. To my mind, though, equating these two regimes is not only logically and historically untenable but also very dangerous morally. Dangerous because it invariably presents the story as one of a struggle between good and evil, thus putting back in place what it wants to deny. Good and evil are gauged by the number of the dead, leaving me at the mercy of ideologies that wish to make decisions for me or have my cooperation, to relieve me of personal responsibility. To me, these efforts to equate the two regimes, while emotionally understandable and temperamentally easy to follow, point up how deeply shaken we are to see that we more or less defeated fascist ideology and communist ideology collapsed under its own weight.

The effort to equate the two is logically untenable because two things that may have similar characteristics can be distinguished only by their differences. If these two things were identical in every respect, there would be no need to give them different names. When, however, we wish to define those two things on the basis of their similar characteristics, we have no third term for their commonality, and, curiously, we call a communist who acts like a fascist a fascist, while we never call a fascist who acts like a communist a communist.

Lastly, the attempt to equate the two is untenable in terms of their histories. One notes that it was possible to establish an antifascist coalition quickly, practically, and effectively; but although attempts were made to form an anticommunist coalition, it proved impossible to establish it or make it effective even in the long run. Fascism, based on an ideology of national self-interest, could be defeated in the bloodiest war the world has seen; some efforts may have been made to defeat communism, the basis of the ideology of human equality, but "peaceful coexistence" between democracies and various socialisms—a coexistence that, seen from the rear windows and back doors of the secret services, was not as peaceful as had been hoped—came about precisely because of their failures.

If we defeated one ideology and the other ideology collapsed by itself, we have reason to be shaken and confused. And with this emotional reason, it is convenient to reach again for the tried-and-true concept of collaboration in order to measure personal responsibility; as in fact many people, frightened by what has been seen from the back doors and rear windows of the secret services, have done. The only question is, If we have spent the past thirty years in "peaceful coexistence," tending not to belligerence but toward a rather pragmatic attitude, then who is shaving whose head? After all, it wasn't only our poor, poor Sascha Anderson who worked in both directions. Pope Paul VI suspended his moral considerations when he received János Kádár. The queen of England invited the unsavory Ceauşescu couple to dinner. And Helmut Schmidt, by the fireplace in the D.D.R. guesthouse in Güstrow, chatted with Erick Honecker; he wore a solemn face, but still, the circumstances were friendlier than for Sascha Anderson with his Stasi interrogators. And if the era of "peaceful coexistence" had been one in which some people basely collaborated with the devil while others with death-defying courage entered the devil's lair to soothe the fury of the beast, then we would have it easier now. But it is not like that. Both the good and the evil men had their suits made by the same London tailors, and they paid friendly visits to one another's caves in the interest of their mutual realization that the largest conflict had to be avoided at all cost. Of course they didn't have contact with just anybody, but everybody was in touch with somebody. And while looking at the cave paintings, drawn according to local customs, people reassured one another of their good intentions. I do not claim that this versatile, well-mannered contact was not a good idea, but what we should be asking now is, How moral was it?

5

Sascha Anderson betrayed his friends. I wouldn't think of trying to excuse him. And I wouldn't think of it first of all because that same year I received a similar proposal, and it never occurred to me to accept it. One does not betray one's friends, and in such a situation not even one's enemies. One betrays no one, informs on no one, and if one does, he is a dishonorable person. But I don't think this is more than a moral indictment, and stopping here and saying no more would mean that I had understood very little of the logic of the era that urged me, in return for small favors, to be dishonorable.

They knew about me too, whom I made love to and when, on whom, how, and with whom I was cheating; they knew all sorts of things that theoretically only two people should have known, or rather no one—except me. Still, selected pages of the secret data of my life were lying in a thick dossier on the desk. I was closeted in a room with two men. Naturally, they wanted to blackmail me with the data they had. Of course they also dangled a carrot before me. But just because I would not accept the role they wanted me to play—for aesthetic reasons mostly—I don't feel authorized to mount a moral high horse. I can guess who might have helped them obtain the data, but I want no amends from those people either, or rather, I *especially* want no amends from them. Yet I would not dare take the liberty to play the judge, and not because they did not beat me up and therefore I did not have to cross the magic threshold of humiliation as others did but because, despite my refusing the role they offered me, I still had to accept, or did accept, the generally valid maxims set up for all eternity by "peaceful coexistence," along with all the pragmatism it entailed.

I was summoned for the purpose of amending the data about me, and though this was not legal, I complied. I did not protest when they locked the door on me, though it was hardly to my taste nor was it necessary to lock me up in an office with two strange men when it was they who wanted the additional information. I did not behave dishonorably, but neither did I turn into a hero or resistance fighter. I did not return the slaps, and a provocative grin did not appear on my face. I knew what they wanted. I was not afraid of them because I was not afraid of myself. I knew that if they made cooperation a condition of my planned trip abroad, I would no longer want to go. I also figured out how I could say no—with no hint of provocation—in a way that would not instantly mean being forbidden to travel to any destination at all. And with that, I was already up to my neck in the logic of "peaceful coexistence." But just because it can be very expedient to pretend to be more stupid than one is, this does not make one's behavior ethical. If in a locked room I argue, however expediently, in the interest of avoiding big trouble and also of extorting a small favor, I am still talking to the people who locked me into the room. This is how my practical victory becomes my moral defeat.

I left the room with no little self-satisfaction, and to this day I remember how nicely the spring sun was shining outside. But I also remember that in this beautiful sunshine I tried to rejoice in my cleverness so that I would not have to acknowledge my moral failure. This, ladies and gentlemen, was how the thirty-year practice of "peaceful coexistence" played out in action. This was my adult life, set up for eternity. This practice was sanctified by the Helsinki Conference of 1975 when it stamped its huge seal of approval on the division of Europe arranged at the Yalta Conference and in return offered up its basket of human rights with its alluring contents.* This was the logic that the pope, the queen of England, and Helmut Schmidt followed. Although at small focal points

---

* The Organization for Security and Cooperation in Europe began international discussions on security and other issues that led in 1975, at the Helsinki Conference, to the Helsinki Accord, which among other things gave support to the Universal Declaration of Human Rights of 1948. The thirty-five signatory states, which included the Soviet Union and the nations of the Soviet bloc as well as all the western democracies, agreed to respect the principles set forth in the accord's "baskets," as its subdivisions were called, and these included such basic civil and human rights as freedom of association, movement, opinion, and press. They also agreed to meet regularly to assess progress among the signatories—Editor.

of resistance it should have been possible to turn the logic of this situation inside out and say that instead of small favors I should have chosen the illogical moral minimum, nonetheless, the Hungarian Democratic Opposition, the Czechoslovak Charter 77, and the Polish Solidarity all had to understand what the framework was within which they could make this choice.

I am locked in a room. I cannot go too far because then I may never get out. Negotiate while you can, for if you don't, you'll have given up hope. Better to go slow than to act unreasonably. If you make yourself defenseless, I cannot protect you. Don't make a speech in the name of truth, and don't preach about good and evil; look for what is reasonable today.

And if after all this, people want trials like the Nuremberg Trials and, once again trotting out the concept of collaboration, hope (at the price of equating communism with fascism) to sidestep their own moral and aesthetic standards, they would not only be quickly forgetting this whole era and their entire adult lives, but be finding a way to cover up a basic sickness of European civilization that we ought to deal with intelligently on the basis of personal responsibility. For there are a few things that thinking and feeling people should not forget.

We should not forget, first of all, that humans are physically and mentally, existentially and morally very fragile beings. And these fragile beings had been living in systems that had been set up for eternity. And though for three decades the great western democracies may not have approved of them, for all intents and purposes they accepted these systems' supposedly eternal political weight and, with this hardly objectionable gesture, managed to make it hopeless for the few people who accepted neither the reality of the systems nor their dreams of eternity, who were compelled to call them *un*real in terms of daily human life and existence. And if only a very few of these few thinking people stayed the course— for not only did the Stasi persecute such an attitude, but it was also considered a hallucinatory nightmare by the great western democracies whose politics were based on practical realities—then what could the large majority of people possibly have done? All those physically and mentally, existentially and morally fragile beings who, deprived of all real hope, lived on in these systems designed to be immutable and eternal, had but two possibilities: either they could accept the system and thereby, within its frameworks, strengthen it, or they could reform it and thus de facto confirm that the framework was eternal.

For many long years I was torn between these two impossibilities. Acceptance was not morally justifiable, but if one took seriously one's own wish for reform, in a couple of short steps one came up against the arbitrary limits of that framework, which should have been blown to pieces; rationally, one should become a revolutionary, not a reformer. Quite a few people wanted to see such a revolution, and theoretically one could take part in preparing for it, but not practically, because it would have been senseless to create a military conflict between the two systems, and Europe, aghast at the Soviet suppression of the Hungarian Revolution of 1956, would not have risked this. If not before, then on August 21, 1968,* it became clear that the great western democracies in their pragmatic way were willing to support only reform movements and only if they stayed nice and calm, within the framework. And in their very pragmatic way they voted, though with an aching heart, for acceptance rather than reform. Thus from a moral standpoint it was not the first period of the system that was darkest but, through the good offices of western democracies, the second one, which has encompassed our common adult life.

One had to be a most sovereign independent being not to walk into the dead ends of acceptance or reform and at the same time not to go insane, commit suicide, or drink oneself to death. I, for one, know very few people like that. By the early 1980s a peculiar situation had arisen: the great western democracies were more interested in maintaining the frameworks than were the people who lived within them. For western democracies, "peaceful coexistence" had become nothing more than the result of their practical view that, while political systems are not eternal, their voters would not approve if we were to say how we saw the end of the inhuman system we lived in—partly because they were not interested, partly because they were very interested in peaceful trade with us, partly because the system was not *that* inhuman, partly because they too believed in the ideals of social equality or at least of social balance, and mainly because they could not afford to get entangled in a hopeless adventure for the sake of some moral ideals. It was better to continue to wait, to negotiate, and to compromise.

---

* On this date, troops from the Soviet Union and four Warsaw Pact nations invaded Czechoslovakia to bring an end to the reform movement there, initiated during the previous spring by the government of Alexander Dubček; Soviet tanks in Prague ended the reformist initiatives for "socialism with a human face" that Czechoslovak citizens overwhelmingly supported—Editor.

For those of us who spent our lives in this system, the only hitch in this very pragmatic reasoning was that we could hold up our heads while waiting for the end of eternity—or throw a bridge toward negotiating—only if we had some assurance that what we saw was just a semblance of eternity or we really had a chance to negotiate. We had no assurances of the first; the second was given only to the gentlemen who, above our heads, visited one another in their respective caves. Erich Honecker had no choice but to issue the order that anyone attempting to scale the Berlin Wall must be shot. At the sight of this desperate weakness, Helmut Schmidt said to himself, Well, I am going to pay a visit to East Germany, and thus I will provide some relief for those who haven't even tried to climb the wall. In front of the fireplace the two men talked about how humane it would be if at least pensioners could cross the East-West border freely and separated families could be reunited. Honecker had to agree to this not only because that way he could call his system humane but also because he had spent so much money on ammunition he hardly had anything left. Although Sascha Anderson's illegal activity weakened Honecker's negotiating position because it could have been more proof of how humanly unbearable and untenable the East German system was, Honecker did not make him vanish from the face of the earth; he meant to demonstrate that the system was not all *that* untenable, so Schmidt could come for a conversation, and he, Honecker, might, in return for easing some restrictions, be able to squeeze enough money out of Schmidt to ensure the eternity of his system for at least another day. And the reason Sascha Anderson was no obstacle to this solution was that he too had to realize that if he disappeared from the face of the earth, Helmut Schmidt would only protest, if indeed anyone even noticed his disappearance. And Helmut Schmidt could not have gone so far as to support Sascha Anderson overtly or even covertly, partly because his voters would not have approved and partly because he could not then have sat down to negotiate with Honecker and exploit the latter's visible weakness to extort, in return for a small sum, some humanitarian concessions. And Sascha Anderson could console himself by knowing that though he had betrayed his friends and never taken a step that was not dictated by Honecker, the both of them were undermining a system that Honecker could not even maintain without Schmidt's support. He could also keep alive, among the very friends he had betrayed, the hope of resisting this eternity.

Evil suffered a defeat, but not because the good was victorious. One cannot arbitrarily measure the same thing now by its practicality, now by its morality. At most, one can say that although this little "peaceful coexistence" of ours was not too particular morally, it allowed for the resolution of everyday little problems with a minimum of bloodshed. But can one say that our actions of yesterday satisfied our moral requirements? What became a characteristic feature of the societies functioning in the framework of "peaceful coexistence" was that we who lived in them did not think of the world in terms of good and evil. This is the framework, this is my allotted space for movement, these are the factors affecting me, these are the restrictions, and given all this, I have to decide what I should or should not do and what does still belong or no longer belongs in the realm of the doable. An entire generation grew up in these circumstances; the next one was born into it. In the circumstances of a "peaceful coexistence" we acquired those basic rules of pragmatic thinking of which today we should make good ethical use. And if there was anything that helped bring about the collapse of those systems set for eternity, beyond their own inviability, it was that it is impossible to maintain a system based on an ideology when people are thinking pragmatically. And now here we are, standing on the ruins, facing the inevitable question, To what extent was our practical thinking affected by moral considerations? This question must be answered by each and every one of us, individually. We must sit down, nice and proper, and pour ashes not on one another's heads but on our own. Whoever does not do this, and would like to answer by turning to some earthly tribunal, is clinging to one of the old bankrupt ideologies, busily mouthing hollow maxims, or wishing for a sweet little new ideology modeled on the old pattern, that might redeem this miserable world without individuals' having to redeem themselves.

The task of modern democracies should be to establish equal relationships among independent persons as well as among independent states; and none of these relationships should have priority over any other or over our relationship to nature. There is no doubt that modern democracy in this century has failed in this task.

But as opposed to the proselytizing and world-redeeming ideologies, modern democracy is at least trying to do the job, meaning that I do what must be done, or I don't; I do it today, but not tomorrow. It is hard to imagine a democracy's failing because of someone else's fault and not because of mine.

6

A characteristic feature of "peaceful coexistence" was that everyone—I emphasize, every one of us—acquired the basics of a pragmatic thinking that made personal morality relative, thereby also learning to excuse or explain away the lack of personal responsibility in a situation judged as bad or unavoidable. But now I would like brazenly to return to my own case.

When they locked the door on me in that room of the Interior Ministry on Andrássy Road and asked that upon my return from abroad I should report on whom I had met and what we had talked about, they immediately justified this very polite request by saying that "because of the increased tensions in foreign affairs, our homeland now finds itself in desperate straits," and therefore they needed every little bit of information, even on matters that might seem insignificant to me. They would not ask me to do anything dishonest, they simply needed my help; in other words, would I aid my country?

However, one could no longer delude oneself in those years into thinking one had a country. No, by the beginning of the 1970s the last little hope for a country that could be reformed was gone. Everyone was left with one imaginary and one real country, and the stretch of no-man's-land between them was a true minefield. In the evening, everyone could withdraw to his or her imaginary country, but in the morning one had to go across the minefield because that was the only way to reach the real country. If one was not blown up by a mine, did not commit suicide, or did not drown in alcohol, then in the evening one could return to the imaginary country and continue to nurture one's desires, memories, obsessions, and fantasies. That is how it was, and I was not naive. I knew what they were offering me. If I decided that going abroad was more important than staying at home, they would immediately give me the obvious explanation: I would serve my country. But I had no reason to be indignant about such an explanation. On the one hand, as a citizen I accepted the existence of various secret services and, if they existed, their job somehow had to be done. And I had my own job to do. The worst that could happen was that the two jobs were irreconcilable, and then they would find someone more suitable than me. On the other hand, and this is more serious, if I had started arguing with them about the country,

I would have not only made myself a laughing stock but in a very coarse manner given legitimacy to an illegitimate situation that I barely countenanced with my silence.

I did not get to my feet, I did not hit back, I did not grin, and I did not even say no. On the contrary, I said I would be glad to report to anyone at any time of the experiences I had on my travels, only I saw very little sense in it since my life was an open book and I usually recounted my experiences in public. Here we did get into a little argument. They knew very well that I was not being allowed to publish anything. Again, in response I did not get up or spit in their eyes; lying audaciously, I told them I had no knowledge of such a decision. But then how to explain that my writings were not seen anywhere, though they knew I worked regularly? Simple, I work, but I do not publish. They asked, Would it not be much simpler if I helped them, and in return they would help put an end to this unpleasant ban on publication of my work? That is when a tiny voice of minimum moral courage piped up in me: don't reply; pretend you did not even hear it! Of course they understood I was ashamed of the whole business; the question of how I made a living without publication had occurred to them too. Where did I get the money for such an expensive trip abroad? Was I being kept by a life companion, a mistress, or a they-don't-even-know-what-to-call-her, well, some woman to whom, on top of everything else, I was unfaithful? Wouldn't it be a pity if she found out with whom I was being unfaithful? If by accident one of my letters wound up in her hands? And why did I want to go to Italy and Germany, why those countries? Whom did I want to meet there?

This last question I could answer very precisely. I was curious about places that were important in the life of Thomas Mann. I wanted to visit Rome, Munich, and Lübeck, and if that was what interested them, I'd be happy to tell them about my visits, but I was sure their interests lay elsewhere. They played their roles, I played mine; neither was less transparent than the other, and both were equally false. The younger of the two men spoke very intelligently, with well-chosen words in friendly tones; the other one growled constantly, occasionally even yelled at me. This too was part of the game. Still, it was the younger who after an hour and a half kicked the chair out from under him, slammed shut the cover of the thick dossier of my data, slapped it hard, and yelled, "That's enough!" And I thought, Well, here we go, it will start now. But it was not the beginning of a nightmare one could have expected in the light of Béla Szász's or István Eörsi's experiences; that was how the whole thing ended.

This was a very pragmatic sentence. It meant they would look for someone else. Yet out on the street I did not feel the rapture of victory. And not because I had any pangs of consciousness about lying. The problem was solved; that was one thing. I wasn't inept; that was another. But the moment when in the interest of a clever and inventive solution I uttered the words that I'd be happy to report to anyone at anytime, and I had thus morally annihilated myself, the added proviso—that I saw no sense in such a report—was already in vain. Or maybe it wasn't even that one sentence that tortured me; its ironic meaning was obvious enough. It was that short phrase: I'd be happy to.

From the standpoint of pragmatic thinking, one must say one of the following: yes, but; on the other hand; however; actually; in another sense. But one's personal morality can tolerate the rule of neither *wenn* (if) nor *aber* (but); it knows only yes or no. I cannot say that this is unimportant or a mere stylistic offense, and I cannot blame my own moral irresponsibility on anyone else. I wanted to solve a problem, and to do that, I had to leave the imaginary country into which I withdrew on August 22, 1968, in the hope that I might protect myself morally. And then I stepped on a mine, and the mine exploded.

With that short phrase I legitimized within myself the social arrangement that offended my moral sense. Of course one can look for extenuating circumstances. After all, if I had not on some level given evidence of legitimizing the situation, I would have had no opportunity to resolve the matter. That was the logic of "peaceful coexistence." But for me, this phrase, this "I'd be happy to," was even then a sign that in the interest of resolving my situation I legitimized something whose legitimization I no longer felt was acceptable. I admit, I'm making a mountain out of a molehill, but still I must say there is no difference between the logic with which Sascha Anderson resolved his situation and the logic with which I resolved mine. If there was any difference, it was in the levels on which we perceived our respective situations within the framework of the same logic.

Sascha Anderson most probably, and dead seriously, accepted as valid, the eternal reality whose existence Erich Honecker hoped to ensure for at least another day. And I said to myself in late August 1968 that I no longer wanted to accept things the way they were and had been but did not want reformism either, because I wanted nothing at all from that promised eternity, which did not mean that I did not receive some benefit from it. Helmut Schmidt saw this better than Honecker; the pope and the queen of England relied on more solid traditions than did Mrs. Ceaușescu or even Mikhail Gorbachev. There are differences among these things, and to forget this would be just as wrong as to forget the bitter, even if inspiring, truth that it is futile to build one's personal morality on the necessity, practicality, or usefulness of one's actions; this simply does not work. Having said all this, and having defined my own not very heroic position, perhaps I can speak more exactingly of the general aspects of the problem. And I still do not wish to speak of others' morality or immorality only of the unavoidable logic of the historical situation.

7

As the 1960s began, there was a public discussion in Hungary about the relationship between power and morality. Whoever could read between the lines saw what it was really all about. Should I admit that nothing could have happened except as it did, and in that case should I become a follower of Kádár? Or should I realize that exactly because nothing could have happened differently, it wouldn't be very propitious to be a Kádár follower? If I endorse or even merely recognize the reality of the overwhelming force that drowned the will of the majority in blood, my own personal morality loses credibility. If, however, in defense of my own personal morality I do not recognize this reality and am even less inclined to endorse it, how should I talk about it? Conversely, would silence be tantamount to recognizing it? The debaters had to smuggle these questions across the border between political fantasy and political reality carefully, so as not to be blown up on the first mine with a huge bang.

One side would have liked to say that this power, just as it was, was immoral, but instead it claimed that all power was immoral. No, not so, said the other side, common sense would not allow for such a claim because first of all one must distinguish among mechanisms of power, and secondly communist power was moral because it served the greatest possible number of people, while capitalist power was immoral because it functioned in the interest of only a thin stratum of society.

An intellectually paradoxical and morally unacceptable situation was created. The well-intentioned commentators who somehow still wanted to say that the current regime had no legitimacy and therefore was immoral, lumped together all forms of state power from fascism to democracy, and they ended up very far from the prevailing realities and also from the truth; their words could be understood as, at best, poetic hyperbole or metaphor. Those who remained within the confines of the realities, though distinguishing among different forms of power, ended up with a formula according to which even the worst form of socialism was better than the best form of capitalism, clearly demonstrating the worthlessness of their moral ideas.

It was probably necessary to counter this morally worthless idea with a well-intentioned one holding all forms of political power to be immoral, but if my thinking is based on a necessary and useful little deception, then my moral idea is just as worthless as the one I judge to be worthless. And in the following decades these two ideas not only grew deep roots but somehow blended together. Although it was impossible to find proofs that even the best form of capitalism was worse than the worst form of socialism—for this had no reality—it was possible not only to find evidence that all forms of political power are immoral, but also to say that this necessary and useful moral relativity meant and defined my personal moral standards.

We might say that during the period of "peaceful coexistence" these false ideals formed the basis of morality and moral relativism became the consensus. Concepts of political morality and of the legitimacy of power became unpleasantly entangled, and yes, one should have spoken the very words that could not be said out loud.

A power may lay claim to any kind of morality only if it receives its legitimacy from its voters, but the legitimacy of a power structure does not mean that I must accept its politics as moral. If the majority decides to choose this or that form of politics, thereby legitimizing a governing power, it does not follow that I, whether belonging to the majority or a minority, should or am allowed to give up my own moral values, all the more so because these are my only guarantee that politics will not turn immoral and therefore lose legitimacy. Legitimized power is merely a precondition for political morality; the only guarantee of political morality is personal responsibility. But personal responsibility does not have different levels that can be gauged by usefulness or necessity. I am its sole custodian, and only I can represent it.

By the late 1980s the problem was not that such ideas could not be voiced openly, but that people, having become very comfortable in their moral relativism, never thought of doing it. Helge Leiberg, whose studio was destroyed by Stasi agents and who once was one of Sascha Anderson's friends—that is to say, victims—says now, with a certain resignation, "The Elbe kept flowing gently while we lost our sense of how human beings should relate to the world around them."

So-called citizens hurrying to vote in so-called free elections were choosing not between party platforms but between fantasies that on the basis of well-understood principles of self-interest and on mechanisms of moral self-defense they had nurtured within themselves for thirty years in the safety of their homes and in a state of hopelessness. Today we have socialist, Christian, fascist, democratic, national, and liberal fantasies, but these intellectual categories have no more substance or reality than they did yesterday. Whether we fantasize as voters or as politicians, we find behind the fantasies the pragmatism of our daily, ugly little compromises and the sad, futureless experiences of our apathetic moral relativism. We have not started new lives, but have only continued the old ones. We would like to draw a long red line and say, The bad lasted up to here, and here we shall have the good. To perform this false action, it is not only necessary but also useful to have at least one Sascha Anderson.

8

Probably everyone would like to draw a long red line and say, Good ones stand over here, bad ones over there. It is now the Germans who are trying desperately to make such an effort, but it is no accident that the Czechs, the Slovaks, the Poles, and the Hungarians have not yet dared hang out in public, unashamedly, the dirty laundry of their secret services. I sincerely hope that they won't either.

Even the most democratic state should keep discreetly quiet about the work of its secret service. Democratic parliaments have watchdog committees, but they too are under an oath of silence. They have plenty to keep quiet about. A democratic, law-abiding state probably cannot do everything or anything it wants, but whatever it still must do may be difficult to reconcile with the moral standards on the basis of which its citizens live their lives. The chief as well as the agents of the secret service—only on duty, of course—measure their activities not by standards of beautiful or ugly, good or evil, but by necessity and usefulness, by what is in the interest of the state, which may not necessarily be made public. Chief and agent, in this context, are individuals whom the state, in its own well-conceived interest, has exempted not from physical education but from ethics. And if tomorrow, in the state's own well-conceived interest, it must exempt someone from ethics, then it cannot expose someone else for a moral offense today.

The Germans probably risked the magic trick because they suddenly found themselves with two of what others have only one of. And they probably only meant to convey that they had to throw away the worse of the two and keep the better one out of necessity. They could have done it more quietly, but maybe their hearts had grown heavy at the sight of the ruined lives of their compatriots. Perhaps their sense of morality had become flexible too during the years of "peaceful coexistence." Maybe they were carrying moral burdens from earlier times. At any rate, they now gave notice to the world that they had chosen to go with their good secret service and therefore had to show what their evil secret service was like; if they were already doing that, they could also name the agents of that evil. They seemed to be claiming that although the activities of a good state's secret service should be kept secret, friends should not be betrayed in the service of an evil state. And that is a rather puny moral lesson.

They could not go as far as to indict every agent of evil, for while there is a law against a person's acting on behalf of a foreign nation, there is no law, neither in a good nor in an evil state, against being an agent of one's own state or against betraying one's friend in the performance of one's duties. No one with an intact moral sense can claim this is correct: a betrayal committed as part of doing one's job cannot be considered a chivalrous offense when it ruins or even snuffs out the lives of others; no one has the right to ruin anyone else's life even in the interest of the state. But it will be possible to pass a law forbidding the betrayal of friends, even in the interest of one's state, only when all nations, in a common decision, decide to do away with secret services. Until that distant day, whether I live in a fascist, communist, or democratic state, the task is fatefully entrusted to me. Buffeted by their moral and legal doubts, the Germans unfortunately went so far as to create a legal framework for public moral judgment. In such a process it was not the police doing the investigation but the accused, or the victim, whom public opinion judged irreproachable. In this process concerning morality, it was the press and not the prosecutor who raised the charges. No lawyer could properly defend the accused, and the verdict, as is usually the case with moral judgments, was pronounced by public opinion—considering itself above reproach—at the hairdressers, in the stairwells, on television, in pubs and bars, in literary salons.

If I were to formulate my words very politely, I would say that this is an emergency situation. My gentle-penned German colleagues, however, are talking about the necessity of self-examination. In that case, I must put more pressure on my own pen, because I cannot imagine starting a self-examination with the examination of someone else.

Sometimes a disadvantageous situation has advantages. The Poles, Czechs, Slovaks, and Hungarians are not in an advantageous enough position to reveal which was their good and which their evil secret service. These nations too have material evidence, but not enough to use it to parade the workings of evil against the backdrop of their own irreproachability. Even on this level they cannot deal with their own material. And luckily for them, when the need for self-examination arises, this is the more advantageous situation. Why did it become such a burning issue for the Germans—especially for them—to call evil by its name once they had refuge in the trenches of the good? To this question it is they who must give the answer.

First published as "Szegény, szegény Sascha Andersonunk" in *Esszék* (Pécs: Jelenkor Kiadó Kft, 1995).

Work Song

When building my house, I worked alongside the head craftsman, who was about my age. I found him congenial, and I think he felt the same way about me. Of course we talked while we were working. Our discourse progressed on a free association basis. He would think of something and then, as if in passing, verbalize the thought between two movements, and I would do the same. Our attention was divided between the work and the independently arising thoughts. Conversations of this kind don't really differ from a decent work song. Monotonous physical exertion seeks a mental complement in words, and the harmony of the two helps stabilize the peaceful fellow feeling between two people.

The basis of peaceful fellowship is equilibrium. But equilibrium can't be established once and for all; it must be sought continuously. In this respect, we both had to make some effort. In the flawless, unhindered, and effortless execution of the movements required by the job he had an advantage over me, but he would have to have been a big dolt if he'd tried to lord it over me because of his expertise and experience. He was ahead, and I could not overtake him; he was the master, and I only a helper— and a temporary one at that. Not only did he have to be careful to share his knowledge gradually with me, but he also had to do certain little jobs that, according to the unwritten rules of his trade, were not among his responsibilities. A truly wise man is considerate not out of the goodness of his heart but because it is in his deepest personal interest to choose not what seems at the moment like the most advantageous or comfortable solution but what would be the most advantageous solution in the long run. Had he not helped me bridge the immense gap between us in professional know-how, I would have been even clumsier in trying to help him, and an unpleasant additional burden, there would have been nervous tension between us.

In the work song, I was in the more advantageous position. Not that I would constantly and immediately share my thoughts, occurring unexpectedly and uncontrollably, with anybody; on the contrary, I had the upper hand because I don't like such behavior, indeed find it detestable. Fear is cautious and often bids us choose carefully. Therefore I had acquired some experience in categorizing, in finding connections or making distinctions among thoughts that involuntarily arise in me. Had I taken advantage of my experience, I would have found many of my partner's free associations absurd or repulsive and rejected them firmly. But I found it more enjoyable to try to fathom the more profound meanings of his thoughts, which he sang out involuntarily, and to determine their origin, than to say something that would create senseless tension between us. We looked out for each other, and as I began to appreciate his ability to respect the integrity of another person, he worried less that I might violate the existing relationship between us, which was more important to us than anything else. We did everything to revere in each other the ability to respect the other person—as if to say that only the attributes we recognize in another person can we also respect as our own.

After a few weeks the moment arrived when two men, left to themselves, might admit they were filled with the warm feeling of friendship. In the searing summer light we were digging a ditch. It had to be about twenty meters long and almost two meters deep. We were standing between the yellow marble-smooth clayey walls and kept bending up and down but not even the tops of our heads could be seen from outside; only the sky was above us. He was working with a pick and spade; I followed him with my shovel, heaving out the heavy clumps of loosened earth so that not even the tiniest grain would roll back down the growing piles of dirt. At such a depth the smells are different and words have a different sound. It is as if you were standing in the violated secret primordial life of the earth, not to mention that you are spending the day where you will wind up in the end. It was then that he happened to say he hated Jews because they disgusted him. I quickly asked if all Jews disgusted him. He said there were no exceptions. From his categorical reply I came to the not surprising conclusion that his hatred was probably caused by his disgust and that his disgust was a prisoner of his hatred. When a feeling so desperately clings to an emotion—with tooth and nail, so to speak—there is no room left for the reasoning mind, let alone for another person's reasoning. I could entrap his hatred only if I let him know that this time, with me, he had made an exception and therefore gone against his own rock-solid conviction, by unconditionally hating a half Jew or by half hating someone who is not a Jew at all.

There's no denying his statement caught me unprepared, though I wouldn't say I hadn't expected it. I fancy myself a person who can tell if someone feels the need to make this kind of admission, wishing and hoping for a sense of camaraderie, and who also knows in advance when this need will be felt. It is a matter of insight into human nature, of life experience. Once, for example, I rode 250 lulling kilometers with a driver, and having studied his state of mind, on the return trip I was weighing whether his liking for me would be expressed at the city limit or only close to our final destination, when we would turn off Fehérvári Road onto Andor Street. But I gauged the level of the driver's friendly attraction correctly, and I wasn't off the mark. In the case of the builder there was no miscalculation either; only the mutual friendly relation blunted my preparedness. Most of the time I enter these games with great curiosity, and my curiosity is seldom ruffled by being personally offended. My point of departure is that one can't argue with feelings. The most one can ask the other person is if his emotion is really appropriate to the feeling that clings to it. This can be done quite thoroughly, though it's a tricky business because a hot, cherished emotion likes nothing less than questions. And if a mere question makes the emotion lose potency, the feeling can no longer cling to it so securely. "Tooth and nail" will need a new handhold. It is a whole other question, of course, where a person might find the handhold in his or her mental constitution.

The following day we were in the same ditch. Our movements were the same, the sky was the same blue sky, the smell was the same, and the freely associated words did not sound any different. This time he happened to say that he hated Gypsies and if he had his way, he'd exterminate every last one of them. My brain clouded over, and immediately I began to shout. Between the world's going dark and the shouting, how-

ever, many things occurred to me. If I had not felt so friendly and if on
the previous day I had not considered as some sort of success that my
questions could poke holes in his hatred, his new declaration would probably have not touched me so personally. I had a friendly feeling for him
precisely because I trusted his mental capacities and his moral judgment.
I was disappointed not in him but in myself, in my own judgment; my
insight into human nature had suffered a serious blow; the previous day's
partial defeat was now total. That's what hurt so much. And how could I
stay with such a man? If I did, I couldn't stand being with myself. Not
because he hated Gypsies—if he didn't hate Jews—but because my own
disappointment caused me pain, and I had no words to counter that, only
a feeling of disappointment and helplessness—and hence emotion.

My mouth was poised for shouting, but my mind still had time for
sober consideration. If I started to scream, I'd then have had to look high
and low for another expert craftsman like my partner, and because of an
inevitably futile ideological dispute, the construction of my house would
come to a halt. I didn't care; let him go anyway. And I could hear that my
emotion was louder than my common sense. And I was already shouting.
I shouted something to the effect that whoever wanted to kill was a killer,
and if he wanted blood, blood would flow, and if ten years from now
blood would be flowing again in great streams, let him remember that it
was flowing from just such talks, from these kinds of words and nothing
else. He did not leave off working. He must have had worries similar to
mine. If he left, he'd have to admit he had been disappointed in one of his
feelings and had failed to find common ground with someone precisely
where he had looked for it; he'd have to be dissatisfied with himself: he
had proved to be a poor student of human nature. For a long time our unbearable silence continued. And then, between two movements, he said
that I should go ahead and shout at him anytime with no hesitation;
shouting would never offend him because someone else's shouting only
made him laugh. This response did not lack a certain elegance.

Not only was there no laughter, but for days we said nothing to each
other. But then, as usually happens, we had so many anxious issues about
the work that we had to find a way to exchange some words. We returned
to the customary work songs. Not a week had gone by, however, before he
declared that he hated gay men. They all should be caught and castrated,
every one of them, with jackknives. With my persistent questioning I

had deprived him of Jews; with me he could not go on hating Gypsies because that would make me shout; still, there remained the question, What should we do with these poor homos? It was as if he were offering me a last chance. Putting me to the test in this way meant no small risk on his part because he could check the credibility of his own hatred only through my feelings. I looked up as if expecting to see not a grown man but an innocent and awkward child. He was bending down for something, with his back toward me. Even if I'd seen his face, I'd probably have found no explanation. What I really wanted to do was to kick him in the butt so he'd fall on his face. I said not a word. I decided to become an opportunist and not take homos under my protection; I'd leave them to him. Let him peddle and strut his hatred wherever and however he wanted. My silence, though, must have given him pause. Or his anxiety about gay men must have been so great that he had to fill the air with talk about them. He told me his banal experiences; I became fed up with them. He kept asking questions, and getting no answers. I busied myself with work; he carried on his dialogue with himself. He related his own imaginings and fantasies, deviating by not an iota from the most common ones. I was listening without being irritated; at most, I pitied him. Everything he said I found unworthy of reply. He clung to his hatred; therefore he clung to the subject. I had no response to that either. He clung so much to his hatred that he talked it to death, or more correctly, he clung to it so long that he talked it to pieces, and that, after all, is healthy. He accomplished alone what he could not have done better even if I had not kept my peace. From the castrating jackknife he arrived at the rather grandiose conclusion that people differ greatly one from another.

The great turning point of our story is still to come. On a nice day six different craftsmen were working on the house, each with his apprentices: carpenters on the open roof, plumbers on ladders, pipe fitters in the ditches, joiners in the windows, electricians everywhere, and so on. Their presence was matched by appropriate levels of noise and work songs generated by their labor. Everyone was talking at the same time against the background of constant hammering, chiseling, grinding, rasping, and sawing; there was an unstoppable stream of yelling, laughing, cursing, and jabbering. Everybody picked something of his own to tell somebody else, who responded also with something of his own, not necessarily related to what had preceded it. My partner had recruited the other work-men and was the one who supervised their work. He and I had neither spoken to nor seen each other for hours because I took up my place be-hind the house and was diligently cleaning leftover mortar from previ-ously used bricks. He probably did not suspect I was anywhere nearby. Sometimes the various motifs of the verbal cacophony found a common channel, but then either the work made the men stray from the exchange of views, or they deliberately strayed, using their work as an excuse not to have unnecessary arguments. Sometimes it all sounded like a choir; some-times ambitious solos surfaced; sometimes different groups seemed to be singing in rounds. The volume rose and fell, and the instrumental accom-paniment was constantly changing.

Suddenly they were talking about a recent crime that at the time had the whole region in great excitement. The crime, in which blood and semen intermingled, had been committed by two young Gypsies. The craftsmen were cutting into one another's words, raising their zeal to fever pitch; each man analyzed the crime according to his own fantasies, especially when suggesting punishments. On the whole, the fantasies were similar; none of them very innovative, but the sanguinary compo-nent kept increasing. They spelled out what they would do to the two Gypsies, coloring their descriptions and trying to outdo one another, squelching through the bloody details of the horrible act. My ears told me that my builder had ceased to sing his own work song; his silence was ever louder. In the meantime, the choir seemed to be stirred by the con-viction that no torture would be sufficient for the perpetrators, and even too much of it would not be enough. I kept sitting on the ground, clean-ing the bricks. Now they also sang the song of hatred for law and order, for in the eyes of these good men the expected court verdict could be nothing but mere infamy. I could not even imagine what the concluding cadenza of this choral piece would be. Impassively I continued to clean my bricks. I felt we were approaching the finale when I heard the sten-torian bass of my friend. His voice rose calmly and majestically. His emotions could perhaps be measured only in the volume of his voice, for only there lurked the impulse of trembling. He thundered that whoever wanted to kill was a killer, and if they wanted blood, blood would flow. That is what he thundered about, word for word. And if ten years hence blood would again be flowing in streams, let them remember that it was flowing from just such talks, from these very words and from nothing else.

Suddenly there was quiet. The accompanying instruments came to a halt. The ensuing silence was one of stupefaction. And then, after a little while, there was the sound of a tentative saw, a grinding wheel, a screeching screw cutter, a rattling, susurration, and hammering, but for a long time, for a very long time not a word under the blue sky. But a little later, with a "give me that," a "put that over there," cautiously words stole back into the song.

First published as "Hatodik levél" in *Talált cetli és más elegyes írások* (Pécs: Jelenkor Kiadó Kft, 1992, 2000).

Minotaur

"Shouldn't he be given a kid, Joseph?" Even when the bell does not ring, the full moon makes Joseph start, as if someone had rung. Even when it was not asked, in his sleep Joseph always heard the question. He waited for the second ring. Whenever he was not sure, he waited for the second ring. Mary was puffing gently in her sleep; there was no second ring. The moonlight. He sat up in bed. "Did you take down the chicken, Joseph? Is he still eating the chicken, Joseph? Shouldn't he be given a kid, Joseph?" Carefully, so there would be no reason to listen to questions, he slipped out of bed. The room is vaporous with Mary's sleep. To the window. He scurried swiftly so as not to make the floor creak, sat down behind the curtain. The filled-out moon looked down from the height of six stories into the blue ring formed by six galleries. As if he were sitting deep in a well. He may have been praying. He waited for the bell. The bell might ring at any moment; as if he could have predicted when. "Dear God! I thank you for waking me in this late hour of the night. Almighty God! Grant me peace and quiet, and grant the same to all who dwell in this house . . . and grant me strength to get up when they ring the bell. And guide on their way those returning home who will ring the bell, and grant me strength that I may welcome with love the returning lambs. Lamb of God, have mercy on me! My God, my Father, save me from evil. From my sins." What if they rang now? Could he leave while talking to God? *Yes.* But was it not Satan who said yes? *No.* And am I not saying yes and no to myself, as I please? *As it had been foreordained.* He lowered his

head. May it be so. In place of the moon, in the dark, under his lids, a
shiny puddle remained. And from the room, vaporous with Mary's sleep:
"Did you take down the chicken, Joseph?" "I did, I did," answered
Joseph, quickly, panting, from behind the curtain. Mary's gentle blowing
and puffing in her sleep. "Are you asleep?" Joseph asked from behind the
curtain. The smell of the room vaporous with Mary's sleep and her gentle
puffing in her sleep. "She's asleep," said Joseph quietly. They were not
ringing the bell yet. He waited for it. Even if they rang, Joseph would
not turn on the light when the moon was full. When the moon's time
filled out, he started, as if they had asked him or rung the bell. He started
up even when they did not ask him and did not ring the bell. The chance
of being startled. He could sit under the window, in the niche between
the wall and the curtain. He could look at the blue lights of the six galleries, their sharp shadows. He could pray. He could search for the
method. How to hear in advance the inevitable shrill voice that kept
ringing in his ears. The first vibration of the voice. The certainty that he
hears it. He could stretch his neck to be closer to the source, if only by a
few centimeters. If he slept, he waited for it in his sleep. If he slept, he
awoke with a start. By the time he did, the bell ceased ringing. Only the
debris of ringing remained in his ears. Did they ring? Did they? If he was
not sure, he waited for the second ring. If it came, he got up. Did not
sneak or scurry away from the questions. Mary was not puffing. He shuffled into the kitchen, took the key off the board. In times of the full moon
he did not turn on the light. In times of the full moon he stood by the
window and looked up. The black shadows of the galleries, the blind
light of the windows. As if from the depths, from the well. The filled-out
moon from between, behind, and above the squat chimneys. If they
rang, he paid no attention to other noises. By the time he returned,
the questions were waiting for him. He knew he was not awakened by the
questions or the bell. "Did you check the steel door, Joseph? Who was it,
Joseph? Why don't you answer when I ask you, Joseph?" In times of the
full moon, even if they did not ring, he started up as though they had.
"Shouldn't he be given a kid, Joseph?" Carefully, not to have to listen to
questions, he slipped out of bed. Sat down behind the curtain. He could
pray. He could imagine the shadow as it stops before the gate. As it turns
the corner, he could imagine the sound of footsteps, the tapping, the
swishing of coattails, male tapping, female swishing. Tapping and swish-

ing in front of the umbrella maker's shopwindow. The shadow as it stops
by the gate; the hand rises; the finger fits itself to the bell button. The
finger, as it presses the button. He could imagine himself, as he was sitting here. The electric circuit as it is closed by the pressure of the bell
button. He could start for the kitchen, without paying attention to other
noises. He could unhook the key from the board. Open the door. He
could look at the steel door; is it closed? But when the moon was full, he
did not turn on the light. He could go down the creaking wooden stairs,
cross the yellow tiles of the courtyard. As if walking at the bottom of a
well, in circles. He could open the main gate, hold out, and then wrap his
palm around the coin. "Who was it, Joseph? Why don't you answer when
I ask you, Joseph? Joseph, did you check the steel door? Tell me, Joseph,
why do you torture me with your silence? Tell me, what have I done to
deserve this torture, even at night, in the hours of rest? Joseph, why are
you doing this to me? Joseph, are you alive at all? Sometimes I believe
you are not alive. Am I living my life locked up with a shadow?" He
could answer. Or not. "It was a woman on the sixth-floor gallery; it was a
woman, Mary. You see, I'm answering. Whatever I can, I answer; to you,
Mary. I checked the steel door; it's locked. Mary, relax, the steel door is
locked, as always. I have no intention. Far be it from me to torture you
with my silence, but what should I do with my silence, Mary, what
should I do at night when we are left alone with my silence in the hours
of rest? Why do you torture me with your questions, Mary? Tell me,
Mary, why are you alive at all? And I haven't been alive for twenty years.
Why must I, locked together with a living being, why, Mary?" They
could answer each other. Or not. "How much did you get from the
woman, Joseph? Are you sure that woman lives on the sixth floor and is
not a sneak thief who exploits your weakened eyesight?" "I got two
forints from the woman, Mary." "Give it to me!" "I put it on the table."
"I didn't hear it knock against the table." "I put it on the table, actually
not on the table, I threw it into the money box, Mary." "I didn't hear it
jingle. You're lying, I didn't hear the jingling. May God forgive me for
saying things like this, but you're lying, I did not hear the coin jingle,
Joseph. Joseph, hand me the money box! Joseph, why aren't you moving?
Joseph, if you put it in the money box, then give me the box. Go
on, Joseph, move! You think you can pull a fast one on me? You think
you can take the food out of his mouth? From him?" "That woman

started for the sixth gallery. I heard when she took her key out of her handbag. I heard her open the door. And I heard her close the door." "Very nice! She took out her key, you say. Her skeleton key! You're contradicting yourself, Joseph, contradicting, Joseph, as always, right smack into the middle of the noose. I'll expose her for you. Joseph; that woman is a sneak thief! I haven't the slightest doubt. Come to your senses! That woman took out her skeleton key. You heard that, you said. Nice! She started for the sixth gallery, you said; well, of course. And in the meantime she stole back the two forints from you. What is a woman who nowadays would give you two forints if not a sneak thief who can steal it back right away? Do you have any proof, Joseph? Only the money can be your proof, Joseph!" "I can't find it." "You can't find it." "I put it right here on the table." "Very nice. Before, you said you put it in the money box, Joseph. And before that, you said you put it on the table. Because you didn't want to tell me about it, you wanted to deny it. You stole it. There was no woman, and she didn't give you two forints. If she did, she stole it back. If she gave it to you, you stole it. Oh, God, how are we going to buy him a chicken, a kid, if you steal the money, if without batting an eye you deny your simplemindedness when they steal money right out of your hand? Murderer." He could keep his peace. Or not. He could answer. "It was a woman, Mary. She gave a two-forint piece. That woman. Started for the sixth gallery. I couldn't be sure, but I felt it in my palm that it was a two-forint piece, I did. I can distinguish that coin very well from other coins. I can really do that. The only other thing I think it might have been, apart from possibly my having made a mistake, was that she gave me a fiver, a fiver. But something like that, nowadays, from that woman, from a woman like that, who starts for the sixth gallery, who took out her keys, I did hear it, Mary, I heard the clicking of her handbag, you know, Mary, sometimes these women have handbags with metal locks that click. She took her key out of a handbag like that. I heard it. I heard her feet touch every step, not to mention hearing my own steps, Mary. But it's impossible, Mary. It's impossible that she would have given me a fiver, impossible. I was coming, and as I approached, creaking on the wooden stairs, I heard her steps, every one of her steps on the sixth gallery, not to mention, Mary, my own steps. From there, from the sixth gallery, one can hardly hear footsteps unless somebody wears shoes like that woman's. You can barely hear, from there, directly under the chimneys, while I am cracking and snapping, no matter how careful I am, sometimes I even rumble on our wooden stairs, and I tried to exert, to exert all my energies, Mary, but while I am making my way, stepping, crack and snap, and rumble, I must pay attention to the steel door too, to the steel door, but I heard it, Mary, not to mention the snaps and cracks of our stairs, that old wood creaks because of its dried-out joints, but I heard the keys, and I was telling you about this before, I hear her key that she took out of her handbag, Mary, from her handbag, the one I told you about before, I hear her key as she, I can hear it, fits it into the lock, opens it, takes out the key, walks in, closes it, fits it in, locks it, and by then I was standing in front of the steel door, I felt it with my hand, it was still locked, as always." "If once you'd left it open, Joseph? If once you'd forget to close it! Why don't you answer me, Joseph, why don't you answer me, Joseph?" "You didn't ask me, seems like you didn't ask me anything, Mary." "What would happen, Joseph, that's what I was asking, Joseph. What would happen, Joseph, that's what I was asking, if once you did not forget, if once you forgot to close it, that's what I asked. If just once you did not turn the key in the lock, as the woman I was talking about did. If only once you'd done what I wanted you to do. If once, only once, you did. If only you gave me the money. If only you had put it in the money box. If only you'd put it on the table, and given it to me, so we could buy a chicken and a kid. Did you take down the chicken, Joseph? Is he still eating the chicken, Joseph?" The bell rang. "The bell, Joseph. Can't you hear? The bell. The bell. Why don't you move? Where are you? Why are you torturing me? Joseph, where are you? The bell is ringing. Can't you hear the bell? Go on, Joseph, move! Can't you hear it?" "I can't." Another ring. "They rang, can't you hear! Can't you hear? I am asking you. Can't you hear it?" "I can, Mary." "Why don't you move, why? Why do you want to tempt fate? Go. Can't you hear?" He could go. "The money. Be careful!" He could unhook the key from the board. "Murderer!" When the moon was full, he never turned the light on. Only once. He could open the door. He could look at the steel door: Did you check the steel door? He could creak his way down the wooden stairs with the loose joints; he could cross the yellow tiles of the courtyard. As if shuffling at the bottom of a well, in circles. He could open the gate, stretch out and then wrap his palm around the coin. "Who was it, Joseph? Joseph, did you check it? Why don't you answer? Why are you torturing me with

your silence? Tell me, what have I done to deserve this? Even at night, in
the hours of rest? Joseph? Aren't you going to answer me?" "I am answering you, you see?" "Who was that, Joseph?" "That woman." "How much
did you get from the woman? Are you going to answer?" "Whatever I can
answer, I answer, Mary." "Did you put the money in the money box?"
"No." "On the table? Why on the table? Why don't you answer? Give me
the money, Joseph. Move. Give me the box, Joseph. Do you hear me?
Where are you? Are you going to answer me?" "I am behind the curtain,
under the window, in the small niche where I feel good. From where I can
look up at the chimneys, where I can wait and pray." The moon is not
there yet, among the chimneys. The gray debris of shadows fills up the
well of the courtyard. No one is ringing the bell. Mary's puffing in her
sleep. "Are you asleep?" The smell of the room vaporous with Mary's
sleep and her gentle puffing in her sleep. "She's asleep." Among the
chimneys a purple beam is climbing slowly down the slope of the roof.
By the time it reaches the iron railing of the sixth gallery it is red. Yellow. And then it turns into light. It is split along a sharp line, a sharp
line cuts the tiles of the courtyard in two, yellow. In two, light and shade,
diagonally. Mary is puffing gently in her sleep in the depth of the vaporous room. In the courtyard a little boy is circling, around and around,
on a bicycle. Pops into the light, disappears in the shade. Rings his bell
from time to time. Disappears in the shadow, emerges into the light,
around and around in circles, on the bicycle. From time to time, the
smooth gliding of the rubber wheels turns into creaks. He rings his bell.
Mary is not puffing in her sleep, gently. "Where are you?" she asks. "I am
here, behind the curtain, under the window, in the niche where I feel
good." "Very nice. And you don't think that you might soil the curtain,
grease it up with your body? The starched curtain? That doesn't occur to
you, does it? Who is out there in the courtyard?" "Nobody." "Who is out
there in the courtyard? Do you hear? Aren't you going to answer? Who is
in the courtyard? You think you can just deny it? I can see it on the ceiling, I can see its shadow, somebody is out there. Ringing the bell, can't
you hear it? The bell. I can hear somebody out in the courtyard. Who is
that out there in the courtyard? Whose shadow do I see going around in
circles on the ceiling? You're not answering? Do you hear? Where are
you?" "By the window, between the curtain and the wall." "Still, even
now, you still say nobody? It doesn't bother you that you might dirty up

the starched curtain with your body? Somebody rang, do you hear? Do you think it's any good denying it? Do you? Tell me, why? Why should I, Joseph? Joseph, tell me, why? Why not? Joseph!" He could answer, "No, Mary, why would I deny that somebody is out there in the court-yard? Far from it. There is nobody in the courtyard. I will relate to you what is happening in the courtyard." "You will relate?" "There are three trees in the courtyard. A maple, an oak, and a plane tree." "What kinds of tree, Joseph? But there were no trees at all in the courtyard!" "They have grown since then. They grew in the courtyard, a maple, an oak, and a plane tree; they have grown since then." "God, Joseph, why are you deny-ing that someone is moving about among the trees in the courtyard when I can see his shadow on the ceiling as he moves about the trees, around and around." "Why would I deny it if someone was really walking among the trees, Mary?" "Why?" "Nobody is moving about under the trees, Mary, among the trees, on the crowns of trees; in the foliage of the trees only the wind is moving, the breeze is moving the leaves of the trees, that is what you see on the ceiling." "You're lying." "I will relate what is hap-pening among the trees." "Relate? You're lying." "On the maple tree, sparrows are sitting. They are chirping, as sparrows usually do. Can you hear it?" "I will expose you, Joseph, I'll expose your lies, Joseph, do you hear me?" "On the plane tree, turtledoves are sitting and cooing. Can you hear it? And now something is happening in the air between the plane tree and the maple tree." "And the oak, are you leaving out the oak, Joseph?" "And now something is happening in the motionless air be-tween the maple and the plane tree." "You said the wind, Joseph! I'll ex-pose you!" "In the motionless air a tiny bird appears. The sparrows notice the tiny bird and stop chirping. One of the sparrows takes off from one of the branches. Oh, if I could tell you, Mary, which bird from which branch! It is chasing the tiny one. Now I can see. Yes. No. I can't see it well. That's not the tiny bird, it's a june bug. June bugs fly so awkwardly. It's coming between the two trees in the motionless air like an airplane. Mary, the sparrow, one of the sparrows, which one I can't tell you, is now chasing it. Pounces on it. Misses. The june bug is fleeing. Clumsy. Mary! Fleeing! The sparrow, now from below, upward. But Mary! Now two sparrows are chasing it, now three!" "What is happening, great God, what is happening around the three trees, Joseph? Joseph, why don't you answer me when I need an answer most?" "It's over." "Oh, Lord! What happened, Joseph, what happened in the courtyard, why don't you continue?" "I can't see it." "Very nice. You can't see it, you say, it's over, you say. That's what you answer me when I'm in need. Very nice. If you could see the whole thing well, how come you couldn't see the end of it, Joseph? That should do, Joseph. It's over. Stop, Joseph. Don't answer. Let's be quiet. You really think, Joseph, that you can, you believe that you can still dupe me with your stories? Your stories? Don't answer, Joseph. You don't know, you say, it's over, you say. You got yourself into a nice little contradiction, Joseph, a little contradiction, Joseph, as always. Right smack into the middle of the noose. I will expose it all. Those three trees, Joseph. You say, acacia, poplar, and chestnut, those three trees, if they had grown up since then, as you say, if the wind were moving in the foliage, in their crowns, if a breeze were moving the leaves of those trees, as you say, in the motionless air. But how could it move the leaves if the air is motionless? You can't answer that, can you? If there is a wind or just a breeze, don't answer, Joseph, then the air is motionless? Enough of this. We'd better be quiet, Joseph. Do you feel it? Much better if we're quiet. Do you hear me? Answer me! I have exposed you. Answer me! I know why you're silent. The little boy. Call the little boy, Joseph." Disappears in the light, emerges from the shadow. The little boy is circling about, around and around and around. "What should I say to him?" "First the address, Joseph, how will you address him, we always start with the address." He could answer her. "Do you remember, Mary?" "Don't waste our time, Joseph, what should I remember, Joseph? Start with the address, as in a letter. Do you hear me?" "Little boy." "Joseph, that's not good. Start it the way you'd start a letter, otherwise you'll scare him away. Do you hear me?" "Dear little boy!" The little boy is wheeling around in circles, the rubber wheels are gliding like silk on the smooth yellow tiles, from time to time the wheels creak. "Is he answering you? Why isn't he answering?" "He doesn't answer, Mary, the little boy does not answer." "Louder! The address, Joseph, let's repeat the address louder! Little boy, we'd say louder, dear little boy, we'd say louder. Do you hear me?" "Little boy! Dear little boy!" "Good God, Joseph! Louder!" "My little boy, dear little boy!" "Good God, Joseph! Joseph, be quiet! I don't want to hear it." "My little boy! My dear little boy!" "Joseph, no! Oh, Joseph, why are you torturing me?" "Little boy! My dear little boy! Mary! It's no use, Mary! Mary, I did start with the address, as in a letter. Mary, he doesn't want to hear it! Mary, I started the way we used to, with the address!" "Joseph, why are you torturing me? Joseph, what is happening? Joseph, maybe you'd better. What is happening with the birds, Joseph? Why don't you answer me?" "He does not respond to my voice. Mary, he does not respond to my voice. Mary, nothing else is going on, but the little boy doesn't answer, my little boy, dear little boy! He is wheeling around in circles in the courtyard, nothing else is happening. The rubber wheels sometimes glide like silk, sometimes creak. Can you hear it? Now he disappears in the shadow. Now he appears in the light. He rings his bell. Do you hear?" "Enough! Do you hear? Joseph, I don't want to. Do you hear? Let's be quiet about him. It's better that way. The silence. Do you hear? I hate him. He left us. We'd better be quiet, Joseph." He could answer or not. "He didn't leave us, Mary." "Did he go away? I can't see him on the ceiling. Did he go away?" "The little boy has gone away, Mary, he is not wheeling around in circles anymore." "He's let himself go, Joseph. I'm not surprised. Why don't you answer? Have I exposed you? You've no answer to that, do you? He ended up with rogues and knaves. What have you to say about that, Joseph? If only he hadn't ended up with rogues! You're not answering, you can't answer, can you, Joseph?" "He has gone away, Mary, disappeared. Does not appear in the light, does not disappear in the shadow. He hasn't left us, Mary. He started with rogues." "He ended up with rogues, Joseph. What do you say to that? Aren't you answering? Why don't you answer when I'm asking you, Joseph?" The sediments of light fill up the well of the courtyard. Grayly. Mary was puffing gently in her sleep. The moon is there. Among the chimneys a blue beam is climbing slowly down the slope of the roof. It does not reach the depth of the courtyard. And then, light. Along a sharp line it is split into two, light and shadow, the tiles of the courtyard, yellow. Mary in the depth of the vaporous room. "Did you take down the chicken, Joseph?" Even when nobody rang the bell, Joseph started, as if somebody had rung. He wasn't sure of it, he waited for a second ring. Mary was puffing in her sleep, gently. There was no second ring. Joseph sat up. Carefully, so as not to have to listen to questions, he slipped out of bed. He glided swiftly, so as not to make the floor creak. He could stop by the window, he could look up. The filled-out moon looked down from the height of seven stories into the circle of galleries. As if he were standing deep inside a well. He could go on. He could open the steel door. He could go down the stairs. "Did you grease the steel door, Joseph? Have you ever thought that somebody, maybe that woman, might want to know what door squeaks so loudly in the night, in the hours of rest?" Stairs. Two steps down. He could pull the steel door behind him. "Did you grease the steel door, Joseph? What shall we do, what do you think we shall do, if one day somebody might want to know what's behind the steel door that squeaks so irritatingly in the night? Even in the hours of rest, Joseph? Are you going to answer me?" Sixteen steps down. The stretched-out hand bumped into the wall. "My right is the one in which I hold the pencil. My left hand is the one in which I don't hold the pencil. So, to the left." The palm was feeling the wall to the left, feeling its way forward on the left. Three steps; he knew the way. The stretched-out hand bumped into the wall. "My right hand is the one in which, so to the right, let's go." The palm was feeling its way to the right. For four steps. There he found the crack. Easily he squeezed through it. Into a hollow black silence. He could not see its limits, ever. It could have been a hall. A plaza. Or the tiled floor of the courtyard, above which the house might have been walled in. If he stepped back, he was not sure he would find the crack through which he had squeezed himself so easily. And now forward, anywhere. Only not to move. If he moved, the noises would graze the silence and he wouldn't hear it. He only hears the breathing. His own. And the silence in the pauses of the breathing. If he moved, the silence would toll in the pauses of the breathing. It is not dark, it is light within the darkness. The darkness is light. Invisible. To hear the sound in the brief pause of breathing. To start off in the direction of the sound in the invisibly dark, light space. Anywhere, forward. Silence. The first tremor of the sound. He could raise his hand in front of him, for protection. Nothing. With his unprotected blind body forward, anywhere. And always, for a long time, nothing. As if the palm had felt the wall approaching, the space is finite. Nothing. As if something could slam against his face at any time. A silently flying bat, a spider in the middle of its web. Nothing. Panting, shuffling. His own noises. But nothing. "I know the way. I can't get lost." It is as if he could be hit in the chest, stabbed in the back, by somebody, with the knife he is holding in his own hand, anybody. As if it were his own heart, the chicken is moving in the sack. As if he had been standing here from the beginning of time and only his heart had moved; the chicken in the sack. As if his vulnerable blind body were moving forward in this darkness. As if the hollow black silence were his vulnerable body. The chicken is squirming in the sack. As if some light were glimmering somewhere but it cannot be determined where. Maybe forward, maybe backward. The light is not certain, the glimmering uncertain. The uncertainly glimmering dark is moving and tolling. The steps can be heard, as if he were walking in place, always from the same spot, and the puffing too, but it is his own puffing. The minutes are passing. One hour fills the other. Perhaps to the rhythm of months, years, or seconds. Fatigue and hunger are no obstacles. Only the dark. Thick. As if moving in a black mass, and stopping would mean being locked into the thickness of the dark. He is sweating. Feeling the unerring path of the drops. The drops of sweat are headed downward. From his forehead to the protuberance of his brow, from his armpits, along his ribs, toward the waist, from the root of his nose to the rim of the upper lip. That is how he feels the paths of the sweat drops. The widening of his pupils is becoming painful, but the direction of the glimmering is uncertain. "You know the way." He knows the way; nevertheless, the light always blinds him, suddenly. Even though it is only a tiny bulb at the end of the corridor. The corridor is long. He is turning, yet the light of the tiny bulb remains ahead of him, at the end of the corridor, even though he is turning. The chicken stirs in the sack, as if his heart were moving. His pupils cannot shrink small enough not to hurt. "I'll leave the light. I know the way." He is sweating. He grows deaf. He knows he should be hearing sounds, the sounds of his own movements, but all he hears is a booming. The corridor is long, gray, and curving, and no matter how he turns, the tiny lamp is there, blinding, at the end of the gray corridor. As if silence were booming so evenly, the deafness. A mercilessly large ocean locked in a shell. "I know the way very well. I'll leave the light, I must hear the sound." The bell is ringing. As if he had heard the ringing. He is waiting for the second ring, but the first one does not cease; it is long. The drops of his sweat are headed downward, steadily. Steps. Sixteen steps down, and the long gray corridor winds on, with the tiny light source at its uncertain end. Thirsty. He feels neither hunger nor fatigue, only thirst, tormenting. Parching in the hollow of the mouth. "I know, it will pass." The corridor veers away from the light. As if he were not moving but the corridor carried him; the turning would take him by the arm, leading him forward, ever lower, downward like the steady roll of the salty drops of sweat, downward. The lamp winds up being behind him. The downward spiraling corridor, the corridor, winding in ever-narrower circles, is glimmering grayly; the glimmering of the distant light source from behind his back, eternal dawn. "I know it well. This time will pass." As if he were going backward. In the twilight glimmer, the curving of the long gray corridor guides him backward, toward the tiny incandescent lamp. His pupils are dilating, painful. Backward, forward. "I know it. Forward until I cover as much as I did backward. I can't get lost." His pupils became smaller, dilate. He feels no fatigue or hunger and no thirst either. He is struggling with his eyelids, not to let them close. He is sleepy. The steps lengthen, his peculiar shuffle is receding. As if he were receding. Distant, uncertain shuffling. He must know that it is his own. As if he could also hear the gentle trampling of cow hooves in the distant shuffling and puffing, and the tolling morning bell too. Struggling. He knows: if sleep had closed his eyelids, he would lose his way. And then he could start all over, from the beginning. "The most dangerous time. I know it." The steps shorten. To test every step in advance. "I know. The pits must be here somewhere." Every step must be felt and tested in advance, lest he fall into the pit. His soles feel it, the ground is even. Softer than concrete, harder than packed earth. His foot would feel the edge of the pit, but it does not. He is inching forward. As if fog were descending, soft and thick. He separates his own searching from his own steps, his own shuffling, and from the noise of his puffing. His heart moves. As if it were thrusting blood into the arteries for the last time. Silence. He should know that it is not real darkness and not real light that he sees behind his eyelids. He is listening to the cowbell. It is not the morning peal of church bells, but the evening bell of the cows. He should know these are not real sounds, he should hear the real silence, he should know that the shuffling and the puffing ceased. Silence. But he can't hear the silence. "The smells! I know them. I can smell them, I know them." His heart does not move anymore, the evening bell of the cows recedes in the fog, the chicken stirs in the sack. "I have arrived." Silence. As if carried by the wind, the smells rise and sink in short waves, as if driven by a breeze. There he is, lolling in front of his feet. He is snoring. In a slow, human rhythm. His sugary, stifling smell is being raised and lowered by a breeze, carrying it away, bringing it back again. "It's me, Joseph, don't be afraid!" Joseph offends the silence. "Don't worry, I've brought the chicken.

We plucked it, just the way you like it. A living, plucked chicken, the way you like it. Do you hear me? I've brought the chicken. Do you hear?" He is lying in front of his feet, the odor of his body rises and falls, approaches and recedes, as if moved by a breeze, in slow, human fashion he is snoring. "I am Joseph, but call me your father, you hear? Lift your head and say, 'Have you come, my father? Have you brought the chicken, my father? A plucked living chicken, the way I like it? My father, Joseph!' Do you hear?" He is in a deep sleep, he is snoring. "Wake up, my son! Do you hear me, son? Awake! Don't be afraid. I am Joseph, your father. Your mother sent the chicken, plucked, scalded, but still alive. The way you like it. Your mother sent it, Mary. Do you hear?" The chicken does not stir in the sack. He could lift the sack off his shoulder, cut the string that keeps the sack's mouth tight. As he lifts the sack from his shoulder, he feels the knife in his hand. The handle of the knife, the edge of the blade; he feels its length too. The body at his feet has a greasy glow. He is snoring in a slowly rhythm. Rolled into a ball, the greasy body hovers in the amniotic fluid of its own smell. The ribs are raising and lowering his wide chest. If he could insert the knife between the fourth and fifth ribs. *No.* The blade would be just long enough. Now. "Go ahead, Joseph, move!" In front of his feet, the body stirs. Now. No. "The blade would be just long enough if I inserted it between the fourth and fifth ribs. Unerringly into his heart." He is not snoring anymore. Moving about in front of his feet. *As it had been foreordained.* Silence. "Don't be afraid, my son! I am Joseph." Joseph offends the silence. "I have brought the chicken, don't worry. You hear me? Plucked live chicken, the way you like it. Your mother prepared it, plucked it in scalding water. You can gore it with your horn, smell its blood, with your rough tongue you can lap up the spurting drops. The blood. You like that, don't you? Wake up, my son! Do you hear me? It's me. Why don't you answer?" As if his heart had moved, thrusting new blood, the chicken stirs in the sack. He feels the knife in his hand, the length of the blade. "Go on, move, Joseph! Can't you hear me? Joseph? If once, just once, you did what I don't want you to do! Do you hear?" *Yes.* "If only once you did what I wanted. Joseph!" *No.* "Why do you want to tempt fate, Joseph? Why don't you move? Come on! Just this once, only once, Joseph. Move, can't you hear me? Between the fourth and the fifth ribs. Unerringly. Joseph, can't you hear? The bell. Why don't you move, why don't you tempt fate, Joseph?" The body, there, in front of his feet. The handle of the knife, the length of the blade, he can feel it. He could cut the string holding the sack's mouth tight. The chicken whooshes from the sack. The body, there, in front of his feet, is rising. Glows greasily in the sweet husk of his stifling smell. The wide arcs of his ribs raise and lower his chest. His looming horns, his bull's testicles swaying. The body, glowing with the grease of light, rises to its full length. *As it had been foreordained.* He can get started. Bull's horn after the chicken. His legs won't carry him. If he were in the corridor, the corridors would guide him back, forward. He can get started. With the sweetly stifling smell of the body in his nostrils, listening to the sounds, with dilating and narrowing pupils searching and avoiding the light, and feeling the darkness with dilating pupils, he can start his way back. "I know him. I don't want to. First, I would insert the knife between the fourth and the fifth ribs, tear the skin, until I reached your heart with the blade of my knife. Do you hear me, my son? Why don't you answer? I don't want to." It is quiet. The chicken's wings flutter in the silence, somewhere in the uncertain darkness its heart is beating, a frantic rhythm. He feels the handle of the knife, fatigue, hunger, thirst. Bull's horns tussling with the chicken plucked in scalding water. Sleepy. He can start back, forward. He knows: if sleep had closed his eyes, he could start off again, again. "I know him." Carefully, not to make the floor creak. Gliding swiftly, not to hear the questions. "Did you take down the chicken, Joseph? Is he still eating the chicken, Joseph?" Even if she hadn't asked, Joseph heard the question. To the window. Mary was puffing gently in her sleep. Behind the curtain. The filled-out moon looked down from the height of six stories into the blue circles of six galleries. As if sitting at the bottom of a well. He could pray. He waited for the bell. "Dear God! I thank you." And from the depth of the room vaporous with Mary's sleep: "Joseph, is that you? I though I heard steps, your careful, fearful steps. Have you come back, Joseph? Or only my hopes? Joseph, is that you here? Somewhere. Where? Where are you? Probably behind the curtain where you feel good. Very nice. If you knew how much has happened while you weren't here. The bell rang. It was that woman, probably that woman from the seventh gallery, the slut. But I didn't open the gate for her, Joseph, I was on my guard. I know she would have given me a two-forint piece so she could steal it back. A female thief, no doubt of it, Joseph, a sneak thief, I got very tired. I needed all my strength not to hear the bell ring, and if I did hear it not to go to the kitchen for the key. Not to shuffle across the courtyard. Not to open the gate. Not to accept the money that she would steal back from me. I needed all my strength, it exhausted me. I got all tired out. Should rest, we both should rest, Joseph, it's almost time for cleaning. Joseph, why don't you answer me? You've been away for so long, and I would so much like to hear your voice. All right. I won't keep anything from you. If I already started, I'll tell you the whole thing. Joseph, my little boy was here too. His shadow on the ceiling, around and around. And your birds too. Your birds were here too, do you hear? On the trees, among the trees. I called to your little boy, he didn't answer. He went away. He abandoned me. All your hopes are in vain, Joseph, in vain you sit there behind the curtain, in vain you soil my curtains with the grease of your body, he won't be coming back. He degenerated. Ended up with rogues. He has forsaken us. Joseph, did you take the chicken down? Joseph, I am afraid of you. May God forgive me, but I am going to expose you, Joseph, I did not hear the creaking of the steel door. What do you think we'll do if someone starts asking questions about the door that creaks so irritatingly in the restful night, Joseph? Now he's the only one left, we can't kill him. Did you grease it, or did you lock it, Joseph? Did you lock it, or did you leave it open? Or maybe you didn't even open it, Joseph. Did you wolf down the chicken yourself? I'm scared. I'm scared of you, Joseph. Please, show me your palm. I'd like to be sure. Why don't you move? Joseph, please, just once. Where are you? I know, behind the curtain, sitting in the niche between the wall and the curtain where you can feel good, where you can rest. If I have to, I'll wash and starch the curtains every day, Joseph; you won't reach your goal. It's no time to rest yet, Joseph; the time for cleaning is approaching. Joseph, I'd like to see your hand. Your bloody hands. I'd like to taste the blood because I'm scared of you. This is not the chicken's blood, Joseph, this is human blood on your hand. Are you going to answer me? Or should I expose you? Say the following to me: No, Mary, this is not human blood on my hand, you are mistaken, Mary, this is not human blood. You are mistaking the taste of chicken blood for the taste of human blood; say it to me. Joseph, why don't you answer? Please. You see, I told you everything that happened. Joseph, I'd like to know what happened. Are you going to say anything? I'd like to know whether or not you are a murderer. I'd like to know what is next. Are you just going to keep quiet? I know I talk a lot, but I don't want to know our silences, Joseph. You're not answering? Oh! How am I to go on living like this? It's over. Joseph, let's break every tie. God wishes to sanction our divorce. Enough. Let's limit ourselves to the most essentials. And formally. Do you hear what I am saying?" A sharp line splits into two the tiles of the courtyard, diagonally. "Joseph, the time of cleaning has come. Would you wish us to drown in filth? You are wide of your mark. It would be a very shallow revenge, Joseph. Do you hear what I am saying? Go on. Joseph, stand up from behind the curtain, on your feet! Bring in the vacuum cleaner. Plug in the vacuum cleaner. Under the furniture too, Joseph. Under the furniture, the dust gathers into balls; first we have to get rid of those dust balls, Joseph. Take the vacuum out of the room. Have you? Bring in the broom. Let us sweep, Joseph! Under the furniture too. The balled-up dumps of dust. Move faster. Let us do our work cautiously and thoroughly. Maybe you are counting on my drowning in your filth? You are wide of your mark. Take out the broom, Joseph. Have you? The wet rag, bring a wet rag, Joseph. Wipe the floor with the wet rag, to remove the last dust motes. Stop panting. Inhale prudently. Keep working. You are cleaning up your own filth. I have cleaned up after you long enough. Take out the rag. Have you? Joseph, I am tired, very. The time to rest has not yet come. Bring a dry rag. The furniture. The smooth surfaces. Thick dust on everything. Open the window, I am suffocating. Take out this rag, bring another one. Have you? Taken it out? Bring another one. Where are you? Why are you so slow? The time to rest has not yet come. Why would you want to tempt fate, Joseph? Come on! Why don't you answer? Why do you torture me with your silence? Very nice. Everything is nice. We have worked. Now we may rest. The time of resting. We deserve it. At last we may rest. Joseph, please read to me from the newspaper. What news? The most important news items, but briefly. What is happening in the courtyard, Joseph? I would like to hear it. Do you hear? Don't deny me the news. I see the shadow on the ceiling, don't deny it. Do you hear what I am saying? Joseph, I see that something is happening in the courtyard. Don't deny it. Did you take it down? Did you check it? Who is that? I see his shadow on the ceiling. Joseph, don't say that this is the little boy, no, this is not the little boy, don't call to him, no more lies, there are no trees, tell me a story. Joseph, would you tell me a story? This is not the shadow play of the foliage moving in the motionless air. Somebody is out there in the courtyard. Why are you silent? Answer me. Just this once. Did the bell ring? Joseph, answer, for the last time. Do you hear what I am saying?" The filled-out moon among the chimneys. Its light, along a sharp line, splits the tiles of the courtyard in two. Black, yellow. "Yes, Mary! He is standing in the shadow. He is here. He is looking into the light, he is blinking. He is moving. Pops into the light." "His shadow I see on the ceiling, I can see it. His shadow. Joseph! What happened? Answer me. His bull's horns. He may start out. Pops into the light? I can see his shadow. On the ceiling. Joseph, are you keeping quiet? What happened? Good Lord, Joseph, why don't you continue?"

First published as "Minotaurus" in *Leírás* (Budapest: Szépirodalmi Könyvkiadó, 1979).

Fate and Technique

I should like to say some familiar words.

Defeat. Loss. Collapse. Bankruptcy. Devastation. Poverty. Hunger. Inventiveness. Stench. Hopelessness. Helplessness. Sorrow. Illness. Weakness. Pain. Reduction. Torment. Cold. Dust. Gloom. Melancholy. Doubt. Uncertainty. Desperation. Cunning. Joy. Confusion. Resignation. Stifling. Forgetting. Humiliation. Isolation. Self-accusation. Rebuke. Complaint. Anger. Revenge. Self-deception. Lying. Gratification. Dependency. Cowardice. Vulnerability. Remembrance. Daring. Rebellion. Failure. Injustice. Disenfranchisement. Bondage. Absolutism. Restriction. Fear. Anxiety. Breathlessness. Shame. Modesty. Lack. Suffering.

I haven't even mentioned a few, more painful words. Interrogation. Beating. Torture. Execution. And deathly silence.

I should like to say some more familiar words.

Agreement. Construction. Progress. Hope. Development. Employment. Expansion. Order. Building. Investment. Returns. Profit. Success. Joy. Jealousy. Envy. Competition. Cheating. Cautiousness. Attention. Ambition. Talent. Standard. Quality. Balance. Fragrance. Abundance. Welfare. Surplus. Selfishness. Enjoyment. Saturation. Possessiveness. Pleasure. Measure. Moderation. Criticism. Consideration. Toughness. Inconsiderateness. Openness. Power. Cheerfulness. Benevolence. Seriousness. Erring. Starting Afresh. Aloofness. Sensitivity. Independence. Sterility. Coolness. Loneliness. Isolation. Consciousness.

And I haven't even mentioned a few other, quite significant words. Creativity. Sovereignty. Spontaneity. Freedom.

Neither of these word groups could be used to characterize a single person because no one can by himself separate his failures from his successes, his sufferings from his joys, his defeats from his victories or his stench from his fragrance, but perhaps these two principal word groups are nonetheless useful when characterizing the techniques and the essential conditions for organizing society that have determined the perimeters of our personal lives in the past forty years: not the theories and ideologies but the reality of our lives.

In one word group stands the person who is at the mercy of his fate, and in the other the person who organizes his own fate; the one strives to survive and endure what the other tries to shape and arrange. This is a big difference on the level of personal experience, and an enormously large one on the level of personal desires, goals, modes of operation, and choice of means. I have no doubt that in the coming decades of our common life we shall misunderstand one another because of these differences.

I should like to talk about a set of phenomena that a like-minded Greek would call, on the one hand, predestination (*tyche*), which may happen as a will of some god, and, on the other hand, dexterity (*techne*), a mastery of some skill, proficiency, finesse, or deceitfulness; we today would call these two fate and technique. The person in one word group lives out his fate without being able to shape or arrange it, therefore has no technique to deal with his fate; the one in the second word group, though he has the technique, in reality does not know what it is he is shaping and arranging. Their priorities are different within the same duality; one sees too far, the other too close, and neither has much of a chance to understand the other. I wouldn't say they have no chance at all, because their sensibilities continue to operate in terms of their duality, but their activities and thinking work in terms of their priorities. And this means not only that they have problems understanding the other, but their own personal lives consist of nothing but a logical series of painful misunderstandings. And from this we may conclude that we have here not just a simple confusion in communication, but a kind of communicational confusion stemming from the confusion in their self-awareness and awareness of the world. They no longer consider this a duality; the one gives priority to world-awareness while the other gives it to self-awareness.

The person left to his fate perceives events as he does natural phenomena, carelessly universalizes his own situation, and considers his activities compulsion; the person who organizes his fate delimits the sphere of his activities strictly, individualizes his situation, and considers events malleable through various agreements. The thinking of a person left to his fate is regressive, derives cause from effect, looks to the past for explanation, and refers to justice; the thinking of the person who organizes his fate is progressive, derives effect from cause, prefers to find acceptable compromises in the present, and refers to the law. The person left to his fate has only a history but no individual story; the fate-shaping person has only his individual story but no history; the former harkens back to the eras prior to the French Revolution because he must find morally justifiable paradigms for his compulsion to survive and to conform; the latter perceives all history as the story of individualization and prefers not to look back to premodern times. The one compulsively remembers; the other compulsively forgets. The language of a person left to his fate is therefore always personal and intimate but not individualized; the language of a fate-shaping person is always individualized but gives a wide berth to anything that might allude to intimacy or be personal. One leans more on tradition, the other on actuality; one gleans more from the magical and mythic content of consciousness, the other from that of mental consciousness. The manner of speaking of the one is colored by an unpleasant slowness, an archaic and provincial air; the other is eager to demonstrate, just as unpleasantly, alacrity, timeliness, and being well informed. The person left to his fate finds himself in the collective identity, the fate-shaping person in the individual identity.

Their communicational confusion is easily described, for we can see clearly the behavior patterns and usage schemes that stand behind the mentality of each—just as we can understand fairly easily that Bulgarians shake their heads negatively when they mean yes and nod approvingly when they disagree, and that the British use not the drive-on-the-right but drive-on-the-left rule on their roads. The communicational confusion is, however, worsened because behind the behavior patterns and usage schemes stand not only contradictions we attribute to the historical situation or to differences in cultural levels in various geographically defined areas, but confusions of self- and world-awareness that are characteristic of Europe's civilization as a whole.

I should like to demonstrate this connection with a very simple example.

Out of sheer courtesy one person asks another, How are you? Although worn thin from use, the question survives unharmed because right behind it stands the duality of good and evil; embedded in it are curiosity and a desire for recognition, a process of control and self-control and, varying with the quality of the reply, truth and falsehood, honesty and dishonesty, rejection and the empathy, the supposition and conclusion—everything, in codes, on which value judgment is built, which is the prerequisite of both self-awareness and world-awareness.

When two persons left to their fate meet, a response like "I'm fine" can cause a great shock, because it would mean that in the misery that is the life of both persons, the respondent is rejecting solidarity with the other. Usually, when such people want to be courteous, they must strive to describe as vividly as possible—and to outdo one another in the depiction—their unbearable, intolerable fate in all its details. They do this even when by chance they happen to feel good, because their collective identity, expressed in this elementary courtesy, demands that they do not burden each other with accounts of well-being. This is the very opposite of what elementary courtesy demands from people who shape their own fate. When they meet, the basic interest of both parties is to avoid burdening each other with news of bad feelings, even if they happen to be in bad shape. If they did otherwise, they would have to entrust to a relative stranger the confidential information that they have been shaping their fate badly, that they have failed, that they have been losers, and in that case they would be casting doubt on the functional capacity of the all-encompassing theory on which the collective identity of fate-shaping people is built. The former persons compulsively simulate; the latter compulsively dissimulate.

It is no wonder, then, that when a person left to his fate meets a person shaping his fate each is shocked by the other's response. The inevitable impression in both is that the other has violated the rules of elementary courtesy, even though their simulation and dissimulation concern the same thing, fate. But neither of them has insight into their compulsion to simulate or dissimulate about fate. What in the eyes of one seems unreasonable whining, because within the duality of good and evil he has given priority to the good, appears as unreasonable boasting in the eyes of the other, because he has given priority to evil within the same duality. Their meeting becomes even more painful when they offer advice

to each other. Think of a dog, vehemently wagging its tail, coming up
against a cat whose tail is erect but motionless. They unavoidably fall on
each other because what in the language of the one means curiosity and
willing friendliness in the language of the other means distrust and the
intent to attack.

Until now, not even for the sake of simplicity, I haven't mentioned
that one of these persons might be an East European and the other a West
European. Such a distinction would be justified only if there were differences in their mentality and in the levels of their same-directional developments (that is, in everything either included in the mastery of some
skill, proficiency and experience, or derived directly from them), and also
if I were dealing with easily distinguished groups of people who with
various methods shaped and arranged their fate because they had different
ideas about what they were shaping and arranging. In the case we are
considering, unfortunately this is not so. One of them knows what he
should shape and arrange but lacks the technique for it; the other has
the technique but doesn't know what he is shaping and arranging with
it. Therefore what I see between them is not so much a difference as a
connection of distorted views stemming from their different makeup,
which they happen to hide from each other by simulation and dissimulation or by the schematic contrasts of their geographical and political conceptions.

I don't believe it is mere coincidence that the nation-states of citizens
who shape and arrange their own fate succeeded in harmonizing the legal
and economic frameworks of their geographically distinct lives at the
very moment that saw the collapse of the regimes that had striven for
global hegemony and that had made it totally impossible for their citizens, left to their own fate, to shape or arrange their life conditions.

It is likely that the ideologically based effort to achieve global hegemony brought to life an ideologically based separation, but this separation tried to maintain in one geographical sphere the very ideals,
considered common around the world, that the other ideology hoped to
disseminate across every continent and every nation. The former became
geographically separated but held on to the global standards of the once
shared ideals; the latter lost the legitimacy of its global nature for it had
to undergo a political separation. What the two had in common was an
unbridgeable chasm between theory and practice, between ideology and

reality, though the one had developed a penchant for simulation and the other for dissimulation. One can easily see that to create a unified Europe when elementary conditions for a European union were lacking, and when a common cultural community was denied, is no less impossible than to create equality when fraternity is lacking and when elementary conditions of personal freedom are denied.

So indeed I suspect some sort of connection: when the national communities of people who shape and arrange their own fate chose to see the time as ripe for stepping out of their national frameworks and establishing a new identity for themselves in a legal and economic community, based on a shared ideology, at precisely the time when the politically and ideologically separated communities of people left to their fate had exhausted their mental and economic reserves (gained during the era of supranational societies), and therefore could not rise to the challenge of establishing a new identity. Separation cannot be enforced; universalization had been a fiasco.

Yes, 1989 was the year of collapse for the communist experiment, which had hoped to create by forceful expansion a universal freedom based on equality; but it has denied that freedom to individuals, among whom, therefore, it could not ensure fraternity. In the same year, a huge leak developed in the other experiment, which, to the detriment of equality and fraternity, had tried to enforce a way of organizing geographically and politically separate societies based on individual freedom. The difference is apparently great, for it seems that the collapse was primarily economic while the fatal leak was political, in which case we could still hope for the vitality of at least one of them. But not only did the collapsing regimes submit to the regimes that sprang a leak, the invoice for which was far from economic in nature, but it also became clear that modifications had been made in the common universal ideals preserved in separated geographical regions. The concept of freedom had been supplanted by the concept of equality before the law and the concept of equality by that of social balance; the concept of fraternity had been completely forgotten while the necessary separations were implemented.

The actual operation of their social structures, which is based on reduction and separation, makes the human communities that are willing to transcend their national frameworks unfit to validate the global ideals they have voiced for forty years. The peoples of the eastern part of the continent would like at last to realize these ideals, but they keep collapsing, falling back into their national frameworks, while the global ideals, by which peoples in the west adjusted to conditions of separation, become nonfunctional.

Everything that has happened and is happening between the two suggests the bankruptcy or at least the serious malfunction of Europe's entire civilization, and I fear that the economic collapse on one side cannot be remedied because on the other side the communications breakdown cannot be eliminated politically. What seems in Prague, Budapest, and to an extent even Berlin like an insurmountable bankruptcy of civilization may appear in Zurich, Paris, or Frankfurt as merely a surmountable communications breakdown. If someone witnessing the latter speaks of a bankrupt civilization, that person is thinking of fate; and if someone witnessing a bankrupt civilization speaks of a communications breakdown, he is thinking of technique.

Fate means, simultaneously, timeliness and timelessness, the actual and the contingent, while technique, according to its original meaning, refers to the many skills, mischief, pranks, and deceit the sum total of which can make useful the thread that the youngest fate, Clotho, spins on her distaff; can arrange the portions that Lacheis metes out; and suggests that sense can still be made of what the oldest fate, Atropos, makes inevitable. Seeing the connection between "*tyche*" and "*techne*," a Greek whose thinking is similar to mine might say that there are things in this world that owe their genesis to fate—these stem from nature (*phusis*)—and there are things brought into existence by the skills of a trade (*techne*) and made usable by human accord (*nomos*), often in the form of law based on consensual agreement. Nomos, however, can enjoy no priority over nature because things stemming from nature are more powerful, and therefore it would never have occurred to this like-minded Greek to grant techne priority over tyche, as we do, just as it would never have occurred to him, when analyzing tyche or striving for agreements based on a mastered skill, not to act in full cognizance of nature's power.

For thousands of years the function of these interconnected concept pairs has not changed, though the role of fate has been taken over by divine Providence. And though the inner emphases of the connections changed substantially after the seventeenth century, we are thinking more or less of the same timeliness and timelessness that the Greeks must have had in mind when they spoke of nemesis, or the Romans when they mentioned *fatum* (fate), when we refer to creativity, as do the people who shape and arrange their fate, or ingenuity, as in the case of people accepting their fate. One shapes one's situation, which can be neither reasoned nor predicted in advance, now advantageously now disadvantageously. Our reasoning and calculations are, however, no longer impeded by fate's appearing in the image of things stemming from nature, nor guided by divine Providence in ways incomprehensible to the human mind.

This shift in the inner emphases may be characterized as nemesis gaining ground over fatum. For the last three hundred years, thanks to the *lumières* (Enlightenment) we think of fate as something we receive according to our merits or, thanks to *Bildung* (liberal education), of a fate within which, even if it is predetermined, we should strive for the merits due to shapers of fate. Before then, thanks to divine Providence, we had to think of fate as something that was simply our lot, rigid and unchangeable. Thus it is understandable why the person at the mercy of his fate hearkens back to the ages before the French Revolution, while the person shaping his own fate looks to what happened afterward. And it may also be understandable why the latter person is seized by incomprehension and abject terror at the sight of fatum, which he exchanged for nemesis, and why the person at the mercy of his fate feels that personal merits are self-deception, since his life is inevitably controlled by fatum. And it is also easier to understand why one person may desire the kind of fate that is in the hands of nemesis, and why another person's nightmare is the kind of fate in the hands of fatum. This slight difference has existed in European history for only the last forty years, and the history of the critical shift in emphasis is but three hundred years old. But the movements of these notions are based on nearly a thousand years of a culture based on these common concepts that has kept itself separate from other civilizations or, in the name of those concepts, has tried to force itself on other civilizations. Regarding the concept of time, there is no difference between the western man prey to his fate and the western man who shapes and arranges his fate. Whether one simulates or dissimulates, one's concerns are focused on the same thing; already at breakfast one wants to know what supper will be; one's concept of time is determined by a wish that cannot be limited to the present. Whether one thinks one's fate is in the hands of fatum or of nemesis, one should be armed with an image of the future that neither fatum nor nemesis can grant one.

At present, western civilization has one general and one specific concern regarding its image of the future. The general concern is that though it has been successful in widening somewhat the very narrow opening that the tyche of an economically and politically integrated city, state, or even entire continent grants for techne, for human pranks, ingenuity, and mastery of skills, still, nature declares its power precisely in accordance with differentiated technical abilities and the quality and quantity of their structures, and therefore differentiation and structural arrangements mean not that western civilization controls its fate but rather that it can control its fate much less than it had hoped to three hundred years ago. It has neglected the power of nature to the same extent that it has managed to exchange divine Providence for human accord.

In this context, western civilization's special concern is that people subject to their fate tend to think of fatum when they speak of usable life techniques, while people shaping and arranging their fate tend to think of nemesis, which dispenses fate according to individual merits.

I cannot tell whether man indeed controls his fate, in which case he must resist destructive elements, or has no control over his fate, in which case he can at best afford only pranks and artful activities against those elements. And while I also cannot tell whether the level of differentiation and structural development is really a criterion of a thing's quality (I have no data to support such a claim), nevertheless I must state that I believe it is so. The forty years of cold war and "peaceful coexistence" merely deepened the problem that three hundred years of common civilization had been lugging along, unable to solve. It is notable that two political systems collapsed for lack of a coherent civilization, and what remains in their place is no less revealing.

A fascist utopia is one ethnic community's idea for the future, perceived by all other nations or ethnic groups as a method of destruction. A communist utopia is an idea for a common future, but it is not a method. The pragmatic thought of democracies, alien to these two catastrophic alternatives, is not an idea for the future but only a method. When speaking of the communications breakdown that makes contact so difficult between persons shaping and arranging their fate and those who are prey to their fate, we might say that lack of utopia and revulsion against it are staring each other in the eye. To proffer a lack of utopia to those who find utopias repulsive but still want to know what they will have for supper is at least as senseless as trying to fill the lack by revulsion.

We can attempt to avert the communications breakdown only if we assess the method based on human accord from the viewpoint of fate, and consider acceptable only those accords that ensure the primacy of nature. If, however, a very small group of people continue to think their way of getting supper is to threaten everyone else's supper, not only would the communications breakdown worsen, but the ecological crisis would deepen too.

Adding the ecological crisis to the breakdown in communications produces the bankruptcy of civilization.

First published as "Sors és technika" in *Esszék* (Pécs: Jelenkor Kiadó Kft, 1995).

Meeting God

Whether one is asleep or awake, it is very rare that one meets the living God. I, for one, have never met him, though it's also true I've never thought I could aspire to such a meeting. My fellow humans' ambitions in this direction I follow not so much with incomprehension as with indulgence. Whoever prays to God does so on the premise that he might enter a dialogue, and if he is already talking to God, he might, according to his own intuition, ask for some little thing like happiness, money, victory, courage, insight—one thing or another. My problem with these petty objects of prayer is not that God should not be bothered with such requests, and my question is not whether God would hear and acknowledge the verbal manifestation of my distress, but rather, I think that a person with such prayers gives inevitable proof of how little faith he has in Providence. And if this is so, why and to whom is he praying? Although theologians striving for safe and unchanging dialogue probably think otherwise, I find it more than enough to entrust myself to my breathing and my bloodstream.

Quite some time ago my travels took me to an unknown street of an unknown city in an unknown region. It was before the merciful spring rains, on a sunny morning, and the dry wind blowing from the fields chased funnel-shaped clouds of dust across the unpaved street. The air was fairly warm, as if summer had already come, but on the bare skeletons of trees and bushes the buds were only just gathering their juices. A prolonged and insidious devastation had swept through the region; the yards were dirty and disorderly; the roadside ditches were full of long-decomposing contents of upended waste bins—ripped plastic milk containers, rusty innards of machines—and the wind was flipping the pages of a decaying book. In one courtyard I saw some gutted cars; in another, among the half-rotted support poles of a crumbling vine arbor pigs were rooting in the ground, but I didn't think they'd find any worms, because after the winter drought the worms too had withdrawn to deeper and less airy layers of the earth.

Small children were sitting around in the middle of the road, bending over some object or toy, and since my route took me in their direction, I headed toward them with rising curiosity. It had been years, maybe decades, since I had seen children sitting and playing in the dust of a street, and it seemed as if I were walking among deeply buried memories. I stopped by them, and my surprise was so great I couldn't speak, though I wouldn't have had the chance to do so, for they paid no attention to me. There may have been six children in all, and they were pushing a small cart around in the space between them. They were grimy and in rags, but they seemed very healthy. I was amazed too at the little cart, the likes of which I had not seen for a very long time; it was carved from some hardwood and by hand. But the main reason for my surprise was that the children were speaking French. Do it now; look out; not that way, this way; keep it going—they were shouting simple things like these, which I could understand. I thought maybe a French kindergarten was operating in the neighborhood, though I hadn't heard of it, and a French kindergarten would have been out of place in such a devastated, poverty-stricken environment.

How could I have wound up here? I quickly searched my mind, but I could not even remember having left home. I heard footsteps behind me. I turned around and saw a very lovely, thin adolescent girl approaching me. She was barefoot and wore a much-laundered summer dress. No matter how warm the spring sun was shining, this dress too was at odds with the prevailing weather conditions. But I was in trouble not only with the time and place but also with my unabashed observation. She looked at me very sternly, as if to say I shouldn't disturb the little ones, even though I wasn't bothering them. When she reached me, she grasped my arm; from her grip I understood I had no reason for fear. My arm felt good in the pleasant warmth of her palm. She did not smile. She too spoke French;

her touch reassured me. She said I would soon meet God, but it was my
job to look for him.

I did not respond. I wouldn't have known what to say. She let go of
my arm. She did not take offense at my silence because she could feel
what I was thinking. Even if I had had something to say, I preferred not
to speak incorrectly, for ruining the sentences to be formed might cause
physical pain. And I saw no way not to ruin them. She repeated that I was
the one who had to look for him and added that she would accompany
me. There was nothing encouraging in this, and I didn't need the encouragement, but what was good in what she was saying was the hint that in
my search words would mean exactly what they were meant to mean. I
would search, she would go with me; I had to find him, and she would
know where I could find him—a very nice sharing of tasks between two
people. And I promptly set off.

When one sets out on a search, one must be prepared in one's soul for
a long journey. To the right, a narrow little street opened from the wide
road. Softly the girl followed me; her feet made gentle clapping noises as
she kept just a step behind me. Here I turn, I thought, because if I had to
search, I could search anywhere and I might find him at any time. The
little street led up a hill where very close to one another stood some
whitewashed houses or rather small cottages. But I could take only a few
steps. Behind the first house, by the picket fence, there stood God.

He bowed his head slightly as if for some reason, maybe because of
me, he had to be a little ashamed, and then he glanced up at me with a
powerful look. He was no farther than three paces from me. He was tall,
bony, and lean. His furrowed, suntanned face was like that of an old out-
door laborer; his clothing reinforced the impression: loose, faded pants, a
shirt discolored by the sun. He rested one hand, like a heavy hammer, on
the fence; the other, balled into a fist, he kept inside his pocket. He
hadn't said a word, and naturally, neither had I. But if I said that we
looked at each other long, I would not be exactly correct. Perhaps I
should say that from his visage I felt exactly what is written: it is oneself
that one cannot feel when looking into the eyes of God; neither can one
feel the world, for he turns all that into himself. Therefore what I can say
is that nothing was left of me except the mere ability to see, which in
turn was no longer distinguishable from his seeing.

What I saw was a deepest of deep darkness that was a pupil: faintly gray, perhaps tainted with a little green, and surrounded by a network of aged and bloody capillaries originating in the corners of the eye. But then I was restrained by some unknown persons. Or more correctly, they removed me from this deepest of deep dark pupil, and thus I was retransformed into my feelings of indefinable content. I was a helpless patient in their hands, but they were doing their job, with no ill intent, when they wrestled this body, paralyzed by helplessness, to the dry ground before the presence of God; they were more like doctors who come with the ambulance. They had to work fast, and my only reproach to them would have been for removing me from that deepest of deep dark pupil, which, even in the midst of pain, remained a joy. I became blind in the overwhelming whiteness; white was fluttering everywhere around me, flying and swishing on the wings of the white smocks of doctors and male nurses. Here and there the blue sky flashed through the white fluttering, and there was a flash of the picket fence blackened by old rains, a vibration of the whitewashed walls of houses among the endless other layers of whites, and it seemed that I no longer had any clothes on, that my naked body had been covered with leeches, and that various extensions of gadgets were led to many points on and into my body through its many openings.

And then all I saw was a hand holding up the final test results. The hand held a test tube with my blood in it. I was staring at the showing of my blood locked in the test tube. For God's visage it was enough to touch it with a glimpse. With that glimpse he was reassured of what he must have known of me earlier and what was identical with what I had thought of myself. And in light of this, I was correct in sensing that he had to be ashamed for me. He spoke. His voice was strong and hoarse.

"You don't want to live." I had nothing to say. I was indeed thinking what he already knew—in spite of the fact that I was alive. And then a smile was getting ready to be born on his old face. Which could not have meant anything more than he had once again caught someone at this devilish little deception.

First published as "Nyolcadik levél" in *Talált cetli és más elegyes írások* (Pécs: Jelenkor Kiadó Kft, 1992, 2000).

Parasitic Systems

It began as if it were a harmless military exercise. With an alert.

Two of my mates and I were given the task of taking certain brown envelopes from officers of the general staff to the encoders and, once they were processed, carrying the envelopes to the radiotelegraphers—and then doing the whole task in reverse. It took me weeks before I realized I had not been transferred to just another army base; I was at the headquarters of the Hungarian Military Intelligence Service. Pretending to hurry, we kept walking back and forth with the brown envelopes across the spacious quadrangle of our base, where the cloudy November sky seemed to be pressing down all the smoke from all the coal-fed stoves in the surrounding area.

It made no difference to me what job I'd have to do for the two years of my regular service. I was glad not to be going berserk with idleness and glad that I could do work for which I was professionally qualified. I reproduced files, produced ID photos, and enlarged clumsy amateur pictures taken by officers. But everything was secured with iron bars, locked up; I could not even leave the darkroom without permission. Now, however, events were following one another rapidly; we were moving more freely in the winding corridors of the buildings. Yet no one expected anything real to happen. After the Cuban missile crisis one learned to live with the idea that neither side would dare take the irrevocable step.

In a dictatorship, the meaning of secret is transformed because the dictatorship carefully and in a very special way rewrites the meaning of every word.

The sentry on duty at the encoders, shoving the top-secret envelope sealed with red wax at me, told me without hesitation what was inside it. The United Nations Security Council had been called into session. But who cared? The superpowers were always provoking one another; one could hardly keep track of the many causes for which those council sessions were called. It was doubtful that among the countless lies and distortions there was still room for a person with common sense. There was no chance of obtaining distortion-free facts, and that is why everyone was exchanging reliable information with everyone else, and everyone voluntarily returned to the primitive age of communication and believed only what he saw with his own two eyes. The superpowers' mutual distrust had become ossified in everyone's mind, and between the stones there was a sense taking root that one could not be certain about anything, that facts did not exist, and everything was just words, empty words.

All well and good, but this time, within a few hours of the alert, borders were closed. Austria halted traffic on the Danube. Romania and Hungary responded in kind. This prompted me to tell my mates that they should follow closely what was happening. One of them managed to stay alone with a radio set in an empty office. He confirmed that the Security Council was indeed in session. Something had budged, begun to move; news was pouring forth from wire services, intelligence agencies, and military attachés; crossing the quad, I did not have to pretend to be in a hurry. President Tito of Yugoslavia, in a diplomatic memorandum to the Hungarian government, protested the violation of international agreement regarding navigation on the Danube. The Danube fleet was placed on alert. The neutral states of Europe declared a general mobilization—disguised as military exercises. Most suspicious of all, not only the notoriously mendacious Hungarian Radio but also the very unreliable Radio Free Europe said not a word of these developments. We were locked in from every direction.

The following morning the muscle flexing continued. All signs indicated that the defense ministers of the Warsaw Pact states were in session in Prague. The brown envelopes were no longer sealed. From West European capitals East European ambassadors were recalled for consultation. Russian diplomats and journalists were expelled from those same capitals after being accused of being secret agents. The real secret agents continued their work and detected troop movements along the Italian border. It was reported that submarine docks in Norway had been emptied. Roads

leading to Turkish airports were guarded by soldiers. We noticed that
some of our staff officers who had been wearing civilian clothes now
joined their fellow officers in being seen only in uniform, complete with
holstered handguns. The radio still did not seem to know anything, and
the November smoke cloud sat heavily over the mute quadrangle of the
base.

There was a young high-ranking officer with large, melancholy eyes
who had sought every opportunity to talk to me. He knew when I was
going to lunch with my buddies; he followed me and then called out to
me when I was going between two buildings. His approach could not be
interpreted as anything other than what it was. I quickly took advantage
of him and asked if this was just a military exercise or the real thing. He
was a slender dark-skinned man with razor-sharp features, his black hair
continually falling on his brow. We were standing in a dim corridor; he
shrugged his shoulders a little, looked at me with doleful eyes and did
not reply. Looking out the window, I saw people moving on Buda's narrow streets as if nothing were happening. It occurred to me that I should
notify my loved ones, but how? And wasn't it my moral duty to notify
the unsuspecting outside world? There were telephones on almost every
desk, but not everyone had access to outside lines. The impending danger
received confirmation that day, when the earlier flood of news was followed by several hours of silence. As if the world were holding its terrible
breath and thinking things over just one last time.

At dawn I was obliged to inform my relief that in Kansas the silos of
intercontinental missiles were open.

He looked at me, gaping, and jumped out of bed; we stood facing
each other, my humiliating trembling infecting him too. We knew what
was waiting for us.

He got dressed and ran off, and I took off my clothes. I had to lie
down in the same bed he had just left. I tossed about in the warmth of his
body.

If the slot of the lock is in a vertical position, it means peace. If that
certain key is inserted and you turn the slot to a horizontal position, it
means war.

It hardly mattered that in a few hours it became clear that the whole
thing was only a simulation. Helplessness, confinement, fear, and enforced silent endurance carved another deep groove in my memory, and

distrust settled into it like a lasting experience; it became the psychic reality of my life. Although today we know what happened, the memory of it cannot be erased, and even if no one turned that certain key, it is known only too well that the paranoid thinking of the cold war had devoured common sense.

At the very same moment when, on the smoky quadrangle of the headquarters of Hungarian Military Intelligence Service, I realized that I had been had and that my life had no other reality, George Blake, one of the most successful military spies of all time, in the literary circle of a London jail had just completed making arrangements with two inmates, about to be released, for the ways and means of his own escape. Also at the very same moment, Günter Guillaume, who had succeeded in becoming a mole in the party apparatus of the West German Social Democrats, was giving up his profitable tobacco business in Frankfurt. At the same time that a Buddhist monk doused himself with gasoline and set himself on fire on a Saigon street, a mere two hundred meters away Ambassador Henry Cabot Lodge, Jr., was just setting the parameters between paranoid thinking and common sense, when he wrote to President Kennedy about the proposed assassination of President Ngo Dinh Diem that "we have taken the road from which there is no honorable way back."

The archives are open. One can learn how the great parasitic world systems were built into and worked inside each other, and who had what role or who wanted what role for himself in either of them. I was sitting in the secret power center of one of the world systems. Care was taken to keep me away from sensitive material, and I also took care to keep away from it. Still, I could not say I had another, personal life. In sober self-defense I kept to all the regulations lest it might occur to someone to use me for something other than what I was being used for. I did not want to know anything. It was as if someone who had to go through the door a hundred times a day were being careful not to touch the doorknob.

I was extremely excited to know what was being done in the place, if only because of my own plans as a writer. Yet it was not out of caution that I pretended to be uninterested. I had to delude myself. Whatever I learned was more than enough to regard it as morally unacceptable. But it did not occur to me to deny my services because of moral principles. I thought I was fortunate to be able to observe my own false-bottomed reality from such an unusual perspective. Occasionally I took pleasure in imagining what would happen if I decided to enter the adventurous, dangerous life I was observing.

There was a basic rule of behavior whose strictness was not to be doubted. In no circumstance were rank-and-file personnel to recognize anyone outside the military base. I had very little time left until my discharge when, riding on an almost empty streetcar, I felt someone's eyes on the back of my head. The young officer was indeed there, in civilian clothes, standing on the open platform. I didn't know how he'd got there, but he'd no doubt reached his high rank by outstanding achievements, of which popping up on a moving streetcar out of nowhere was certainly not the most morally dubious one. The streetcar was rattling along Verpeléti Road, but we still hadn't turned onto the bridge. He came closer. If I wanted to, this was the opportunity to choose for myself a life that would be more dangerous from every perspective than the life I had lived until then. There was something profoundly dramatic in his enormous dark eyes, and strange as it may sound, he needed my help. While clattering across the echoing body of Petőfi Bridge, I several times refused to help him yet was unable, as many times, not to return to his eyes. We kept standing next to each other, struggling and silent, hanging on the straps, both of us deep in our own infinite sorrow, on guard to see how the other, in his excitement, would violate the behavior code. This is something one can see and hope for on the other's lips and in his eyes. Our sorrows differed not in their depth but in their nature, making it even more attractive. At Boráros Square I got off as quickly as I could. He followed me without a word. The winter of 1964 was a hard one; we made creaky noises in the filthy frozen snow across the square. In the dark crowd we had to wait a long time for the bus. Within each other's body heat we were standing still in the freezing cold. Anyone who has grown up in a dictatorship sometimes tends to suspect that it wants to make him vulnerable to blackmail. He does not believe his own eyes, and he does not even realize this is so. And he becomes like a prickly plant and shrivels up, receding into his prescribed life. I left with the number 23 bus, in the midst of the pressing throng.

In a dictatorship it is very difficult to determine the proportions of one's participation and one's refusal. Four more years had to go by before I could, and it was not I but the combined military forces of the Warsaw Pact that determined the final proportions when in 1968 they overran

Czechoslovakia. Only now am I fully aware of the many decisions I made back then—without available information. While windshield wipers on Hungarian military vehicles ceased to work because of all the spit expectorated by Czechoslovaks lining the streets, and as the Hungarian soldiers riding in the vehicles trembled and wept, President Johnson in a confidential telegram reassured General Secretary Leonid Brezhnev that he would honor the Yalta Agreement. But one did not have to be familiar with the telegram or the text of the famous Yalta note to know that one's civilization had caved in and the collapse would bury him. This too was accepted by the democratic half of Europe. Its life-denying lies, couched in its ritual protests, could no longer be concealed. It spectacularly relinquished its own freedom to act and, in compensation, strengthened its own separation. It restricted equality and solidarity to internal use and reduced them further to equality of opportunity and the maintenance of social balance. "Fraternity" was erased from its dictionary. It did not desert its universalistic ideals but, with its practical and pragmatic thinking, severely restricted their sphere of influence. In political decisions it abandoned the sensible primacy of public interest and declared that self-realization and personal interest were economic necessities. And finally it could not resist exchanging the critical spirit for opportunism. "Into the azure they pop their cocks / all who wanted a future . . ." wrote the era's great Hungarian poet, György Petri, at the sight of nicely ripening European crops. For lack of something better to do, I resigned, walked out, and turned my back on the system to save my soul, though I knew there was no resignation or asceticism that would not make me look ridiculous.

The two great eras of the cold war, first confrontation and then coexistence, are probably among humankind's best-documented eras. Theoretically, with the help of this extensive documentation, nothing stops us from separating out the various intentions and levels of the pathological simulations and chronic dissimulations that characterized the parasitic systems facing each other. The way to delineate their common reality most faithfully is probably via their intertwined illusions.

Only a few lonely historians show any interest in the past. Public opinion is averse to the mere mention of the commonality of the past. Citizens of the new democracies have opted for total memory loss. They have no wish to inquire into what happened during their long isolation because it would be hard to adjust the cheerless reality of their coded language and paranoid role-playing to their actual needs, to readjust their egalitarian socialization to match their individual needs. One is incapable of doing that. And if someone were to attempt it, he would clearly see that the life experience acquired in the isolation of dictatorship is adequate for survival but not for the life gained by surviving, that he may know a great deal about the strategy of selfishness but not enough of the responsibility he owes to himself, and that since others know so little of it as well, he cannot organize an independent life with them. He had been developing the reproductive, not the productive abilities of his intellect. Even as an adult he is unfamiliar with the creative powers of his individuality, but he is very proud of the merciless extremes of his inventiveness, of which he should be ashamed. He does not know what to do, within the law, with his infantile egoism, not because capitalism does not offer playing fields for that egoism—there are plenty of those—but because egoism in the great, well-established liberal democracies is based on the idea of enjoyment, not on the compulsion of survival. The reasons the two kinds of egoism cannot be reconciled are not moral but generic.

Behind the hedonistic egoism based on the pleasure principle, the very rich and centuries-old criminal past—original amassing of capital, slave trade, wars of conquest, Christian missionary work and colonialism—stands in the bright light of an enlightened social contract according to which the bestial desire to amass wealth and the raw instinct to pursue pleasure must be restrained by self-discipline and the cultivation of self-knowledge; it must be redeemed by the mechanisms of solidarity and social security. But even today, nothing stands behind the egoism of the compulsion to survive—save the bestial desire to acquire among the peasantry and petit bourgeoisie, given Eastern Europe's traditional lack of capital. In place of the aesthetics of moral consensus and transparency there is at best a musty dimness along with the noisy swagger of self-pity, for we are the perennial losers. The accruing historical disadvantage indeed appears irremediable. The prohibition against brutality fixed in international agreements inconveniently impedes the intentions that egalitarian socialization (based on the compulsion to survive) would allow, even encourage, or indeed hold as sacred economic necessities.

In the interest of your own and your family's prosperity, you have to circumvent the written law; a contract is only worth the paper it's written on, the given word means nothing, you must rob the hostile state without giving it a thought. Many attempt this sad plan, but if they actually carry it out and accumulate significant capital, they must realize that in the circumstances of globalization their competitive chances are sorely limited. The geographically larger half of Europe, because of the continent's uneven development, is made up of open societies in which people, not as individuals but en bloc, are noncompetitive. The strong democracies would welcome the elimination of inequality between east and west only if it were in their interest to live with the enduring disadvantages of European integration. At the moment, however, their advantage is in fact increasing, because the Schengen borders* are more or less identical to those of the cold war, and as a result, the moral consensus between the two Europes worked out during the cold war does not hold beyond those borders. The future will not see a significant national bourgeoisie in the new democracies, and there won't be a strong middle class either; and one doesn't fear what doesn't exist. The eastern nations have no political representation free from the influence of extremist ideals or prepared for even elementary negotiations. And the governments of the old, great democracies cannot and do not wish to see more than four years ahead.

In Europe we have two great systems that, given the differences in their inner structures, not only cannot integrate but, it is to be feared, may find it difficult to coexist peacefully. The war in Yugoslavia was only the first signal of this likelihood.

Because of the functioning of totalitarian regimes and the cold war, the difference between east and west is greater than ever before. We can see in Germany that this difference has strengthened political extremism in both halves of the continent. Gerhard Schröder was right: neonazism is not an East German problem but has become again a German problem, for West Germans refuse to this day to acknowledge the nature of the difference between them and the East Germans and do not take it into account. The East German state collapsed ten years ago, but the legacy of its secret life strategy is intact. There was no reason for it to perish. It col-

---

*The Schengen Agreement, signed in June 1985 by Belgium, France, West Germany, Luxembourg, and the Netherlands, allowed for common immigration policies and a border system that removed posts and checks among the signatories and harmonized external border controls for the entire "Schengen area." A total of twenty-six countries—including all the European Union states except the Republic of Ireland and the United Kingdom, as well as Iceland, Norway, and Switzerland—have now signed the agreement, and fifteen have implemented it—Editor.

lapsed not because capitalism was in essence more humane than socialism, not because people suffering under dictatorships judged democracy
to be better and became its adherents, or because the undifferentiated inner structures of the socialist societies, inadequate for creativity, proved to
be noncompetitive in a world experiencing its third technological revolution. It collapsed because over several decades millions of people—the
same people who in the name of egalitarian ideals were compelled to
endure privation and a scarcity-based economy—driven by the bestial
desire for accumulation had like moles gnawed and chewed away the
socialist state from under themselves. They too wanted their bananas;
now they have them. Now they are gnawing away at their democracy,
something of which they have neither experience nor knowledge. If it
were otherwise, the new democratic political parties and governments
would not have accepted leading roles in legalizing corruption and in
robbing and criminalizing society. Or the churches, so proud of their ec-
umenism, would be interested in more than finding ways, in the name of
reparations, to take more from the poorest segments of the population.

The citizen of the new democracies has in principle neither affections
nor emotions he might safely use in his new situation, but this is exactly
what is familiar to him. With great inner conviction he has returned to
his role-playing. He allows himself to act according to his parasitic intentions and behave according to the rules of egalitarian ideals. He wants to
get rich at any cost but wishes for a socially balanced society in which
everyone, except he, will pay taxes, and the tax money will be distributed
equally so that he gets more than anyone else. Or if this doesn't work,
he'd wish for a nationalist police state that, for racial or historical reasons,
would deny his neighbor things it would naturally grant him. Citizens
of the new democracies have returned to simulation as if even under the
law they were not free persons. Just as they once simulated socialists, now
they simulate the democrats. And why shouldn't they go on being simulators, when the citizens of the old democracies have not given up dissimulation? The latter haven't exactly rushed to examine the mental and
spiritual consequences of their cold war past.

As if the picture could not be further refined, given the materials
found in the open archives, the old democracies preserve the image of a
bipolar world. At the time of German unification, Chancellor Helmut
Kohl envisioned for himself blooming landscapes so he would not have to

acknowledge the realities of the new German territories that were clearly visible to the naked eye; ten years later Chancellor Schröder, because of his chronic lack of personal experience, still thinks of them as something completely strange and alien to him and to his constituents. Kohl's weighty informational deficit and Schröder's painful political slips of the tongue stem from the same cold war dissimulation. The one, for lack of knowledge, ignores the facts of which the other admits awareness, though he does not wish to deal with them. Where they try to arrange life in geographically separated conditions and based on universal ideas and ideals, dissimulation becomes a necessary component of life. For close to forty years the left in Western Europe had ignored the reality of the existing socialist systems in the east, while the right made good use of them in its arguments. This would have been all right if they had been able to separate their true information from their propagandistic illusions consistently. But neither the left nor the right managed to do that. Their sense of reality suffered great injuries during the cold war, and with the facts of these injuries they had overwritten the universal ideals.

In discourse about the cold war, the anticommunist argument, which, given its erstwhile prevalence, literature records as the "traditional" fundamental principle of the cold war, stands in direct opposition to the anti-imperialist argument, which historians call the revisionist fundamental principle. According to the first, the cold war was caused by the Soviet Union's aggressive and treacherous desire for expansion, while the second blames the cold war on American economic imperialism. The common thread in both principles is that the evil was caused by the other. If it indeed had been caused by the other, why should I take responsibility for it? At most, I'd defend myself; on occasion I pretend to feel empathy for the victims, at other times I even pretend not to notice the crimes committed. When economic necessity trumps fundamental principles in politics, the relinquishment of universal ideals, with which those in power wish to establish a common life, is explained by referring to common sense and practical reasons. The Berlin Wall fell, the politics of "peaceful coexistence," which was to last forever, lost its meaning, but the bipolar world, with all its rituals and methods of argumentation, remained.

Was the cold war confrontation really justified? Was the political rending of Europe's two great historical regions necessary and unavoidable? Did the dual vision of its politics cause irreparable damage? At least these three naive questions about our common past should have been asked during the last ten years. For if the damage was not justified, what was the mistake, and who made it? If it was not necessary to divide the continent (and the world) in two, in what circumstances is unification possible? If with the false-bottomed politics of "peaceful coexistence" a third world war was avoided, though this very gain doomed the bipolar world that was meant to last for eternity, then where was the mistake in believing in the permanent maintenance of a bipolar world, and what practical losses resulted from the faulty political calculations?

In the absence of questions, citizens of the old democracies may continue to cling to the beliefs and appearances with which they succeeded in covering up the social and moral realities of their separation for so long. They opted for partial amnesia; they measure things with a double standard, and accordingly they offer the new democracies isolation, because for themselves they would like to have at least a controlled separation instead of integration.

It is hard to believe they are unaware how dangerous this game is.

First published as "Parazita rendszerek" in *Esszék* (Pécs: Jelenkor Kiadó Kft, 2001).

At the Muddy Source of Appearances

Mutual understanding is what I should be talking about, this lovely and idle pipe dream, but to my great regret I can talk only about the lack, the appearance of understanding, the painful reality of gray and hopeless weekdays.

Frankly, I see little chance for us to understand one another.

Not only as civilizations, peoples, or nations in general, but first of all as you and I, he and she, people pleasantly spending time together, every one of us, personally—the way the ailing Schiller or the deaf Beethoven had hoped we would. This is what is not working. And maybe it is time to acknowledge it. The last missed historical moment is only just behind us—when the Hungarians opened the borders, the Czechs took off on their velvet slippers, the Romanians, trembling and with wanton joy, slaughtered their two tyrants, the Germans with bare hands fell on these concrete walls—as if for the first time in ages the hope of a sensibly ordered common life were flashing before us. Even if we did not all speak the language of freedom in the same way, in principle there should have been mutual understanding among us. But in the very next moment after the flash, the long dark past reached out for everyone, and everyone—with his own past, according to his own disposition, and in his own voice—stifled the lovely melody rising from the chorus of people who were finding their liberation. Deaf Beethoven would have seen nothing but helpless, empty gaping.

First the French, most competent in matters of freedom, began to gape, and then, true to their old customs, the British joined in; the Germans, hesitant at first, soon judged that it would be a good thing to join this general and enthusiastic mouthing. The Scandinavians, the Italians, the Spanish, the Greeks, and the Portuguese did not even bother to strain their mouths too much with gaping. Later, under presidential guidance, the Czechs began; the Hungarians, not ever to be left out, also gaped, and so did the Austrians, who have a specially developed sense for empty mouthing; the Poles, who had earlier and alone given their vocal cords a good workout, gaped too. Let us not forget that in the end only a few hungry, half-naked, and barefoot Albanians did not gape.

Once again we had the deathly silence of restorations past: the well-mannered and spiritless mouthing of a well-rehearsed grand choir of traditional European hypocrisy, never once penetrated by a single word or sigh of human suffering. What remained were the sacred appearances. The silence of mirrored halls, the silence of festive dinners, the silence of crystal chandeliers and of rolled-out red carpets mercifully absorbing the footsteps of political criminals and visiting mass murderers. Chaos, smoke, blood, migration, and genocide, raped girls and women; mothers who send off their own sons with the message to kill, rape! A war that of course no one wishes to see or hear.

Lately I've had the definite impression that this whole mutual understanding, as an intellectual challenge, political task, and moral duty on which our strict and exacting upbringing was hitherto built, is not working very well for us. How could it when even lovers understand each other only when they open their mouths for something other than speaking and even though amniotic fluid always comprehends both mother and embryo at once?

Reason is a very thin membrane over the human world, and it is now pierced by animal instincts, now ripped open by winds. It might be better to admit that at best we have some inkling of what reciprocity is, but mutuality is beyond us.

Of course I do not believe that there is a person remaining who'd be willing to admit much of anything to anyone or that there is an admission or confession that would find understanding ears.

Humanly and spiritually Europe is in such dire condition that it has no thinker who can credibly proclaim the bankruptcy: it doesn't work; I have nothing in reserve, I've erred, I'm exhausted, I can't bear it anymore.

One would be ashamed to utter out loud such compassion-hungry, sensible sentiments.

In the last fifteen years the best minds have given themselves over to the cult of appearances and illusions, because the paying public wants to hear nothing but jokes and success stories. Recently, when someone tried to rattle off for me a few characteristically old-fashioned sentences about his personal fiascos, I too grudgingly adjusted my expression to one of empathy. Grudgingly because I was thinking, What can one possibly say about all this? If you can't bear these woes, don't! It wouldn't be such a great loss if you jumped out of the window. Maybe we should leave room for appearances, for the illusion of empathy, but the air is thick with these unpronounced, secret sentences.

Perhaps it is not by chance that in the early days of the recent Balkan war one of Germany's best-known pundits did utter some of these secret inner sentences. The message he sent to the sides slaughtering each other was that they should go on killing each other until they grew bored with it. We cannot allow uncivilized people to disturb our peace with such senseless wrangling.

To judge by these sentences, there are two completely different Europes: one is satanic, sheerly brutal; the other, however, has always maintained, as it does now, its angelic innocence and noble self restraint. When those few German sentences went to press, the last dreams of a moral responsibility sustained in the realm of pure reason were shredded. Those few sentences meant that in the Europe of perfect, excellent beings, in this best of all possible worlds, neither the last remaining little memory of the long-dead God nor human intellect, venerated as divine for two hundred years, could exercise any control over personal selfishness. To understand others is neither my job nor my responsibility, and above all, it is not my wish.

Kant is gone, and the well-known German pundit's later recantation was in vain. The moment when, despite his intentions, upbringing, and most profound convictions, he uttered those few sentences had been more truthful than his recantation. For a long time now I also would like to shout loud into the face of the sufferers and the ruined ones:

If you can't bear it, drop dead. Don't bother me with your troubles; kill yourself. Starve if you have nothing to eat, but do it quietly. Be cold, freeze, but don't let me hear your teeth chattering.

I am not joking. I know what I'm talking about.

Fifty years ago the city of my birth was bombarded for 102 days. It was razed to the ground. Nothing was left standing. Remnants of bridges poked out of the Danube for a long time after. In all likelihood, I am seriously wounded myself.

My first memory is of an air attack while I was turning on a stairwell landing; the light of the burning roof reflected on the wall opposite me. That horrifying blast of explosion is my first memory: the deafness, the breathlessness, and the wavering blood-red wall as it hurtles toward me.

And until the time when hormones brought my body to maturity, it never occurred to me that there should be, could be, or perhaps actually *was* another, gentler and more innocent, more enlightened world in which people didn't have to have several dead relatives and friends all at once—heroes, martyrs, hangmen, and victims. Or that there should be a world in which life was something other than inevitable loss, in which having a hand or leg or eyesight today that might be lost tomorrow would not be considered the greatest good fortune. The blind felt their way through the rubble with their white-painted iron rods. The lucky ones received wooden arms or legs or had real crutches or a decent stick. Pieces of skin were singed or burned off faces, limbs, or whole bodies: the memorials of incendiary bombs. There were shrapnel and bomb fragments, frayed edges of gashes in human flesh, missing noses and ears, splinter injuries, and myriad bluish gray and crimson scars. Those who were scraped out from under the ruins sounded as if they were whistling when they took a breath. And those who came back from the camps wore tattooed numbers on their arms.

All this is inscribed on my eyes as it is on everyone else's, and that is why no one will convince me that there are two Europes. There is only one Europe, that of the injured. And the boundaries of mutual understanding are far from being geographical ones. I look at France from Vichy, Germany from Stalingrad and Auschwitz, and I think of England strictly from Gandhi's viewpoint. There are those who understand themselves and those who do not. Having been born at a later date is no panacea, because there is no generation now and there won't be one in the foreseeable future that can get by without wartime wounds. We are the ones who pass on what we received directly into the flesh of each succeeding generation; we make it course through the nervous systems of others ten thousand times a day. We initiate everyone into the ritual of destruction.

If we can speak at all about mutual European understanding, and not only about its lack or the superficial appearances of it, the real question would no longer be why some European nations, more experienced in democracy and enjoying freely elected governments, did not help the new democracies get on their feet when it was their moral responsibility to do so or why, serving their own short-term interests, they forced them to their knees when they wanted at least to stand up on their own. Rather, the question would be, Why don't their chosen thinkers come to their senses at last? Why do they fail to articulate, loud and clear, a single, humanly comprehensible, realistic sentence? I cannot help here, because the functional theories of my own system keep me from doing so, but I shall examine the functional error, for after all, the danger increases in direct proportion to the measure of neglect, and therefore I beg you, if you have any ideas how to organize this common life, please let me know. The cult of illusions and appearances probably does not allow such a sentence, or perhaps it does not occur to anyone.

The peoples in European nations more experienced in democracy, and their freely elected governments, are working not to strengthen democratic traditions and correct their errors or to eliminate democracy's functional disorders, but rather to establish new hierarchical relationships. There is no dialogue, and these nations do not want to have one. Instead of natural integration, they offer controlled isolation to the new democracies, and for themselves they suggest a controlled separation. They leave no doubt about who is setting the direction, who does the controlling, who has the right to say anything about how things ought to be, where the limits of politeness lie, and, in general, who the master of the house is. Of course things are probably all right just the way they are. Though it is clear that the greater the chaos, the more forceful and more arbitrary the dictates of these old democracies become, and they screen all the more carefully the daily information reaching their regimes. This is very familiar. The spirit of the Congress of Vienna and of the Kremlin has smoothly returned to the same baroque halls.

In conclusion, I should like at least to tell my own story to the end.

I left off with the remark that until my body, with the help of hormones, reached adult maturity, I had not noticed that my own warlike world was perhaps not quite natural. But then I discovered how velvety skin was, how smooth and flawless our brows. And if there were two un-injured persons in this wondrous world, then there must also be a life in which there was nothing but beauty. At first it was just the sight of the tattooed numbers that disturbed my newly acquired sense of bodily well-being. Why didn't they hide them? Why did they keep reminding me of this horror? And then there were the scars, the ripped flesh, the raw-edged scabs; I was disgusted by missing limbs, the stumps, and those whistling sighs. If I were like that, I wouldn't set foot on the street. Bod-ily well-being does not make you more tolerant or indulgent, as simple logic might lead you to expect, but rather more intolerant. I hated them. They sullied the blue sky. Thirty years had to go by before I could dare confess even to myself what half of Europe, terrified, now suppresses and keeps to itself, now hatefully whispers, and occasionally spits in my eye. I understand, because I too would have preferred to shout in their faces, Why don't you stay home, why are you still living, what are you drag-ging yourself around for?

And though I had never satisfied this barely restrainable urge and never shouted into anyone's face, I could not avoid the punishment.

In the jungle of the city, in some awful lair in our neighborhood, there lived an elderly woman who was always walking the streets, insofar as she could walk, and who was always screaming at the top of her voice, some-times in Hungarian, sometimes in other languages. Her greasy gray hair reached for the sky; her tattered filthy clothes and frayed bags stuffed with leftovers hung pitifully off her body. Everyone knew her story. The six-story tenement where she lived had collapsed. The cellar vault was torn open, and a steel beam had kept her captive under the rubble like a trapped animal. They found her by chance three days later. One of her legs had to be amputated, but people could not erase from their minds the insanity of those days and nights. She had no wooden leg. I don't know why she did not get one; she was poor, she had no one. A rough wooden peg replaced the missing leg, and someone had fastened a piece of rubber to the end of it so it wouldn't make such a racket.

One sunny morning this woman stopped in front of me on the side-walk crowded with people. She appeared to be smiling chastely, almost shyly, as if wanting to say or ask for something, and in a situation like this a well-mannered young man naturally leans closer. But she did not say or ask for anything, only opened her empty mouth to scream. Listen, people, this is the young man who made my mouth stink! People on the street stopped to listen. And the woman leaned so close to me that the breath of her scream hit my face.

Why did you stink up my mouth? She screamed the words slowly, syllable by syllable. How can I defend myself against you?

I did not misunderstand the questions. The soul can see. That long moment taught me many things.

First published as "A látszat zavaros forrásainál" in *Élet és Irodalom*, March 24, 1995.

The Citizen of the World
and the He-Goat

On March 24, 1999, the day NATO began bombing military targets in Yugoslavia, the law lords in London approved the extradition of the former Chilean dictator, the ancient Augusto Pinochet, to the Spanish authorities.* I don't believe the simultaneous occurrence of the two events was coincidental. In this last year of the century something has cracked, shifted, something of whose effect and extent the daily news reports say very little.

The lords' decision touched on a problem that has concerned all fair-minded persons for several centuries and for which no one has found a satisfactory solution to this day, not even for oneself; least of all for one-

---

*NATO's bombing of Yugoslavia followed its long-standing warning that it would attack if Slobodan Milošević's government refused to sign the internationally brokered peace plan for Kosovo, the Yugoslavian province, largely populated by ethnic Albanians, that had been subjected to a Serb campaign of "ethnic cleansing." Kosovo had wanted to secede from Yugoslavia but accepted the plan's arrangement for its autonomy; NATO air strikes began a day after Milošević refused to agree to the plan.

In 1996 a Spanish judge ruled that his court had jurisdiction in a case of international terrorism, genocide, and crimes against humanity brought against General Pinochet by the families of some of the victims of his regime in Chile (1973–89). In October 1998 London police, acting on a Spanish warrant charging General Pinochet with these crimes and requesting his extradition, arrested the former dictator, who had come to Britain for medical treatment. The extradition proceedings eventuated in the High Court's ruling in March 1999. (Later Pinochet was judged too ill to stand trial; he returned to Chile, where he faced many legal efforts made to lift his immunity from prosecution there, and where he died in 2006)—Editor.

self, I'd say, because on a tribal basis almost everyone hastens to show understanding and breathless forgiveness for crimes committed by members of one's own family or nation. Despite tribal customs, however, it remains a generally accepted moral imperative that there should be not two standards but only one by which to judge errors, infractions, and crimes. This is a very delicate security question. The standards of marble halls, dazzling with their brilliant crystal chandeliers, of dim interiors of churches, of riotous and haughty academies, of bloody battlefields, and of hushed libraries all must be reconciled within one person, and then among all persons in a single state, so that they can be reconciled among different countries.

On the medieval marketplace of Pozsony (Bratislava), wrought into the gate of the old city hall, is a well-worn iron yardstick. Any buyer of textiles could use it to ascertain that the merchant had made no mistake or the merchant could check whether his own yardstick had satisfied the requirements people had for units of measurement.

There is no moral yardstick on display anywhere. There are, however, a few conspicuously naive, stubbornly recurring questions that are impossible to answer and impossible not to answer. These questions are, I think, equivalent to the wrought-iron yardstick.

If a state, keen on being lawful, without ado catches, brings before a judge, sentences, and locks up a filthy little pickpocket from the marketplace, how can it let arrant rogues and mass murderers, having completed their dastardly deeds in the morning, enjoy their afternoon tea in the company of crowned heads only because they are rich or because they are statesmen? Are deceptions, robbery, and murder included in, or do they in any way follow from the principle of state sovereignty? Does the personal integrity of heads of state not suffer damage as the result of mass murder committed in the name of state interest? In this genre of state sovereignty, Europe at the end of the century has a few unforgettably shameful snapshots: of Pope Paul VI receiving Hungary's Prime Minister János Kádár; Queen Elizabeth II of England honoring Elena and Nicolae Ceauşescu with a banquet; Colonel Karremans of Holland, commander of the UN blue berets in Srebrenica, and Serbian General Ratko Mladić clinking champagne glasses in the company of their dashing adjutants; Margaret Thatcher demonstratively taking tea in the impeccably appointed residence of General Pinochet, under house arrest in London.

On that March day, frought with decision, the law lords declared that they did not wish to continue the approach that rulers and governments of England, even if in the interest of the British Empire, had thought appropriate for several hundred years. As one of them aptly put it, "It is not one of the functions of a head of state to commit acts which are criminal according to the laws and constitution of his own state or which customary international law regards as criminal."

Similarly, NATO's first air attacks also signified a difficult, no less consequential decision.

I note with some trepidation that the dates of two subsequent events also coincided: the appeal submitted by Pinochet's lawyers was rejected by their lordships on the sixty-sixth day of the war in Kosovo (May 27), the same day that the International War Crimes Tribunal in The Hague announced its indictment of Yugoslav President Milošević and issued a warrant for his arrest. As if fate, destiny, providence, history, or whatever we call it wanted to confirm its earlier declarations with a demonstration of unprecedented force.

That gesture of confirmation suggests there is no way back. If Augusto Pinochet, in spite of the Chilean government's sensible political and legal arguments, is turned over to the Spanish authorities, it is not possible that Slobodan Milošević would not be indicted, however many diplomatic reasons are cleverly argued. The great power mechanisms of democracy work in parallel. Although this makes the work of incumbent politicians, diplomats, and international jurists more difficult and may further unsettle and divide public opinion, it cannot paralyze any of them; put another way, it gives them no excuse for their temporary paralysis.

In my view, that these democratic institutions are working in parallel is the only guarantee that out of the useful elements of chaos and anarchy we may still create a more transparent, more just, and more predictable European order. Some lawyers fear exactly the opposite: that with these decisions the principle of state sovereignty has suffered a serious blow and that the international community will have a hard time recovering. I would not fear this, for everything that has happened and is happening probably has deeper implications, and the changes resulting from them are more essential for the principle of state sovereignty than the need to protect that principle from these changes. I would have been more fearful had the international community, because of the accepted interpretation of the principle of state sovereignty, tolerated genocide or for diplomatic or legal considerations had continued to allow the Federal Republic of Yugoslavia or its president to commit further genocide. But since it very correctly saw no legal justification for such tolerance, state sovereignty came to mean something different from what it meant yesterday.

It probably means that from now on states will not be permitted, even within their own borders, to do what they will with their own citizens. And other states will be reluctant to recognize their sovereignty if they do. It does not follow from the definition of sovereignty that states and heads of states have the right to categorize their citizens according to religion or ethnic origin. Nor does it follow that nations have cradles somewhere (unless in some museum). A head of state, citing raisons d'état or historical rights, may not order people's houses blown up and their residents chased out, may not confiscate personal documents or money, may not expel people to foreign countries, because all this is forbidden by the Universal Declaration of Human Rights. And a head of state cannot do this even if the majority of citizens in his country so wish it and influential intellectuals express no opposition. There is no such sovereignty anymore, and it is shameful that there ever was.

If what I see is true, these changes in the violence-riddled history of sovereignty mean that for the first time the Universal Declaration of Human Rights—almost sixty years after its birth—was validated. Violation of those rights sanctioned the bombing of military installations. The principles of state sovereignty and the inviolability of heads of state were reinterpreted from the standpoint of that hitherto rather worthless document. Diplomacy during all those earlier years, in the interest of maintaining a double standard, had made no effort to reconcile the UN Charter with the Declaration of Human Rights. If Security Council members could veto the decision of other UN members even when the Universal Declaration of Human Rights called for action, then I as a layman had to doubt the seriousness of the member states' intentions regarding human rights. So what we are talking about now is not that under the NATO air attacks a perfect edifice of international law had collapsed, but that its imperfection became visible to everyone. The great gap between the two basic documents was exposed, widened so hugely by the exigencies of the cold war and by the interests of the signatory states' infinite comfort, then filled with the corpses of half a century's mass killing.

I see the situation as exactly the opposite of what opponents of the air attacks, citing legalities, claim it to be. It is not that sovereignty has been damaged, but that we, earlier, based on customary historic law, had derived rights from it that cannot be reconciled with the Universal Declaration of Human Rights. We accepted the cold war logic that the declaration was merely a recommendation, a suggestion, a basket of offerings, a mere desire, a declaration that should not be taken seriously whenever it clashed with the special interests of the signatory states, but that one of those states might immediately refer to it when it was in its interests to do so. We accepted all this, though our watches all ran synchronized to Greenwich mean time, and in the Bratislava City Hall's gate there is only one yardstick.

The international community of states could set new standards for international life by thoroughly analyzing the last fifty years and by thoroughly and seriously reconciling the requirements of the two universal documents. Among other things, the principle of sovereignty ought to be redefined. The constitutions of the international communities should be harmonized, to make clearer where the boundaries of tolerance and permissiveness are and who is allowed to use what kind of weapons, and when. This would better define not only the rights of citizens but also the responsibilities they have to one another. We would better know the individual citizen's and the head of state's personal responsibilities toward others, and the concept of others would not be defined by the boundary of the next village. Individual states within the United States would no longer be allowed to make separate decisions in matters such as capital punishment; no individual member state of NATO could conduct a punitive war against the Kurds. This would not be a standard that measures now what was practical, now what was decent. The sovereignty of a state and the inviolability of a head of state would endure as long as each kept to the uniform rules of the international game. And the community of democratic states would not recognize as legitimate any rules that were not based on the two universal documents. If all this were possible, from now on no head of state would be compelled, in the interest of noble goals, to consult with common criminals about law and order in marble-laid halls with rococo decor where the fragrance of the flowers, though they are changed in the vases every day, cannot overcome the stench of male bodies reeking with unreflective passions.

I have been writing all this in the conditional mode, as if it were some pipe dream, though the first salvo of this enormous change, despite rumors to the contrary, has actually been fired.

After a ten-year delay the old world finally budged from its decaying positions. Not in one day; working out the new system of values will probably take up a century. European governments realize that no matter how great a burden it is, Russia cannot be separated from the continent, just as the United States realizes that China cannot be separated from the world. If, however, with these new realizations they attempt to keep one another in check, as they did during the cold war, they will condemn themselves to helplessness and won't be able to solve problems of hitherto unknown proportions regarding their own populations. And these negative possibilities do exist, because those institutions and political structures that took root during the cold war and, tamed, served well the critical era of peaceful coexistence, have been nearly untouched since the collapse of the Berlin Wall.

There is not, and in the last decade there hasn't been, a single moment of true dialogue between the two parts of the once bipolar world, with their different experiences and different human knowledge. In the absence of the dialogue, and not only in the new democracies but also in the old ones, the incense of counterreformation is wafting, and the mechanisms of anti-*Aufklärung*, of anti-enlightenment, have wormed their way into superannuated structures.

The territorial, economic, and spiritual isolation of the communist-bloc countries came undone after the fall of the Berlin Wall, but they did not cease to exist. The old democracies very rapidly realized how expensive European integration might be, and in their fear they stabilized, in certain points even strengthened, their own traditional separateness. In December 1998, for example, NATO quietly made clear that it had no plans to widen its military alliance beyond the inclusion of Poland, Hungary, and the Czech Republic. Within a few days, however, at the conference in Vienna of the European Council, it was acknowledged that admission of new members into the European Union would be deferred indefinitely. Still, at the end of March 1999, the same statesmen who would have preferred to preserve Europe's cold war boundaries, still proudly displaying their sparkling teeth, had to realize that although they really meant to do something in Kosovo, they had no place to put their gasoline cans, there were no roads where their tanks could roll, and this situation was still part of Europe's reality. Therefore, in the interest of gasoline cans, they presented the immediate and unconditional possibility of expanding both NATO and the European Union, an announcement that was no less anarchic than the earlier announcements had been. And it was the same with their later forgetfulness with which by late May they had drawn a veil over their January decisions and their April promises.

The stronger the older democracies' ambitions for separation, the greater Europe's destabilization and disorientation. The smaller their need for a continent-wide dialogue, the greater the chances in the new democracies for postcommunist and neofascist ideas, which recognize no dialogue and strive for autarchies and isolationism. Ten years of separatist politics has succeeded in making the cost of expansive European integration so prohibitive that the new democracies' internal instability indeed threatens the security of the old ones. It seems that in London, Brussels, Bonn, and Paris there is a failure to this day to acknowledge that Serbia, defending its *autistic* isolation as a national peculiarity, is neither unique nor rare, because in Albania, Bulgaria, the Czech Republic, Estonia, Croatia, Poland, Latvia, Lithuania, Hungary, Russia, Romania, Slovakia, Slovenia, Ukraine, and heaven forfend, even the new German territories there is a Serbia that is bigger than Serbia. The great mechanisms of dictatorships, though not healthy or intact, are still functioning on various levels, and they do want to survive their anticipated fate. And this, no matter where we look at it from, is the larger part of Europe, and not a mere region of it.

Put briefly, this means that the citizens of former Communist countries in the era of peaceful coexistence had no realistic choice but to give up their desire for freedom and accept dictatorship for their lifetimes and longer. But the traditionally democratic societies did not come out of this horrible process unscathed; in the real and desirable avoidance of a third world war, they forgot about the moral price tag attached to the politics of peaceful coexistence. Their premise had been that the only possible way was also the moral way; they lived with this belief, and their deep conviction of its truth permeated the inner life of the European Community. They failed to notice not only that people living on the other side of the Iron Curtain had to swallow, along with the principle of peaceful coexistence, the principle that dictatorships were necessary and real, but also that their former left-handed marriage with the dictatorships continues to confuse their own perspicacity and moral feelings. They had lived

in this morganatic marriage with a system whose real nature they refuse
to acknowledge to this day. Had they bothered to become acquainted
with their partner, they would have realized they could not live together,
and if they had made the effort to do this at least retroactively, they
might recognize the unpleasant consequences of their disorientation, dis-
information, and amoral decisions.

Except for a few outstanding journalists, no one will acknowledge
that to remedy the anarchic and chaotic conditions of distant and foreign
countries, of no particular interest to tourists, we should recognize not
only those conditions, but also the old democracies' false sincerity and
profound ignorance about them, the consequences of their own autism
and unawareness. An autistic person probably does not understand what
it is he does not understand; perhaps he has no wish to understand. His
mind wriggles and writhes separately from his senses.

Regarding the forms and conditions of human coexistence we have no
new treaties, and the old ones are useless. Two autisms, of different character and origin, have met, and thus war has become the only usable and
symbolic language for festive declarations. Yet we cannot say that the
meaning of last year's or the last decade's events are completely obscure.
And their significance is presumably no less than that of the three earlier
interrelated dates in the history of civil emancipation.

Those who doubt the legality of the decision made by NATO's nineteen member states are probably right; initiating air attacks was not legitimate in the given legal frameworks. But it does not follow that we
should ignore the fragility of these legal frameworks or their contingencies conforming to the standards of a bygone era, those dangerous areas
of friction that the fundamental reality of democracies cannot endure:
NATO took a great risk when, bypassing China and Russia, it decided
not to be bound by these intolerable legal frameworks. But we can consider the air attacks as expressive of the old democracies' great power ar-
rogance only if their goal lacked a universalistic character. Strangely, the
military aims of the old democracies evince far more enlightened and universal principles than the aims they pursue with their daily separatist
efforts.

Enlightened and universal goals have unavoidably aggressive traditions associated with them, which the European public, imagining itself
as refined and content as it is with its own separateness and double standards, no longer wants to acknowledge.

It is interesting to note that in February 1689 the creators of the Bill of Rights in the British Parliament failed to ask permission of the religious and secular authorities to deprive their church and their king of almost all their privileges and to declare, alongside the principle of monarchic sovereignty, that of their own. They forbade the king to levy taxes or rescind laws; without their approval the king could not raise an army in peacetime; the church could no longer serve as a court or issue sentences, and so on; in thirteen points they violated the divine order. The Declaration of Independence could not have been very popular either in monarchy-loving circles. In the proclamation in Philadelphia on July 4, 1776, the American patriots went far beyond their British counterparts, for they declared that their rights were related to the inalienable rights of individual citizens, and thus they deprived their king of the last crumbs of his sovereignty. And compared with the preceding conditions of law and order, the passing of the Déclaration des droits de l'homme et du citoyen on August 26, 1789, in the French National Assembly was a feat no less arbitrary. There it meant the end not just of royal sovereignty but of the tyrant king. These arbitrary legal maneuvers to reinterpret the meaning of state sovereignty in the name of the people's sovereignty overthrew the monarchy to ensure the simultaneous happiness of as many people as possible. Although I do not claim that the happiness of many people can be ensured by legal, political, security, or military means, with bombs or the guillotine, it is one of the great realities of life that people endeavor to achieve happiness by just such means, yet these are also the ones from which they recoil in horror.

The world does have an unenlightened, animal-like face. Theoretically, its brute features are supposed to be integrated into both conservative and liberal politics, yet they have been forgotten because peace and, above all, prosperity are so agreeable. And bestiality per se confuses the leftist humanistic and messianic view, just as the actually existing socialisms did with their serious criminality. But theoretically abject fear should have become superfluous by now. The unexpected military adventure in the last year of the century announced, in its own symbolic language, the wish to hearken back to the great aggressive historical and legal tradition that mediates between the humane and the bestial. The Kantian "citizen of the world" that Jürgen Habermas writes about has not only brains but also hooves and long nails; he constantly wants to rape someone, and he reeks with the penetrating stench of the he-goat. This tradition of Kant and Habermas cannot afford not to show man's animal face—that is, his own most personal animality—because it wants to humanize that face, and if we didn't see it, we wouldn't know what on earth needs to be humanized.

It is interesting to note from this perspective, regarding the legality of the events and methods of action, that some of the governments themselves were reluctant, or hesitated, to act in accordance with the brutal demands of the European enlightenment, while their electorates, in accordance with democratic rules of the game, albeit for the most varied reasons, did not wish to have any of these things done (not like this, or maybe not like that, or not now), things that otherwise they constantly demand and hold their governments accountable for. During certain brief periods the great civilized edict of emancipation works with an inexorable logic. The governments of the nineteen NATO states despite all their vacillation, doubt, and internal debates did not dare *not* follow this logic in 1999. The decision regarding the air attacks and the military strategy against Serbia unconsciously obeyed civilization's inner command concerning the permanent humanization of coexistence, and this expressed a rather practical political awareness, an awareness that the European Union, for reasons of convenience, cowardice, sensibility, natural self-defense, ignorance, and bestial selfishness, had successfully avoided and rejected for ten years.

If during the coming years the European continent wants to modernize itself because *pro primo* it does not want to lag behind in global economic and technological competition; *pro secundo* it is not content with using heavy weaponry at its borders to prevent worldwide migration; and *pro tertio* it realizes that globalization is not the result of the evil machinations of stock exchanges and multinational conglomerates, but the very opposite, since a high-level general provision for very large societies cannot be ensured without a global infrastructure—if, then, Europe does not wish to lose out in the process of continued modernization and the establishment of security, and does not want to delay further the creation of international norms that manage and make global tendencies transparent—because it does not want to see its living standards drop as its democracies' functional capabilities decline, which is to say because it does not wish to fall back into anarchy and chaos or, worse,

to rot and revert to some form of dictatorship—then European integration in the widest possible geographic sense is no longer avoidable. And
it can be brought about only as an integration of highly developed
democracies.

A partial recognition of this was first heard from the lips of the German foreign minister Joska Fischer. He himself seemed a bit alarmed by
it, because he must have known that the French foreign minister Hubert
Védrine would have preferred an army over integration, and the British
foreign secretary Robin Cook was completely unaffected by the thought.
Fischer must also have known that plans for a common army cannot substitute for integration plans. He may have also known that in the midst
of war one should speak of the necessity of integration, even though a
new wave of separation and isolation might soon engulf and sweep away,
for a long time to come, the hope and achievements of integration; therefore, instead of a grandiose plan for European integration, a more modest
plan, dealing with order in the Balkans, should be put on the table.

In the war against Yugoslavia, the democratic European states reached
a terrible and illusion-free moment of self-recognition. After a ten-year
delay they had to acknowledge that because of their own traditions, restrictions, needs, and constraints, they could not avoid the utopia of a
complete European integration, together with its painful consequences,
but neither could they attain it. Societies of very different mentalities
were coming face-to-face with one another and with themselves, and seeing one another's activities, they had to conclude that they did not understand one another, did not even understand what it was they did not
understand in themselves. Therefore they were in principle incapable of
integration.

Time was truly jolted out of joint. When Serbs swarmed into the
streets with bull's-eyes on their backs and foreheads to demonstrate solidarity with their own brutal state and to offer themselves as possible sac-
rifices, the international military coalition not only declared that the war
was not against the Serbs but also, putting its considerable military
know-how to the test, did everything possible to avoid making those
demonstrators targets (though it could not protect the Albanians, with
whom it had declared solidarity *against* the brutal state). The Serb mentality matches no known form of common sense or behavior, while the
NATO ambition flies in the face not only of common sense but also of all
known experiences of warfare.

To reach a mutual understanding of these opposing languages of isolation and separation, we would have to do a huge amount of linguistic, anthropological, and ethnographic fieldwork, and the results would have to be handed over to philosophers, historians, and sociologists for systems analysis. This would keep the best minds of every European nation busy for quite some time. A very accurate three-dimensional spiritual map of Europe would have to be drawn up. As the first step, the personal and technical conditions for this multidisciplinary work would have to be established. As the second step, they would have to gauge the cultural, religious, and ethnic boundaries and fault lines along which communication difficulties have traditionally arisen and conflicts erupted in Europe. As the third step, they would have to discover what the concerned parties along these borders and fault lines mean by commonly used words and concepts, what they would like them to mean, how they assess and evaluate the words and concepts used by people on the other side of the borders. And these findings, along with all their magical and mythic rituals and customs, would have to be clearly spelled out in every European language. In this phase we would already have an enormous, multilingual dictionary that could be used like a kaleidoscope. As the fourth step, these parallel descriptions would have to be translated back from every European language into the languages of the parties in conflict or with communication problems, and they in turn, in one of the main intermediary languages, would have to respond to all the points concerning them. Only then would the picture appear before us in all its cultural plasticity, and only then would it become visible from every angle. Moreover, the peculiar, the local, and the special, with all their connotations, would for the first time be embedded in the material of those major intermediary languages that now swallow and conceal instead of revealing and making their own, national, ethnic, religious, and regional connotations according to their own linguistic properties and philosophical rules, or that sweep them aside as useless debris until the next conflict. As the fifth step, every entry of the completed work in its multiannotated form would have to be presented in every European language. Since the entries would take their places in the multicolored field of the various concepts, philosophies, languages, and analyses, their analogies, symmetries, and exceptions would become clearly visible.

In short, to be able to speak articulately about what we need and obviously want to speak about, we must prepare the first Great European Encyclopedia.

In the European experience, always satisfied with its own bestiality and always drowning in its own opportunism, such an insane proposal, or anything like it, would be considered a nightmare and within half an hour would be consigned to oblivion. European experience walks along a different path. But if people who want to make some use of their minds delved into this intellectual and mental adventure, they would soon realize that three of their great concepts, saturated with political meaning, but to be undifferentiated in the future—Western Europe, Eastern Europe, and Central Europe—were no longer serviceable. It might also become clear that in the era of the cold war and peaceful coexistence, the function of these concepts, borrowed from geography, was to help the old democracies give a name to their separation from and opposition to the territorial isolation of the dictatorships. Theoretically, since 1989 these two ambitions of separation and isolation, each presuming the other, should have no purpose and neither should the concepts have any relevance—if only the cold war and peaceful coexistence had not made, on both sides, for a very characteristic socialization that predetermined the mentality of several generations, and if the structures of the democratic and dictatorial institutions had been altered. But they weren't. On the contrary, to this day the old democracies ensure their own separation and hide their structural problems with the help of these concepts of Western, Eastern, and Central Europe, even though this goes against their own universal needs, and the new democracies, also with the help of these same concepts, continue with the mental and intellectual structures that ensure the survival of dictatorial institutions and militate against strengthened democratic thought.

The borders and chasms that make it impossible for Europe to define itself as an independent power or, at least, after the experience of two world wars, allow it to stand on its own feet do not appear where or how they have been opportunistically depicted. The few people working on a Great European Encyclopedia would have this as their next discovery. But they can be discerned. There is a strong mental demarcation line between monarchies and republics, for example. And there is an even bigger fault line between the colonial powers and those European states that never had colonies, or only minor ones, and those that themselves lived under colonial oppression. And among the first group there is a significant difference between those who almost without hesitation gave up their colonies or let them disintegrate and those who brutally tried to hold on to them. The main stem of the European Union today is made of former colonial powers. It could hardly be otherwise, since the administration of Europe may be achieved only by nations with imperial experience. The experience necessary for governance is joined, however, by unchecked imperial aspirations with which, almost with the precision of a timetable, England and France thwart the long-range interests of European integration and, in the process, usually engage the assistance of Germany, which, if only for the potential promotion of its power, considers such a privileged position flattering.

The colonial foundations of the European Union today are derived not from the weight of artistic and material value gained from several centuries of human trafficking, slavery, and global plunder, though these deeds have had a part in it, but from the enormous knowledge accumulated during the centuries of experience in governance of foreign lands. This knowledge gives these societies a disciplined inner structure, an exceptional self-discipline that probably only the Spanish, French, Dutch, and British possess. However, from the standpoint of the virtual European community, it makes a difference whether or not this accumulated knowledge is well screened and humanized. In the Bosnian war it seemed unscreened, raw, and beastly. When the U.N. Commander, the French General Bertrand Janvier, freed his soldiers from captivity at the cost of Dutch blue helmets standing idly by as their charges from Srebrenica were taken away and slaughtered, France, with the intervention of President Chirac, put its own universal ideals into its pocket and with its other hand produced, from the other pocket, its unchecked colonial habits left over from Algeria.

There is an even more significant, historically even deeper fault line between the individual peoples, nations, and states of Europe; it runs along the disparity of their levels of urbanization. Sometimes it runs not between individual states but between regions. In Hungary east of the Danube, one lives at a different level of urbanity from that west of the Danube, just as in northern Germany the urban mentality is quite different from that in the south. There are nations in Europe with an independent philosophy, with philosophers but no independent philosophies, and with not even any philosophers. There are nations whose modern history is under the influence of the Reformation, others more influenced by the Enlightenment. There is a significant demarcation line between the states of Europe whose history is replete with democratic experiences and those more experienced in dictatorship and despotism. Europe can be divided into zones showing the level of technological training and technical development: in certain zones the productive spirit rules and in other zones the reproductive spirit, and there are zones in which not even the latter can rule. The continent's cold war partition, however, has a seemingly lasting particularity, and in this context the geographical distinction is indeed telling. Civic emancipation had taken place and can be considered complete in Western Europe; the peoples of Eastern Europe are not emancipated but in every conceivable way live in bondage. They are not emancipated as children, as women or men—even if they are homosexual they are not emancipated—and they all are in bondage in relation to their states. It is as if two different species were living on either side of this deep dividing line. And then there are the familiar religious borders, the chasms between Catholics and Protestants, between Catholic or Protestant Christians and Orthodox Christians, between Christians and Muslims that once again are redrawing the well-known maps in unprecedented ways.

As for why the Serbs, with the approval of their clergy, murder Albanians, we know nothing more or less than we do about why mature Irishmen of one tribe, on certain days of the year and in the name of Christ, want to march through certain parts of a city carrying their tribal emblems or why mature men of the other tribe feel it necessary to reciprocate this ritually bloody senselessness, also in the name of Christ, on other days of the year.

Universalist notions and needs can only be given meaningful content by comprehensive and well-structured knowledge. Today the governments of democratic Europe and European public opinion possess no such knowledge—either in war or in peace.

"A világpolgar és a kecskebak," first published in German in *Die Zeit* (Hamburg), July 15, 1999.

Clogged Pain

Once, on a fairly empty bus while I was chatting with someone, something unexpectedly crashed down from the ceiling and knocked me on the head. The blow was strong enough to make me buckle, but I felt no pain. Serious pain is usually very insidious, and it takes time before one feels it. This time my mouth gaped, and the familiar world stared back at me, dumbly. The frightened little screams around me seemed to recede, yet my senses recorded everything more dispassionately than before. In fact I felt that what was happening to me was quite wonderful; the only thing that disturbed my calm, mental enjoyment was something streaming heavily into my eyes and down my nose. I came to when it reached my lips. Blood.

I was struck with the same powerful blow when I realized that for fifty years I had understood nothing, nothing at all, and still don't understand today, perhaps don't even want to understand, anything about what others—contrary to what their own well-functioning senses tell them—consider the real world, their everyday life, with which they are well content. Not only do I not understand their gestures, motivations, and intentions, but I don't understand their ways of reckoning time. And so what until then I had thought of as my strength became my weakness. I could see clearly that with my eternal storytelling compulsion I might have succeeded in backing out of the eternal present tense of the real world, driven by raw instincts and mundane interests, suspending my presence in that world, in a way, and managing to protect myself, but at the same time my life had definitively and irrevocably installed another person in me: a stranger who, in the universal disorder that has recently come upon us, is completely defenseless. Over fifty years he used up all the reserves of his ingenuity; he had nothing left with which to delude himself. And there is no one else to deceive, for everyone sees that this most perfect real world not only tolerates systematically committed evil deeds but desires them, turns them into business, abets their commission.

This person must perish. Logically I cannot insist that he live even if I perish with him. He no longer has any real emotions. His instincts do not function properly, either. In every situation his narcissistic attention is focused on examining which emotion goes with which instinct. He knows a great deal about this; he cannot be fooled easily. Controlled instincts, however, leave no room for real emotions. Or interests. He is unfit to live. Only those who can see all this are fit to live, who know this is so yet don't look over their shoulders and don't circumspectly ask what our common future will be like if the situation is like this. Self-defense has no other tools. I must look either from too close up, so as not to see what was done to me, or from too far off, so as not be affected by what I am doing. There is no sensible mind, nor could there ever have been one capable of comprehending and fully recording the devastations of World War II. In the light of the Balkan war one can clearly see the half-century-old omissions made by what remained of common sense.

Slowly I too should learn this more ignominious reckoning of time. If someone deliberately refuses, for decades, to look back at the devastation left behind him, it is not likely he'd want to have a picture of his tomorrow. Days, weeks, months, and years may slip away imperceptibly in his conscience. In the absence of memory there wouldn't be hours either; events would have neither beginnings nor ends, no select or exceptional moments. *Fin sans fin de siècle.* Unending end of the century. And this is not necessarily frightening since Christian chronology is nothing but a cultural agreement that Europeans made, at their own risk, among themselves, and the stars, and the gods. And it won't last forever either. It could easily be broken.

The infusion, taped to my hand, was dripping slowly into me. Every droplet lengthened, as if considering whether to descend farther and only then submitting to the force of gravity. As if I might still have time to record permanently, at least for myself, the more important things. Covered with a single sheet and attached to various instruments, I lay naked on my back in a huge hall in which there was no day or night. Behind barely drawn green curtains the more serious cases were wheezing, moaning, pleading, farting, and rattling in their throats, naked as when we were born, men and women together. Occasionally some odious stench wafted my way.

I must say I wasn't thinking about literature. Who thinks about literature anyway? My brain was wiped clean, with no trace of anything I had ever done. There was not even the memory of having to remember something, though clearly before me were every intimate intention, reason, direction, passion, mechanic, and compulsion of all my work until then, what one might call the writer's technology. But not a single subject of that work. It was as if I had finally managed to peel off its style from one of my sentences.

Perhaps the art and literature of the end of this century may best be characterized by this peculiar and very dubious success. Having robbed themselves of their subjects, they still have very strong style. It seems to me that *la condition humaine* is no longer a subject. Neither is the common human situation, or the personal situation, not yesterday's situation or tomorrow's, but only the styles of all these. As if beguiled in the palace at Versailles, we were enjoying the wonders of its interconnected mirrored halls but wanted to forget that the courtiers urinated in the stairwells and the ladies were filthy and lice-infested. The duc de Vendôme issued his orders of the day from the chamberbox in his room and cheerfully dined while evacuating. In the royal theatre the duchesse de Bourgogne gave herself an enema but held its results in check until after the sumptuous postperformance dinner and the fatiguing chitchat in the king's inner chambers. She claimed the enema invigorated her whole being and kept her from swooning in the stifling halls.

Art and literature at the turn of our century do not see the various aspects of life as a whole; they fluctuate between the extremes of a single thing; they sterilize or brutalize, disinfect or criminalize their subjects. These artistic gesticulations are driven by raw panic, which may be understandable, since there was much to fear during the dark restoration that followed the war. Cold war dreams gave birth to monsters. The only remaining sensible means of preserving democratic order where it existed was an open political struggle that in the long term justified and strengthened democratic political traditions. In the eastern half of Europe, however, the only sensible political way out of tyranny was senseless rebellion. Indeed politics lost its traditional meaning in this region, and in the mind of every decent person turned into a nightmare. Because of this significant divergence, Europe in fact fell apart, though a single thin thread invisibly kept it together: the hitherto unknown, or rather never openly recognized, primacy and mindless cult of politics.

Western Europeans construed fate as if it were something to be decided on and influenced by one's politics; Eastern Europeans lived their entire lives believing that along with political destiny, fate had also been wrested from their hands. The two interpretations are not interchangeable. Yet by the end of the century the Versailles-style intellectual elite in both Europes had let the nails on their index fingers grow long the better to point an accusing finger at politicians or to gauge out politics altogether. It was probably these obligatory exercises that made the elite forget its own responsibilities, which it could not share or transfer. They are an exclusive part and parcel of the elite's activities and not necessarily identical with civic responsibility. There were other reasons why these responsibilities were forgotten. The concept of artistic responsibility, which along with the concept of humanism perished in the ashes of the crematoriums, was cleverly redeemed during the postwar skirmishes with the political concept of artistic commitment. This latter, which could not accommodate stylistic or structural issues, kept the encounter with anti-authoritarian political movements free and unhindered.

The profound, lasting, and destructive effects of that encounter can be still seen clearly today, though the old idea of artistic commitment has long since been relegated to the past. The role of the human person has been taken over by political or ideological formulas, and in this sense a person no longer has interrelated qualities but rather is made up of emotions and opinions, or as a countereffect to the brutal changes, a provocative stylization has appeared that hopes to bypass everything political and ideological by replacing the depiction of human traits with the channeling of creative passion into the *means* of depiction. The strength of one method is its resolutely political view; the strength of the other is a resolutely aesthetic one. One rewrites the traditional European human landscape with political concepts, the other with aesthetic ones. But both rewrite it. And the rewrite, in both cases, means that the creative artist has pushed his way in front of his subject.

The century's end Versailles-style elite does not come to its senses even at the sight of tragedies, does not remember that it may have forgotten something and therefore cannot remember what it was it forgot. And if it comprehends at all what is going on around it, it does not examine, as a first step, its own professional responsibility—its created works—but instead hurls its civic wrath at its freely elected political representatives, who nonetheless are staunch defenders of its day-to-day interests, at people whom theoretically, according to democratic rules, it could vote out of office. But the elite do not do this. For if the governments indeed tried to put Europe in order according to logical rules, instead of leaving it mired in chaos, there would be serious consequences. The Versailles style of life to which the elite has grown accustomed would have to be given up. From its throne resting on its completed lifeworks, it would have to admit professional bankruptcy.

I don't want to point my finger at politicians. I should like somehow to break with this tried-and-true habit, which is shamefully hypocritical.

My own profession and other related ones are in dire straits—not morally, but in the most narrowly professional way. Ariane Mnouchkine gets succinctly to the heart of it. "In the West, one often has the impression that actors have been trained to speak through clenched teeth: Look, everyone, how well I conceal all my feelings." Of course we may interpret this as the new quality of European art at the end of the century, because the situation is the same in Eastern Europe too. There the audience's impression is that actors have been trained to open their mouths at seven in the evening and until eleven keep shouting at the top of their voices: Look, everyone, I still have plenty of inner feelings left, plenty. The difference between the two is that what the intellectual elite of Western Europe tries to solve with forced dissimulation, the intellectual elite of Eastern Europe attempts by constant simulation. What one side compulsively keeps silent about the other compulsively talks to death; in neither case do we learn what the person is feeling—if he or she still feels anything.

This simulation and dissimulation have one real and one illusionary subject. The illusionary subject is the unnamed emotion; the real subject of the unnamed or unelaborated emotion is, however, history or, by another name, fate. The illusionary subject must carefully cover over the real subject since for many long decades the art and literature of our century's end not only had no opinion on it, but because of the war's traumas had to strike from the dictionary the very concepts of history and fate. Only by dissimulation can they help themselves cross the yawning gap. A human landscape rewritten with the help of political and aesthetic concepts is one of the most essential means of this dissimulation. Somebody, for some reason, is unable to express something. Somebody, for some reason, is not allowed to express something. Suppressions and screams. These are very intense gestures. With these intense emotional gestures the intellectual elite of our century's end covers up the truth that it has had no independent idea about the fate of humanity in Europe. And since almost no one feels an obligation to tell us something about this, European literature has been taken over by stylists, politicians, ideologues, and craftsmen skilled in philology. They have already sterilized and brutalized everything. That is all the end of the century has to show in its self-defense, which of course is the general public's self-defense. We no longer wish to see anything that might remind us of sufferings endured; we would not know how to cope with such things by traditional means. Probably the only kind of destruction that can be accepted is the one for which the culture has a prepared rubric. If there is no such rubric, the pain and shame will not subside with time.

No matter who survived it or where and how, no matter who perhaps had not yet been born, the pain and shame of World War II has reached everyone and stuck in our throats. This culture cannot abide the destruction. Operating that enormous apparatus of simulation and dissimulation is merely a desperate effort at self-defense. Despite it, the shame and pain that had been choked back for fifty years erupted at the sight of the Balkan war. Still, the self-defense mechanism will most likely be far stronger than the sense of responsibility that flickered dimly during that war, if for no other reason than that the simulators and dissimulators are very pleased with themselves; one might say that they are unstoppable in their obtuseness and shortsightedness. They created the politics, economics, and aesthetics of simulation and dissimulation systems that seem much easier to reconcile with one another than with common sense. Their politics consists of national or big power selfishness raised to a universal level. Their state budgets are made up of mutual, global, and lasting indebtedness and multilateral corruption. Ugliness, vulgarity, lack of proportion, superficiality, and the cult of criminality are the components of their aesthetics. The perfect state system is here, ready for use. Yet the system of simulation and dissimulation does have a weak point· it has been unable to create an ethics worthy of itself. And during the Balkan war this was the fault line along which the entire edifice cracked.

An ethics could only have been built on what art and literature in our time did not and could not provide, the independent view of humanity and fate. The problem is not that one cannot live with a chronic lack of basic ethical principles. The problem lies elsewhere. The chronic lack has gradually, almost imperceptibly, undermined the institutions we have inherited from previous centuries. That they were designed for something else, in different measure, we have only just discovered, quite suddenly. An ethics would be only an intermediary stage. What makes the system of simulation and dissimulation unable to function is not a lack of ethics but differences about the view of humanity and in the scales of traditional institutions. If we stop operating the system, the result is social catastrophe; if the system operates, it not only is unscrupulous but will deepen the ecological catastrophe.

This is the only recognizably encouraging factor in the entire bankruptcy. The civilization declares that it will not submit to the enormous apparatus of simulation and dissimulation It declares that what can be done is not necessarily sensible and what is sensible is not necessarily ethical. It declares that democracies do not reconcile personal intentions with national interest or national intention with universal interest according to sensible and ethical standards. It declares that the level of civilization is no guarantee of the quality or permanence of culture. On the contrary, the higher the level of civilization, the more fragile culture becomes. And this is not as general a rule as we should like to make ourselves believe—which is to say that we should not only be on guard against a great social and ecological catastrophe but also be aware that this civilization makes everyone individually fragile; it exposes every person individually to destruction.

My heart broke down after fifty-one years of dedicated hard work. It stopped. But this did not mean I had reached the end of something or that my seeing or thinking ceased; what happened was that I tumbled into another dimension along with them. From the dark womb, one tumbles into the dim birth canal where a benevolent force carries one toward the light. In the moment of death one probably relives one's birth—not figuratively but literally. I turned over several times and saw the dim ribbing of the birth canal; as I approached its oval entrance the light grew ever greater. I had not reached the opening yet. I knew this was the time I was leaving my life. My mother's open labia were not quite symmetrical; the oval pulled a bit to the right. The enormous moving force that was turning me over and carrying me along was unusual, but my observation was not at all unconscious. I was unable to be born; not even my mother could give birth to my death because three and a half minutes later measured by worldly reckoning, the three people working on my body, two doctors and a nurse, brutally brought me back so that I should continue to live, suffer along with them, and along with them enjoy my suffering. Yet somehow, my consciousness remained stuck to some extent in the hereafter because for *it*, it was sweeter not to see things torn into their component parts.

They returned me, and I too immediately returned with my memory of the world. My conscience was working normally, but from then on it began to establish connections among seemingly unrelated and distant things. It connected the historical and political upheaval with my earlier favored and much-cherished belief that I was strong and healthy. Nowhere else could I have experienced more profoundly the miserable chaos of human beliefs and presumptions than on that hospital bed, half dead and chained to an insensible civilization. Here what our famous civilization says is indeed very different from what our even more famous culture says.

It was as if my cultural conscience were sticking out its tongue at my civilization-driven conscience. Because if I really don't understand what others call reality, then I shouldn't understand it; I should perish. Saint Augustine claims that death is sweet when it is in the order of things. Yet here, the human body—no matter how ready it is for death, how eagerly it wishes for it, how contented it is with it—is thrown to the ground, knelt on, given terrible electric shocks on its breast. As if the conscience rooted in civilization, as opposed to the cultural conscience, were shouting that it wants to live at any price.

They had exposed me to fire and broken my ribs. They had embittered my own perfect death. They yanked me back into that disgraceful and irresponsible present tense that they serve with their instruments and deify with their technology. This is the nature of lifesaving; it takes its stand on the pure instinct to preserve existence and rears on up from there. But lying there again, having been torn from my mother's womb for the second time, I had to pay dearly for civilization's success. I could do no other; I kept breathing despite my strongest conviction. We have no currency with which to pay this price. Our culture is not designed for such a transaction.

Émile Cioran's aphorism that says every suffering human being is a public menace may be inscribed as the motto above the thunderous bankruptcy of our century's end. Cioran is dead. There is no other side, no beyond, where I might close accounts with him for composing this absurd, destructive sentence. But I don't need to. He knows by now that he built his life on a false premise. Better to say everyone who wants to avoid suffering is a public menace.

First published as "A megakadt fájdalom" in *Talált cetli és más elegyes írások* (Pécs: Jelenkor Kiadó Kft, 1992, 2000).

Way

If on a wintry night someone would turn into Klauzál Street from Rákóczi Road without meeting anyone, come to a stop, and then move on under the dark windows and reach the open-air market of Klauzál Square, where at this hour, between one-thirty and two in the morning, the stalls are deserted and, forgetting some of his emotions while balancing others on the tip of his tongue or tasting them in his throat, would cross that short section of Dob Street that takes one from Klauzál Square to Kertész Street, and then, before turning, would look up at the lighted windows of the Fészek Club and keep on pressing forward without staring at the display window of the Apisz store—whoever undertakes this walk must inevitably notice that in Kertész Street there are incomparably more cars parked than in Klauzál Street, though they are mostly old vehicles and almost all of them dirty, but even this observation would be no cause for distraction, because if someone, following my example, conforming of course only to his own needs, between one-thirty and two in the morning continued his sentimental stroll by turning from Rákóczi Road into Klauzál Street and then, having crossed Dob Street, progressed along Kertész Street, without walking too slowly though not hurrying either, he could be sure that in about eight minutes he would reach, opposite the darkened building of the Music Academy, the intersection of Kertész and Mayakovski streets.

First published as "Út" in *Leírás* (Budapest: Szépirodalmi Könyvkiadó, 1979).